CAFFEINE NIGHTS PUBLISHING

SHAUN HUTSON

CHASE

Fiction to die for...

Published by Caffeine Nights Publishing 2019

Copyright © Shaun Hutson 2019

Shaun Hutson has asserted his rights under the Copyright, Designs and Patents Act 1998 to be identified as the author of this work

CONDITIONS OF SALE

All rights reserved. No part of this publication may be reproduced, stored in a retrieval system, or transmitted in any form or by any means, electronic, mechanical, photocopying, scanning, recording or otherwise, without the prior permission of the publisher

This book has been sold subject to the condition that it shall not, by way of trade or otherwise, be lent, resold, hired out, or otherwise circulated without the publisher's prior consent in any form of binding or cover other than that in which it is published and without a similar condition including this condition being imposed on the subsequent purchaser.
All characters in this publication are fictitious and any resemblance to real persons, living or dead is purely coincidental

Published in Great Britain by
Caffeine Nights Publishing
71 Buckthorne Road
Thistle Hill
Minster on Sea
Isle of Sheppey
ME12 3RD

caffeinenightsbooks.com

British Library Cataloguing in Publication Data.
A CIP catalogue record for this book is available from the British Library
ISBN: 978-1-913200-04-6

Cover design by
Michael Knight
Massillusion.co.uk

Everything else by
Default, Luck and Accident

Also by Shaun Hutson:

ASSASSIN
BODY COUNT
BREEDING GROUND
CAPTIVES
COMPULSION
DEADHEAD
DEATHDAY
DYING WORDS
EPITAPH
EREBUS
EXIT WOUNDS
HEATHEN
HELL TO PAY
HYBRID
KNIFE EDGE
LAST RITES
LUCY'S CHILD
MONOLITH
NECESSARY EVIL
NEMESIS
PURITY
RELICS
RENEGADES
SHADOWS
SLUGS
SPAWN
STOLEN ANGELS
THE SKULL
TWISTED SOULS
UNMARKED GRAVES
VICTIMS
WARHOL'S PROPHECY
WHITE GHOST

Hammer Novelizations
TWINS OF EVIL
X THE UNKNOWN
THE REVENGE OF FRANKENSTEIN

ACKNOWLEDGEMENTS

Thanks always seems too inadequate a word for some of the people who help, support or just have faith in me while I'm writing a book but, until someone comes up with a better word, that will have to suffice for the following individuals.

I'd like to thank my publisher, Mr Darren Laws for all his support and faith. Thanks, mate. Also, a huge thanks to everyone at Caffeine Nights. A special thank you to Michael Knight.

Many thanks to my agent, Meg Davies.

I'd also like to thank Jonathan Sothcott (whose knowledge of obscure horror films is breathtaking) and Damien Morley. Matt Shaw, Emma Dark, Graeme Sayer, Jo Roberts, Claire and anyone else I've forgotten.

I would also like to thank Cineworld Milton Keynes (where I seem to spend most of my spare time), particularly Elizabeth, Sonya, Alun, Phillip, James, Phil, Jake, Daniel, Ben, Alex, Charlotte, Nathan and anyone else I've forgotten or who's left by now.

And big thanks too for The Broadway Cinema in Letchworth.

My thanks to Gary Farrow as well (despite his taste in football teams).

My Mum and my daughter deserve far more than just a thank you but, for now, it'll have to do. They know I mean so much more.

And, as ever, a massive thanks to you lot. My readers. The most loyal, the most critical and the most valued.

Let's go.

                                        Shaun Hutson.

DEDICATION

Everything I do and everything I write is for my daughter, Kelly.

This is no exception. As always, it comes with all my love. Even though I tell you, you'll never know how much you mean to me.

Chase

SHAUN HUTSON

'There falls no shadow where there shines no sun.'
                                    Hilaire Belloc

PART ONE

'The Hawk swoops down on its prey. So does the Indian.'
Black Elk – Oglala Sioux Indian Chief (1863 - 1950)

THE CHILD
COLORADO, USA

The child had stopped crying half an hour earlier.

It had screamed, kicked and thrashed when he'd first taken it and in between mumbled entreaties to release it, it had cried almost incessantly. But now it was still and quiet as if all the fight had left it and all the tears had simply been used up.

They didn't all scream and cry and fight back. Some seemed to accept their fate almost noiselessly while others struggled.

This one had struggled.

He was barely eight. Dressed in a pair of jeans, holed at the knees, a grey t-shirt and a pair of trainers that had seen better days. The T-shirt was soaked with sweat and one of the trainers had been torn as the boy had been dragged into the back of the van.

Now he sat silently, bound at the wrists with heavy rope that had cut into the flesh in places. His feet were bound too but now he just sat motionless, looking around, stretching his jaw to try and relieve the discomfort of the thick tape that had been dragged across his mouth to prevent him shouting. His cheeks were damp with tears and he looked around the room he was being held in with wide, fear filled eyes.

He had no idea where he was and no idea why he was there, and on both counts he was lucky, for had he realized the reason for his presence in this place then he would probably have started screaming and crying again.

He sniffed and continued to look around, both afraid and also puzzled by the bleakness of the room he found himself in.

The walls were bare brilliant white plaster. They were so white they were practically luminescent. There wasn't a mark on any of them and the boy wondered if someone came in every day and re-painted them such was their perfectly pristine nature.

And covering these walls was transparent plastic that reminded him of the kind of food wrap his mother used to place around his sandwiches before she placed them in his lunch box on a school day.

The thought of his mother made the boy whimper again.

What he wouldn't give to be with his mother now. What he wouldn't give to be with anyone *now as long as he was free of this white room and the ropes that held him prisoner.*

She would come looking for him. His mother would come. So would his father and they would find him. He was sure of that.

He sniffed back more tears and shuffled uncomfortably on the bare wooden floor.

There was a single door to his left, but even that was covered by the same transparent plastic that hung on the walls like a second skin.

The boy pushed himself back against the wall and managed to straighten up. He felt uncomfortable. There was a horrible dampness around his groin where he'd wet himself earlier, the fear of being snatched having overcome him at that time. He felt uncomfortable but he felt ashamed too. Boys of his age weren't supposed to wet themselves.

He looked down at the wet patch on his jeans and felt like crying once again.

Off to his left he heard movement and the door swung back on its hinges, causing the plastic sheeting to billow.

A man entered the room.

He was carrying a small holdall and the boy looked at him, shuffling backwards against the wall as though he was attempting to melt into the plaster itself.

He could feel the terror rising swiftly inside him once more.

The man unzipped the holdall he was carrying and dug his hand swiftly inside.

When the boy saw what he'd taken from within it, he began to shake uncontrollably.

ONE

David Carson closed the lid of the laptop and looked across at his wife.

'Done,' he said, smiling.

Amy Carson hit the mute button on the TV remote, jammed a piece of folded paper into the book she'd been reading and moved closer to him on the sofa. She leant over to kiss his cheek.

'Thanks,' David said, turning his face to kiss her on the lips. 'I deserved that.' He pulled her more tightly to him.

'Is everything ok?' Amy enquired.

'I was just finalizing us picking up the RV with the company in the States.'

'Ooh, the RV, get you,' she said, prodding him with one index finger.

'What do you want me to call it? A bloody camper van? It's a bit more than that.'

'A mobile caravan?' She giggled.

David looked at her with mock disdain.

'It's a lot more than that, I can give you the exact specifications if you like,' he said, trying to look stern but failing miserably.

'No, don't do that,' she said, shaking her head. 'I don't care how many bloody horsepower the engine is and all that shite.'

David smiled.

'I just hope we'll be able to manage driving on the other side of the road,' Amy went on. 'I mean over here if someone cuts you up the worst that happens is that they shout at you or stick two fingers up but they've all got guns in the States haven't they?'

'Well, I wasn't planning on forcing anyone to pull a gun on me,' David said. 'And not everyone carries guns you know. We're not going to a shooting range for our holidays. You've been watching too many films. And the easiest way to avoid accidents once we're there is for me to drive.'

Amy jabbed him with her index finger again.

'Cheeky,' she said. 'I'll go on my own if you cast any more aspersions on my driving.'

'I wasn't casting aspersions I was just saying it might be easier for me to do the driving. You and Daisy can take pictures or play eye spy or something.' He laughed.

'I don't think we're going to have to resort to playing eye spy,' Amy chuckled. 'Daisy can't wait. She talks about it every day. "When are we going Mum?" "How long do we have to fly for?" "Are we going to see any cowboys?"'

'We might see some cowboys,' David mused. 'If I take a wrong turning and drive through Texas by mistake.'

Amy moved closer to her husband, one hand resting on his thigh.

'We need this holiday,' she said, quietly.

'Tell me about it,' David smiled.

'It's taken long enough to save up for it.'

'Well, things haven't been easy have they?'

David opened his mouth to say something then contented himself with just a shake of the head. He didn't particularly want to discuss what had made their lives less than idyllic during the past two or three years.

Some things were best left unsaid. Like any married couple in their early thirties they'd had problems to solve (some of which they'd managed and some they hadn't) and obstacles to overcome both professionally and privately but all they wanted to do now was look forward. It had, David told himself, been too long since they were in a position to do that.

The thought of spending two weeks driving across America in an RV with just his wife and his seven-year-old daughter was the only thing he wanted to think about at this particular moment in time.

Until he heard the thud from the floor above.

TWO

David sighed and hauled himself to his feet.

'Do you want me to go?' Amy asked.

'Finish your book,' he said. 'She's probably dreaming. I'll see to her.'

Amy nodded, glancing at her husband as he made his way from the room and out into the hall. Seconds later she heard his footfall on the stairs as he ascended.

Amy flipped open her book again, her gaze flickering over the words but as she glanced at the page nothing seemed to be registering. She turned back a couple of pages and realized that she'd have to re-read some of the book. Her mind hadn't been on it from the time she'd started earlier that evening. She put the paperback down and turned her attention back to the TV, flicking channels.

There wasn't much on. The usual diet of reality shows, talent contests and desperate fame seekers was interspersed with the national news (an endless array of depressing stories as far as Amy was concerned) and repeats. She settled on a re-run of an American crime series, rapidly tired of it and found herself grinning at an old episode of *South Park*.

It was coming to an end when the living room door opened and David re-entered.

He was carrying their seven-year-old daughter.

'I can't sleep, Mum,' David said in a high-pitched whining voice. 'Dad said I could come down and say goodnight, Mum.'

He tickled Daisy gently and she giggled, her long blonde hair flying around her head as she wriggled in his grip. He sat down next to Amy, still holding his daughter who waited a moment then scrambled over to her mother. David shot out a hand and grabbed her by the neck of her SpongeBob SquarePants pyjamas and she giggled again.

'You're supposed to be asleep,' Amy told her.

'Dad said I could come down and say goodnight,' Daisy told her.

'You said goodnight two hours ago,' Amy reminded her. 'Have you been to sleep? Dad read you a story like he always does.'

'He read one about a cat that died and went to heaven,' Daisy said. 'It was really good.'

'Sounds lovely,' Amy said, raising her eyebrows.

David grinned.

'Your mum bought it for her last Christmas,' he explained.

'It was really good mum,' Daisy explained. 'This little girl had this cat called Tiddles and he died and she was upset but...'

'You can tell me about it in the morning,' Amy said, trying to sound stern. She prodded Daisy's nose with one index finger and the little girl chuckled again.

'And I was thinking about going on holiday too,' Daisy

confessed.

'You can tell me about that in the morning too,' Amy added. 'Bedtime.'

'But Mum, I can't wait,' Daisy said excitedly.

'Well you'll have to wait,' Amy reminded her. 'We all will.'

'Will we see Mickey Mouse?' Daisy continued. 'And Cinderella? And Harry Potter?'

'He's not a Disney character,' David smiled. 'And we're going to the Grand Canyon.'

'Will we see him though?' Daisy persisted.

'Only if you go to bed right now and go to sleep,' Amy told her daughter.

'Can I have another story?' Daisy asked.

'A quick one,' David said. 'A very quick one.'

He scooped his daughter up into his arms and Amy stood too, reaching out to embrace her daughter, planting a kiss on her cheek before David turned away towards the door.

Amy patted him gently on the backside and he looked back at her and smiled, raising his eyebrows suggestively.

'I won't be long,' he said.

Amy smiled and once again heard his footsteps receding upstairs.

He was back in less than ten minutes.

'She's flat out,' he said, sitting down beside Amy once again.

'That was quick,' Amy told him.

'She was tired. All the excitement's worn her out.'

They sat in silence for a moment, Amy resting her bare feet on her husband's lap. He closed his hands around them, massaging gently.

'Are you sure we can afford this holiday?' she said, finally.

'Yes,' he said, his gaze never leaving the TV screen, his hands still gently stroking her feet.

'You're sure?'

'We've saved for years for it, we'll be fine.'

'I know, David, but…'

'No buts. No more worrying. No more questions. Right? We all need this holiday and we're taking it.'

Amy nodded.

'I love you,' she murmured.

'Well that's a good job, because I love you too,' he grinned.

Amy smiled, the expression widening as David lifted one of her feet and kissed the instep.

'Time for bed?' he asked.

'Yes please,' Amy breathed.

He pulled her closer to him.

'We should make sure Daisy's asleep first,' Amy said, running one index finger over his cheek.

'Why, because you make so much noise?' he murmured.

They both laughed.

David pressed the OFF button on the remote.

'No one says we have to go upstairs,' he announced.

Amy smiled and kissed him.

And in that moment, David Carson was aware of nothing else in the world, not even the rain that had started to fall outside and was pattering on the windows.

THE GATHERING
COLORADO, USA

The cellar was well lit.

Flooded with cold white light from the wall and ceiling fluorescents that crackled and buzzed like angry insects.

There were two large wooden worktops on either side of the wide subterranean room, both covered with an array of tools ranging from bolt cutters to blow torches. A chainsaw hung on the wall above one of them, the blade and chain oiled. There were several cans of gasoline pushed into one corner of the room and it was towards one of these that a tall man with a thin face and balding head walked. He picked it up and shook it to ensure that there was sufficient fuel inside then he turned to the fifteen or twenty others people gathered in the cellar.

A number of them nodded approvingly as he wandered back to the centre of the room to join a shorter stockier man who was standing beside one of the roof supports. The thick wooden pillar was a foot or more across.

It easily supported the weight of the boy who was tied to it.

He was barely nine years old. His body held firmly to the pillar by thick rope that had been wound around his waist, chest and arms. There was a piece of dirty rag stuffed into his mouth to prevent him speaking but he made little sound, staring wide-eyed at the interior of the cellar and the people who gazed at him.

As the man with the gasoline approached, he looked in that direction and struggled momentarily against the ropes that bound him, but it was a perfunctory movement with no real hope of success. He was held too securely.

The smaller man moved closer to him and pulled the gag free, wrenching it from the boy's mouth and tossing it aside. The boy let out a deep breath, as if the gag had been holding the air in his body like a valve. He shuddered against the rope for a second, seeing that the shorter man was holding something but not quite sure what it was. Even when the man stepped in front of him, the boy wasn't certain what the shiny metallic material was.

Only as it was wound around his head did he realize it was barbed wire.

The barbs cut into his flesh easily as it was pulled tight by the man who was wearing thick rubber gloves to prevent cutting himself. He had several lengths of wire and wrapped each one swiftly and expertly around the boy's face and head, ignoring the blood that spurted from the wounds that opened.

The boy made no sound except a muted gurgling, doubtless due to the fact that his tongue had been cut out with a pair of secateurs only hours earlier.

Blood ran from his mouth down his chin, mingling with the fresh crimson that was now pouring down his face from the wounds left by the barbed wire.

The shorter man looked directly into his eyes for a second then took another length of barbed wire and wound it securely around his forehead and brow. The sharp barbs punctured one eyeball and clear vitreous fluid mingled with the blood running down his face.

The boy was shuddering now, his body jerking and straining against the ropes, his head occasionally slamming back against the wooden pillar he was tied to but he remained conscious.

He was still conscious when the tall man began splashing him with gasoline.

He could smell it as it soaked into his clothes and stung his ravaged skin. When some of it trickled into his torn eye he shook violently and tried to scream.

The two men stood before him for a moment, looking him up and down, one of them turning towards the watching group.

A woman at the front of the group nodded vigorously and the tall man pulled a lighter from his pocket and held it before the boy, allowing him to see the small flame that was burning there.

'Do it,' someone called.

'Burn him,' another added.

'Burn,' several others called.

The boy looked directly at the lighter flame.

'Burn.'

The word reverberated around the cellar, chanted now by the entire group it seemed. It grew louder, more frenzied. There was desire and despair in the noise that filled the cellar.

'Burn.'

The man with the lighter took a couple of steps backwards, away from the boy, dropping to his haunches beside a puddle of gasoline. It had spattered all around the boy and the pillar he was secured to, streams of it soaking the floor of the subterranean room

The tall man lit one of these streams, moving back as it ignited, the gasoline erupting, flames racing along the trail until it reached the boy. He disappeared in an explosion of yellow and white flame that engulfed his body in an instant.

It wasn't long before the stench of burning flesh began to fill the cellar and those watching clapped and cheered. Some embraced each other.

They stood watching the boy's body burn.

THREE

At first David thought he was dreaming.

He heard the sound and thought it was the residue of some subconscious excursion, but as he stirred and turned his head towards the bedroom door he realized that what he'd heard had not been imagined.

Outside the window there was a sudden explosion of white light and David winced as he realized that it was lightening. The storm must have come on during the early hours because he could also hear distant rumbles of thunder too as he swung himself out of bed, trying not to wake Amy in the process.

The sound he'd heard came again.

'Dad.'

He hurried out of the bedroom and across the landing to Daisy's room.

He found her sitting up in bed, the duvet pulled up to her face and her head turned towards the window.

'Dad's here,' David said as he crossed to her, closing his arms around her. 'Did you have a bad dream?'

'I heard the noises outside,' Daisy told him.

'The thunder,' he told her. 'It's nothing to worry about.'

'What is it, Dad?'

'It's just the clouds bumping together. I used to tell you that when you were little, do you remember?'

Daisy smiled and nodded but a particularly violent flash of lightning wiped the smile from her features. She grabbed David and clung to him.

'It's OK,' he said. 'It's only lightening. You always get thunder and lightning when there's a storm, you know that.'

'So, if thunder is the clouds bumping together, what's lightening?'

David got her to lay down, sitting on the floor beside her bed he held one of her small hands within his own.

'When the clouds bump together they make thunder,' he said, pointing towards the window and waiting for a rumble which duly arrived. 'the lightening is like sparks where the clouds crash.'

A brilliant white flash illuminated the room and Daisy sucked in an anxious breath but David merely squeezed her hand.

'It won't hurt you,' he said, smiling. 'When I was a little boy my Dad used to tell me that thunder was God farting.'

Daisy giggled.

'Granddad used to say that,' she said, her little body shuddering as she laughed.

David's grin broadened.

'He used to say lots of things,' he explained.

They sat in silence for a moment, both of them looking at the window, listening to the elements beyond. The pounding of the rain and the celestial firework show that periodically lit the room with white light and filled it with thunder.

'Do you miss him, Dad?' Daisy said.

David squeezed her hand.

'Yes I do,' he whispered. 'Do you?'

Daisy nodded.

'He used to make me laugh,' she said, quietly.

David swallowed hard.

'He was a good man,' he said, softly, his voice catching. 'And he loved you.' He reached around and tickled Daisy who giggled.

'Is Grandad in heaven now then, Dad?' she asked finally.

David raised his eyebrows and nodded almost imperceptibly.

'He's probably organising everyone up there,' he added.

'Mum doesn't believe in God, does she?' Daisy said.

'What makes you say that?' David asked.

'I heard her say it one time. She was talking to Auntie Julie and she said she didn't believe in God.'

'Well, that's mum's opinion, isn't it?'

'But why doesn't she believe in Him?'

David sighed.

'Well, when her Dad died, before you were born, Mum got very angry and upset and she sort of turned against God,' he explained.

Daisy nodded and rubbed her eyes.

'Not everyone believes in God do they, Dad?' she asked.

'Not everyone,' he explained. 'Different people believe different things. It's their opinion. No one's right or wrong, just different.'

There was another flash of lighting and rumble of thunder.

'God's farting again, Dad,' Daisy chuckled.

David leaned forward and kissed her on the forehead.

'You go back to sleep,' he said, getting to his feet.

'Perhaps it's Granddad farting,' Daisy added.

David laughed, pausing at her bedroom door.

'Sleep tight, princess,' he said. 'I love you.'

'Love you too, Dad.'

David left her bedroom door open a fraction, standing motionless outside it for a second before turning and heading back to his own bed.

Outside, the storm continued.

THE HOUSE
COLORADO, USA

The house wasn't quite in the middle of nowhere but it was pretty close.

Approachable only by a single track that cut practically straight across the countryside for almost five hundred yards once it branched off the service road, it stood in a slight dip in the ground that made it almost invisible until any visitors were within fifty yards of its front door. This, coupled with the trees that grew on three sides of the structure, helped to make it look as if it were hiding from the world. Something that might be an admirable quality to some but might hamper its sale to others.

Solitude was one thing but isolation was something quite different, and the distance from the nearest town might be something that would make the house difficult to sell.

That was one of the thoughts in the mind of Thomas Erikson as he guided the Dodge Durango along the dirt track, muttering to himself each time it passed over the many deep potholes that scarred the ground. He knew the house had been empty for more than a year and he knew that whoever had lived there had obviously never had the approaches to the building levelled to provide a smoother driving surface, but this was appalling.

Erikson saw the next pothole approaching and managed to guide the Dodge around it, just clipping it as he drove by. It jolted the vehicle and he shook his head irritably.

Off to the right there was a small building that he thought at first had been used as a stable, but as he glanced at it he saw that it was windowless, the tiles on the roof were discoloured and missing in many places. If the house was in a similar state of disrepair, he told himself, then it was going to need a hell of a lot of work before anyone parted with their hard-earned money to purchase it. And considering the length of time the property had been empty, there was no reason for him to expect it to be anything other than a mess both inside and out.

When the tenant had died, the bank had been anxious to sell the property in an attempt to recover some of its money and now Erikson was to inspect the house and put a price on it with a view to a sale.

As he drew closer to the building his heart sank even more.

Even from a distance he could see that the outside of the building would need major repairs and decoration.

The area directly in front of the house was overgrown, the grass and weeds almost knee high in most places.

Erikson muttered to himself and brought the Dodge to a halt, sitting behind the wheel for a moment, allowing the song that had been playing on the radio to finish before he switched off the engine and clambered out of the vehicle.

He stood in the sunshine looking at the house for a moment then approached it slowly, his expert eye taking in details here and there.

At the end of the overgrown path leading to the front door Erikson stopped.

He sucked in a deep breath, his gaze fixed on the front of the house.

And, as he stood there, he wondered why every single window frame was sealed with thick black tape.

The front door was the same. Erikson walked up to it and ran his index finger slowly along the black tape, feeling the smoothness, checking the extent of the seal.

He glanced up and saw that the top of the door was not only covered in tape but it was also nailed shut, each metal spike driven through the tape.

Erikson glanced down at the keys in his hand and realized how useless they were. He would have to find another way in.

Twenty minutes later he stood at exactly the same spot shaking his head.

Every single door and window on the property was similarly sealed.

Some had been nailed, some welded closed, but each opening was impenetrable and each was then covered by the same thick black tape, in many places applied in three or four thicknesses.

Thomas Erikson shook his head and wondered how the hell he was going to get inside.

FOUR

The morning brought no respite from the rain.

It was still hammering down but at least the storm had passed. In many places water had laid on the road, the drains having long ago overflowed, unable to cope with the sheer volume of water that had fallen during the night and continued to fall from a sky the colour of wet concrete. News bulletins had already talked about possible records for the amount of rain falling in a twenty-four-hour period and there was, they promised, no respite from the downpour which had been as unexpected as it had been torrential.

Amy stood at the front door and slid her hand into her coat pocket to double check she had her car keys. Satisfied she had, she glanced up the narrow staircase from the hallway.

'Daisy,' she called. 'Come on.'

David emerged from the kitchen, a half-eaten piece of toast in his hand.

'Are you sure it's OK for me to take the car?' Amy asked.

'Yes,' he told her. 'Frank's picking me up.'

'Frank?' Amy said, raising her eyebrows. 'You hate Frank.'

'I don't hate him, he just talks too much and besides he offered me a lift in to work and a lift home so...' David allowed the sentence to trail off.

'You're just using him,' Amy smiled.

'Frank's OK, he just needs to know when to shut up.'

'He's probably lonely since his marriage broke up.'

'I'm not surprised his wife left him.'

'You're horrible.'

David kissed her on the cheek as he passed her, hurrying upstairs, the piece of toast still in his hand.

The prospect of going to work ignited one of a number of emotions in him dependent upon his frame of mind. The overriding feeling was of tedium. The sheer physical act of sitting at a desk and answering phone calls all day wasn't taxing in any way shape or form but it was the sheer waste of time that David objected to. There were surely so many more things he could more usefully be doing for eight or nine hours a day he told himself. Exactly what those things were he wasn't sure but there had to be something more productive than selling shirts for a company whose idea of customer relations was closer to servile than service. He'd applied for a position at a very successful independent Cinema, organising their programming, about twenty miles away but was still waiting to hear and patience had never been David Carson's strong point.

Daisy ran out of her bedroom and almost collided with him. David scooped her up in his arms and hugged her, tickling her as he put her down again, making her giggle.

'How long until our holiday, Dad?' she asked.

'Four years,' David joked.

Daisy giggled.

'No, really, Dad,' she protested.

'Not long,' he told her. 'Now go. Mum's waiting. Have a good day at school. Be a good girl.'

Daisy nodded enthusiastically and sped off down the stairs, jumping down the last two steps to land in the hall with a thud.

'Love you, Dad,' she called, breathlessly.

'I love you too, princess,' he answered.

David stood at the top of the stairs watching his wife and daughter, waving, when Amy finally hustled Daisy out of the front door into the rain beyond. She closed the door behind her and the house was suddenly silent.

David paused at the top of the stairs for a moment longer then continued on into the bedroom to finish dressing, swallowing the last of his toast in the process. He knew that Frank would be arriving to pick him up at any minute. Frank was always on time. Always.

David glanced out of the window once again, shaking his head as he saw how hard the rain was hammering down. The clouds in the sky were like dirty grey rags thrown at the heavens by some irate giant and there were certainly no signs of the downpour ceasing or even easing up. David glanced inside his wardrobe and selected a thicker jacket then he trudged down the stairs once more and stood at the front door waiting.

The car he was waiting for pulled up within moments and David sucked in a deep breath.

'Back to the world of dreams,' he murmured then he sprinted towards the waiting car.

FIVE

If anything, the rain was getting worse.

It hammered against the windscreen and even with the wipers on double speed, Amy had trouble seeing. Two or three times she slowed the car almost to a stop when visibility became too impaired. There was hot air blowing into the car in an effort to keep the inside of the windscreen clear of condensation but the heat was also beginning to become oppressive and Amy lowered the driver's window. Rain spattered her and she tutted irritably.

'What's wrong, mum?' Daisy said, peering out of her own side window, drawing one index finger through the film of condensation.

'Nothing, sweetie,' Amy told her.

'You're not going to swear, are you?' Daisy enquired.

'Why should I do that,' Amy chuckled.

'Dad does it when he's driving.'

'Oh, does he?'

'Only if some silly fucker cuts him up though,' Daisy elaborated.

'What did you say?' Amy snapped, attempting to inject some false indignation into her voice but failing miserably.

'That's what Dad says,' Daisy said, nodding and still looking out of the side window.

'Well, Dad's very naughty,' Amy said, concentrating on the road ahead and easing her foot off the accelerator slightly as the car ploughed through a particularly deep puddle.

'Are you picking me up from school, mum?'

Amy turned the wheel, glancing in the rear-view mirror, concerned that the van behind her was too close in such treacherous driving conditions. She pressed down gently on the brake, eager to show the driver of the vehicle that he was too close. She wished she had an illuminated sign across the back window that spelled out BACK OFF. Unfortunately, she didn't, so she had to rely on touching the brake again when the van showed no sign of falling back.

Amy didn't usually mind the school run. She had become accustomed to the slow-moving traffic on the way and then the dash to work afterwards. It was a chore but a necessary one. The school Daisy attended was a good one and any parent knew that finding a good school was half the battle when considering a child's education. Fortunately, the primary and secondary school were combined so there wasn't the usual trauma of leaving one school then making the step up to the bigger one when the time came. Children in the primary school made regular trips to the secondary part of the building so the environment wasn't so alien to them and the frequency of those visits increased as they neared the age when that move would materialize.

Daisy had nothing like that to worry about for at least three years, Amy thought, glancing across at her daughter who was still gazing happily out of the side window.

Amy glanced in the rear-view mirror again, slowing down as she took another corner, concerned by the sheer amount of water lying on the road. Waves of it sprayed up on both sides of the car as she turned.

Behind her, the van edged closer once again.

'Jesus,' Amy muttered, irritably. 'What is wrong with this guy?'

Daisy looked across at her mum then peered between the two front seats, glancing back in the direction of the van.

The driver was wearing an orange high visibility jacket and, from where Daisy sat, he looked as if he was glowing. His face looked almost the same colour. There was a man with a beard sitting next to him and Daisy frowned when she saw that he was picking his nose.

She turned back, seeing her school looming into view ahead of them.

Scanning the pavements leading to the building she could also see a number of other children being delivered into the care of the educational authorities for the day. One of them she recognised.

'Mum,' she shouted.

Amy gripped the wheel and felt her heart pounding at the sudden explosion of noise.

'There's Kelly,' Daisy said. 'Look.'

She was pointing towards another girl and her mother who were walking along in the rain, trying to avoid the deepest puddles.

Amy slowed the car down, glancing again into her rear-view mirror. She was surprised to see that the van had disappeared. If it had turned into a side road she certainly hadn't noticed but she was just grateful for the fact that it was no longer behind her. She sounded her hooter and the girl on the pavement and her mother looked around in the direction of the car. They both waved.

Daisy was already zipping up her coat, anxious to get out of the car and reach her friend.

'Kelly's mum will be in the usual place at half past three,' Amy said, ruffling her daughter's hair.

'Ok, mum,' Daisy said, pushing the car door open.

'Hey, haven't you forgotten something?' Amy said, wide eyed.

Daisy looked puzzled.

'A kiss for me,' Amy informed her.

Daisy chuckled, kissed her and hurried off to join her friend.

'I love you, sweetie,' Amy called.

'Love you…'

The door slammed shut on the last word.

Amy waved to the other girl and her mother, checked her rear-view mirror once again then drove off. She should, she guessed, be at work in less than thirty minutes, as long as the roads were still passable. If there was too much water lying on the thoroughfares around her workplace she might not be able to get in. It had happened before.

The rain continued to fall.

SIX

David Carson pushed the microphone away from his mouth and exhaled wearily.

'Customer Service would be great without the customers,' he said, reaching for the plastic beaker of water on his desk.

He glanced at his screen, noted that it was time for his break and hauled himself to his feet.

At the desk next to him, Frank Breen raised a hand.

'Want some company?' Breen asked.

David smiled, resisted the temptation to say no and headed for the exit door. Breen followed him and the two of them made their way downstairs to the canteen.

'This rain is bad isn't it?' Breen said, hurrying to keep up with David. 'I saw two people building arcs on the way in.' Breen guffawed at his own joke.

David raised his eyebrows by way of acknowledgement.

The newly decorated and re-furbished headquarters of Raymond Walsh shirts was fifty miles north of London. A call centre (or contact centre as the HR department preferred to call it) and warehouse had been built on the site of an old carpet wholesaler and the entire operation had moved up from its previous flagship location just off Oxford Street in London.

As David pushed open the door of the canteen and made his way across to the vending machine on the far side of the room he was relieved to see that there was no one else on their break. Someone had left a copy of *The Independent* on one of the tables so he got himself a hot chocolate from the machine and sat down with the paper.

Frank Breen joined him a moment later, spilling half his tea on the table as he sat down.

He grabbed some tissues from the dispenser on the table and wiped up the beverage, muttering to himself.

'Ah well,' he said. 'No good crying over it.'

David looked quizzically at him.

'Spilled milk,' said Frank.

'It's tea,' David reminded him.

'But it's got milk in it.'

David nodded.

Frank Breen was in his mid-fifties. A tall and slightly overweight man with glasses. He was completely bald on top with just a halo of hair around the top of his head.

'Are you looking forward to your holiday then, young man?'

Breen wanted to know.

'I can't wait, Frank,' David told him.

'You're going to the States aren't you?'

'We've rented an RV. We're going to drive across Colorado.'

'Sounds like fun.'

'Well, we're looking forward to it. We're just going to relax for two weeks.'

'How do you get the RV? Will it be waiting for you at the airport?'

'No, there's a shuttle bus to take us to the rental location. Then we just transfer our luggage, get in and drive off. Simple as that.'

'The Rocky mountains are in Colorado aren't they?'

'Yes, we're hoping to drive through the foothills at least.'

Breen nodded.

'I don't go on holiday since my wife left me,' he said. 'It's not much fun on your own.'

'I can imagine.'

'I was going to take my mum but she doesn't get around too well. She's 91. I thought of just taking her to the seaside for a couple of days but, like I said, she doesn't get around too well. Bad legs.' He sipped at what was left in his cup.

'You live with your mum don't you, Frank?' David asked.

'I had to move in with her after my marriage broke up,' Frank told him. 'I couldn't afford to stay where I was. I had nothing saved and the pittance they pay here certainly does nothing.' He looked down. 'It's humiliating. A man of my age living with his mother.'

'It's not your fault,' David said, quietly. 'Circumstances change situations don't they?'

Breen nodded gently.

'*Feels like times have changed,*' he said slowly, in a not particularly convincing American accent. 'That's a quote from a film, you know.'

'Which one?'

'*Pat Garrett and Billy the Kid.*'

'The Sam Peckinpah film?'

'That's the one,' Breen said, excitedly. 'I loved his films. *The Wild Bunch, Major Dundee, Straw Dogs.*' He smiled wistfully. 'I took my wife to see *Cross of Iron* for our anniversary one year.'

'That's probably why she left you, Frank,' David murmured.

The two men sat at the table for a moment longer, both of them staring ahead.

'Is your son looking forward to the trip?' Frank Breen said, finally.

'My daughter,' David corrected him.

'Oh, yes. Your daughter,' Frank muttered. 'Is she looking forward to the holiday?'

'She can't wait.'

'I never had any children,' Frank said, quietly.

'Why not?'

'Just never got around to it. I never got around to a lot of things. It's a bit late now though.'

'It's never too late, Frank.'

'That's easy for you to say, you're young.'

'You talk as if you're an old man, you've got years in you yet.'

'Really? Can I have that in writing?'

David looked at the older man who was gazing down into his cup as if seeking some kind of inspiration at the bottom of the murky liquid within.

'People talk about second chances,' he said, softly. 'But there aren't really second chances.' He looked directly at David with sadness in his eyes. 'Not for people like me.'

'I think there are second chances, Frank.'

'Are there? What would you do differently if you had another chance, David?'

David shrugged.

'If you could change anything about your life, if you could even influence your own destiny would you?'

'My own destiny? That's a bit deep for a coffee break, Frank.'

Frank Breen drained what was left in his beaker and put it down on the table.

'If you lost someone close to you, what would do?' he asked, flatly.

'Bloody hell, Frank. Deep, and now depressing.'

'I was just thinking aloud.'

'Well, if they're the kind of thoughts you're having, keep them to yourself,' David said, trying to smile.

'When I lost my wife I wondered what I could have done differently,' Frank said.

'You didn't lose your wife, Frank, she left you,' David reminded him.

'It was as if she'd died,' Frank said. 'I felt as if she'd died. She wasn't with me anymore, she might as well have been dead. I would have done anything in my power to bring her back to me. Wouldn't you do that, David? If you lost someone you loved wouldn't you do everything you could to bring them back? No matter what the cost?'

David nodded slowly.

'Yes, I would, Frank,' he said. 'Yes, I would.'

'I think anyone would,' Breen murmured. 'But you never know until you're in that position, do you?'

'How many people get a second chance at anything?'

'I suppose you just have to hope but, to be honest, hope is in short supply sometimes.'

David nodded and glanced towards the windows where the rain was still lashing down.

THE CHURCH
COLORADO, USA

The church was a small whitewashed structure that stood on the northern bank of a wide but shallow river. The bank rose sharply on the northern side, almost a sheer fifteen or twenty foot drop that rose from the surface of the water before levelling out into scrubland. Grass grew around the building as sparsely as hair on the head of a balding man. There were three or four stunted trees in the area leading up to the main entrance, but all seemed leafless irrespective of the season. When the wind blew through their branches it sounded like dry bones rattling together. The applause of dead hands.

There were no roads or tracks leading either up to or away from the church. At one time there had been a dirt track which had been flattened by the passage of many vehicles but no one had visited the church for years. Not for the purpose for which it was designed anyway. In the long hot summers, the barely visible remains of the track had been eroded so that it simply looked like the rest of the barren earth around the building.

The ground sloped down gently towards the bank and, below, the river ran past, no more than four or five feet from surface to bottom even at its deepest point. During the summer it frequently dropped to half that depth and would have been easy to cross had anyone bothered to try.

On the southerly bank grass grew thickly, almost lustrously. Trees too, towered over the landscape, leaning over the river and providing cover for the birds and animals that made their homes there.

The Northern bank was, it seemed, shunned by wildlife.

Mice had nested inside the church at one time and there had been a bird's nest in the bell tower, but no more.

Built as a monument to God, the church looked as if it had been abandoned by the Creator and those who, at one time, had sung praises to His name within its walls.

Exactly whose land it stood on no one seemed to know. If the barren patch of earth upon which it stood was the property of anyone then they obviously didn't care too much about it. Even if anyone had wanted to enter the church, the large wooden planks that had been hammered across its main doors would have prevented that simple act. It remained neglected and forgotten, in time to crumble and rot away just as anything else that had been discarded.

On the other side of the river a large crow sat in the branches of a tree gazing out across the gently flowing water. Finally, it left the branch, rising high into the clear blue sky on its black wings, soaring out over the river and then towards the church on the other side.

It flew high over the church as if some kind of primal instinct were driving it as far from the edifice as possible. Why it flew so high it didn't know. Why it wanted to avoid the building it had no idea. Some primordial instinct forced it away from any close proximity to the battered building.

Had it swooped lower and closer, it may well have heard the faint sounds coming from the forgotten and dilapidated structure.

SEVEN

Amy Carson sat back from her Mac screen, massaged the bridge of her nose between her thumb and forefinger and blinked myopically. When she looked at the screen again, the image that stared back at her looked no better than it had when she first looked.

It was a mermaid. A generic, cliché of a mermaid. And after the mermaid it would be a rabbit, or a fairy or a puppy or something else excruciatingly cute, probably decorated with sparkles. Amy smiled to herself. That was the way here, everything was pink, sparkly, cute and cuddly. That was the Eskimo way.

Unlike most publishing houses, Eskimo Publishing was situated not within the grimy and noisy confines of a big city like London but in expansive and beautiful countryside. Housed in a converted farm building, it had been in existence for more than fifteen years and had been growing rapidly since it's foundation. One of the main reasons for its growth was not the quality of the product it delivered but the company's ability to deliver illustrated books and toys so cheaply. The printing was done in Taiwan or China. The books themselves were usually eight or ten page 'board books' aimed at very young children who were going to do little more than chew them when presented with them. A team of editors and designers (of which Amy was one) were from a diverse range of backgrounds, very few of them having previously been in publishing, gathered together every day to hasten through more of the cut-price product that had made Eskimo such a force in children's publishing.

Amy had been in her current position for the last two years and, despite the fact that the money was poor, it was the relaxed atmosphere and working hours that had appealed to her. The novelty, however, had worn off fairly rapidly. Amy had always wondered how a company, so resolutely determined to crush all creativity within its employees, had managed to flourish but that vexing question was one that she considered less and less these days.

There were strict guidelines that had to be adhered to in order for each book or activity pack to maintain the Eskimo style. Certain colours were anathema (on the orders of the publishing director). Even some words were taboo (on the orders of the publishing director). Words like 'mischievous' or 'naughty'. Words that (on the orders of the publishing director) didn't sound right. Words that someone, somewhere, might be offended by. Everything had to be safe and predictable. Everything had to be right. Nothing new or original could be attempted for fear that it failed. Cliché was the order of the day. So, work was done within these strictures and restraints and it was all done on budgets and schedules that prevented even the smallest amount of employee input. That was why their turnover of staff was so high.

'Amy.'

Hearing her name made her jump and she looked up to see who was standing so close to her.

It was Alan Knox, the editorial director. He was wearing his usual practised smile and looking down at her with the kind of expression a lion might wear if it had stumbled on a crippled zebra.

'Yes, Alan?' Amy said, trying to inject a little enthusiasm into her voice. Alan liked enthusiasm and positivity. He liked team work. He liked anything that had just come out of the latest management manual.

'How's Magical Mermaid coming along?' Alan asked, moving from one foot to the other as if he was about to spring forward and run a sprint.

'It's coming,' Amy said. 'It's not particularly magical at the moment but I'm getting there.' She pointed at the screen which showed a mermaid (the Magical Mermaid of the title) sitting on a rock beside the sea, gazing wistfully out at the ocean and the gently breaking waves.

'Not sure about the colour of that seaweed,' Alan said, pointing at the clump of withered plant that was pictured along the bottom of the illustration. 'It's a bit dull. A bit murky.'

'Shall I try green instead of brown?' Amy suggested.

Alan sucked air through his teeth and his face showed the kind of expression he might have worn if Amy had suggested inserting a red hot poker into his anus.

'Not green,' he winced. 'Try teal.'

'Teal? It's seaweed.'

'Yes, but Frank doesn't like green. Teal is more of an upbeat colour.'

Amy raised her eyebrows.

'Let me know when you've done it,' Alan smiled and walked away towards the nearest desk to Amy's. 'Oh, and by the way,' he added, spinning around and pointing one index finger at her. 'Don't forget we've got our meeting later.'

Amy nodded sagely and carried on with her work.

There were four pods set up in the large room, each of them peopled by two editors and two designers. It was the duty of these two 'publishing pairs' to check the art work and text that was sent into Eskimo by the large numbers of freelancers who actually completed their projects. These freelancers weren't referred to within the company as writers or artists but as 'packagers', something which, Amy thought, spoke volumes about their abilities. Present on Amy's pod was Carl, who was about thirty but acted as if he was twice that age, and Stephanie who was in her mid-twenties and as irritating as anyone Amy had ever had the misfortune of meeting. Enthusiasm was fine but she ran around the office as if she'd just snorted a kilo of cocaine, washed down with pure caffeine. However, she did suffer from migraines which, Amy thought, was a blessing in disguise because when one struck her it at least shut her up for a couple of hours.

Both she and Carl were editors, or passed for them. They were basically project managers who thought they were creative and defined that creativity by the number of books they worked on and how much they'd contributed to them, although correcting spelling mistakes in an eight page version of HICKORY DICKORY DOCK hardly seemed to qualify as great creativity as far as Amy was concerned.

She glanced at her watch and noticed that it was approaching one p.m. Lunch time. She blinked myopically and yawned.

'Are we going for a walk?'

The question came from Nicola Gray, the other designer on her pod, who was sitting opposite her.

Amy nodded.

'I need to clear my head,' she told Nikki, who was four or five years younger than her. 'And it looks as if it's finally stopped raining.'

She glanced towards the large picture windows that afforded views of the countryside and saw that the rain had indeed stopped falling. There were several deep puddles on the ground but there was a long winding driveway that cut across the land surrounding the buildings making up Eskimo publishing, so there would be enough firm ground for them to walk on, Amy thought. She would be glad to get out of the office for an hour.

She always was.

THE INFECTION
COLORADO, USA

The term hypodermic comes from two Greek words meaning beneath the skin. The man holding the needle in front of him had no idea why this should enter his mind, now of all times.

But it did. He merely sat gazing at the syringe he held as if it were about to impart all the secrets of time and the universe to him. The untold secrets of humanity, creation and evolution all contained within a small plastic syringe, its long hollow needle and the almost clear 50ml of fluid it contained. He smiled to himself.

Fifty millilitres. The measurement might not be correct but the only way he could discover that was by trial and error. How many attempts he would have to make before he finally got the correct measurement was unknown. He hoped that this latest attempt would be more successful.

One hundred millilitres had been too much. Twenty had been too little. Or, had it been the composition of the fluid itself, not the actual amounts that had caused the previous failures? He couldn't be sure. He knew he had to continue with his work in an attempt to isolate both the correct measurements, and also the correct composition. There were other imponderables too. Even if the amount was right, if the composition was correct and everything else was favourable then perhaps it was the location of the injection that was wrong.

He sucked in a deep breath and gazed more intently at the syringe.

Into a vein or into a muscle?

He shook his head. Did it really make a difference? He had made the last two injections directly into the base of the skull.

On both occasions, the recipient had been dead within an hour.

There had to be a better place to put the needle. Somewhere on the body that would allow swift absorption of the injected liquid but also somewhere that would allow time for the newly introduced substance to adequately reach those parts of the anatomy it needed to reach.

He continued to gaze at the needle, watching as the light glinted on the elegant steel tip. It was a shorter needle than usual and thinner. This would allow easier insertion into the part of the body that he chose.

The man got to his feet and turned towards the other side of the basement. That was where the child was secured.

Held to a wooden table by a combination of rope and straps, it had not moved much in the last ten minutes. Its struggles had gradually receded since he first brought it down here, as if it realized that fighting against the restraints was pointless. Occasionally it would strain against the straps but, apart from that, the only sound it emitted was a low sob every now and then.

As the man walked across the basement the child began to struggle again, jerking against the straps and ropes for a moment or two as it heard the footsteps approaching. The man slowed his pace, his hand shaking slightly as he lowered the syringe. He knew that the child would scream or shake or try to escape again when it saw the needle.

They always did.

But then, he reasoned, no matter what he did there would be screams and crying and suffering.

That was the way it had to be.

He stood over the child, running appraising eyes over it.

A girl of ten or eleven. She was a pretty little thing. Or she had been at one time. The cuts and sores on her face had negated the dainty beauty he had noticed when he'd first taken her. Her lips were swollen and bloody, cut in several places where she'd chewed through them. The flesh there wasn't very strong and her teeth had cut easily through the tissue. Her fingernails too were bloodied and broken, from where she had scratched at her own body but also from where she had attempted to escape by clawing at the walls of the small room he'd imprisoned her in shortly after snatching her.

He looked down at the child, regarding her evenly.

She lay still, unaware as yet that he held the syringe. When he raised it into view she began to struggle again, her eyes bulging wide with terror.

And then he realized where the needle must go.

He wondered why he hadn't thought of it before. The solution seemed so obvious. He leaned over the child using one hand to hold her head steady, then, he brought his other hand up, his thumb already poised over the plunger of the syringe.

The girl tried to scream but the rag that had been secured in her mouth by a length of rope prevented that exhortation.

It was probably just as well.

The man leaned closer and brought the syringe close to her face.

He steadied it and aimed the needle at her eye.

EIGHT

Amy knocked lightly on the door, waited a second then walked in.

Trying to control the quite irrational nervousness she was feeling, she smiled efficiently and slipped into the room, noticing immediately that there was another figure present too. One she hadn't been expecting.

Seated behind the desk, Alan Knox waved her in, pointing to the small wooden chair that had been placed opposite him.

To Knox's right sat the individual Amy hadn't expected to see.

Carla Sheringham was in her early thirties and head of Eskimo's HR department. She was an attractive woman who towered above most of the other staff in the organisation, her three-inch heels boosting her already considerable height to close to six feet. Fortunately, she was sitting down now and Amy also sat, exchanging brief pleasantries with Carla who had her iPad before her and occasionally tapped at the screen for reasons best known to herself.

'Carla's going to sit in on our little chat,' Knox said.

'Am I getting the sack?' Amy asked, trying to smile. 'Usually HR only turn up when someone's getting the sack.'

'We don't use that word, Amy,' Carla interjected, smiling and raising her hand to her mouth.

'Well, whichever word you use,' Amy went on. 'Am I getting it?'

'As you know,' Knox continued. 'Eskimo has recently been purchased by a major American company and, inevitably, there may be some staffing issues. Stream-lining that's been requested by the new owners.'

'Cuts in staff,' Amy offered.

'Possibly,' Knox conceded. 'We don't know yet but we just wanted to make people aware.'

'There could be changes here and they might affect the levels of staff required,' Carla added.

'And I could be one of the ones losing their jobs?' Amy asked.

'No, no, no,' Knox said, waving a hand before him as if he was trying to clear the air of a bad smell. 'No decisions have been made. We're just allowing people to prepare for the possibility. Just giving them the heads-up.' He smiled.

Amy nodded.

'These new owners are looking for a specific kind of employee,' Carla added. 'They're very community minded.'

'Meaning?' Amy asked.

'We see ourselves as a big family here at Eskimo,' Carla went on.

Amy sighed, wearily.

'We work hard together and we play hard together,' Carla went on.

'The social side of the company is nearly as important as the business side,' Knox added. 'That's why so many social events are organised by Carla and her department.'

'But you don't come to many of the staff social events do you, Amy?' Carla said looking devastated. 'You didn't come to the Christmas Party or the barbecue, did you?'

'And you don't come to the end of month pub lunches,' Knox intoned.

'And you didn't come ice skating last month either, did you?' Carla added, sadly.

'I have things to do outside work you know,' Amy said. 'Most of the staff in there are younger, they don't seem to have any interests outside work and the people they work with. I have a husband and a child.'

'I've got a family too, Amy,' Knox chimed in. 'But I find time to join in. I have a son called Corrado, you know.'

Amy ignored the temptation to tell Knox that was *his* problem. Anyone who named a child Corrado needed a slap as far as Amy was concerned.

'I've heard you mention him,' she said. 'Once or twice.'

If he caught the sarcasm in her voice, Knox didn't comment on it.

'So, you can understand the concerns we have,' Knox went on. 'It's important to interact with your colleagues out of work as well as in it.'

'Why?' Amy said, flatly.

'To foster the feeling of one-ness,' Knox told her, a smug grin on his face.

'I come to work to earn money, not to make friends,' Amy announced. 'I have friends outside work. Friends *I've* chosen, not ones that the company thinks I should have.'

Carla and Knox both looked suitably distraught. They glanced at each other then at Amy almost apologetically.

'Well,' Knox said. 'We've told you the situation.'

'So you're threatening me with the sack if I don't socialise more?' Amy told him. 'That's about the size of it isn't it?'

'No, no, no, not at all,' Knox went on. 'I like you Amy, I want to help you. I'm just telling you the way it is. The company that purchased Eskimo is very keen on a community spirit.'

'And any staff who don't toe the line are out, is that it?' Amy said.

'It isn't like that,' Knox told her, a self-satisfied smile on his face.

'They're already planning a summer party at the home of the new Managing Director. There'll be a special marquee erected in his garden and it'll give employees from here and from the parent company the chance to mingle. We're all expected to attend.'

'Why?' Amy wanted to know. 'So he can show off his big house and remind us all *we'll* never earn that much money?'

'That's a very negative attitude, Amy,' Carla murmured, a look of displeasure on her face.

'I'll go and sit on the naughty step shall I?' Amy retorted, shaking her head.

'It's important to have a good work stroke leisure balance,' Knox told her.

'I agree,' Amy offered. 'But I prefer my leisure time away from the people I work with.'

'All the staff here can bring a guest to the summer party,' Carla added. 'The new company will pay for accommodation over that weekend.'

'My husband hates socialising even more than I do,' Amy chuckled.

'Well, that's unfortunate,' Knox proclaimed. 'As I said, this company really does value its employee's presence at events.'

'I'm not the only one who feels this way you know,' Amy protested.

'Well, we haven't heard anyone else speak the way you have,' Knox assured her.

'Perhaps they're scared of losing their jobs,' Amy said.

'This has nothing to do with that,' Knox sighed.

'It has *everything* to do with that. If my work was below standard I could accept this,' Amy told him. 'It's not is it?'

'Your work is fine, Amy,' Knox elaborated. 'You could be a little more adventurous sometimes but....'

'What's the point?' Amy snapped. 'Everything I do that isn't specifically requested is rejected anyway.'

'Not everything,' Knox chided.

'Nearly everything,' Amy continued. 'You should just give us guidelines to follow instead of pretending we actually have any creative input at all.'

'I'm sorry you feel like that,' Knox muttered.

'None of these staff cuts are confirmed yet, Amy,' Carla

offered. 'We're just letting people know the situation.'

'Warning them you mean?' Amy muttered.

'That isn't how we see it,' Knox said.

'So there's nothing wrong with my work,' Amy enquired. 'Just with my socialising?'

'We have the annual rounders day coming up,' Carla told her excitedly. 'You didn't come last year, if you could make it this time around that would be super cool.'

'I'm busy that weekend,' Amy said.

'You don't know which weekend it is,' Knox reminded her.

'Well,' Amy sighed getting to her feet. 'Whichever weekend it is I'm busy.'

She looked at them for a moment then turned towards the door. 'Shall I send the next victim in?'

'Yes please,' Knox murmured, looking down at his notes.

Amy slipped out.

THE CAPTIVE
COLORADO, USA

At first he thought he'd gone blind. When the boy opened his eyes there was only darkness. Thick, impenetrable darkness. He swallowed and shook his head as if that simple action would force away the gloom but, of course, it didn't.

Only after a few seconds did the boy realize that he had been blindfolded.

A piece of thick dark cloth had been wound around his eyes and the top part of his head, pulled so tightly that it was making his head throb.

The man who had wrapped it so securely around his head had been strong and he had needed that strength to subdue the boys struggles.

The boy remembered being grabbed from behind as he walked towards his home, the feeling of terror and helplessness as he was lifted off his feet, hands gripping his throat and face. Then he had felt the stinging injection in his back and the coldness that seemed to fill him.

That was all he remembered. Everything shortly after the injection had been darkness as he'd fallen into unconsciousness. How long ago that had been he had no idea but it felt like a long time.

He tried to move his arms but he couldn't and, as he slowly regained his consciousness he realized that this inability was caused by the thick leather restraints around both his wrists. There were two more securing his ankles.

As he tried to sit up he realized that there was another one around his chest, holding him down as surely as if he had a boulder on him. He strained against the straps once again but it was useless.

'You can't get away.'

He heard the voice close to his head and snapped it around towards the direction from which the sound had come.

'This is the way it has to be,' the voice went on.

It was deep. A man's voice but not one he recognised.

'I would say I'm sorry for what I'm going to do to you but I'm not. It's necessary you see.'

The boy heard footsteps moving around him and the next time he heard the voice it was in a different place. Closer to him now.

'I know you don't understand that,' the voice continued. 'But it doesn't matter. It doesn't matter what you understand. It wouldn't help if you understood. I've still got to do what has to be done. I've still got to hurt you.'

The boy pulled against the restraints once again.

He felt a hand on his forehead and he gasped.

'No,' the voice whispered. 'Struggling won't help. And what we're doing here is a good thing. It will help others eventually. I know you won't appreciate that but it's true.'

There were more footsteps and the boy realized that the owner of the voice was walking around him again, his footfalls echoing inside what was obviously a large room.

'This has to be done,' the voice went on. 'Not just to you but to others as well. There have been others before you and there will be more after you. And they will all be purified the same way. With pain.'

The boy jerked hard against the restraints, his breath now coming in gasps.

'Pain is the only way to remove the infection,' continued the voice. 'The contamination. When a wound is cauterized, fire or heat are used to burn out the impurities and seal the veins and arteries. The heat is a cleansing agent. And in this case, pain is the thing that cleanses.'

The boy felt a hand rest lightly on his thigh and his fear finally overwhelmed him.

He began to urinate, unable to help himself.

'It's strange the effects that fear has on people,' the voice went on. 'Effects that no one can anticipate. Pain is the same. No one knows how they will react to pain, especially when it is applied in a measured way. A controlled way. The way you will undergo it.'

The footsteps were loud again. The owner of the voice was on the move once more and when the boy heard words spoken next time they were close to his right ear. Again, he jerked his head around towards the direction from which they were coming, still unable to see as much as a chink of daylight through the thick folds of material obscuring his vision.

'There is a purpose to this,' the voice proclaimed. 'A purpose and an end result. Evil must be cleansed. It must be removed from this world and only by the inflicting of pain can that evil be exorcised. When a person is in truly excruciating pain they haven't got time to think about right and wrong, morality or immorality or any other kind of philosophical matter. They only know that pain. It has a kind of purity to it. It's untainted. They are untouched for the moments they are suffering.'

The boy could hear his captor breathing heavily close to him now, as if speaking the words was itself an exhausting job.

'I've known what I had to do for a long time now,' the owner of the voice told him. 'But knowing and being able to carry out the task are two different things. It takes strength of will as well as physical strength. But that's something else you wouldn't understand.' There was a chuckle which sounded horribly menacing as it echoed inside the room.

'Evil flourishes in this world,' said the voice. 'And it will grow stronger unless it is checked, because too many people are content to ignore it. They won't fight back. They won't try and defeat it. To fight it you have to use extreme methods. You must have stronger will than the thing you're fighting against.'

The boy felt warm, stale breath in his face as the owner of the voice bent close to him.

'I wish you could understand that, if nothing else,' said the owner of the voice. 'You are doing good by your suffering. You are helping ultimately by enduring your pain.' There was a heavy silence in which the boy heard only low breathing and then, the voice once more. 'And now we must begin. Your pain must start. Because if it has no beginning how can it have an end?'

The boy began whimpering as he heard the footsteps moving away from him, only to return a moment later. It was then that he heard the sound of metal against metal. What the owner of the voice was holding he could only guess and the thought sent waves of terror coursing through him once more. He struggled violently for a second then lay still.

'What I do I do in God's name,' the voice murmured. 'It is time.'

The boy would have screamed for mercy and help if his tongue hadn't already been torn out.

NINE

'Good day?'

Amy Carson merely raised her eyebrows as Julie Taylor spoke the words.

The two women had been friends for the last ten years ever since they'd both worked together at the local government offices. They saw each other every day when Amy came to pick up her daughter and, every day, she repeated her gratitude to Julie for picking Daisy up from school and caring for her until Amy picked her up. The two of them went out once a month religiously. For a meal, to the cinema or just for a drink but those meetings were important to them and helped cement a friendship that had flourished so easily and was as strong as ever.

'You should leave that place,' Julie said as she closed the door behind Amy. 'All you ever do is moan about it.'

'I wasn't moaning,' Amy reminded her.

'You didn't have to,' Julie smiled. 'I can see the look on your face.'

'And if I leave there where am I going to go? The company that just bought Eskimo own most of the other children's publishers too. They're taking over the fucking world.'

Julie smiled.

Amy smiled back, despite herself.

'You were talking about going freelance not long ago,' Julie reminded her.

'I'd be terrified the work would run out,' Amy explained, wandering through into the kitchen where she sat down on one of the wooden chairs around the table. Julie poured her a cup of tea then sat down beside her.

'The girls are fine,' she said, answering Amy's unasked question. 'They're playing upstairs in Kelly's room.'

Amy nodded and sipped at her tea.

'Is it just work that's bothering you?' Julie asked.

'What else would it be?' Amy enquired.

'I just wondered if David was OK,' Julie offered.

'He's fine,' Amy told her. 'And no, he's not drinking again if that's what you were getting at.'

'I'm here if you need to talk, you know that.'

'Trust me, Julie, if David had started drinking again I'd tell you. You'd know about it.'

The two women sat in silence for a moment then Julie cleared her throat.

'Do you ever worry he's going to start again?' she said.

Amy raised her eyebrows.

'I don't think about it,' she said. 'He hasn't touched a drop for over a year. He's settled in his job. We're getting back on our feet. He wouldn't jeopardise that. Not again. He knows what he put us through the first time.'

Julie nodded.

'This holiday is like the final piece in the jigsaw,' Amy went on. 'The last thing we need to tell us that we're over all that shit. That it's all in the past.'

'Are you sure about that?'

'Yes, I am,' she said flatly.

Julie reached across and squeezed her friends hand.

'And you're sure *you* won't start drinking? Having to drive across Colorado?' she asked, her voice heavy with mock concern.

Amy laughed.

'What's wrong with Colorado?' she said, smiling. 'It has more sunshine every year than Florida I'll have you know.'

Julie laughed too.

'So you've done your research I see,' she said. 'I just thought you might have gone to Disneyland or somewhere that would have suited Daisy better.'

'She can't wait,' Amy said. 'We just need the break, Julie, and I think being away from other people for a couple of weeks will do us all good. Standing in queues for three hours to get on rides at Disneyland wasn't really what we wanted.'

'So, you just drive for two weeks?' Julie said.

'No, not just drive. We stop and get out and walk around in fresh air. We stay in hotels sometimes. We do whatever we like for two weeks,' Amy explained. 'And we haven't done that for a long time.'

Julie was about to say something when there was a thumping from above them. Moments later, Daisy and Kelly rushed into the kitchen, Daisy making straight for Amy who swept her up in her arms.

'Right,' she said. 'We'll leave you in peace. Daisy, go and get your things from upstairs and we'll go home and see Dad.'

Daisy scrambled free and dashed back out of the room with Kelly in pursuit.

Amy got to her feet and headed towards the front door, digging in her pocket for her car keys.

'At least the rain's stopped,' Julie noted, glancing out of the window. 'I was beginning to wonder if it was going to.'

Amy nodded, standing in the hall and watching as Daisy came hurrying down.

'Don't run on the stairs,' Amy called and Daisy slowed her pace, finally standing beside her mother in the hallway.

Julie opened the door, her arm around her own daughter. She watched as Amy and Daisy walked out towards the waiting car. She and Kelly waved as the car pulled away.

TEN

David Carson slumped into the passenger seat of the car and slammed the door shut.

'Careful,' Frank Breen said, hearing the thud. 'I'm rather attached to this car.'

'Sorry,' David breathed.

As the engine started so too did the car radio. Immediately David recognised the song that was playing.

'*Baker Street*,' he said, nodding his head. 'I love this song.'

'Gerry Rafferty,' Breen added. 'Very talented man. He went insane you know.'

David looked at his older companion.

'Insane?' he said.

'Well, he had some psychological problems,' Breen elaborated. 'Just goes to prove that money isn't everything.'

'Oh, don't start that again, Frank,' David said, dismissively.

'It isn't. It can't buy happiness.'

'It can buy *anything*.'

'All the money in the world wouldn't bring my wife back to me,' Breen said, wistfully.

'Frank, trust me, if you had all the money in the world, I'm sure your wife would find you attractive again.' He smiled to himself.

'What would you buy if money was no object?' Breen wanted

to know. 'If you had millions.'

'After a nice house and a decent car, I'd put money in a trust fund for my daughter.'

'Why?'

'So she wouldn't have to go through the shit I've had to go through because I'd got no money,' David said, smiling.

'She'd turn into a spoilt little brat without work to do.'

'No, she wouldn't. She appreciates everything she's given. She always has. She's a great kid.'

'Your wife's brought her up well then?' Breen grinned.

David nodded.

'I take none of the credit,' he said, happily. 'She's got her mum's good character traits.'

'She must have some of yours.'

David shrugged, glancing out of the side window as Breen drove.

'I'm not sure I've got any good ones, Frank,' he said, quietly.

'There's good in everyone, David. Don't put yourself down.'

'I wasn't. I was just making a point.'

'Would you change anything about your life if you could?' Breen asked.

'Not again,' David grinned. 'You asked me that at tea break.'

'Well would you?' Breen went on.

'Of course I would. All the bad things.'

'They say everything happens for a reason, don't they? So, even the bad stuff that happened, happened for a reason.'

'If you say so, Frank. I just want to forget the bad stuff.'

'What does not kill me makes me stronger.'

'That's Nietzsche, isn't it?'

'It's on the opening credits of *Conan the Barbarian* and that's good enough for me,' Breen smiled. 'I suppose that's true. When you get through bad things it gives you strength.'

'Do you feel stronger because your wife left you?'

Breen shook his head.

'So, that's bollocks then isn't it?' David insisted. 'And I certainly don't feel any stronger since I gave up drinking.'

'Gave up?' Breen said, glancing at him. 'Why did you give up?'

'Because I had a problem with it.'

'Were you alcoholic?'

'I don't think I was. Alcoholic, to me, is two or three bottles of vodka a night. I wasn't drinking anything like that much.'

'It can creep up on you though. Without you even knowing.'

David nodded and returned to his vigil out of the side window.

'People can lose everything when they're addicted to drink or substances can't they?' Breen went on.

David merely nodded. He was already angry with himself for even having mentioned the fact that he'd had a drink problem. Exactly how that problem had affected him and those around him he had no intention of discussing now or at any other time with Frank Breen or anyone else. He'd barely talked about it with those close to him, he certainly wasn't going to break his self-imposed silence with a work colleague.

'Everyone copes in their own way, Frank,' he said, finally.

'My father used to drink,' Breen told him. 'I can remember when I was a kid seeing him sitting around with his cans of beer.'

'It's not a good look, is it?' David chuckled.

Breen smiled. 'No, it isn't. I suppose it's an escape. Just like drugs or sex.'

David glanced briefly at his companion.

'Or porn,' Breen went on. 'Some people have porn addictions, don't they?'

'So I believe,' David said, looking out of the side window again.

'When I was out of work I used to look at porn a lot,' the older man went on. 'Too much if I'm honest.'

'What's too much?'

'When you're looking at porn at seven in the morning you know you've got a problem.'

David raised his eyebrows.

'I used to go in to chat rooms,' Breen went on. 'I think I just wanted the company as much as anything. It wouldn't have mattered whether they were talking about flower arranging or having sex with pigs, it was just nice knowing someone else was there.'

'I know what you mean, Frank,' David said, wearily, wishing his companion would shut up.

Breen looked as if he wanted to say something else but exactly what it was David never found out because they drove the rest of the relatively short journey in silence.

THE THEORY
COLORADO, USA

It had to be children.

He had thought about it many times and he was convinced that the subjects of the experiment must be children. They were untouched, untainted and yet to be corrupted by the vagaries of everyday life. They still looked at the world through innocent eyes. They trusted. They loved unconditionally. Their personalities were yet to be twisted by the torments and pain they would experience as adults.

It had to be children. And preferably children aged from five to ten. He wondered if he was being too specific but then dismissed his own doubts. If his work was to be successful then he would have to keep that kind of specificity.

It was like working with a blank canvas.

Teenagers had already begun to develop the kind of traits they would manifest in adulthood, he reasoned. Also, they were far more suspicious. It wasn't so easy to dupe a teenager.

Grown men and women had too much psychological baggage, it made the tests more difficult to judge.

And, they were more difficult to catch.

The man walked back and forth slowly from one side of the basement to the other, his mind racing, his fingers intertwined behind his back.

How often he would have to carry out his experiments he had no idea. There were no precedents that he could rely on. No research that he could refer to that would offer a guide to him. All the work was his so all the trial and error was also his. There was no one to turn to for help. He was alone but he relished that. If he was alone then he had no one else to rely on. There were no others who would interfere or try and change his mind. The only thoughts and ideas that counted were his.

He had lived alone most of his life. Unlike many he had never been uncomfortable with his own company or his own thoughts. His mother had once said to him 'if you don't like your own company then don't expect others to like it either.'

It was sound philosophy that he had retained. One of the many pearls of home spun wisdom that she had imparted to him during his life.

She'd died more than ten years ago, the victim of a stroke that had unfortunately left her paralysed down her left side, incontinent and incapable of all but the most rudimentary of speech. What she had become had hurt him even more than her eventual passing. To see a woman who had been so vital and alive reduced to nothing more than a mumbling zombie had been almost intolerable for him.

Her death had been something of a relief if he was honest. Towards the end she had barely recognised him anyway. Talking to her had been fruitless and pointless if he was really honest. He hated himself for admitting that but what else was he to do? He visited her grave once a week, taking a large bouquet of tulips and roses each time. He would clean the black marble headstone and keep the plot tidy, always finding something to do when he arrived.

Even now, a decade since she left him, there wasn't a day that passed that he didn't think about her. He missed her. He missed the woman she had been before the stroke.

The house had been hers and, when she died, it had passed to him. No one visited any longer. But that was fine as far as he was concerned. He didn't want people coming around. He didn't want anyone snooping or sticking their noses into his business.

He looked around the basement, his eyes alighting on one part of the large subterranean room. He nodded to himself. There were things he needed.

He decided to drive into Denver for them.

The drive would help him to think straight, to clear his head. And when he was finished, he would drive around to the airport and have a coffee. Something he often did. He liked the airport. He could melt into the crowds easily. He was faceless there.

And there were always lots of children.

ELEVEN

'Can we have pizza for dinner, mum?'

Amy glanced at Daisy who was sitting in the passenger seat pulling at a loose thread on the sleeve of her school blouse.

'Yes,' Amy said, smiling. 'We'll call in and get it on the way home.'

'Can't you just ring up when we get home?'

'Why?'

'Because I like it when the man brings it to the house,' Daisy giggled. 'Especially when he's on that little motorbike.'

Amy smiled and shook her head.

'Do they have pizza in America?' Daisy wanted to know. 'Do they have it where we're going?'

'They love pizza in America,' Amy informed her.

'And McDonald's?'

'And Burger King and KFC and lots of others we don't have over here.'

'Have you and Dad been to America before?' Daisy enquired.

'Yes, sweetie, but we went to New York.'

'Did you like it?'

'We loved it.'

'Can we go to New York next time so I can see it as well?'

Amy smiled.

'Of course we can,' she said.

'Why didn't I go with you when you and Dad went?' Daisy wanted to know.

'Well, you sort of went with us because I was pregnant at the time so you were in my tummy, just not actually walking around,' Amy told her daughter.

'I wonder if American children are like English ones,' Daisy mused, still pulling at the thread on her cuff.

'I think children all around the world are pretty similar,' Amy offered. 'The good ones are good and the bad ones are bad.' She grinned and nudged Daisy, turning the steering wheel and slowing down slightly as the traffic ahead of her began to brake. The warning lights at the approach to the level crossing about a hundred yards ahead were already flashing and, as Amy tapped gently on the wheel, the barriers began to fall. She stopped the car and stuck it in neutral, glancing in her rear-view mirror to see that the road behind them was clear.

Ahead, the barriers of the level crossing were down. The train should be passing very shortly. After that they should be home in less than fifteen minutes.

Daisy sat up and unbuckled her seat belt, kneeling on the edge of the seat so she could get a better view of the train she knew would be passing shortly.

'Sit down, sweetie and put your seat belt back on,' Amy instructed.

'I want to see the train,' Daisy told her.

'You'll be able to see it with your seat belt *on*,' Amy told her.

'Now strap yourself in again.'

'Mum,' Daisy tutted.

'Or no pizza,' Amy told her, raising her eyebrows.

Daisy instantly did as she was told, the snap of the belt echoing inside the car.

'Can we go on a train in America, mum?' she asked, pulling at the belt once it was secured again.

'Maybe,' Amy told her. 'If we get time. We'll be in the RV most of the time.'

'Is it like a bus?'

'Well, sort of but there'll only be you, me and Dad in it and we can drive wherever we like.'

Amy glanced at her watch and then at the dashboard clock. The train was close now, she could hear the rumble even from this far back. The trains that passed were only local services. Two or three carriages at most and occasionally a goods train towing trucks full of God knows what. There was a small station just beyond the level crossing that looked crowded if there were more than a dozen people on the tiny platform and Amy looked in that direction as the rumbling of the train grew louder. Again she glanced at the rear view mirror, jabbing the button close to her right hand to lower her window. It was a little stuffy in the car and condensation was building up on the inside of the windscreen.

Daisy pointed excitedly as the train finally rumbled past.

The noise given off by the passing train completely masked the sound of the lorry behind them.

Amy never even heard it roaring towards them and, even if she'd heard it she would have been unable to do anything.

Its brakes had gone. Simply failed to slow it down or stop it. Some kind of electrical fault. Something faulty in the engine.

Something.

At the last moment, Amy turned in her seat and saw the huge juggernaut hurtling towards them, its hazard lights flashing impotently.

She even saw the terrified face of its driver.

The lorry was doing just over fifty when it hit Amy's car.

TWELVE

David Carson had known pain in his life. Physical pain and emotional pain. He'd also known sadness and depression. But, as he sat in the bare walled room of the hospital the feeling he was consumed by now was desolation. There was no other word to adequately describe the numbness that consumed him.

He knew that there were two other men sitting in the room opposite him but what they were saying barely registered any more. They may as well have been speaking a foreign language. Their words seemed to come from miles away, projected from some parallel universe or some part of deep space. Yes, that was it. He was in some kind of black hole. A black hole that was growing steadily larger from inside him. Perhaps this was what cancer felt like, he told himself, but he felt no physical pain. What he felt was devouring him, eating him a tiny piece at a time but it wasn't killing him. Was it? Could a person die from the effects of so much devastation and misery? Perhaps he would find out soon.

He needed a drink, that was the only thing he was absolutely convinced of. By Christ he needed a drink. As someone once said, and he didn't remember who, *'I'd give my soul, just for a beer.'* And he would have done. His soul, his heart. Everything he had.

He couldn't even remember how long he'd been at the hospital, let alone in this room. Time had ceased to have any meaning for him. It ticked by now as surely as it did on the clock mounted on the wall of the room. The ticking was all he seemed to hear.

Tick, tock. Tick, tock. More minutes of your life passing and fading. More minutes that you'll never get back. Wasted and lost.

Wasted and lost seemed to describe David Carson fairly accurately at this moment in time.

There was a low table in front of him and someone had placed a Styrofoam cup filled with either tea or coffee there, presumably for him to drink. David could only look blankly at it, as if he wasn't sure what to do with the brown fluid.

Every now and then a word would penetrate the apparently invisible force field that had been placed around him. Words like 'condolences' or 'sympathy' or 'apologies.' There had been other words before that which he had understood. Words he'd heard before this feeling of desolation enveloped him. These words had been 'car crash,' 'fatality,' 'accident' and words of that ilk.

David had heard them all.

Now, he saw one of the men get to his feet and move across to the vending machine in one corner of the room. He returned a moment later with another Styrofoam cup which he placed beside the first he'd presented David with. How long ago he'd put the first one down David couldn't remember. Time, like words, had lost its meaning.

'Mr Carson.'

He heard his name and looked up.

'Mr Carson.'

Again, someone spoke his name.

David looked at each of the two men in turn.

'Are you sure you want to do this?' the first man continued.

David sucked in a deep, painful breath and rubbed his eyes. There was still moisture on his cheeks from his tears earlier but it had virtually dried by now. He looked directly at the man who was speaking. A tall man in his late forties who was dressed in a brown suit with a white shirt. The tie he was wearing was undone as was his top button. He looked tired and pale. David knew how he felt.

'You don't have to do this,' the man went on. 'You should rest.'

David shook his head and finally reached for the nearest Styrofoam cup. He took a sip, wincing when he realized how hot the liquid inside was. At least, he reasoned, he could feel something.

'Do you want one of us to come with you?' the second man asked.

David cleared his throat.

'No,' he said, taking another sip of the brown liquid which he still couldn't identify.

'It is hospital procedure...' the second man began.

'I'll do it alone,' David told him, flatly. 'That's the way it should be.' He leaned forward, resting his elbows on his knees, his head bowed. There was a button on the floor beneath the table and David wondered where it had come from. Had someone accidentally pulled it from a jacket or skirt? What had been going through *their* minds while they sat in this room? Had they felt the way he felt now?

And in the grand scheme of things, did it matter? No it didn't. David clenched his teeth together, suddenly filled with a quite disproportionate feeling of anger. Fuck whoever had sat here before him. Fuck them. Fuck their lost button. Fuck their lives. He exhaled and straightened up.

'How long's it been now?' he wanted to know.

'Three hours,' the second man told him.

'And you're sure?' David said, quietly.

'Mr Carson...' the first man began softly.

'Tell me again that you're sure,' David hissed.

'We're sure,' the first man murmured.

David got to his feet, shooting out a hand to grip the back of the chair, afraid he was going to topple over but he shook his head and clenched one fist, digging his nails into his palm so hard he almost drew blood.

'I'm going now,' he said, his voice catching.

Both men rose too.

'If you need any help, Mr Carson,' the second man offered.

David shook his head.

'No,' he breathed. 'It should be me.'

'You may feel that way but it doesn't have to be...' the first man protested but David merely waved the protest away.

He sucked in a deep breath then spoke the words softly.

'I should be the one who tells my wife our daughter is dead.'

THE PRIEST
COLORADO, USA

The Starbucks he was sitting in was quiet. There were only a dozen or so people seated inside, sipping at the various different coffees on offer.

They were the usual denizens of the establishment. Shoppers taking a break. People meeting friends. Those who wanted a rest and a drink during their busy day. Just normal people. Ordinary people.

The man sipped his own decaffeinated caramel macciato and glanced around at each of the other people in turn. He wondered where they were going. Where they had come from. He mused on what kind of lives they had. Were they happy? What was happening in their private lives? He sipped at his coffee and fixed his gaze on a couple in their thirties who were seated close to the main doors of the building. They were an attractive couple, she was dressed in jeans and a baggy top with her long blonde hair pulled up into a bun on her head. The man opposite her kept reaching out to touch her hand, brushing the back of hers gently with his fingertips. On more than one occasion she gripped his hand and held it, gazing into his eyes.

Their laughter would occasionally punctuate the low murmur of conversation that filled the Starbucks. He watched them furtively for a moment longer then reached into the pocket of his jacket and pulled out a small notebook. There was a biro jammed into the ring binding and he took this out and began doodling on the top of the page.

The other scribblings there were meaningless to anyone but him. Words and rudimentary pictures or patterns that meant nothing and had probably been drawn, like now, just to pass the time. There were more important words and symbols towards the front of the notebook but he kept those hidden from any prying eyes. They were for no one but himself. They were not to be shared.

Not yet.

He turned his head sharply when the woman with the child walked in.

The child was about five. A pretty little girl in a dark blue coat and hat, her dark hair cascading over her shoulders. He watched her as she wandered across to the counter with her mother, glancing through the glass at the cakes, cookies and other food within. Her mother was pointing to some of the items and he saw the little girl motioning towards a large piece of chocolate cake. He heard laughter and then saw the assistant behind the counter selecting a piece of the gateau, handing it across the counter as the mother fumbled in her bag for money and the little girl jumped up and down delightedly a couple of times.

He pushed the notebook back into his jacket and took another sip of his coffee, wondering where the woman and her child were going to sit.

He was still wondering when the priest walked in.

The priest was a wiry, grey haired man in his late fifties. A pair of spectacles were perched on his long nose and his ears stood out against his head, accentuated by the fact that his hair was cut so short. He moved with difficulty across to the counter and he seemed to have difficulty putting weight on his left foot. Exactly why, the man who watched him, could only guess. Perhaps, he mused, a slight smile touching his lips, it was some kind of judgement from God for something he'd done wrong. What could a priest do that would anger God so much, he wondered. The thought fascinated him.

He watched the priest order his drink then wander to the end of the counter to wait for it. The people nearest the counter nodded to him and the priest responded. He smiled warmly and crossed to their table, obviously enjoying the *interaction.*

As the man watched, he felt the hairs rise on the back of his neck. He was sure that now was the time. When the priest sat down. Then it would be right.

He sipped more of his own coffee and kept on watching.

Only occasionally did he look at the little dark haired child.

THIRTEEN

'David, I can't do this.'

Amy stood before the mirror in the bedroom looking at her reflection and when she spoke, the words were barely audible. She was dressed in a black jacket, a white blouse that was almost luminous it was so perfectly laundered and a black skirt that reached to just below her knees. Thick black tights and black shoes completed an outfit she hadn't worn since the funeral of her aunt five years earlier. But now, she was wearing it for another funeral. Not of a distant relative but of her own daughter.

She raised a hand to brush away some strands of hair from her face and saw that her hand was shaking.

It had been almost eight days since Daisy's death, days which had been difficult enough to endure but now, as the funeral approached, Amy had discovered new depths of despair and uncertainty. Organising the funeral itself had been bad enough. With the help of her own mother, and Julie Taylor in particular, she had managed it. *That's what friends were for.* Or whatever that particular cliché was. Inside the undertakers had been the worst. The woman who had greeted them had emerged from behind her desk with outstretched arms and immediately embraced her. It was an act probably of genuine but, Amy suspected, well-rehearsed caring and she shrank from it. Similarly, when the woman had asked what kind of music they wanted played at the funeral to remind them of Daisy, she had been unable at first to respond. Julie had taken over at that point and Amy had been intensely grateful for that.

Amy had been like a zombie since Daisy's death, refusing the offer of tranquillisers despite the fact she was finding it increasingly difficult to sleep. Feelings of helplessness, pain and rage seemed to be all she felt now. Her world was composed of those three emotions. Nothing else. She hated herself for it and she hated herself for withdrawing from David but she couldn't help it. People said she needed time to adjust but Amy was beginning to wonder if she would ever feel any different.

From the other side of the room, David joined her, holding her shoulders gently.

'I said I can't do this,' Amy replied.

'I heard what you said,' he murmured, softly. 'But you can. We both can.'

'I can't,' she insisted. 'I can't sit in that church and hear a vicar talking about her. I can't. And I can't stand beside a hole in the ground while they put our daughter in it. I can't.'

Tears began to roll down her cheeks but David pulled her close to him.

'You can do it because you've got to do it,' he told her. 'We've got to do it for Daisy's sake and for the other people who are there. Other people who loved her.'

'I don't care what anyone else thinks. She was our daughter, no one else's. How can they know what we're feeling?'

'They can't,' he said, forcefully. 'They can never know.'

Amy looked into his eyes and saw the desperation there.

David wished he could say something that would make her feel better. He wished there was some profound and far reaching words that would make sense of this whole situation. But there weren't and he knew exactly what she was feeling and he felt the same way. He just wanted this day to be over. He didn't want other people telling him how sorry they were and offering condolences. Was any of that going to bring Daisy back? No. He wanted a drink. That was the only thing he knew for sure. He wanted a drink more than he'd ever wanted one in his life. And then he wanted another and another. He wanted to pour alcohol down his throat until he felt nothing and remembered nothing. Until the whole day and the whole situation just passed him by. He wanted to swallow booze until he blacked out and knew nothing of what was going on around him.

David Carson wanted oblivion.

From somewhere downstairs a voice called. David sat Amy down on the end of the bed then moved to the landing and peered over to discover the source of the voice.

It was Julie Taylor who was standing at the bottom of the stairs looking up, a small handkerchief already balled up in one hand.

'The cars are here, David,' she told him.

'Thanks, Julie,' he said. 'We'll be down in a minute. If you could just help sort everyone else out. Get them into the right cars.'

Julie nodded, hesitated for a moment longer then retreated back into the sitting room where others waited. Other family members, other friends who had come to pay their respects. David stood motionless for a moment then headed back into the bedroom where Amy was still sitting on the end of the bed, gazing at the floor.

'We've got to go,' he told her, quietly, pulling on his jacket. 'The cars are here.'

Amy didn't answer.

'Amy,' David insisted. 'Come on.'

He clenched his teeth until his jaws ached.

'It's not fair,' Amy murmured. 'Why did it have to be her? I was driving that car and I got out without a scratch. It's not fair.'

'We can't do this now,' he told her, helping her to her feet and holding her close. 'We've got to be strong. For Daisy. For each other.' He looked into her eyes and saw the pain there because it was a reflection of the agony he felt himself and he knew that all the empty words and platitudes in the world weren't going to make one scrap of difference to how they were both suffering. It would be a long time before anything meant anything again. Maybe that time would never come again but here and now wasn't the place to consider that.

He felt Amy shuddering against him, her sobs almost soundless and it was all David could do to hold back his own anguish but he knew that the time would come when he'd be unable to restrain himself. That time was yet to come.

He used his handkerchief to wipe the tears from his wife's face, holding her desperate gaze for a moment longer.

'All right?' he asked, his voice catching.

Amy nodded almost imperceptibly.

'Ready?' he went on.

'Don't leave me, David,' she said, quietly. 'Don't leave my side today. Please.'

'I won't. I won't ever leave you. Not today or any time.'

She sniffed back more tears and then they both walked slowly towards the stairs and on into what they both knew would be the longest day of their lives.

ANOTHER SACRIFICE
COLORADO, USA

The man sipped his coffee, wiping his mouth with the back of his hand. He looked again at the little dark haired child and checked to see that no one else inside the Starbucks had seen him gazing so raptly at her.

The Priest certainly hadn't seen him. He was too pre-occupied with what he was doing. No one else seemed interested in anything but their own business. The man took another sip of his coffee and looked at the child again.

He wondered how loud she would scream when he cut off her fingers.

Sometimes they passed out when he did that. That was no use of course. The purification could not be carried out adequately when they were unconscious. He had tried it that way once or twice in the past but he was convinced that they had to be awake during the entire process or at least as much of it as could be accomplished before the body simply shut down. Loss of blood sometimes caused premature unconsciousness and this was something else he had been forced to consider. Cutting the throat too early was a pointless exercise because it caused blood loss so severe that the subject only clung to life for five or six minutes after the cuts were made. The same had happened when he'd tried removing a leg too close to the hip. Severing the femoral artery caused exsanguination as rapidly as any wounds to the throat. He had been surprised to see the speed of demise the first time he'd tried. Within minutes the body had been white and lifeless, apparently empty of life fluid. The smell had been startling too. An overpowering coppery odour that had taken quite some time to recede.

Perhaps he would start somewhere else. Once she was secured he had more time to consider the possibilities. Possibly severing the toes would work, but of course this would also cause pain extreme enough to cause unconsciousness. There were ways of keeping them awake of course and one in particular was useful in more ways than one.

Pouring gasoline, or even lighter fuel, into the eyes usually ensured that they remained conscious.

The additional pain caused as the corrosive fluid seared the eyeballs was just a useful addition to the pain he would inflict anyway.

The man took another sip of his coffee, his gaze now alternating between the little dark haired girl and the priest. The little girl was eating a piece of cake with a fork that was too big for her to manage comfortably and pieces of the confection kept falling back onto her plate but she persevered and the man smiled as he saw her chewing happily, sometimes looking up at her mother as if for reassurance. Her mother stroked the little girl's hair on more than one occasion and said something that the man could not hear.

He saw the girl's dark hair gleaming beneath the lights inside the building and it made him think again.

He could scalp her.

Once she was secured and immobile he could take a knife and carve her hair from her skull. It seemed fittingly ironic that Red Indians had used that technique in the past and now he was considering using it on the next child. He was, after all, following their teachings, he told himself. Cutting the scalp from the skull would cause intense pain, he was sure of that, but it wouldn't cause death. There were no major arteries in the scalp, certainly nothing to compare with the carotid in the neck or the femoral in the thigh.

The man nodded to himself and sipped more of his coffee. It was something to consider he mused, pleased with himself.

There were so many techniques to try and he would do that when he got the chance.

The little girl finished her cake and put down her fork, reaching for the small glass of milk her mother had bought her. She chattered happily to her mother who was also eating cake.

She was an attractive woman in her late twenties but the man had no interest in her. She would be of no help to him. It was her daughter he was interested in. He wondered where they were parked. If they were meeting anyone later.

He wondered how easy it would be to snatch the child in the crowded mall.

He closed his eyes for a moment, screwing his eyelids together until white stars danced behind them. Then he let out a deep breath and sat back on his seat, sipping his coffee once more, casting another glance in the direction of the little dark haired girl.

She hadn't seen him looking at her. They never did.

He smiled again.

FOURTEEN

Amy and David stood beside the front door waving as enthusiastically as they could, watching the last of the mourners leave.

It had been Amy's mother who had taken her leave last and, only after repeated assurances from both Amy and David that they would be all right. They would cope. They would get to bed early. Whatever hopeless platitudes were offered they had answers for them and had finally persuaded Amy's mother to clamber into the taxi and allow herself to be driven home. She had, Amy observed, cried more than they had. Not that it was a competition of course. There were no winners anywhere today. Certainly none at the funeral or the little gathering afterwards. If anything, Amy had found it easier to contain her own grief because of the outpourings of others. She didn't know why but wondered if she was still trying to maintain some pretence of strength in the face of such overwhelming sorrow. David was the same. Terrified that to lose control once would signal a loss that could not be recovered. The threat of that complete collapse hung over them like the clouds gathering now in the distance.

David closed the door and followed Amy back into the house.

Most of the food had been eaten. Finger sandwiches, sausage rolls, pasties and any thing else that could be classed as buffet food. On more than one occasion, Amy had wondered where the quaint ceremony of feeding the mourners after a funeral had come from. She had probably heard somewhere but it wasn't at the forefront of her mind. She had moved through the entire day in something of a daze, clinging to David's hand or arm for most of the time, wondering why she hadn't cried more.

It felt as if there was some kind of lock on her emotions. If that lock should be removed then, she feared, she may well never stop crying. There was too much pain and anguish stored inside her. To release some of it would inevitably lead to a flood she knew she would not be able to cope with.

During the service and particularly at the graveside, she had struggled to keep those feelings in check. Especially when she heard others crying. The sounds had been carried away on the harsh wind that had swept periodically across the cemetery as Daisy was laid to rest, but they had registered in her mind before being buffeted by the breeze as surely as Autumn leaves. At least two people had walked away from the graveside, unable to tolerate any longer the soul crushing solemnity and sadness. Amy wished she could have joined them. She had felt hands squeezing her shoulders and arms occasionally during the priest's litany. Gestures of sympathy and condolence that she appreciated but which counted for absolutely nothing. There was nothing that could penetrate that veil of numbness that had descended upon her. It was as if she was unconscious and yet still aware. Standing motionless at the graveside while her child was lowered into the depths.

She closed her eyes when the coffin reached the bottom of the grave. No matter what she couldn't bring herself to look at it. The screaming finality of it seemed to hit her like a train and she turned towards David who forced back his own pain to hold her while the priest finished speaking.

Even now, Amy could not remember how she had got from the graveside back to her house where she now stood waving goodbye to those who had suffered through the day with her.

As the taxi pulled away she and David turned and headed back into the sitting room.

He was already clearing plates and glasses away.

'Leave it,' she told him. 'I'll do it tomorrow. It'll give me something to do.'

'No,' David said, flatly. 'I'm not leaving you with this.'

'Please, David,' she said, softly. 'Just sit with me.'

They seated themselves on the sofa, the oppressive silence in the room closing around them like an invisible hand.

Amy slipped off her shoes, dropped them on the carpet and drew her feet up beneath her, her head resting against her husband's shoulder.

'It's so quiet,' she murmured.

David nodded.

'Shall I put the TV on?' he offered. 'Or some music?'

Amy shook her head and they sat within that cloying silence for what felt like an eternity. They felt like strangers, neither knowing what to say. Neither willing to break the oppressive stillness. When words finally escaped they came from Amy.

'How can that priest stand there and talk about God like he did?' she murmured.

'What do you mean?' David enquired.

'He kept saying that God was merciful. That God was kind,' she muttered. 'What fucking bullshit.'

David pulled her closer.

'I thought that when my Dad died,' Amy went on. 'But I felt it even more today. What kind of God allows little children to suffer the way Daisy suffered?'

David kissed the top of her head, desperate for something to say but failing miserably.

'I don't want to know about God and how good and how merciful he is,' Amy breathed. 'If He was merciful then our daughter would still be alive.' She looked heavenward. 'Fuck God. If He's abandoned me then I'm doing the same to Him.'

She spoke the words with such venom that David shuddered.

FIFTEEN

David Carson turned over in bed and glanced at the luminous numbers glowing on the clock beside him.

3.17 a.m.

David groaned, let out a long almost painful breath and blinked myopically

in the darkened bedroom. As he shifted position he looked at the other side of the bed and it took him a second to realize that he was alone. He reached out to touch the area where Amy would normally be but she was, as he had first thought, gone. Normally he could hear her breathing when he woke in the night but not tonight. There was no reassuring sound rising from that side of the bed. No warm sleeping shape beside him. David sighed and swung himself out of bed, padding across the bedroom to the door where he looked out on an equally dark and gloomy landing.

He could hear no sounds of movement from anywhere in the house and there was no tell-tale strip of light beneath the bathroom door indicating that she was in there. As far as he could tell she may be downstairs. David made his way slowly down the steps without turning the light on. Moving about in the darkness somehow seemed easier. He felt a part of the shadows. They hid him and welcomed him. He wished they had been there during the day so he could hide from the prying eyes of the other mourners. Hiding seemed a very enticing prospect at this particular time in his life.

He reached the bottom of the stairs and stood there quietly for a moment, glancing around but seeing no other indication that his wife was on this level of the house either. He checked the kitchen where plates left behind by the other mourners had been taken from the dishwasher and stacked on the table. Then he looked in the sitting room but there was no one there either. Earlier in the day the room had been crammed with people, speaking in suitably hushed tones, offering sympathy and help if it was needed.

David was ashamed when he thought of his own emotions that afternoon. In addition to the overwhelming grief and sense of loss he'd felt he was also consumed with anger. Rage that these people around him were not feeling the same soul-destroying pain that he and Amy were feeling. How could *anyone* know what they were feeling? If they'd been in the same position then they would have known but none of the guests at the funeral had been, had they? He paused for a moment, looking around the sitting room again.

Why? Hoping to see Daisy hiding behind the sofa as she loved to do?

He took a deep breath.

You're never going to see that again. Get used to it.

David closed the door behind him and made his way back up the stairs. As he reached the top he heard a sound coming from one of the other bedrooms. From Daisy's room.

He moved towards the door, moving as slowly as he could so he didn't step on one of the creaky boards. The silence was almost oppressive as he approached the door, ears alert for the slightest sound now. He could hear something as he leaned closer to the wooden partition. There was a large multi-coloured sign on the door that proclaimed;

DAISY'S ROOM

She'd made it a couple of years ago at school and it featured a small photograph of her, smiling happily surrounded by her toys. David reached out with one index finger and touched it tenderly, his eyes filling with tears.

The door suddenly swung open before him and David stepped back, his heart suddenly racing.

'What are you doing?'

Amy was standing at the threshold of the door, looking out at him with questioning eyes.

'I woke up,' he told her. 'I wondered where you were.'

Amy stepped back into the room, seating herself on the end of the small bed. She picked up the small stuffed Dalmatian she'd been holding.

'Dummy dog,' David murmured looking at the little toy.

Amy nodded.

'I remember buying this the day she lost her dummy,' she said. 'She lost it in a sand pit when she was playing and I couldn't find the bloody thing. I bought her this little dog to take its place. She never needed a dummy again after that, did she?'

'I remember,' David told her, sitting down beside her. 'Do you remember that little doll she used to carry around with her all the time when she was about eighteen months?'

Amy nodded.

'I took her for a walk one day in her pushchair and she dropped it in the river,' David went on. 'I had to get on my hands and knees and fish it out.' He managed a smile. 'I nearly fell in but I got the doll back. That was all that mattered.'

'Memories are all we're going to have from now on.'

'Good ones.'

'But to know that there won't be any more.'

He snaked his arm around her shoulders, pulling her closer to him.

'Have we done anything to deserve this?' Amy said, softly.

'What do you mean?' he wanted to know.

'You know what they say about Karma, that if you do something bad then something bad will happen to you eventually. What if...'

David cut her off.

'What could we have done that's bad enough for us to lose our daughter?' he said, irritably. 'Don't even think that. No one deserves to feel like this. Nothing we could have done would have caused this to happen. Don't even think that.'

Amy nodded and they sat silently for a few minutes, surrounded by the stillness until she spoke again. 'How do we do it, David?' Amy asked, helplessly. 'How do we go on without her?'

He wished he had an answer.

SIXTEEN

David Carson fumbled in his jacket for his house keys. As usual he felt the same contradictory feelings he always experienced when he got home. He was glad to be back but there was also a feeling of something best described as dread. As much as he hated work, it at least offered some respite from his own unrelentingly painful thoughts. The distraction was welcomed. When he was working at least he had no time to consider his own situation or to think about the death of his daughter. Any respite from the barrage of thoughts was to be seized. When he got home he was fully exposed to the memories and desperately aware of his failure to cope with them.

Raw pain had subsided into a dull ache for him. Like an open wound that was slowly closing and leaving behind thick scar tissue, his despair had become more deep seated now.

He pushed the key into the lock and turned it, stepping into the hallway.

The house was quiet. It always seemed to be quiet these days. David told himself that he had probably come home many times in the past to find it in a similar state but now, without Daisy around, it just seemed as if a constant cloud of stillness had settled on the building and it's interior, never again to be broken by the sound of her voice.

Don't start thinking about that now.

David sucked in a deep breath and walked into the sitting room. It was empty. He wondered if Amy had gone to see her Mum or one of her friends but, as he turned he saw that her coat was hanging up in the hallway and she would, he told himself, have told him if she wasn't coming straight home.

'Amy,' he called.

No answer.

David wandered through to the kitchen but she wasn't there either. He moved to one of the windows and glanced out into the small back garden but there was no sign of Amy out there. There was mug on the kitchen table and her handbag was there too. He was even more convinced that she was at home now or at least had been home but, he reasoned, she wouldn't have gone out again without her handbag. She didn't go anywhere without that and he could see that her purse was still inside. He made his way upstairs.

In their bedroom he found Amy's work clothes strewn over the bed, discarded as if they'd been torn off hastily. That wasn't like her.

'Amy,' he called again, moving out onto the landing once again.

As he did he heard the sounds coming from Daisy's room and he hurried towards the door, pushing it open.

The sound was Amy sobbing. Sounds of such anguish that it almost froze him in his tracks for a second.

She was kneeling beside Daisy's bed, her head on the animal pattern duvet, her hands gripping the material as if she was afraid it would escape her clutches.

David didn't speak he just knelt beside her, putting his arm around her heaving shoulders. She turned towards him without speaking, her sobs continuing. He could feel her whole body trembling as he held her, each spasm causing her to shudder. David clung to her helplessly knowing there was nothing he could say or do that would stem this tide of despair now. It was as if the dam had finally broken. Every emotion she had been battling to keep in check had finally forced its way through and she was drowning in the deluge.

Even when she finally looked at him, her eyes puffy and red rimmed, her cheeks soaked with tears, she couldn't speak. The words wouldn't come. David ran his hand through her hair, kissing the top of her head in a comforting gesture that, he was all too aware, was too insignificant.

She snaked her arms around him and held him, not wanting to break contact with him, knowing that he was the only other person in the world that was feeling the kind of agony that was now ripping her soul apart. He was the only one who understood the depth of despair she was feeling. United in their inconsolable grief, they remained where they were, surrounded by the tangible memories of their daughter and wishing that there was some way they could have her back.

It was a long time before either of them spoke but it was Amy who finally murmured some muted words.

'I can't do it, David,' she blurted. 'I can't do this.'

'Do what?' he wanted to know, tears now pouring down his own cheeks.

'I can't go on like this.'

'Please go to the doctor, Amy,' he urged. 'Get something.'

'Pills you mean?'

'Get whatever he'll give you. You need help.'

'What about you? Why don't you?'

He hugged her tightly.

'I want to help you,' he said, quietly.

'You've got a right to grieve too, David.'

'I know and I've done nothing but grieve since she died, believe me.'

'You haven't said anything.'

'About what? What good would it do?'

'Have you spoken to anyone about how you feel?'

'Would I tell someone else what I won't tell you?'

He kissed her on the forehead and felt her hold him more tightly.

'Get some help, Amy,' he murmured. 'Please. I love you too much to see you suffering like this.'

'He'll give me Valium or something. Just fill me full of tranquillisers. I'll be like a zombie.'

'As long as he does *something* for you. Promise me you'll make an appointment.'

She stroked his forearm gently as he held her.

'Amy, promise me,' David said again. 'I love you and can't stand seeing you like this.'

'I love you too,' she said, softly. 'And I will get help, I promise,' she murmured.

SEVENTEEN

As Amy sat in the doctors surgery the same thoughts kept circulating inside her mind. Spinning round and round like a pebble in a blender.

Why am I here? What can anyone do to help me?

She glanced at her watch, realizing she'd now been waiting for more than thirty minutes. Amy was about to get to her feet and walk out when she heard her name being called over the intercom.

She smiled despite herself, thinking how unbearably cheerful the doctor sounded as he announced her appointment. She stood up, striding briskly towards the corridor that led down to the surgeries. There were four GPs at the practice and the room she wanted was the last one on the right at the end of the corridor.

She glanced up at the nameplate over the door, knocked, and then walked in without waiting for acknowledgement.

Doctor Stephen Jacobs was in his early forties but sported a shock of grey hair that would have been more appropriate on a man ten or twenty years his senior. He stood up when Amy walked in, gesturing towards the chair beside his desk. She seated herself and took a deep breath.

'What can I do for you today?' Jacobs asked, sitting back in his swivel chair.

'I'm not sure you can do anything,' Amy told him. 'I only came because my husband wanted me to. He wants me to get some antidepressants.'

'And do you think you need them?' Jacobs asked. 'I know your husband does but do you?'

'I think I need something. Whether it helps or not is another thing.'

'What's caused your depression?'

Amy opened her mouth to speak but the words wouldn't come. She was afraid that if she told him everything she needed to that she'd be in tears after the first two or three sentences. She ran a hand through her hair and shrugged.

'My daughter,' she began, finally. 'Was killed in a car crash.' She exhaled deeply, almost painfully.

'When?' Jacobs enquired. 'How long ago?'

'Two months,' Amy told him.

'Have you felt like this for two months? Why didn't you seek help earlier?'

'It's all I can do to get out of bed most days,' she told him. 'It's been getting worse though. That's why I'm here.'

'Are you working?' the doctor enquired.

'On and off,' Amy confessed. 'I've been in a few times but it's difficult. I've used up most of my holiday allowance by now.' She smiled but there was no humour in the expression. 'I can work from home so I've been trying to do that but..' The words trailed off into the empty air of the consulting room.

'I understand,' Jacobs said. 'I'm very sorry.'

'No you don't understand, doctor,' Amy said, smiling thinly. 'No one understands. No one understands that kind of loss unless they've experienced it.'

Jacobs nodded.

'Have you spoken to anyone about it?' he wanted to know. 'Loved ones? Friends? Relatives?'

'What's the point? It's not going to bring her back is it?'

'Neither are antidepressants, Mrs Carson,' Jacobs reminded her.

'Talking about it isn't going to help,' Amy persisted.

'Well, normally, I would recommend some kind of cognitive therapy before prescribing tablets. To talk about what happened with others who..'

'Talking isn't going to help,' Amy interrupted. 'My daughter is dead. If I talk for three hours straight she's still going to be dead when I finish talking isn't she?' Amy closed her eyes. 'Please, just give me some antidepressants.'

'Have you thought about suicide?' Jacobs offered.

Amy shook her head dismissively.

'As an alternative to antidepressants?' Amy said, bitterly. She shook her head. 'What good would that do?' she said, wearily. 'And my husband's lost a daughter it's not fair that he should lose a wife too is it?'

'I have to ask,' Jacobs said almost apologetically. As he spoke he leaned forward and began flicking through a large book on his desk. 'How's your husband coping?' he asked.

'He's been brilliant,' Amy said. 'If it hadn't been for him I don't know what I'd have done, how I'd have gone on. It isn't fair on him that I'm like this all the time.'

'And he was the one who advised you to come here?'

Amy smiled.

'I think he's fed up with me,' she admitted, twisting her wedding ring gently.

'Do you have any religious beliefs, Mrs Carson?' the doctor wanted to know. 'Sometimes people with strong beliefs find comfort...'

'I don't believe in anything,' she said, flatly. 'I lost my father eighteen months ago. If there's a God, He and I aren't on speaking terms any more.'

Jacobs nodded gently.

Amy took a tissue from her handbag and dabbed at her nose.

'I know this is probably a pointless question, Mrs Carson,' the doctor continued, writing something on a piece of paper. 'But you haven't got any holiday booked have you? Anywhere that you and your husband could go to just get away from what's happened. Even if it's only for a weekend. The change of environment can sometimes help believe it or not.'

Amy let out a hollow laugh and nodded.

'We had a holiday booked in America,' she said, quietly. 'We were going to cancel it when...'

'If you can go then you should go,' Jacobs said. 'The break will do you more good than any amount of antidepressants. It'll be good for your husband too.'

Amy sighed and got to her feet, turning towards the door.

'Thank you, doctor,' she said, walking across the room.

'Mrs Carson,' Jacobs said. 'I'm very sorry for your loss but things will get easier. I promise you.'

Amy pulled the door open.

'Will they really?' she said, flatly. 'Can I have that in writing?'

And she was gone.

THE CONVERSATION
COLORADO, USA

The Priest pulled his iPhone from his pocket and put it on the table before him, setting down his coffee next to it then he checked to see if he had any calls.

There were two from numbers he recognised immediately and another from one he did not. He nodded to himself and decided he would check his Facebook page before he left Starbucks. He had asked a friend to set it up to make the church appear more modern and accessible but there had been little response locally or nationally. A few people had left crude and, on one occasion, revolting messages on his wall, but other than that there had been little interaction. He decided to leave the page up for another week and then, if things hadn't improved, remove it once and for all.

He took a sip of his coffee, aware of movement close to him.

'Father.'

The word startled him for a moment but then he looked up and saw that the man was standing over him, looking down.

'I'm not disturbing you am I, Father?' the man asked.

'Of course not,' the priest said.

'I saw you come in,' the man continued. 'I wondered if I could just speak to you for a minute. If you've got time of course.'

'Sit down,' the priest said, motioning to the chair opposite.

The man accepted the invitation and settled himself, putting his own caramel macchiato down.

'I wanted to ask you something,' he said. 'If you don't mind.'

'Of course not but if it's a spiritual question you might be better off asking your own minister, I..'

'It's not a spiritual matter,' the man interrupted. 'At least I don't think you would class it as that.'

'Go ahead.'

'Have you ever encountered real evil in your time as a priest?'

'There are all kinds of evil,' the priest offered.

'I mean true evil. Irredeemable, satanic evil?'

The priest regarded him warily for a moment.

'I've seen what I would consider to be evil. Suffering. Pain. Hopelessness.'

'That's not real evil,' the man snapped through clenched teeth.

The priest looked at him again, sipping slowly at his coffee.

'Then tell me what you *mean by evil,' he said, evenly.*

'The kind of thing that twists men's minds. The sort of evil that challenges God.'

The priest considered the question but, before he could speak, the man went on.

'Do you believe evil is in all of us from birth or do we acquire it?' the man continued. 'Do we collect it like we collect loose change?'

'I think some people are born evil, if that answers your question.'

'But we're all shaped by things in our lives aren't we? Things we're exposed to?'

'Some people believe that.'

'But not you?'

The two men locked stares.

'I think there is a dark side to every human heart and soul,' the priest said. 'And sometimes it's hard to control. Not everyone is capable of controlling it.'

The man sipped his caramel macchiato, his gaze fixed not on the priest now but on the table between them.

'Some Red Indians believed that a child would bring about the end of the world,' he murmured. 'They believed that hundreds of years ago. I wonder if they still do.'

'Red Indians,' the Priest said. 'You mean native Americans?'

'Does it matter what you call them. You know what I mean. Some tribes believed that all the evil of the world was contained inside children and that by destroying that evil they could rid the world of it.'

'So they killed the children?'

'Those they thought were carrying evil. By doing that, they thought they were cleansing their world. I think that's good.'

'But what about the children who died?'

'If they were evil what did it matter?'

'Life should always be cherished.'

'Even the life of an evil person?'

'All life is sacred.'

The man shook his head gently.

'Doesn't the church believe that all children are cursed with original sin.'

'The Catholic church does.'

'What if they're right? What if the Indians were right?'

The priest looked warily at the man.

'I don't know what you're getting at,' he said, a note of exasperation in his voice.

'Wouldn't you want to remove all the evil from the world if you could?' the man enquired. 'That's part of your vocation isn't it?'

'For everything evil there is something good,' the priest said.

'I hope you're right, father.'

The man looked down at the table top for a second then he locked stares with the priest once again.

'I have seen infected children,' the man said, quietly.

EIGHTEEN

The British Airways A380-800 is two hundred and thirty-eight feet long, has a wingspan of two hundred and sixty one feet and is almost twenty five feet high from the bottom of its wheels to the top of its fuselage.

Powered by four Rolls Royce Trent 900 engines it can reach speeds in excess of five hundred and eighty miles an hour.

David Carson knew all these facts about the plane that he was sitting on because he'd read the laminated leaflet in the pocket before him at least five times since the aircraft left Heathrow thirty minutes ago. It was, he told himself, better than gazing out of the window or thinking too much about where he actually was. He hadn't flown much in his life but when he had it frightened him. It was like the old joke, he told himself, it wasn't the fear of flying that scared him it was the fear of crashing. Yes, he knew it was statistically more likely that he could die on the road in an accident (a statistic that seemed even more painfully relevant now). He knew all the facts and figures but it still didn't stop him from being scared.

He glanced at Amy who was doing her best to read one of the magazines she'd bought at the airport. He knew she was nervous about flying, she always had been. They'd never been great travellers in the past, they'd never had the money, but they'd worked and saved for three or four trips before Daisy was born and...

He let out a deep sigh. A vision of his daughter flashed into his mind and refused to move.

And why would you want it to move? You don't want to wipe her from your memory do you?

Amy glanced across at him and smiled.

'You OK?' she asked, squeezing his hand.

'Yeah,' he told her smiling. 'Are you?'

She nodded.

'Did you know that if all the wiring in this plane was laid end to end it would stretch from Edinburgh to London?' David said.

'Really?' Amy answered, smiling more broadly. 'Did you read that in that leaflet? You must have read it half a dozen times since we took off.'

'At least half a dozen,' he confessed. 'What about you? How's the article?' He nodded in the direction of the magazine.

'I haven't got a clue what I'm reading,' Amy chuckled. 'It might as well be in Japanese.'

She pushed the magazine into the compartment in front of her and sat back, glancing briefly out of the window.

There was heavy cloud cover but, every now and then, the sun would appear, covering everything with brilliant yellow light. The clouds were obviously responsible for the turbulence that periodically caused the plane to shudder and, each time it did, Amy swallowed hard.

'We should have gone by boat,' Amy said, smiling.

'Knowing our luck, it would have got hit by a plane,' David told her, raising his eyebrows.

Amy squeezed his hand.

'They'll be bringing food round soon,' she told him. 'That'll give us something else to think about. Or we could watch a movie.'

'I don't think I could concentrate,' David confessed.

'Me neither,' Amy added.

'Knowing our luck it'd be *Airplane.*'

They both laughed.

David leaned over and kissed her on the cheek.

'I love you,' he whispered.

'I know,' Amy murmured and he could see the tears in her eyes. He knew that she was thinking the same thing as he was. She was wondering what Daisy would have thought of the plane and the flight. David considered mentioning it but then decided against it.

As if not mentioning her might somehow lessen the pain.

It didn't.

Amy squeezed his hand even more tightly and sat back in her seat. She wished that she could sleep like some on the flight were already doing but she was denied that luxury. She glanced at her watch and saw, with more than a little disappointment, that they weren't due to arrive at their destination for another eight hours. She adjusted her seat again and glanced down the aisle to where the stewardess was serving drinks. David had seen the drinks trolley too although he was doing his best to ignore it.

He undid his seatbelt and squeezed Amy's hand again.

'I'm going to the toilet,' he announced. 'Just get me an orange juice when the drinks arrive.'

Amy nodded and watched him go.

She reached for her magazine and, once again, tried reading the article she'd started. She managed to read the title again; 20 THINGS YOU SHOULD KNOW ABOUT YOUR MAN. That was all she read. She pushed the magazine back into the seat pocket and lay back. She adjusted her headrest and reclined the seat slightly glancing across to see that the stewardess had arrived with the drinks trolley.

'Can I get you something?' she asked, her fixed smile in position as it would have to be for the remainder of the flight.

'Just a mineral water please,' Amy said. 'And an orange juice for my husband.'

The stewardess nodded and set about pouring the drinks.

'Will we be ahead of schedule on the flight?' Amy asked, sipping at her drink.

'It's hard to tell yet,' the stewardess confessed. 'Why?'

'I just wondered,' Amy went on. 'I'm looking forward to getting there and getting off the plane.'

'Are you a bit nervous?'

'My husband and I are both bad flyers.'

'I don't think anyone really *enjoys* it, but try and relax and the time will soon pass.'

Amy nodded.

'I can give you something for it if you like, if it gets too bad,' the stewardess told her conspiratorially. 'But maybe a large brandy would just be best.' She smiled. 'Do you want one for you and one for your husband?'

'Better not,' Amy said. 'We might be drunk by the time we get there.'

Or my husband might.

The stewardess nodded and moved on, turning to deposit two small bags of nuts on Amy's tray table before serving the next passenger.

As she pushed the trolley away, Amy heard a bell ring and she looked up to confirm her suspicions. The seat belt sign had come on again.

The plane was heading into turbulence.

THE CONFESSION
COLORADO, USA

The priest leaned forward slightly, his brow furrowing.

'Infected?' he said. 'With what?'

The man sat back on his seat, a slight smile on his lips, his gaze fixed now on the small puddle of spilled coffee on the table top rather than the priest himself.

'I'd had the idea for a long time,' the man said, quietly, the smile fading as

he began speaking. 'I knew I could do it.'

'If this is a joke it isn't very funny,' the priest said. 'I have things to do and...'

'It's no joke,' the man interrupted.

'What have you done to these children?' the priest insisted. 'Who are they?'

'I don't know their names. Names aren't important. What I did is important, not who I did it to.'

'Tell me what you've done,' the priest said, evenly.

'I don't think you'd understand, father,' the man said, the smile returning to his thin lips.

'Try me,' the priest insisted.

'And when I've told you what will you do?'

'That depends.'

'If I confessed in church you wouldn't be able to tell anyone what I'd said. I thought the sanctity of the confessional was sacred.'

'To Catholics,' the priest reminded him. 'Do you want to confess something then?'

'It isn't a confession, father. I don't feel I have to cleanse my soul. I'm not burdened by the things I've done.'

'Then why did you want to speak to me? There must be things you want to talk about that you can only talk about to me.'

The man nodded and smiled.

'Very astute, father,' he muttered. 'Do they teach you how to listen at the seminary? Or wherever it is you learn to be a priest? Is that one of the prerequisites for the job?' He smiled more broadly but there was no warmth in the gesture. All the priest saw in it was a touch of scorn.

'Tell me about these children,' the priest said, tiring of the man's ramblings.

'The children, the man repeated, nodding. 'The children. Do you ever wish you could have had children, father? Was that one of the sacrifices you realized you'd have to make when you became a priest? Did you never want to be a father?'

'I am a father, I have two children. I had them before I became a priest.'

'That's nice,' the man said. 'Children are so precious aren't they?'

He suddenly cracked out laughing and the sound sent a shiver down the priest's spine. It caused several of the other inhabitants of the room to look around, seeking out the source of the hollow noise.

'What's so funny?' the priest asked, anger beginning to fill him now. He wasn't sure what this man wanted and he felt uncomfortable in his company.

'We're all children of God aren't we?' the man said, now staring fixedly *at the priest.*

'Look, I appreciate you wanting to talk to me,' the priest said. 'But I have got things to do so...'

'You want me to get to the point, I understand. I do have a tendency to ramble on. I'm sorry.'

The two men sat in silence for a moment, the priest looking at his companion, the man running one index finger endlessly around the rim of the coffee cup. He finally picked it up and took a long swallow.

'How old are your children, Father?' the man enquired.

'My son is twenty-five, my daughter is twenty,' the priest informed him.

'Too old,' the man murmured. 'No use to me.' He looked directly at the priest. 'The Indians only killed smaller children you know. They thought that souls were more vulnerable because they were prey to all the evils of the world at a younger age.' He nodded. 'They had no protection you see. As you get older you build up a kind of immunity to evil but when you're a child you have no protection. The evil gets inside more easily. That's why I only use younger children.'

The priest sat back slightly.

'I don't understand,' he said.

'You don't have to understand, Father,' the man told him.

'You still haven't told me what you've done to these children. The ones you say are...infected,' he persisted.

'They were purified,' the man breathed.

'Purified? How?'

'By pain.'

He smiled and, as he did, he slipped one hand inside his jacket and pulled something free.

The priest froze when he saw the gun gripped in the man's hand.

'Thank you for listening, Father,' the man said, then he jammed the pistol into his mouth and squeezed the trigger.

There was a deafening explosion as the gun went off, the sound reverberating inside the Starbucks, mingling with several screams.

The priest almost fell backwards from his chair, his bulging eyes now fixed on the scene before him as the man pulled the trigger. There was no time to stop him or grab for the gun, the priest could only watch helplessly as the bullet tore through the man's skull then erupted from the back of it carrying a sticky flux of pulverized brain matter, shattered bone and blood, all of which sprayed up the wall behind the man. His eyes rolled upwards in their sockets then he slumped forward onto the table, exposing the fist sized exit hole in the *back of his skull. There were several wisps of smoke rising from the dead man's open mouth.*

The priest put a hand to his mouth, hoping he'd be able to prevent the explosion of vomit he felt rushing up from his stomach.

He couldn't.

NINETEEN

David Carson had his gaze fixed firmly on the air hostesses who were still moving around the cabin.

He knew that once they were ordered back to their seats, the turbulence the plane had been flying through for the last ten minutes had increased. It had been a while since he and Amy had flown and, he told himself, they had probably both forgotten that mild turbulence was an almost unavoidable by-product of flying. What they had also both forgotten was just how frightening it could be.

Amy was laying back in her seat, her eyes closed. As if that simple act would cut out the disturbances around her. He could see her swallowing every now and then and, when he held her hand, he could feel her shaking.

'It'll be over soon,' David said, quietly, wishing he could believe his own pathetic attempts at reassurance. 'They'll climb to get clear of it.'

'When?' Amy asked without opening her eyes.

David again glanced at the nearest stewardess who was struggling to serve a drink as she steadied herself with her free hand, almost overbalancing when the plane lurched.

There was a collective groan from the other passengers in the cabin.

Taking a cue from this, the intercom suddenly burst into life.

'Cabin crew, strap in please,' the captain's voice said with a calmness David envied.

He watched as one of the stewardesses hurriedly wheeled the trolley back down the aisle then he glanced up again as the pilot continued;

'We're sorry about the turbulence ladies and gentlemen,' he said with the same even and untroubled tone. 'This is what we call light turbulence. It's no worse than a bumpy road to an average driver so there's nothing to worry about. If it doesn't clear we'll try to find a smoother route for you but we should be out of this in about ten minutes so please just bear with us.'

'Light turbulence?' Amy murmured. 'I'd hate to feel what bad turbulence is like.'

She glanced out of the window and saw that the clouds around them were thick and grey. The sunshine that had accompanied them for most of the trip so far seemed now to have forsaken them.

David nodded almost imperceptibly and reached for his drink, his hand shaking slightly as he raised it to his lips.

There was another bump and it felt as if the aircraft had dropped several hundred feet. He knew this wasn't the case but he gripped the small, clear plastic container so hard for a second he feared he might crush it. The plane levelled out again. Then dropped.

'Oh God,' Amy gasped, looking worriedly at him.

Somewhere behind them a woman screamed.

David jerked his head around in the direction of the sound. This wasn't the high-pitched yelp uttered by a nervous person forced to suffer this apparently endless ordeal. The sound he'd heard, that had filled the entire cabin momentarily, was a shriek of pure, unadulterated terror.

He saw a blonde woman in her twenties struggle to her feet and dash across the aisle towards the toilet. As she did so, a member of the cabin crew also got up, gesturing in the woman's direction.

'Stay in your seat please,' the stewardess called but it was too late, the woman was already at the door of the toilet, dragging it open.

Why the blonde woman would feel safer in the toilet David had no idea but she obviously saw it as some kind of sanctuary and no amount of interference from the cabin crew was going to prevent her from reaching it.

'What's happening?' Amy wanted to know, her voice catching.

'I don't know,' David said, seeing one of the air hostesses struggling down the aisle towards the toilet where the woman had now ensconced herself. A man was also on his feet, rising from the seat next to the one the woman had vacated.

'Please sit down, sir,' the stewardess said as she moved past.

'She's pregnant,' the man offered, as if he was telling the stewardess something that wasn't already abundantly obvious, and also supposing that the explanation was designed to explain his companion's aberrant behaviour.

The stewardess rapped sharply on the toilet door.

'You can't stay in there,' she said. 'You've got to sit down and strap yourself in. Just until we're through this turbulence.'

The plane juddered violently as if to reinforce the stewardess's words. The uniformed attendant shot out a hand to steady herself, almost overbalancing due to the unedifying jolt. David could see the concern etched on her face now and he was beginning to wonder exactly how bad this turbulence really was.

'Please open the door,' the stewardess said more forcefully, banging again.

'Just leave her,' the man in the seat next to her said.

'She's got to sit down and strap herself in,' the stewardess snapped.

She banged on the door again.

'Please, madam,' she called, her face pressed against the door. 'You've got to come out.'

From inside, the stewardess thought she heard crying. She knocked again.

'You could injure yourself,' she called. 'Please come out.'

David, like most of the passengers in this part of the plane, had turned to watch the tableau now. If anything, it at least distracted them somewhat from the turbulence and it's possible consequences. There were more moans when the plane shook again. Amy shot out a hand and grabbed David's arm.

'It's getting worse,' she said, breathlessly.

The stewardess beside the toilet door stumbled, almost falling but holding herself up against a seat as the plane rocked helplessly in the air.

'We're going to crash aren't we?' Amy said, gripping David's arm so tightly she threatened to draw blood.

He wished he could say something to reassure her, to tell her they were going to be fine. He wished he could believe that himself. As the plane lurched violently again, he was beginning to wonder.

There was another deafening scream from behind them.

TWENTY

The stewardess reeled back from the toilet door as it burst open.

She almost overbalanced, startled by the movement before her and also shaken by the latest enormous judder that shook the plane as if some giant invisible hand had grabbed the tail.

As she turned back towards the bathroom door she saw something dark and wet soaking into the carpet beneath her feet, spilling from the bathroom. At first she wondered if the toilet had overflowed, then she realized what the reeking fluid really was.

She saw the blonde woman, standing motionless in the doorway, her hands covered in blood, the red fluid coating her arms as far as the elbows, her face the colour of milk.

The stewardess screamed again.

David turned, rising in his seat to get a better view of the source of the sound. As he did so, he also caught sight of the blonde woman emerging from the bathroom. Exactly what she was holding he had no idea at first. He was mesmerised by her appearance. Drawn to it, unable to look away.

Amy turned too.

They both saw the blonde woman emerge from the bathroom and both of them could see that she was holding something at arms length before her. Something that was about two feet long, something that was covered by a thick coating of dark blood and membrane. Something that was still joined to her by a pulsing, slippery tentacle that stretched from her body to the object she held.

It took just a second to realize that what she was holding was a baby.

It took them a little longer to realize that it had been torn from inside her, through the long gash that was visible from her pubic bone to just above her navel. It yawned open like the bloodied gills of a fish.

The blonde woman walked slowly forward, holding the object before her like a weapon. There was blood and clear fluid dripping from it, spattering the carpet as she moved along the aisle between the seats, her gait even. There was blood flowing from the gash, soaking into her clothes and running down the pale flesh of her legs, puddling where she stepped.

She was saying something quietly, her lips moving almost imperceptibly as she advanced further down the aisle, the child still held before her, sticky pieces of flesh and slicks of blood sticking to it. The stewardess was still backing off, retreating like a vampire before an upraised crucifix. But no one else in the cabin seemed to see what was happening, David thought. They were all sitting bolt upright, staring fixedly ahead, oblivious to the monstrous scenario playing out before them. He looked at the man across the aisle from him and saw that he too was sitting motionless, his eyes fixed on the back of the seat in front of him. There was sweat beaded on his forehead and upper lip but, apart from that, there was no sign of movement from him. The woman sitting next to him was the same. Her face was emotionless, greasy with perspiration, her hair slicked back as if she'd just run a marathon. Her skin was grey. It looked as if it was about to peel away from her bones like old wallpaper.

And she didn't seem to see the blonde woman with the baby either.

No one did.

David looked back in her direction but couldn't see her.

He rubbed his eyes.

'David.'

He heard his name and turned to look at the seat next to him.

The blonde woman was sitting there now.

She pushed her blood spattered bundle towards him and David could smell the blood and viscera on the body of the child. But it wasn't that which made him recoil so violently. It was the child's face.

He was looking directly into the face of Daisy.

His dead daughter smiled back at him and then screamed three words at him.

'Dad, help me!'

TWENTY-ONE

David sat forward with a start, restrained only by the seat belt still fastened across him.

'Jesus,' he gasped, panting like an exhausted dog as he looked around. He could feel his heart hammering against his ribs and there was perspiration on his forehead.

He glanced to one side, expecting to see the blonde woman sitting there but, to his immense relief, all he saw was Amy who was now gripping his hand and looking at him with concern.

'Are you OK?' she said, stroking his hand now. 'You were dreaming.'

'I had a nightmare,' he said, breathlessly aware that the man on the other side of the aisle had heard him and was now looking across with a look of bemusement on his face. 'A terrible nightmare.' He tried to swallow but his throat was dry. He reached for the half empty plastic beaker on the tray table before him and swallowed the contents in one gulp.

'What was it about?' Amy asked. 'The nightmare?'

David was about to tell her but hesitated. Did he really want to to mention Daisy? They'd managed, whether consciously or unconsciously, to avoid talking about their daughter since they left the house and, David told himself, if they didn't speak of her then they wouldn't have to confront that debilitating sorrow and pain they had been feeling since her burial. He looked at Amy then leaned across and kissed her lightly on the tip of the nose.

'I think the turbulence set me off,' he said. 'I'm all right now.'

'I wondered who you were dreaming about,' she told him. 'You kept moaning and sighing.'

'How long was I asleep?'

'An hour or so, you slept right through the turbulence.'

'Thank Christ for that. Were you all right?'

'I took one of my tablets. It soon passed.'

'Thank God for tranquillisers,' David smiled.

Amy nodded.

'I was going to offer you one too but you didn't seem to need it,' she told him.

'Did you manage to sleep at all?' David enquired.

'About fifteen minutes. Better than nothing.' She stretched. 'We're less than half way there.' She indicated the small screen on the back of the seat in front of her. It displayed an electronic route finder image showing their progress from London to their destination. The tiny plane in the image was still making its way resolutely across the Atlantic. There was a time elapsed section on the screen and, almost against his better judgement, David looked at it. They been in the air for less than two hours. He sighed wearily and glanced up at the seat belt sign. It was off so David undid his seat belt and got to his feet.

'I'm going to the bathroom,' he said and made his way down the aisle towards the rear of the cabin. As he drew closer he glanced at the other people on the flight, his eye drawn to a blonde woman seated close to one of the windows. Even a quick glance told him that she was pregnant and David realized that she was the woman he'd seen in his nightmare. He must, he told himself, have spotted her earlier, that was what had caused her to feature in his dream. *Wasn't it?*

She saw him look at her and smiled thinly as he passed. The man she was sitting next to was gazing at the small screen in the back of the seat before him, chuckling occasionally, distracted by what he was watching. David glanced once more at the blonde woman then moved on.

He was relieved to see that the bathroom was vacant and he pushed the door open and entered. He ran some water into the small basin then splashed his face with it, rubbing his eyes and looking at his reflection in the mirror. His skin was pale and, as he raised his hand to his face, he saw that he was shaking slightly. He sucked in a deep breath, held it then splashed his face again, drying it on the paper towels he pulled from the dispenser on the wall.

He stood, his hands on the edges of the sink, just staring at his own reflection, listening to his own breathing.

Christ, he wanted a drink. More than he had for a long time. More than he had since that day at the hospital when he'd arrived to discover that Daisy was dead. He leant forward and deliberately bumped his head sharply against the glass of the mirror.

Stop it. Stop thinking about her. Stop thinking about Daisy.

He clenched his teeth until his jaws ached.

Just one drink wouldn't hurt would it? Just one. One small one. You could control that. If you make sure you only drink a little drop. Just keep control over it this time.

David looked at himself in the mirror.

Get a fucking grip.

He glared at his reflection as if he hated it, sucked in a deep breath and held it until his head began to swim then exhaled almost painfully. He knew if he had one drink it would become two and three and then more than he could count.

Fight it. You've beaten it for so long now. Don't give in.

He shook his head then turned towards the bathroom door, pushing it hard. As he emerged back into the plane cabin he started, surprised to see someone standing so close to the bathroom doors. She moved back as he stepped out.

'Sorry,' she said. 'You made me jump.'

It was the blonde woman he'd seen on his way in.

The one from your nightmare?

David regarded her evenly, trying not to stare at the bump in her belly but he managed a smile and pointed at the bulge.

'When are you due?' he asked.

'A couple of months,' she told him. 'But it feels like it could be tomorrow.'

She laughed.

'Let's hope not,' David said, smiling. 'Do you know what it's going to be?'

'A little girl,' the woman told him. She looked him directly in the eye. 'Like yours.'

THE AFTERMATH

The first two uniformed policemen on the scene ensured that the Starbucks was emptied of people then they cordoned off the building while they waited for the other emergency services to arrive.

One of the men, however, insisted on taking a statement from the priest at the scene.

He escorted the shaken man into the staff room at the rear of the building and sat him down at the wooden table, pushing a glass of water towards him, watching as he sipped it, his hands shaking.

The priest seemed to regain his composure fairly quickly and gave a long and detailed description of his conversation with the dead man and also of the moments leading up to the suicide.

While the priest gave his statement the other uniformed man went carefully through the pockets of the dead man looking for identification which he found in the form of a driver's licence, a social security card and several other items. Word was passed to a unit beyond the mall who quickly found the dead man's car parked in the lot outside.

It was less than twenty minutes later that the forensics team arrived and men in body suits began to pick over the scene, their attention taken mainly with the gun the man had used to kill himself.

In the back room, the priest sat contentedly at the wooden table sipping his water and chatting to the first policeman. The uniformed man was happy to be away from the scene of carnage. He'd only been a policeman for ten months and he'd never seen a dead body up close before. Certainly not one with most of its head blasted away by a bullet. He'd been called to traffic accidents and he'd ridden an ambulance with a man who had suffered a heart attack but he'd never been so close to a corpse as he had been upon discovering the suicide victim. It was the kind of sight he was sure he would have to become accustomed to during the course of his work but it wasn't something he was comfortable with. He hadn't expected quite so much blood.

It had covered the floor of the Starbucks in a crimson pool and there were many fragments of brain and splintered bone floating in the gleaming red fluid. That same cranial mess was also spattered on the walls around the table where the man had been sitting when he'd pushed the gun into his own mouth. The policeman wondered what kind of thoughts had been going through that man's mind to make him take such a drastic step.

When he'd asked the priest about their conversation the older man had sighed and announced that he thought sometimes people were under such terrible pressure in their lives that death seemed the only alternative. He had said he wished the man had sought spiritual help. The police officer had nodded sagely and continued writing.

When the scene had been thoroughly inspected and items had been logged, listed and catalogued, the time had come to remove the body. By then there was a considerable crowd gathered both inside the mall and also out in the parking lot. Exactly what they were hoping to see the policeman had no idea. Did they really want to see a body with its skull blasted apart, he wondered? What did people find so fascinating about death? The same instinct was visible after a bad road accident. People slowing their cars down to peer at the carnage. Watching as the ambulances were filled with the victims. It was a contemptible thing to do and it was beyond the policeman's understanding. Perhaps it was some kind of collective relief, he told himself. A feeling of 'there but for the grace of God go I' that manifested in their rubber-necking and voyeurism. But in his opinion, that still did not excuse the morbid fascination.

As the body was taken to the morgue the uniformed officer walked across the parking lot to the place where the dead man's car was parked.

There, more of his colleagues were checking the vehicle over. Going through everything they could find in the glove box and side pockets of the Buick. There was nothing unusual inside the vehicle itself.

In the trunk there were a number of items that caused raised eyebrows. Not least the knives. Six of them. All monstrously sharp. Wrapped in a piece of thick leather, each bound in white gauze. Every one of them was like a razor and one of the forensic team actually cut his index finger while inspecting the lethal weapons.

There was duct tape in there too. Two dozen rolls of it. Twenty feet of electrical wire. Fifty heavy duty cable ties and several strips of material, some of which was stained. Exactly what it was stained with no one could be sure as yet.

When the driver's identity was confirmed a unit in his town of residence was sent to his address to impart the news of his death, but they found that he lived alone.

No wife. No family. Nothing. And about this time, local journalists began to take an interest. A story began to build. Others began to learn of the man's suicide. Some would read of it or see news of it on social media. For most it was a fleeting moment in their otherwise busy lives.

For others, it was devastating. And dangerous.

TWENTY-TWO

David thought he'd misheard her at first.

He shot out a hand and gripped her arm, his fingers digging a little too hard into her skin.

'What did you say?' he asked, feeling as if his body had been flooded with ice.

The woman looked down at his hand then at his face and tried to shake free.

'You said something about my daughter,' he continued, glaring at the woman now, his face only inches from hers. 'What did you mean? How do you know about my daughter?'

The woman finally managed to pull away from David's grip. She looked angrily at him.

'I'm psychic,' she said, flatly. 'I see things sometimes.'

David looked dismissively at her.

'Like what?' he demanded.

'I see people and places. I don't know how but I've had it since I was a child. Even I don't know when it's going to happen.'

'Did you see my daughter?'

'I saw a little girl with you,' the woman said. 'About seven or eight, dressed in a dark blue school uniform.'

'Jesus,' David gasped, the breath catching in his throat. 'This isn't funny you know.'

'It's not meant to be funny,' the woman protested. 'I'm just telling you what I saw. I saw you and your wife at the airport and your daughter was with you then.'

'How do you know? You couldn't know.'

'I told you, I have some psychic abilities. My mother was the same.'

David shook his head.

'This is bullshit,' he breathed. 'Why the fuck would you say that?'

'I'm sorry if I've upset you,' the woman went on. 'But people usually like to know. It gives them comfort.'

David held her gaze, aware that he was trembling slightly now.

'Can you describe her?' he snapped.

'She was wearing a dark blue school uniform as I told you, I couldn't see her face properly. It isn't always clear. I see *impressions* of people rather than their faces. It's like looking at an old photo, sometimes it isn't completely clear.'

David swallowed hard.

'When did she die?' the woman enquired.

'Three months ago,' David said, quietly.

'How?' the woman went on.

'Car accident.'

'I'm very sorry.'

'So am I.'

'I just thought you'd like to know that your daughter is still with you. Most people like to know if...'

'My daughter is dead,' David rasped, cutting her short. 'And nothing can bring her back.'

'Have you thought of contacting her?' the blonde woman went on.

'No we haven't,' David snapped.

'Perhaps you should. There are lots of really good clairvoyants who...'

'She's dead,' he said through clenched teeth. 'No one can speak to her.'

They stood in silence for a moment then the woman spoke again, one hand resting gently on David's shoulder.

'I'm sorry if I upset you,' she told him. 'I didn't mean too. I only meant well.'

David didn't speak.

The woman slipped past him and into the bathroom, closing the door behind her.

David hesitated a moment longer then headed back to his seat, his mind spinning.

He slumped down in his seat and reached for the beaker of orange juice on the tray table.

Amy looked at him and frowned, seeing how pale he looked.

'Are you all right?' she wanted to know. 'You look terrible.'

'I feel a bit sick,' he lied. 'I'll be fine. Probably something I ate.'

Do you tell her what just happened?

'You know what they say about airline food?' Amy chuckled.

David nodded, distractedly.

'Shall I get the stewardess?' Amy went on. 'She'll probably have something for sickness.'

'No,' David said, quickly. 'Leave it. I'm all right.'

Tell her what the blonde woman said. Tell her about Daisy.

Amy squeezed his hand.

Tell her what? That some crazy woman thinks she's seen your dead daughter? What fucking good will that do?

'OK,' Amy said, quietly. 'Don't bite my head off.'

'There was a woman over by the bathroom,' David began, slowly, motioning over his shoulder. 'She's pregnant.'

'You're not supposed to fly if you're too far advanced,' Amy said, glancing behind her.

'She said she'd got a couple of months to go,' David went on.

Amy studied him, wondering why he looked so troubled.

'Did it make you think of Daisy?' she said, squeezing his hand.

He nodded almost imperceptibly.

'It's not wrong to think of her, David,' Amy murmured. 'I think about her all the time.'

'If you could see her just once more, just for a moment, would you?'

'Of course I would,' Amy said, tears filling her eyes. 'Wouldn't you?'

'What would be the point in having her back just for one moment?'

'Because it'd be better than nothing.'

David turned, hearing something close to anger in Amy's voice. He saw her wipe away a tear, her eyes also coloured with that same rage he'd heard in her voice.

Tell her now. Tell her what the blonde woman said.

'It's all right for you, David,' Amy hissed. 'You didn't kill her.'

TWENTY-THREE

'Neither did you,' he snapped back.

Amy sank back in her seat, wiping away more tears, glancing around to see if anyone else had seen her.

'Let's not do this now,' Amy said, irritably.

'Let's not do it at all,' David insisted. 'We've been over this, Amy. It wasn't your fault, it was an accident.'

'That's easy for you to say, David, you weren't there.'

She looked down the cabin aisle to see where the crew were serving drinks.

'What are you doing?' David asked.

'I need a drink,' Amy hissed.

Before David could say anything, the stewardess had arrived.

'Could I have a Bacardi and lemonade please?' Amy asked.

David shot her an angry glance.

'Can I get anything for you, Sir?' the stewardess asked, passing Amy her drink.

The temptation to ask for a large brandy was overwhelming but David shook his head.

'Just a mineral water,' he said, quietly.

The stewardess gave it to him, dropped another packet of peanuts on each tray table and moved away.

'Thanks for the support, Amy,' David said, acidly, watching her as she took a large swallow from the plastic beaker.

'If you hadn't been talking to that woman about Daisy I probably wouldn't need it,' Amy told him.

'Is that a good idea? If you've taken your tablets?' David asked, nodding towards the liquor as she raised it to her mouth.

'Don't be so superior, David. It won't affect me.'

'I hope you're right.'

'Perhaps your psychic friend would like a drink. You can have one while you discuss Daisy.'

'I was just telling you what she said,' he countered. "I didn't say she was psychic."

'Stupid bitch,' Amy hissed, her sarcasm not lost on David. 'She should keep her fucking psychic visions to herself. What the hell is she doing talking to you like that anyway?'

'She didn't mean any harm.'

'Did you believe her then?'

'It's just strange. How could she know that? How could she know about Daisy?'

Amy shook her head and took a sip of her drink.

'Daisy's dead,' she said, flatly. 'She couldn't know anything about her.'

'She told me what colour school uniform she was wearing.'

'A lucky guess,' Amy said, dismissively.

'She guessed right.'

'Why don't you ask her to contact Daisy then, David? Go on. I'm sure she'll be able to summon her spirit or whatever people like her do.'

'You said you'd give anything just to have one moment with Daisy.'

'But that's not going to happen, is it? What do you think she's going to do, make Daisy appear now?'

'I don't believe it any more than you do,' David protested. 'I was just telling you what she said.'

'My daughter is dead, David. That's it. End of story.'

'She was my daughter too, Amy. You haven't got the monopoly on grief you know.'

A man walking down the aisle glanced at them as he passed, his attention attracted by their slightly raised voices. David shot him an angry glance and the man continued on his way to the rear of the cabin.

'I said not here didn't I?' Amy snapped, undoing her seat belt and barging her way past David.

'Where are you going?' he wanted to know.

'To speak to your fucking psychic, where do you think?' Amy told him, slipping out into the aisle. 'Maybe I should ask her to do a quick séance while I'm in the bathroom. What do you think?'

And she was gone.

David watched her make her way down the aisle to the bathroom. She disappeared inside, slamming the door behind her. David let out a deep sigh and slumped back in his seat.

THE MEETING
COLORADO, USA

'What do we do now he's gone?'

The woman looked challengingly at the two men seated opposite her.

'We carry on,' the first man said.

'How?' the second wanted to know.

'We know what we have to do,' the first man continued. 'We've always known. So we do it. With him or without him. We don't need anyone to guide us. Not now.'

'But he was our leader,' the second man offered.

'We can manage without him,' the first man insisted. 'We agreed with his ideas. We're not sheep who need him to control us.'

'I agree,' the second man offered. 'We know what we have to do. We should continue.'

'How many more?' the woman wanted to know.

'It depends,' the first man murmured. 'We keep going until the required number is reached.'

'Or until we find the one we need,' the woman said, flatly.

The others murmured in agreement.

They sat in silence for a moment then the woman exhaled deeply.

'Why did he kill himself?' she murmured. 'And why do it in front of the priest?'

'Perhaps we should be more concerned about what he said to the priest before he shot himself,' the first man offered.

'What do you mean?' the woman challenged.

'What do you think I mean?' the first man snapped. 'He could have told the priest everything. Our names. Anything?'

'He wouldn't have told him,' the second man interjected.

'Why not?' the first man grunted. 'If he was desperate enough to kill himself then he could have said anything.'

'We would have heard by now,' the woman said. 'We would have heard something.'

'I didn't think he was a coward,' the second man went on. 'I never expected him to take his own life.'

'It takes courage to end your own life,' the woman countered.

'He was a coward,' the second man insisted. 'Why would he do it? After everything he'd done. After what we'd done to help him.'

'We'll never know why he did it,' the first man said. 'Not now. But that's not what matters.'

'What have the others said?' the woman wanted to know. 'Have you spoken to any of them yet?'

The first man nodded.

'Those I've spoken to think we should continue,' he confessed.

'I found the same thing,' the second man told her. 'No one thinks we should stop. We're too close. We can't turn back now.'

'There will be others,' the first man said. 'There must be. We know how many there must be. We must continue.'

The woman sucked in a deep breath.

'Have you spoken to the priest?' she enquired. 'The one who he was talking to when he shot himself?'

Both men shook their heads.

'If we approach him we risk exposing everything,' the first man muttered.

'We have to know what he told the priest,' the woman insisted.

'Then you speak to him,' the first man snapped.

'I say we wait,' the second man added. 'If the police knew anything they'd have been in touch by now. Talking to the priest could just cause more problems.'

The woman ran a hand through her hair.

'Someone will have to go to the house,' she said, finally.

'Why?' the second man wanted to know.

'To see what's there,' the woman told him. 'Make sure there's nothing to tie him to us. Us or any of the others.'

'I'm not going near his place. Not now,' the first man said, flatly

'Who's the coward now?' the woman said disdainfully.

'I'm not a coward,' the first man snapped. 'Would I have done what I've done if I was?'

'You said it was best to keep our distance,' the second man reminded her. 'As far as I can see that includes keeping away from the house.'

'Someone has to go there,' the woman insisted.

'Not me,' the first man told her, defiantly. 'Ask one of the others.'

'And if they find something there? What then?' the second man wanted to *know.*

'Maybe the priest he spoke to has already been there,' the first man murmured, cryptically. 'Or maybe you're just paranoid.'

'Maybe I'm paranoid for a good reason,' the woman corrected him.

The first man got to his feet.

'Are we done here?' he asked, sharply.

'Yes we are,' the woman told him. 'For now.'

She remained in her seat.

'When you've spoken to the others, let me know,' she called after the first man.

He stopped as he heard her but he didn't turn around.

TWENTY-FOUR

David turned as he felt the hand on his shoulder, startled by the touch. He snapped his head around and saw one of the air hostesses standing there.

'I didn't mean to make you jump,' she said, smiling her practised smile.

'I was miles away,' David confessed.

'We're bringing some food around in a couple of minutes and I wondered if you'd like anything,' she said, handing him a small menu.

David was about to thank her but she had already turned to the man on the other side of the aisle.

He glanced at the menu and made his selection then he put it on the tray table, noticing that his hands were trembling slightly. He wondered what was causing the small, almost imperceptible movement. He looked at the liquor in Amy's glass for a second then shook his head. It wasn't that. He smiled to himself. Not the DTs. That was something else. He looked behind him in the direction of the bathroom but there was still no sign of Amy. She seemed to have been gone for ages, he mused. But, then again, it wasn't as if she could go anywhere other than the bathroom was it? If they'd argued anywhere else she could have stormed off but not on a transatlantic flight. He felt a certain amount of comfort in that realization at least. He was already beginning to regret telling her about the blonde woman and her psychic pretensions.

But were they pretensions? What did she hope to gain?

David let out a deep sigh.

He tried to relax, slumping back in his chair, avoiding looking out of the window if he could help it. The sight of blue sky and banks of cloud wasn't so relaxing to him when viewed from 38,000 feet. He sipped from his own beaker, his gaze fixed on the small screen in the seat back ahead of him. There was a film showing, but he hadn't taken much notice of it. He knew it was *The Meaning of Everything*, he would have recognised most films if he was honest. He was about to reach for his headphones when he sensed movement beside him and turned to see Amy standing there, waiting for him to let her return to her seat.

He stood up enough to let her pass and she dropped back into her seat and looked at him.

'I'm sorry,' she said, quietly.

'You don't have to be,' David told her. 'I shouldn't have said anything. I should have kept it to myself.'

'You can't avoid mentioning Daisy for the rest of our lives, David.'

'I know, I don't want to but I shouldn't have told you what that woman said. I was stupid.'

'You were trying to protect me?' she cooed.

'I suppose I was,' David murmured, squeezing her hand.

'She obviously believes it. What about you? Do you believe what she said?'

'I suppose I wanted to. Even though I know it's impossible.'

Amy squeezed his hand.

'I know how you feel,' she said, wearily. 'I think about her every day and how I could have saved her.'

'It wasn't your fault,' David insisted.

'There must have been something I could have done, David. If I'd got her out of the car in time or...'

'You couldn't do anything, you know that,' he snapped, cutting her short.

'But how...unjust was that? I get out of that wreck with a few minor cuts and bruises and Daisy is killed. Where's the fucking justice there?'

'The doctors said it was a miracle.'

'A miracle for me. It wasn't much use to Daisy was it?'

'I could have lost my wife *and* my daughter. I'm grateful I didn't.'

'Grateful to who, David? The lorry driver? He got out without a scratch too didn't he?'

'The hospital chaplain said I should thank God.'

'If that was down to God he's got a fucking warped sense of humour.'

'What the hell else was he going to say? Some people find comfort in that don't they?'

'In God? Good luck. It was the same when my Dad died. They asked if we had any religious beliefs, do you remember?'

'I do. I remember what you said.'

'I said not any more.'

'I can understand how you felt.'

'And then, a year later, it happens to my daughter too. Thanks God.'

'Someone once said that God is a sadist but probably doesn't even know it.'

'I'll second that.'

They sat in silence for a moment then Amy sipped at her drink.

'Didn't your mother suggest talking to a clairvoyant, not long after...' she said, the words trailing off.

'I think that was more for her benefit than ours,' David murmured.

'Maybe she's trying to contact us,' Amy offered.

David looked incredulously at her.

'That's what they say isn't it?' Amy went on. 'That when psychics or clairvoyants see a dead person's spirit it's because that person wants to make contact with the living.'

'How the hell do you know that?'

'I went on the internet after Daisy's death and looked it up.'

'You never told me.'

'What was the point? I knew it was bullshit but I thought I'd look anyway. It's amazing what you do when you're desperate.' She sipped more of her drink.

'You were trying to find ways to contact our daughter and all I was doing was trying to resist having a drink.' He raised his eyebrows. 'That makes me feel so useful.'

'I was so proud of you when you didn't hit the bottle again. It would have been so easy for you.'

'And logical,' he laughed bitterly. 'I wanted to, Amy. Every fucking day and night I wanted to. I wanted to hide from what was going on and what I was feeling. I wanted to hide inside a bottle, just like I had done before.'

'But you didn't.'

He shook his head imperceptibly.

'Perhaps I should have,' he murmured.

TWENTY-FIVE

'I wanted to hide too, David,' Amy told him. 'I still do. Every day is an effort. Just getting out of bed. And when I go into Daisy's room...'

She turned away from him.

'I know, I feel the same,' he told her. 'I can't even go in there most days.'

'But every time I do I can hear her voice and I know she'd still be alive if it wasn't for me.'

'Amy, that's not true. What happened was an accident. There was nothing anyone could have done to prevent it. Especially you.'

'Would you feel like that if you'd been the one in the car with her when it happened? I doubt it.'

'What happened can't be changed...'

'What if it could?' Amy interjected.

David looked at her in bewilderment.

'Changed? How?' he wanted to know.

'If there was some way of...'

'Of what? Of bringing our dead daughter back to life?'

'No,' Amy snapped. 'I might be depressed, David, but I'm not brain damaged. I know she can never come back. But if there was any way to make it up to her. One chance. Just one chance to put right what I did.'

'You didn't do anything wrong,' he said, wearily.

'I think I did and I'm not the only one.'

'What do you mean?'

'Your mother said that she didn't know how I could go on knowing what had happened. She said that no parent should have to bury their child and live with that burden. I got the impression she held me responsible.'

'That's crazy,' David snapped. 'How could you even think that?'

'You'd be surprised what goes through your mind.'

'No one blames you.'

Amy merely gazed blankly ahead.

'Maybe I should have died with her,' she offered. 'It would have been more just.'

'Don't be ridiculous. What good would that have done? I'd have lost both of you. I couldn't have taken that.'

'I didn't feel as bad when my dad died,' Amy went on. 'Is that bad?'

'Of course not. The death of your child is bound to have more impact on you than the death of a relative.'

'They didn't deserve to die, David. Neither of them. It's not fair. There are people who deserve it more than they did. Evil people. People who wouldn't be missed.'

David could only nod.

'Straight afterwards, when I went out,' he began. 'It seemed that everyone I saw had a child with them. I know it was coincidence but it was terrible. And what was really bad was that I resented those people for what they still had. I hated them because I'd lost my daughter. I wanted them to suffer like I was suffering. Just so they knew what it felt like. Do you think that's wrong?'

Amy shook her head.

'I felt the same way,' she admitted. 'I still do.'

They sat in silence for a moment then Amy drained what was left in her glass.

'When it happened, I didn't want to go on,' she said, finally. 'I didn't see the point. It would have been so easy to...' The words faded away.

'To what? Kill yourself? Did you think about it?'

'Once or twice.'

David reached over and squeezed her hand.

'Why didn't you tell me?' he asked.

'What would that have solved?' she wanted to know. 'You were trying to cope in your own way, David. Everyone was.'

'But suicide...'

'I wasn't serious. If I had been I'd have done it the morning of the funeral. I don't know how I ever made it out of the house that day, let alone to the cemetery.'

'I know what you mean. But we had each other to get through

that and we've still got each other now.'

Amy nodded, leaned over and kissed him lightly on the cheek.

'I'm sorry, David,' she said, softly.

He was going to tell her she had nothing to be sorry for but instead he remained silent, gazing at her then beyond to the window and the limitless sky.

PART TWO

'Despair gives courage to a coward.'
English proverb.

TWENTY-SIX

Amy smiled as they walked from the customs desk. She pushed their passports into her handbag and re-adjusted her grip on the handle of the suitcase she was pulling on two wheels behind her like some paralysed dog. She always felt this kind of relief after a flight and the fact that it had been a while since her last one was not lost upon her. The earth felt wonderfully reassuring beneath the soles of her trainers. She felt simultaneously tired but also elated. Glad to be alive she told herself, her smile widening.

David also smiled broadly, gazing around him, taking in all the sights and sounds of Denver airport. Manoeuvring a case and also a hold-all, he narrowly avoided bumping into a large woman in a bright yellow trouser suit who had spotted a relative and was hurrying as best she could towards them without caring what was around her. It was busy inside the terminal, like any airport it was crammed with people coming and going. Beginning or ending their journeys to God alone knew where.

David and Amy made their way out of the main entrance heading for the area where they knew the shuttle bus would be waiting to transfer them to the depot where they would pick up their motor home. David felt a frisson of excitement, at least he thought it was excitement. He wasn't sure whether it was just apprehension at the thought of driving on American roads for the next two weeks, but he pushed the reluctance to the back of his mind, eager instead to embrace this first opening part of their adventure.

They both walked slowly enjoying this part of the journey. The traumas of the flight had passed into memory now. They were here, on firm ground and that was all that mattered. There was nothing to do now but look forward. And that was something they both badly needed to do.

They passed some fountains, water spouting into the air, splashing down reassuringly into the pools that surrounded them. People were sitting on the low wall around the fountains, some sipping drinks, others just taking in the impressive scene. Amy saw people in the shops, buying last minute gifts for loved ones or mementos of their trip. She wondered where so many people could be going to or have come from. It was something she'd always done ever since she'd been a child. She would look at people in a busy street or on a bus or train and invent lives for them. Were they happy? Were they returning to a home they wanted to be in or to one where they faced upset and misery? What did they do for a living? Had they got someone in their lives who they loved and who loved them? All these thoughts tumbled through her mind as she and David walked.

She slowed her pace as David paused momentarily.

'I didn't adjust my watch when we landed,' he said. 'I'm still on British time.'

Amy glanced up and saw a large clock suspended above the entrance to a jeweller's shop on the airport concourse.

'Ten a.m.,' she told him. 'They're seven hours behind us.'

David pulled out the winder on his watch and adjusted the time, nodding to himself.

'Shall we get something to eat and just have a bit of a rest before we pick up the RV?' Amy asked.

'We might as well just get going,' David suggested. 'The sooner we pick it up, the quicker we'll get used to it.'

'Whatever you say, you're driving,' she reminded him. 'I was just thinking about you. You haven't slept much since we left London.'

'I'll be fine,' he told her. 'I don't feel tired.' 'We'll get a coffee and sandwich when we get outside the airport.'

Amy nodded.

The child ran from inside a shop to their right.

A child no more than six years old. A little girl in a bright red dress and a straw hat who was carrying a teddy bear in one hand and a bar of half eaten chocolate in the other. She stood before Amy and David, looked up at them then smiled.

She was about to say something when a tall man appeared and swept her up in his arms.

'I told you to stay with Mommy,' he said, attempting to inject some authority into his voice. He looked at David and Amy, tutted and shook his head. 'Pardon her,' he said. 'She's kind of excited. The airport and all.'

They nodded knowingly.

'Kids,' the man said, dismissively. 'Who'd have them?'

And then he was gone, carrying his giggling cargo back into the shop.

They walked on without speaking.

TWENTY-SEVEN

The waves of practised friendliness and rehearsed camaraderie that poured forth from the man who stood before them was overwhelming. Amy felt as if she should brace herself each time he spoke, such was the torrent of verbiage he unleashed, while retaining a smile that seemed so wide it threatened to crack his face in two.

He was in his early forties and had obviously been doing this for years, she guessed. No one new to this job could possibly manage the same faultless and almost word perfect tirade and appear to actually be enjoying it. The man with the name badge on his left breast that proclaimed MITCH, was a seasoned professional. There might have been small sweat rings beneath his arms, soaking into his grey shirt, but he was definitely a professional. He was balding, his head almost as shiny as the newly polished chassis of the RV he was pointing them towards. It was, he had already told them, the company's Standard Model. Twenty five feet in length and capable of comfortably accommodating five people, it was, he assured them, the most popular model his company leased.

'Have you driven one of these before, David?' Mitch asked, ushering them towards the RV with all the reverence normally reserved for a state funeral.

'No,' David announced.

'Well, you'll be just fine and so will you Amy,' Mitch beamed, urging her to join him as he opened the side door of the vehicle to allow them entry.

'Is it economical on petrol?' David began. 'I mean, on gas.' He smiled.

'It's OK I understand your strange English words,' Mitch beamed. 'And yes, it's fine on gas. It has a fifty-five-gallon tank. The tyres are filled with nitrogen which is also a good fuel saving consideration we feature on all our vehicles. There are a number of fuel saving features within the vehicle itself, like our Tow/haul setting on the shift. You don't have to use the brake so much on hills, it makes driving much easier. But I'll show you all that when we're inside.'

He pushed open the door and waved them both inside, clambering in after them.

The interior smelled of polish, Amy thought, as she glanced around the RV.

'As I said, this is our most popular model,' Mitch went on. 'It gives you a little more room to move around.'

David nodded as he ran appraising eyes over the inside of the vehicle.

'I think it has everything you'll need,' Mitch told them. 'Microwave oven, sink, worktops, refrigerator.' He pointed to each one as he named it, opening two of the cupboards above the sink to reveal that they were well stocked with groceries. Boxes of cereal, tins of food, packet goods and pasta were all revealed as Mitch held the cupboard doors open.

'We always put some groceries in each vehicle,' he announced. 'Just until you have time to stop and get what you really like. You guys might have to do without your roast beef and Yorkshire pudding for a couple of weeks though.' He laughed. 'Or your chips.'

'French fries,' David added.

'You have tried to learn the language then?' Mitch quipped.

'We were thinking that we'd probably have breakfast at a diner most days,' Amy said. 'We don't want to get too far away from civilization.'

'Well, you guys will do just as you want once you get on the road but I would strongly recommend that you enjoy our beautiful country as much as you can during your trip,' Mitch went on. 'What you see from your RV will be much better than what you can see from a diner.'

He pointed out the beds, the shower, the dining area and then led them to the cab (which had another double mattress above it), continuing with his well-rehearsed spiel. Amy heard terms like In-dash air conditioning, sixteen-gallon grey water tank and LP gas twelve volt furnace but she didn't take much notice of them. All she wanted now was to begin their trip. The details didn't seem to matter anymore. They were here. That was all that mattered.

'And of course,' Mitch went on. 'You have maximum blackout capability with the curtains, and the roof vents are also treated to prevent sunlight glare.'

'It's very nice,' David said, nodding.

'Was it what you were expecting?' Mitch enquired.

'Well, it's bigger than I expected,' David confessed. 'It didn't look that big on the online video when we were booking it.'

'It handles like a dream, all our vehicles do,' Mitch assured him. 'You'll soon get used to it.'

'Have you driven one?' Amy asked.

'Of course I have,' Mitch informed her. 'My family and I take our vacations every year in one of these.'

'Where do you go?' Amy wanted to know.

'We just drive around,' Mitch said. 'That's the beauty of a vehicle like this. It gives you so much freedom. We try and find the most beautiful spots and then we camp there. My wife and I have always been interested in the outdoors and we hoped our children would be the same.'

'Are there many wild animals?' Amy wanted to know.

'None that will worry you, Amy,' Mitch chuckled. 'You're not planning on driving up into the mountains are you?'

'No,' David said. 'We're staying on the flat. No adventures if we can help it. Just a nice relaxing drive.'

'Sounds good to me, David,' Mitch said, happily. 'If you do need any help or advice don't forget you can always call our Travellers Assistance line twenty four seven.'

Amy sat down on one of the upholstered seats and looked around at the interior of the RV. David sat in the driver's seat and allowed Mitch to talk him, once again, through the numerous features of the vehicle. Finally, they all got to their feet and Mitch dug a hand into his trouser pocket.

'This is all you need now,' he said and held a set of keys out towards David's outstretched hand. 'Each one is labelled so you don't forget what's what. Do you want to start her up?'

David nodded, accepted the keys and sat down in the driver's seat again. Amy joined him, settling herself in the passenger seat.

David turned the ignition key and the engine roared into life.

'There you go,' Mitch said. 'You've got a full tank, your luggage is already loaded, so you're ready to roll. There are maps in the glove box and, like I said, you can call us on the Travellers Assistance line if you need any help or if you get in trouble. Which you won't of course.'

'All we need is *Born to be Wild* on the radio and we're set,' David said.

Amy nodded.

'Anything else I can do for you guys?' Mitch wanted to know.

'No, thank you,' Amy told him. 'You've been very helpful.'

'OK then,' Mitch went on. 'You know where you're going and you know when you have to have the vehicle at the drop off point.'

David nodded.

Mitch made his way to the door, climbed out and closed it behind him. He walked round to the driver's side of the RV and raised his hand to wave them off.

'I hope I don't stall the fucking thing with him watching,' David said, inside the vehicle.

Amy chuckled.

'Come on then, easy rider,' she laughed. 'Let's go.'

David eased off the brake and the RV moved away.

TWENTY-EIGHT

'How is it to drive?'

Amy sat back in the comfort of the passenger seat and glanced across at her husband.

'Is it as good as Mitch said it would be?' She smiled.

David nodded, his eyes on the wide road they were now travelling on.

'How the fuck does he manage to sound so enthusiastic?' David grinned.

'He's good at his job,' Amy added. 'You should know, you're in customer service, that's how you're supposed to be.'

'I don't want to think about that for two weeks,' David told her. 'All I want to think about is this holiday.' He manoeuvred the RV round a car that had pulled into the side and stepped on the accelerator to take them clear, slowing down again as a huge eighteen wheeler passed. 'Do you want to drive?'

'Not until we're well clear of the city,' Amy told him.

'We should be pretty soon. Is there anything to tell us where to go.'

'I thought you knew where you were going.'

'I do, I just wondered if there were any suggested routes or stop overs or anything like that. Otherwise we'll have to ring Mitch on his Travellers Assistance line for some advice.'

Amy opened the glove compartment in front of her and sifted through the pile of leaflets inside. There were maps, food vouchers, laminates listing places of interest and lots of leaflets giving details of fuel conservation and other aspects of the RV.

'There's a recommended route here,' she told him. 'Denver to Cheyenne. It says here the drive should take a couple of hours.'

'And what's in Cheyenne?'

'It's heading towards the Wild West and the scenes of so many famous incidents you've read about or seen in the movies,' Amy read. 'They even recommend a hotel to stay at in Cheyenne. That might be a good idea, David. You must be tired. First the flight now the driving.'

'I'm fine,' he assured her. 'I feel kind of energised since we arrived.'

'Well, there's an RV park in about a hundred and twenty miles, we could stay there for the night if you like.'

'Let's see how we feel,' David suggested. 'We've got everything we need here, like Mitch told us. We're self-contained. We don't need hotels and RV parks. We could eat under the stars tonight.' He laughed.

'If you can keep this thing steady enough, I'll check and see what they've given us in the way of food,' Amy said, getting to her feet. She swung herself out of the passenger seat and walked with more ease than she expected towards the kitchen area of the RV. She opened each of the cupboards in turn, looking to see what they contained. There were microwave meals, rice, pasta and all manner of other dried goods. The refrigerator was also well stocked and Amy nodded to herself when she saw some appetising pieces of steak among the yoghurts, soft drinks and other items.

'They certainly stocked us up well,' she called. 'There's loads of food here.'

'I'm pretty sure that was part of the price,' David answered.

'Do you want a coffee?'

'Love one.'

She put the kettle on to boil, spooned some coffee into a couple of mugs she found in another cupboard and wandered back to the cab, standing behind her husband as he drove, massaging his shoulders gently.

'If you feel tired pull over,' she told him.

David reached up and gently touched her hand.

'As long as we find somewhere to stay by the time it gets dark,' he said, quietly. 'I don't want to drive through the night. Getting used to driving on the other side of the road is one thing but I don't want to do it in the dark.'

Amy gazed out at the countryside stretching away in all directions and she shook her head gently.

'It's huge isn't it?' she murmured. 'A massive country.'

David nodded.

'The traffic's thinned out a lot too since we got clear of the Denver suburbs,' he told her. 'I don't think I've seen more than ten cars in the last half hour.'

'I didn't expect it to be as green as this,' Amy said.

'It's not Arizona you know,' David said, grinning. 'We're not driving through Death Valley. But then again geography was never your strong point was it?'

She slapped him playfully on the shoulder and turned towards the kitchen where the kettle was boiling. She made their coffee and returned to the passenger seat, placing David's drink in one of the holders. She sipped her own drink and leaned forward to switch the radio on.

'Let's see what American radio sounds like,' she said, smiling.

There were several stations of the usual vacuous pop music that filled the RV courtesy of the stereo system but Amy continued changing stations until she found something different. Finally, a voice boomed out;

'So come and join us this Sunday at our celebration of the word of God and...'

Amy switched it off.

TWENTY-NINE

David had taken to the RV more quickly than he'd expected. He had been slightly reticent about driving a vehicle of such a size and also on the opposite side of the road to that which he was used to, but he'd kept his reservations to himself. There had been no point worrying Amy with his trepidation. It had been something he hadn't really considered when they booked the holiday he had to confess. Not until he'd been confronted by the vehicle had he actually begun to feel the kind of nervousness that comes with driving a rental. And on a different side of the road.

Now, he guided the RV effortlessly along the wide straight roads of Colorado, feeling as comfortable behind the wheel of a vehicle as he had at any time in his life.

He glanced up ahead and saw that there were some thick grey clouds gathering. It was too early for dusk to be building in the sky so he wondered if they were heading for bad weather. He hoped not. It would be unfortunate if their first day in this beautiful country was to be spoiled by rain or something worse.

'What have I missed?'

He felt Amy's hand on the back of his neck and she slipped into the passenger seat, gazing out at the vast panoramic view.

'Nothing,' David told her. 'I saw a couple of trucks and that was it. Did you enjoy your shower?'

'I didn't have one in the end, I just splashed my face with water to wake myself up,' she told him.

'I thought you were quick,' he chuckled. 'Were you scared I'd crash while you were in the shower?'

Amy smiled.

'Mitch was right, though,' she said, grinning. 'This RV has everything.'

'He did tell us,' David reminded her.

'Yeah, about ten times.'

'You wouldn't think there'd be any overcrowding in cities when there's this much space would you?' David offered, making a gesture with his hand. 'So much land.'

'This wouldn't be farmland would it?'

'Some of it might. The rest is just waiting. Waiting until

someone buys it and builds houses on it I suppose.'

'Imagine living out here, in the middle of nowhere.'

'Some people do don't they?'

'My Dad always used to say he liked being alone. He could never understand why people needed company.'

'That sounds like your dad,' David chuckled. 'Anti-social bastard.'

Amy laughed too at the mention of her father.

'I still miss him you know,' she said, quietly.

'Of course you do, he's only been gone just over a year hasn't he?'

She nodded, the smile fading.

'Do you think the time ever comes when you forget about people who've died? When you just can't remember them?'

'I've never thought about it.'

'Will we ever just forget about Daisy?'

'No,' David said without hesitation. 'Never.'

'How can you be sure?'

'Because we don't want to forget her,' he insisted.

They drove a little way in silence, only the drone of the engine accompanied their thoughts, then Amy spoke again.

'I wonder what she'd have said about this,' she mused. 'The flight, the RV. Everything.'

David smiled.

'She'd have loved it,' he said, quietly. 'We'd have had to sedate her she'd have been so excited.'

They both laughed.

'Perhaps I'm just trying to forget why she's not here,' Amy said, after a moment or two.

'She's not here because of a freak accident. A chance in a million. There's no other reason.'

'She's not here because of me.'

David exhaled deeply and shook his head.

'You're the only one who thinks that, Amy,' he said, flatly.

'I'd do anything to have her back. Just for a second. Just to hold her. To tell her I love her.' Amy could feel tears forming but made no attempt to stop them. 'To tell her I'm sorry.'

'You've got nothing to be sorry about,' David told her. 'It wasn't your fault. I've told you that.'

'It doesn't matter how many times you tell me. I'm not sure I'll ever believe it.'

David glanced at her and saw that she was staring blankly out of the windscreen. He yawned, trying to stifle it but not succeeding.

'Are you tired?' Amy wanted to know.

'A little bit,' he confessed.

'I'm not surprised,' Amy told him.

'It's catching up with me a bit now.'

'We should pull over soon. Stop for the night.'

'Is there somewhere near? A hotel or motel or something? Didn't you say there was an RV park?'

Amy flipped open the glove box on her side and sifted through the leaflets inside. She nodded.

'There's an RV park in about eighty miles,' she said. 'A hotel called Pine tree Lodge in about fifty.' She looked across at him. 'What do you think?'

David nodded.

'Pine tree Lodge it is then,' he said.

THIRTY

'I think it's going to rain.'

Amy spoke the words wearily, her eyes fixed on the banks of thick cloud that had been gathering in the West since they arrived at the hotel.

'I thought that earlier,' David replied. 'Better it does it during the night while we're here. I hate driving in the rain.'

'So do I,' Amy murmured.

'If it stays dry do you want to drive for a bit tomorrow?'

'OK,' Amy replied.

'I'm not forcing you into it.'

She turned and smiled at him.

'I know you're not,' she said. 'I'd like to. If you trust me.'

'You'll be fine,' David assured her.

He was laying on the bed in their room at the Pine Tree Lodge, glancing at one of the newspapers left on the table in the centre of the room. Amy continued to stand by the window, occasionally reaching for the glass of mineral water she'd placed on the sill.

In the background, the television set droned on. They'd flicked channels when they'd first put the set on, experiencing the kind of excitement that only comes on a holiday from the novelty of viewing TV in a different country. They checked all the channels, finally settling for a local station and a news bulletin that was still going on forty minutes after they'd first switched on.

'Do we really want to go down into the restaurant to eat?' she asked. 'We could have room service in here couldn't we?'

David lifted his head from the newspaper and nodded.

'What have they got?' he wanted to know.

Amy glanced at the room service menu and raised her eyebrows.

'Are you hungry?' she wanted to know.

'I could definitely eat something,' David confessed. 'I'll have a steak. Just this once.'

Amy chuckled and reached for the phone, hitting the number that connected her with room service.

She placed their order, watching as David swung himself off the bed.

'How long before the food arrives?' he enquired.

'They said about forty minutes,' Amy told him.

'I'll have a quick shower before it does,' he said, disappearing into the bathroom.

Amy nodded then crossed to the bed, glancing at the paper David had put down, then at the television set.

She was about to change channels when the story that was running caught her attention.

'*...missing for three days. Police say they have reason to believe the latest child could have been abducted by the same person or persons responsible for the disappearance of five other children in this area during the past three months...*'

Amy turned up the volume and moved to the end of the bed, perched there as she watched the flickering screen of the television.

'*All of the missing children were aged between five and ten and are believed to have been abducted from crowded public areas like shopping malls. Police have asked parents to be extra vigilant in view of the disappearances.*'

Amy shook her head slowly as she watched.

'*Anyone with information about these missing children is requested to go to their nearest police station or FBI office immediately. More than 1,000 children go missing in Colorado every year although many of these abductions are usually attributed to family members. However, in this case, police suspect that a stranger is responsible for the abductions..'*

Amy held the remote in front of her, ready to turn off the TV or at least to mute the sound but she hesitated when several photos were displayed. They showed each of the missing children.

Two boys and three girls.

Amy knelt beside the screen as a photo of the latest missing child was shown.

'Oh God,' she murmured.

The child was seven. Her hair was blonde and cascaded past her shoulders. The picture that was in shot showed her smiling happily.

Amy reached out and touched the screen.

'Daisy,' she said, softly.

There were definite similarities between her dead daughter and the child on the screen. Same colour hair. Same wide and warm smile.

Amy rubbed her eyes and looked at the screen again.

The picture of the child had vanished only to be replaced by another.

Amy let out a sigh then got to her feet. She retrieved her glass from the window sill and drank what was left in it, gazing out once more at the night sky.

She wandered across to the bathroom, pushing the door open and stepping into the steamy room. The sound of splashing water was coming from inside the cubicle and she could see the silhouette of her husband through the frosted glass door. Amy smiled and sat on the edge of the bath, watching him. For a moment she considered telling him what she'd just seen on the television but she thought better of it. What good would it do? Why tell him? She smiled as she watched him, realizing that he was still completely unaware of her presence.

She watched him wash his hair with the small bottle of shampoo the hotel supplied and, when he was washing the lather from his hair, she tapped on the shower door.

David turned quickly, surprised by the sound.

'Did I scare you?' she said, still smiling.

'Yeah, I thought it was Norman Bates,' he told her, grinning.

David eased the frosted glass shower door open slightly and peered out.

'Are you all right?' he asked, wiping water and shampoo from his face. 'I won't be long.'

Amy smiled at him.

'That's OK,' she said. 'Take your time.'

David washed the rest of the lather from his hair and prepared to turn off the shower.

'No, leave it on,' Amy told him. 'I wondered if you wanted some company,' she said.

David smiled.

THIRTY-ONE

Amy's smile broadened and she began unbuttoning her jeans, sliding them over her slender hips and pulling them down, kicking them away before slipping off her blouse and bra. She hesitated a moment then pulled off her knickers and dropped them onto the floor with the rest of her clothes.

When she was naked she stepped beneath the jets of water.

David allowed her to stand in front of him, feeling her body against his as the jets of water hit her.

'It's hot,' she said, tilting her head back as the water ran in rivulets down her body.

'It's meant to be,' David told her, smiling. 'To wash all the dirt of the road off us.'

Amy chuckled.

She ducked her head forward, soaking her hair then she moved back slightly and reached for the shampoo.

'I'll do it,' David told her, pouring a handful of the liquid into his palm. He smoothed it over and through her hair and used his fingertips to massage the shampoo into the soaking strands. As he did so she moved back against him. He lifted her hair away from the nape of her neck and kissed her there. Slowly, gently. Amy let out a long deep breath and turned her face slightly but David continued kissing her neck, feeling one of her hands reaching back to brush against his thighs.

He used his fingertips on her scalp, kneading gently, pulling the slippery hair so that the long strands were rinsed clean as she turned her head in the jets of the shower.

Her skin felt so smooth as he ran his hands up her arms and over her shoulders. Flesh that was always silky and soft now felt slippery smooth beneath his fingers. He'd almost forgotten how good she felt and how good she looked without her clothes. Amy turned her head a little more and David kissed her lightly on the lips but it wasn't enough for her and he felt her lips part, felt her tongue pushing urgently into his mouth and he welcomed it.

They held each other tightly, almost ferociously, unwilling to let go. Amy snaked her arms around his neck and held on as if she was falling. David moved closer, pressing his growing erection against her and she slipped one hand down to envelope it in her fingers, squeezing it and feeling its stiffness. They broke the kiss as David ducked his head and flicked his tongue over each jutting nipple in turn, sucking the swollen pink buds between his lips, raking his tongue over them as Amy gasped her pleasure.

She increased the pressure on his penis, tightening her grip on his shaft and David slipped one hand between her legs which she parted eagerly. He brushed his fingers over her mound then moved lower, feeling her slippery stickiness there, almost surprised at how moist she was. She moved back against the wall of the shower, guiding him towards her swollen lips, parting them with the tip of his penis which, a moment later, he pushed forward.

He slipped inside her with one gentle thrust, sliding deeper until he was completely enveloped by her wetness. They both gasped from the pleasure and also because it felt as if they'd suddenly rediscovered how pleasurable this sensation actually was.

David stood motionless for a moment, just looking into Amy's eyes then he began to move gently inside her.

She gasped and murmured something he couldn't hear beneath the lashing jets of water but she gripped his buttocks as if to force him deeper and he responded. Each long, slow thrust into her made them both shudder and Amy kissed him deeply, her nails digging into the flesh of his back.

He brushed some strands of wet hair from her face but she merely gripped his buttocks harder and pressed herself against him with an urgency he hadn't felt for a long time. They kissed again and he could feel, as well as hear, her breathing accelerate.

He cupped her breasts, thumbing her nipples then ducking his head to suck them again, drawing them between his teeth.

She said his name breathlessly, rotating her hips to match his thrusts. When he slid one hand down to gently caress her swollen and sensitive clitoris she could control herself no longer.

Her orgasm hit her quickly and almost unexpectedly. Her body stiffened and he held her tightly to him.

He felt her muscles tighten around his shaft and she let out a wail of pure pleasure, her body tensing and flexing as he slid deep within her. For what seemed like an eternity, the waves of pleasure racked her body and she clung to him once more, savouring the sensation but also wanting him to stay where he was. As the feeling subsided she allowed one arm to slip from his shoulders, her body shaking. The warmth that seemed to radiate from between her legs filled her whole body, it engulfed every muscle. She felt as if she was floating.

David increased the pace of his thrusting, eager to reach his own release now.

They kissed as he drove deeply into her, her muscles tightening around him, coaxing him closer to his peak.

She touched his face with her fingers and he looked into her eyes as he felt himself reach his climax. With a loud grunt he felt his pleasure explode. He shuddered as he filled her with his fluid, thrusting as deeply as he could to prolong the feeling. She held him to her, enjoying his release almost as much as he did and, when he finally allowed his penis to slip from her, she kissed him again.

They clung to each other as if stitched together, frozen there beneath the shower spray like a flesh covered statue. She felt his seed trickling from her, mingling with the water, running down her thighs to be washed away in the warm torrents.

If she'd believed in a God of any kind, Amy might have prayed that feeling never ended.

'I love you,' she whispered.

'I love you too,' he told her.

It was all that mattered for now.

THIRTY-TWO

Amy was still in the bathroom when she heard the knock on the door.

Assuming David would answer it, she ignored it and continued drying her hair. When the knocking came again she frowned and peered out into the room, wondering why her husband hadn't heard it.

She smiled when she saw he was fast asleep on the bed. Realizing that the knocking was obviously an agitated room service waiter, Amy pulled her dressing gown more tightly around her and headed towards the door to let the bearer of their dinner in.

There was another knock. Four heavy raps on the wooden partition that seemed to indicate the person on the other side was rapidly losing patience.

As she reached the door she peered through the peep hole but frowned when she saw no one on the other side. He must, she guessed, have got fed up and left it outside. Amy opened the door and glanced into the corridor beyond.

There was no one there.

There was also no food outside the door.

She sighed and thought about calling David, getting him to ring down to chase up their order. She was about to do that when she heard movement further down the corridor.

It was a crash, like dropped crockery, followed by a high-pitched squeal that she recognised immediately as belonging to a child.

Amy stood in the doorway of the room for a moment, her attention towards the sound but then something else began to trouble her.

Who had been knocking on the door?

She had definitely heard the sound. She hadn't imagined it. Even though David hadn't heard it, she put that down to the fact he'd been so tired and, after their lovemaking, had flaked out on the bed.

Then she noticed something else.

Lying about half way up the corridor there was a small stuffed toy.

Amy hesitated for a moment then hurried in the direction of the toy, scooping it up. It was a little white and black cuddly dog, its wide button eyes gleaming beneath the fluorescents that lit the hotel corridor. Amy held the toy tightly in one hand. It reminded her of a toy dog Daisy had owned. She'd bought it for her daughter the day she stopped using a dummy, as a reward. From that day on the dog had been known as 'dummy dog' and Amy smiled briefly at the recollection, then she seemed to remember she was standing barefoot, dressed in just a towelling robe, in the middle of a hotel corridor and retreated back to her own room, not quite sure why she was still carrying the stuffed toy.

She walked back into the room and closed the door behind her.

'Look what I found,' she said, turning towards the bed and brandishing the toy like a trophy.

The bed was empty. David was gone.

Amy guessed he was in the bathroom and tapped on the door. No answer.

She pushed the door open.

The bathroom was empty.

'David,' Amy called, realizing how inherently stupid that act was. If he wasn't in the room and he wasn't in the bathroom then where the hell was he? It wasn't as if the room was huge.

There was a small balcony but it was barely large enough to take one person and she could see through the window that he wasn't outside. She moved back to the bathroom as if not sure whether to trust her eyes or not. The condensation from the hot water of the shower was still fairly thick on the frosted glass door and there were droplets of water on the tiled floor. Amy shook her head, pushed the stuffed toy into the pocket of her robe and headed back out into the bedroom.

As she did so, there was a loud banging on the bedroom door.

Amy froze, confused and disorientated. She moved towards the door and pulled it open without checking the peep hole first.

There was a room service trolley outside the door. A white table cloth laid over it, plates, cups and other crockery and cutlery like some mobile dining table. At one end was a stainless steel cloche.

Amy reached out with a shaking hand and lifted the cloche.

On the plate beneath was the severed head of her daughter.

The eyes rolled in her direction, pinning her in an unblinking stare then the lips moved.

'Mum,' Daisy's disembodied head croaked. 'Help me. Please.' Blood spilled over the lips, running down her chin to drip into the puddle of thick crimson fluid that had already spread from the stump of the neck.

Amy backed away from the trolley, dropping the lid of the cloche which landed with a loud clang on the floor of the corridor. As she slammed the bedroom door and spun round in the room, she caught sight of a figure lying on the bed and saw immediately that the figure bore her own face and body. She stood transfixed, looking at her own body writhing on the bed, legs and arms secured by bloodied lengths of torn sheet. The huge bulge in the stomach rising and falling, the skin ripping as if something inside the belly pressed against the flesh so hard that it couldn't take the strain.

The skin tore like thin material, a head bursting from the blood filled maw of the belly.

It was Daisy's head.

'Mum,' she sobbed. 'Help me.'

Her body followed, tearing its way free of Amy's body, pieces of skin and viscera clinging to it and dripping from it. She pulled herself free of Amy's lower body, lengths of intestines gripped in her small hands. She stood beside the eviscerated corpse, shaking, her eyes rolling upwards in their sockets until only the whites showed.

Amy screamed.

THIRTY-THREE

Amy was still screaming when she woke up.

Propelled from the nightmare she clutched immediately at her belly, glancing down to ensure that the skin there had not been torn open. She was shaking.

On the bed beside her, David put out a hand to calm her.

'Oh God,' Amy gasped, breathlessly.

'Jesus,' he murmured. 'Are you all right?'

Amy nodded, her whole body shaking. She turned towards David and embraced him and he held her close, feeling her shudder.

'What the hell were you dreaming about?' he wanted to know.

She shook her head, happy to feel his arms around her but the visions from the dream still remained and she closed her eyes tightly, trying to force them from her mind.

'I could see Daisy,' Amy said, quietly. 'She spoke to me.'

'What did she say?' David wanted to know.

'She said "help me".'

David swallowed hard.

'That's what she said to me,' he confessed. 'When I had that nightmare on the plane, that's what she said.'

'But we couldn't help her, could we?' Amy said, sadly. 'We couldn't help her then and we can't help her now.'

David sucked in a deep breath but, before he could speak, Amy continued.

'If there was anything we could do...' she began but the words trailed off.

'She's gone, Amy and we have to face that,' David said, quietly. 'We have to move on.'

'You mean we have to forget her?'

'No. That isn't what I mean. But it's like the counsellors told us at the hospital, we've got our own lives to live and we can't do that if we focus on the past.'

'Did you believe what they said?'

'I wanted to believe it. I wanted to think that we could move on with our lives. I wanted to believe that we had lives to look forward to.'

'And do you believe that?'

'I have to believe it and so do you.'

Amy swung herself off the bed.

She crossed to the window and peered out into the darkness.

'In your nightmare and mine, Daisy was asking us to help her,' she said. 'Do you think that means something?'

'It means we both miss her terribly,' David said.

'Don't you think it's strange though, that we both dreamed her saying the same thing.'

David nodded slowly.

'It's coincidence, Amy,' he said. 'Nothing more.'

There was a knock on the bedroom door and Amy padded across to answer it.

She opened it to find the room service waiter complete with a trolley covered by a white tablecloth. Amy looked at him and smiled, stepping back to allow him to wheel the trolley into the room.

'Good evening, Sir,' he said to David, letting down the flaps at either end of the trolley before pointing out the food they'd ordered as if they'd forgotten what they'd asked for. Amy signed the bill then gave him a five dollar note as he turned to leave.

As he reached the door he dug his hand into the pocket of his trousers and pulled something out.

'This doesn't belong to you, does it?' he asked, brandishing the object he'd taken from his pocket.

Amy felt the hairs on the back of her neck rise.

He was holding a small black and white stuffed dog, its glistening button eyes catching the light and gleaming at Amy.

'Where did you find that?' Amy wanted to know.

'It was outside your door,' the waiter told her. 'I wondered if you might have...'

'No,' Amy said, flatly, her eyes fixed on the stuffed dog. 'It doesn't belong here.'

'Just thought I'd ask,' the waiter said, retreating. 'You have a good evening,' he said as he pulled the door shut behind him.

'What's wrong?' David asked, seeing how pale Amy looked.

'That toy he found outside our door,' she said, quietly. 'It was the one I saw in my nightmare.'

THE OFFERING

The room smelled of damp wood, sweat and gasoline.

Situated in the basement, it tended to be damper than the rest of the building and that odour of moist wood was now strong in the air, mingling with the more acrid smell of sweat.

Not that any of the inhabitants of the room were concerned with its smells. They had other things to occupy their minds.

Not least the seven-year-old child that was carried into the room by a powerfully built man dressed in overalls.

He held the child by the shoulders, its hands and feet already bound by thick rope. It was immobile. Only its eyes moved. Flickering back and forth as it looked at the people gathered in the room. A thick piece of cloth had been stuffed into its mouth, held there by more rope, wound so tightly around the boy's head that it had chafed and scraped the flesh beneath the ears and on the jawline.

The man stood the child against a wall and hastily cut the ropes around its wrists with the long double bladed knife he took from his belt.

'Take out the gag,' one of the watchers called.

The big man did as he was told, sliding the blade across the rope, tugging it away then wrenching the cloth from the boy's mouth so hard he almost pulled him over.

Immediately, the child gasped.

He looked at those watching and shook his head.

'Don't hurt me,' he said, his voice cracking.

'Why not?' one of the watchers called.

The boy had no answer for such a brutally direct question and he tried to swallow, a task made all the more difficult by the fact that his throat was so dry. A combination of fear and the fact he hadn't been allowed to drink anything for the last twelve hours.

'Do you know who we are?' another of the watchers called.

The boy shook his head.

'Do you know why you're here?' someone else wanted to know.

Again, a shake of the boy's head.

'What's your name?' a woman close to the front of the group wanted to know.

'Caleb,' the boy stammered. 'My name is Caleb.'

'No, it isn't,' the woman told him, fixing him in an unblinking gaze.

'My name is Caleb,' the boy insisted, shaking now.

'Liar,' the woman said, quietly.

'Liar,' another voice echoed. It came from the back of the group and it belonged to a man.

'Do you know what we're going to do to you?' the woman at the front of the group asked again.

The boy shook his head.

'Or why we have to do it?' another woman added.

'Tell us who you really are,' another voice demanded.

The boy just looked more bewildered.

'My name is Caleb,' he said, breathlessly.

'It won't help you to lie now,' someone told him. 'You should tell the truth and pray that God forgives you.'

The boy looked bewildered.

'Tell the truth,' another voice demanded.

'Tell us who you really are,' a man towards the back of the throng shouted.

'God hates liars,' the woman told him.

'I'm not lying,' the boy gasped. *'My name is Caleb.'*

Even if he'd been able to react in time it's unlikely he would have been able to prevent the man in overalls from grabbing him and slamming him into the wall behind him. The impact knocked some of the wind from the boy and he made a wheezing sound as he was lifted off his feet. His head was spinning and his eyes were cloudy with pain, as he saw the big man reach for the nail gun. It felt cold against his palm as the man pressed it to his flesh.

There was a loud crack as the man pulled the trigger.

Travelling at a speed in excess of 1200 feet a second, the nail tore easily through the boy's palm, ripped through the skin and through the bones before erupting from the back of his hand, driving itself into the wall behind a good two inches.

The boy's screams of pain had barely died away when the man in the overalls drove another nail into his palm, the nail itself penetrating as deep as the flattened head.

He slammed the boys other hand against the wall and pumped three nails into that one too, leaving him four inches off the ground, suspended by the heavy-duty projectiles that held his hands at arms length and left him dangling helplessly like an insect on a board.

The boy was screaming madly by now, enveloped by the pain and on the verge of fainting due to shock. Seeing this, the man in the overalls slapped him hard round the face, the blow so hard it left a bright red welt on the boy's cheek but it did, at least, keep him conscious.

He had to be conscious. He had to feel every searing moment of pain. That was how it was.

THIRTY-FOUR

'It's weird isn't it?' David said, glancing out over the open countryside. 'You could drive for hours here without seeing another car.'

Sitting in the passenger seat, Amy nodded, also taken aback by the vastness of the landscape. She could hear the low drone of the engine and the radio in the background, some vapid pop music, an accompanying soundtrack to their journey.

'It makes it feel as if we're the only people in the world,' she murmured.

'I could live with that,' David said, smiling.

'You'd get fed up with me,' Amy assured him.

'I haven't got fed up with you so far and,' he glanced at his watch, 'we've been driving for two hours already.'

She slapped him playfully on the arm and smiled.

'Are we going to look for another hotel or motel to stay in tonight?' she wanted to know.

'It seems pointless,' David observed. 'I think we should find somewhere and sleep in here.'

'Do you want to find an RV park?'

'Why? We're self-contained. We could find a nice spot and stay the night.'

'I thought you always hated camping.'

'It's hardly camping, is it? We've got a motor home to sleep in. We haven't got to pitch a bloody tent when we stop.'

'Do you remember that time...'

She suddenly stopped speaking.

'What?' David asked.

'It doesn't matter,' she said, gazing out of the side window.

'No, go on,' he insisted.

Amy merely shook her head.

'You were thinking about Daisy, weren't you?' he said.

Amy didn't answer.

'That time you and she camped in the back garden,' he went on.

'How did you know?' she asked.

'Because I just mentioned tents,' David told her. 'I knew what you were thinking.'

'Everything we talk about, everything we do. It makes me think of her.'

'There's nothing wrong with that. I'm the same. I hear songs on the radio and think of her. I hear people talking about a certain subject and I think about her. It's only natural.'

'And it's all we have, isn't it? Memories.'

'Let's be thankful we've got those.'

Amy nodded gently.

They drove in silence for a moment or two, just the engine and the radio for company then David pointed to something up ahead.

'At last,' he said. 'Another car.'

Amy followed his pointing finger and saw a vehicle a few hundred yards ahead.

'I wonder where they're going?' Amy mused.

'Whoever it is could be driving home,' David offered. 'They might live around here.'

'Live around here? There's nothing here but miles of empty space.'

'There must be little towns and farms dotted about.'

David glanced down at the speedo of the RV and noticed that he was doing just over sixty. He eased up on the accelerator slightly as they drew closer to the vehicle ahead. It had seen better days. The back bumper had some dents and the dark green paint was peeling, the chassis rusted in several places.

David checked his wing mirrors then swung the RV out into the road to overtake the other vehicle. As they drew level Amy glanced across and saw that the driver was a man in his early fifties. She raised her hand in greeting and the man waved back happily. Amy smiled as they passed, rapidly leaving the green car behind.

'I wonder if he's got any children,' Amy mused.

'Maybe he's driving to see them now,' David offered.

'I hope so,' Amy added.

David merely glanced at her then returned his gaze to the open road. There was nothing else visible on it for a long way ahead. He leaned forward and eased up the volume on the radio.

'...as many as six children are believed to be missing and local police suspect that the disappearances may be linked.'

Amy glanced down at the radio, turning it up even more.

'The children are all aged between five and ten.'

'I heard this on the TV last night,' Amy said.

'Have they been kidnapped?' David wanted to know.

'I think so,' Amy told him.

David shook his head.

'Christ,' he sighed. 'What kind of person does that to a child?'

Amy had no answer.

'When I heard that last night,' she began. 'I tried to imagine what the parents of those children must be feeling. To know that your child is out there somewhere but to know you can't help it...' The words tailed off.

David nodded.

He reached across and squeezed Amy's arm.

'But the selfish part of me thought that they were luckier than us,' Amy went on.

David looked puzzled.

'At least they've still got the *hope* that they could see their children again, haven't they?' Amy went on. 'We *know* we'll never see Daisy again.'

THIRTY-FIVE

There was a bridge ahead.

David pointed at it with a kind of ridiculous enthusiasm, grateful it seemed, to see anything that broke up the beautiful but increasingly monotonous landscape. During the last two hours they had seen just five other vehicles on the road and nothing around them but flat countryside. The bridge was a welcome distraction. David was even more grateful to see that beyond it were several buildings grouped together around a wide forecourt. He realized it was a gas station.

'Shall we pull in?' he said. 'We could do with some fuel.'

Amy peered at the fuel indicator and saw that they had over half a tank.

'We don't need gas just yet,' she said, smiling.

'We could get something to eat,' David insisted. 'Sample the delights of a truck stop.'

'OK,' she conceded, glancing out of the passenger side window at the river beneath the bridge as they passed over it. It wasn't deep as far as she could tell but it was flowing swiftly beneath them as they rumbled over the bridge.

David took the short off ramp that led them into the parking lot of the gas station. It was huge. A vast area of tarmac that was cracked in several places and looked as if it had been baked dry by the rays of the increasingly hot sun.

There were half a dozen other cars parked there and a couple of motorcycles too.

'At least we won't have to wait for a table,' Amy said, smiling.

David parked and turned off the engine.

As they left the RV they both felt the heat from the sun. Suspended there in the virtually cloudless sky, it covered the entire landscape with its warmth and Amy shielded her eyes as the rays seemed to reflect off the smooth surface of the parking lot and the gleaming white paintwork of the buildings around it.

They headed through the two sets of double doors, past the rest rooms and towards the restaurant which had a large sign outside its entrance propped on a metal frame. The sign proclaimed;

TACO TUESDAY – HARD OR SOFT SHELLS 99 cents each.

'They must have known we were coming,' David said, smiling.

Amy shook her head and followed him into the restaurant.

There were at least two dozen tables inside the huge room but only three were occupied. A couple of heads turned in their direction as they entered, not least that of a young boy of about five, dressed in a *Jurassic World* t-shirt, who was seated with his family at a table near the centre of the restaurant. David saw the boy and glanced briefly at Amy who had also seen the child. Neither of them spoke but he knew what she was thinking. He was thinking the same. Always a child somewhere. Bringing back the memories. They walked on.

There was a counter at the far end of the room with a cashier sitting at the till, she was glancing at the guests and occasionally getting up to wipe down the work top next to her.

'Just like the M6 services,' said David, flatly, gazing around.

Amy retrieved a wooden tray from a pile nearby and they made their way past the glass fronted display cabinets filled with food, towards where the cashier waited.

There seemed to be every variety of food inside the cabinets from salads to hot meals and David felt his stomach rumble.

'What do you want?' Amy asked, also gazing at the food. 'It looks pretty appetising doesn't it? Or maybe that's because we haven't eaten since breakfast.'

'I think I'll try the meatloaf,' David said, pointing at something on display in one of the cabinets. 'I've never had it.'

'Hi there,' the cashier beamed as they placed their food before her.

'Could we have two coffees please?' Amy asked.

'Hey, you're Australian aren't you?' the cashier said, filling two huge coffee mugs with the steaming black beverage.

'English,' David corrected her.

'On vacation?' the cashier enquired.

'For two weeks,' Amy told her.

'Whereabouts in England are you from?' the cashier wanted to know.

'Just outside London,' David told her.

'I've always wanted to go to London,' she told them, setting the coffees down on their tray. 'I'd love to go to England. Everyone looks so polite. I watch *Downton Abbey* all the time.'

'It's like that pretty much all the time,' David smiled. 'Just like *Downton Abbey.*'

Amy jabbed him gently in the ribs then picked up the tray and headed towards a nearby table, close to one of the huge windows, while David scooped up cutlery and sugar from a nearby stand. They sat down on opposite sides of the table, Amy pausing for a moment to peer out of the window overlooking the huge parking lot. David glanced briefly at the other occupants of the restaurant then began eating.

The boy in the *Jurassic World* t-shirt sat next to his parents watching them.

Amy took a sip of her coffee and winced.

'Wow, that's strong,' she said, smiling, reaching for the milk.

'That's trucker's coffee,' David grinned.

He reached out and touched Amy's hand gently and she smiled at him. Then they ate hungrily, enjoying the food before them.

They were still eating when the police car pulled up outside.

THE RECKONING

The man holding the nail gun looked at the others in the cellar then back at the boy.

The boy met his gaze and held it.

'Please,' the boy said.

A word of pleading? Of desperation?

The boy looked at those watching.

The voice echoed around the inside of the cellar then died away like rolling thunder.

'Please help me.'

The voice of a seven-year-old boy suffering the worst pain he had ever imagined but knowing there was no end to it.

Those gazing at him looked more intently as he shook helplessly, tears coursing down his cheeks.

'Please help me,' he repeated, sobbing wildly.

'This is not a child,' another voice added. 'We were right.'

There were murmurs of approval.

'What is inside him must be destroyed,' another added. 'Just like it was in the others.'

The boy shook helplessly, suspended by his transfixed hands, blood still dripping from his palms where the nails had penetrated his flesh.

'What we do is right,' called another, as if those words were justifying what was happening in the cellar. 'We've always known that. We knew from the beginning.'

'And now we've heard,' a new voice added. 'We've witnessed.'

There were more shouts of approval.

The man in the overalls grabbed the boy by the hair and jerked his head round so he was facing the onlookers.

'I've seen and heard enough,' he snapped.

'So have I,' another called.

'Finish it,' a woman shouted.

The man who moved forward from the back of the assembled group was a tall, imposing figure, made more distinctive by the thick moustache he sported. His facial hair, like that on his head, was greying, flecks of silver mingling with the darker brown that was his natural colour. His face was narrow and his skin pock marked but it was his eyes that were most striking. They were brilliant, almost luminescent blue. It was as if someone had lit a strong lamp behind them. He pushed through the group, some of whom stepped aside in deference to the uniform he wore. The sergeant's uniform was navy blue and immaculately pressed, despite the fact that the cuffs of the shirt were faded and had seen better days. A bit like the man who wore it.

'We have to be sure,' the sergeant said, looking first at the boy and then at the group assembled in the cellar.

'You heard him yourself,' one of them called.

'Please help me,' the boy cried, softly.

'He is trying to fool us,' someone offered. 'To trick us into believing he is not one of the evil ones. We must not weaken.'

The sergeant turned and looked at him, holding his gaze, seemingly unmoved by the suffering etched on the boy's features.

Then, with infinite slowness, the sergeant reached out and wiped tears from the boy's cheeks with one index finger.

The boy tried to smile.

The sergeant stood there motionless for a second longer then, in one fluid movement, he drew his gun, pressed the barrel to the boy's forehead and squeezed the trigger.

THIRTY-SIX

'I hope you weren't speeding,' Amy said as she watched the two policemen enter the room.

She smiled as David raised his eyebrows warily and glanced at the newcomers who headed straight to the counter at the far end of the room where the cashier greeted them happily.

'Policemen always make me nervous,' David said. 'Especially when they're carrying guns.'

Amy smiled and continued eating, watching as the two uniformed men collected cups of coffee from the cashier. She thought how imposing they looked in their dark blue uniforms and the taller man in particular caught her attention. He was

a powerfully built man with a thin, pock marked face and a thick moustache. As he passed their table he glanced at Amy and she saw how bright his eyes were. They were almost hypnotic their blue colour was so intense.

His companion was a much less imposing figure who walked with a slight stoop despite his younger years.

The two men seated themselves at a table a few feet away and sipped their coffee.

The young boy in the *Jurassic World* t-shirt also gazed in fascination at the two men.

They both had two way radios fastened to their belts and Amy could hear the devices crackling as the men sat there talking quietly.

David sipped at his coffee and glanced down at the empty plate before him. He patted his belly and smiled.

'That was very nice,' he observed. 'We should be OK until tonight now?'

Amy nodded and finished her own drink.

'Do you want to drive for a while?' David asked her.

'Not yet,' she told him as she slipped from the booth, running a hand through her hair and glancing again in the direction of the two policemen.

The taller man with the thick moustache and the bright blue eyes looked in her direction and smiled.

'Are you folks heading North?' the sergeant wanted to know. 'Into the mountains?'

'Yes, we are,' David told him. 'Well, we're not heading for the mountains but we are going North.'

'Hey, you're English, right?' the sergeant offered.

'Don't hold that against us,' David said, smiling.

The sheriff looked vague for a moment then continued.

'If you're heading North there are some problems on the mountain highways,' he went on. 'Some bad weather coming in.'

'We're not going that far,' David assured him.

The sergeant nodded.

'You're on vacation?' he asked.

They both nodded.

'You have a good time,' he told them then turned back to face his companion who was glancing at his phone, reading a message he'd just received.

David and Amy hesitated a moment longer then wandered towards the restaurant exit.

As they stepped out into the sunlight again they felt the heat of the blazing orb. Amy slipped her sunglasses on as she made her way across the parking lot back towards the RV. David suddenly muttered something under his breath and spun round.

'I'll nip back in and get us a couple of drinks,' he said. 'Here, you take the keys.' He dug in his pocket, pulled out the bunch of keys and tossed it to Amy who caught it and walked on.

As she drew nearer to the parked police car she slowed down, glancing at the sleek vehicle.

It was as she walked past she heard the loud thuds coming from it.

Amy spun round, wondering if she'd imagined the noise at first.

She eyed the patrol car, her gaze travelling over the vehicle, her eyes narrowing.

The sound came again.

Four loud thuds that were unmistakeably coming from the car.

Amy hesitated, looking towards the buildings behind her, wishing that David was here with her. She just wanted someone else to tell her she hadn't imagined the sound.

They came again.

And Amy realized they were coming from inside the car. But how could this be? Even through the tinted glass of the windows she could see that there was no one inside the car and, she reasoned, it was unlikely that the two policemen would have pulled in for a coffee and left an occupant in the car.

She was still standing looking at the car when David re-appeared carrying a bag.

'I got us some snacks for the road too,' he beamed, holding up the bag like a trophy.

Amy didn't respond other than to beckon him closer to her.

'I thought you were going to get in the RV?' he said.

'Listen,' she told him, pointing to the police car. 'I heard something inside the car.'

'What do you mean?' David asked.

'A noise,' she told him, gesturing towards the patrol vehicle. 'Banging.'

He frowned and walked around the car with her.

'If they come out now they're going to wonder what the hell we're doing,' he said. 'Are you sure you heard something?'

'I'm not imagining it, David,' Amy snapped.

The banging came again.

'Shit,' David said, stepping closer to the car. 'It's coming from the boot.'

Amy looked at him as he moved towards the rear of the car.

There was more banging.

'Jesus Christ,' David gasped. 'There's someone in the fucking boot.'

THIRTY-SEVEN

Amy moved nearer to him, her eyes fixed on the rear of the patrol car.

'If they see us they'll come out,' David said, also looking intently at the back of the police car.

He frowned as he caught sight of something on the rear of the vehicle. There was a red smudge on the lid of the boot. Another on the lock.

David was fairly sure it was blood.

More banging.

'David,' Amy said, quietly.

'I know, I heard it,' he muttered.

He looked round in the direction of the building they'd come from then turned his attention back to the patrol car.

'Do we tell them?' Amy said.

'That there's someone in the boot of their car?' David said, still staring at the patrol car. 'I'm guessing they'd probably know that.'

More banging.

'We should get out of here,' David insisted. 'Now.'

'Help.'

The voice that came from the boot of the patrol car was faint, almost muffled.

And, unmistakeably, a child.

Amy shot her husband a petrified glance.

'Help me.'

The voice came again and it was accompanied by renewed banging.

'Please.'

'David, we've got to do something,' Amy said, her eyes wide, the breath catching in her throat.

'Like what?' he rasped, gripping her wrist and pulling her away from the police car.

'There's someone in the boot of that car,' Amy hissed. 'We have to help them.'

'There's someone in the boot of that *police* car, Amy,' David snapped.

'A child.'

'We don't know that.'

'You can hear it's a child.'

'Even if it is what are we supposed to do?'

Amy looked at him helplessly.

'Get it out of there,' she said, anger now beginning to colour her expression.

David shook his head, trying to pull her along with him.

'Come on,' he said. 'Let's go. Whatever's happening it's nothing to do with us. I'm sure there's an explanation.'

'David, a child is locked in the boot of a fucking police car. What kind of explanation could there be for that?' she demanded.

'Whatever it is it's nothing to do with us,' David insisted.

'Let's at least wait until they come out and get back in the car,' Amy protested as she moved across the parking lot with her husband.

'And then what?' he snapped.

'See what they do,' she went on.

David shook his head.

'Give me the keys,' he said.

Amy looked puzzled.

'The keys to the RV,' David snapped. 'Give them to me.'

She slammed the keys into his outstretched hand, glancing back at the police car as David unlocked the RV and clambered in.

'It's not a child,' he said as he slid behind the wheel and started the engine.

'It sounded like a child,' Amy told him, angrily.

'It can't be.'

'Why not?'

'Because it can't be,' he snarled, glaring at her.

'We have to find out if it is,' she insisted.

David shook his head and stuck the RV in drive. He gripped the wheel so tightly that his knuckles turned white.

'David.'

Amy's voice echoed inside the RV.

'It can't be a child,' David said, his voice more even. 'It can't be. It doesn't make any sense.'

'We both heard it,' Amy went on.

'Whether it's a child or not, whoever it is, what the hell are they doing in the boot?'

'We could call someone.'

'Like who? The police?'

Amy swallowed hard, her gaze now fixed on the parked patrol car.

'Follow them,' she said, flatly.

David looked puzzled.

'When they come out, follow them,' she insisted.

'I couldn't keep up with them in this thing,' David protested. 'Besides, even if I could it's not like they wouldn't spot us is it? And what would we say when we caught up with them? How are we going to get a look inside the boot? And even if we do, even if we find something, what are we supposed to do about it?'

Amy didn't answer.

'There has to be a logical explanation for it, Amy,' David offered.

'Maybe we're both hallucinating,' she said, sarcastically. 'That would explain it, wouldn't it?'

David looked at the police car again. They sat in silence for what seemed a very long time then he spoke again.

'They could be inside for hours,' he said.

'Let's wait and see,' Amy murmured.

David switched off the engine.

THIRTY-EIGHT

It felt oppressively hot inside the RV.

Even with the air conditioning on, David could feel the sweat trickling slowly down his face as he sat behind the steering wheel of the vehicle looking out at the police car. The patrol vehicle was still parked where it had been left by its two occupants nearly thirty minutes ago. David wondered if they were *ever* coming back.

Amy also sat gazing at the patrol car, her gaze occasionally flickering towards the buildings where the policemen would have to emerge from. So far, the only people to come out were the family with the boy in the *Jurassic World* t-shirt. She had watched them clamber into their car and head off onto the highway.

Amy sucked in a deep breath.

'We can't sit here all day,' David said, his mouth dry.

'Another ten minutes,' Amy murmured. 'They have to come out soon. They're on duty aren't they? They can't sit in there drinking coffee all day.'

'We should ask them what's in there,' David said, flatly.

'Excuse me officer but who have you got hidden in your car?' she chided. 'Something like that?'

'It makes more sense than following them and trying to break into the bloody car,' he snapped. 'Perhaps there's an animal in there...'

'An animal that calls for help?' Amy said derisively.

'This is insane,' David hissed. 'What can we do anyway?'

'Look,' Amy said, suddenly, pointing.

David saw what she was indicating and nodded slowly. The two policemen had emerged from the truck stop and were heading back across the parking lot towards their waiting car.

David started the engine.

The two men climbed into their patrol car, the taller man slipping into the passenger seat. His companion started the car and guided it out of its parking space, heading towards the road that would lead them back onto the highway.

'They'll see us,' David said. 'They'll know we're following them.' He felt a bead of perspiration run down his face.

Amy said nothing, her gaze was fixed on the police car. She watched as the driver guided it onto the highway then accelerated slightly. There was a truck about two hundred yards ahead which he sped past before slipping back into the inside lane.

David followed, careful not to try and coax more speed from the RV than it was capable of. He thought about overtaking the truck too but decided to sit in behind it. He glanced down at the speedometer.

'And how long do we follow them for?' he wanted to know. 'What's the plan?'

She wasn't slow to pick up the sarcasm in his voice.

'What would you do, David?' she wanted to know.

'I'd mind my own business,' he told her. 'Just like we should have done.'

'There is a child trapped in the boot of that police car, David,' she reminded him.

'We don't know that.'

'We heard it,' she protested.

'We don't know what we heard,' he snapped. 'And even if we did hear something, it's none of our business. It's not our place to get involved.'

'Someone's got to help.'

'Why us?'

'Because we're here. We're the ones who heard those noises. What if it was Daisy in that car?'

'But it's not,' he rasped. 'Our daughter is dead. She is not trapped in the boot of that fucking car.'

'Well someone is,' she shouted furiously. 'And we can help. I can help. I couldn't help Daisy but I can help whoever is in there.'

David glared at her for a moment then returned his attention to the road, realizing that they were gaining on the truck ahead. He eased back on the accelerator.

'No, you can't,' he said, quietly.

'I can help them,' Amy went on.

'It won't bring Daisy back, you know that.'

'I'm going to help,' she said and when he looked at her he saw the tears in her eyes. 'Please.'

They both heard the sound of sirens from up ahead.

The patrol car suddenly pulled out from its position in front of the truck, gliding across into the outside lane of the highway. It accelerated away, its engine roaring.

'I can't keep up with them,' David said.

The patrol car roared off into the distance.

Amy shook her head despairingly, tears now trickling down both her cheeks.

THIRTY-NINE

It felt as if they'd been driving for hours.

David could feel his t-shirt sticking to his back, held there by the sweat that had almost soaked through the material despite the air conditioning inside the RV. Amy too looked hot, her face slick with perspiration.

Exactly how far they'd driven neither of them knew or could guess at. Distance, like time, had become secondary to the one thing they had both become obsessed with during the afternoon. They hadn't seen the police car for almost two hours now. Not since it roared away up the highway had they laid eyes upon it.

The landscape for the entire time they'd been moving had barely changed around them. The same vast expanse of green framed by distant hills and mountains that, no matter how long they drove, never seemed to get any nearer. Every now and then they passed clusters of buildings on the roadside. Too small for towns but the only evidence that anyone at all inhabited this huge and sprawling land.

Amy reached for her drink and swallowed two or three large mouthfuls.

'We might as well stop,' David said. 'I told you we couldn't keep up with them.'

Amy said nothing but merely continued with her endless vigil, her eyes fixed on nothing in particular far ahead on the wide road.

'There's another truck stop in about fifty miles,' she murmured finally. 'They might have pulled in there.'

'And you want me to check when we get there?' David said, wearily.

She nodded.

'And if they're not there?' he challenged. 'What then? How long do we look for them?'

'I want to know what's in that car,' Amy said.

'Why?' David asked, exasperatedly.

'I told you why,' Amy shouted. 'I have to know.'

'It's none of our business, it never was.'

'We can help. There must be something we can do.'

David banged the steering wheel angrily.

'Wouldn't you help if you could?' Amy demanded.

'Helping isn't going to bring Daisy back, is it?' he said through clenched teeth.

'At least I'll have done something,' Amy told him.

'You don't have to do anything. You didn't do anything wrong. You don't have to look for redemption for the rest of your life, Amy.'

'I think I do.'

David exhaled almost painfully. He looked at his wife and was about to continue speaking but then decided that whatever he said would be pointless. Instead he gripped the wheel more tightly and drove on, a headache beginning to gnaw at the base of his skull. He glanced at the sky and saw that there were banks of cloud gathering to the East but they were white and the sky itself was still the same azure blue it had been all day.

'What if they're not really policemen?'

The words startled him.

'What if the men in that car aren't really policemen?' Amy repeated.

'So you think they stole the uniforms when they stole the police car?' David said, trying to keep the sarcasm from his voice but failing miserably. 'And presumably they did that before they locked a child in the boot of their stolen car.'

'Fuck you, David,' Amy hissed.

'It isn't very likely, is it?' he offered.

'It could happen.'

'It could happen in a fucking film, Amy,' he chided. 'Not in real life.'

On either side of them the trees were more thickly planted now and, David noted, the road was beginning to rise and dip with more frequency. To the left there was a barbed wire fence that he assumed marked the boundary of someone's land. On both sides of the road there were also a number of tracks appearing, leading off the tarmac and onto the land beyond.

It was on one of these tracks that he spotted the police car.

It was about two hundred yards ahead, the patrol car almost hidden from the view of those on the highway by some trees and bushes on either side of the dirt track it was parked on. David slowed down, his gaze fixed on the patrol car. Amy looked at him and was about to ask why he was slowing down when he pointed at the car ahead.

She followed his pointing finger and saw it.

'I don't know why they've stopped,' David said, quietly, answering her unspoken question.

He checked his mirrors and noticed that there was no traffic behind then he swung the RV off the road towards the hard shoulder, gradually bringing it to a halt about fifty yards away from the dirt track where the police car was parked.

'Now what?' he said, flatly.

Amy took another sip of her drink but didn't answer him.

'What do we do now, Amy?' David went on, the irritation clearly audible in his voice. He took off his seat belt, pushing it to one side. 'I said...'

'I know what you said,' she snapped, cutting him short. 'I'm thinking.'

'Well, that's the first time since we left that fucking truck stop, isn't it?' he hissed.

She shot him an angry glance and held his gaze.

'We have to get to that car,' she said.

'And what's our excuse for stopping?' David demanded. 'What do we tell them when they ask us why we just happened to stop our RV right behind them? In a country this fucking big, we just happen to pull up right where they are. What do we say to them, Amy?'

Still Amy didn't speak.

'Come on, you're the one with the bright ideas,' David persisted. 'Tell me. What the fuck do we say to them?'

'Just let me think, will you?' she protested, angrily.

'You've had two hours to think,' he reminded her. 'What are we going to say to them?'

'I don't know,' Amy shouted. The words reverberated inside the RV and she got to her feet, heading for the door, anxious to get outside. Desperate to be away from David's questions and enquiring glances. She stepped out onto the hard shoulder, the heat and humidity enveloping her. She walked a few yards in either direction, pacing back and forth on the hard shoulder, feeling the warmth of the tarmac even through the soles of her trainers. She couldn't breathe properly. It felt as if her lungs were shrinking inside her chest and she guessed that wasn't because of the heat in the air but because of the fear and uncertainty that gripped her.

She looked in the direction of the police car.

From where she stood she couldn't see either of the uniformed officers. They didn't appear to be inside the vehicle. But if they weren't then where the hell were they?

'We tell them we're having trouble with our engine.'

The words startled her and she spun around to see that David had joined her on the roadside.

He looked and sounded calmer than he had been inside the RV and he gently held her hand as he spoke.

'We ask them for help,' he went on. 'Tell them that we think there's something wrong with the RV. That's our excuse for stopping.' He let out a long sigh. 'If we can get them to come over to the RV, perhaps we can get them away from their car long enough for one of us to get a look in the boot. What we do after that, I don't know.'

Amy nodded and tried to smile, but she couldn't quite manage that simple gesture.

'David...' she began but as he turned to face her again the words faded, carried away on the breeze that had sprung up.

They both began walking towards the police car.

FORTY

As they moved closer to the patrol car, both David and Amy could see that there was no one inside.

Exactly where the occupants of the vehicle had gone neither of them could imagine but that seemed secondary to the fact that the police car was empty.

David took a step ahead of his wife, glancing around in the bright sunshine, shielding his eyes occasionally when the banks of cloud rolled away to expose the burning circlet in the sky. He could feel his heart thumping hard against his ribs, beads of perspiration trickling down his face and he knew that wasn't solely due to the heat. He tried to swallow but his throat was dry.

Amy moved up alongside him, also scanning the area ahead of her for any signs of movement.

As they drew nearer to the car they were now sure that it was unoccupied. Of the policemen there was no sign.

About fifty yards up the dirt track there was a large building off to the right which David guessed was a barn of some kind. Exactly why the patrol men had stopped here he had no idea but all that mattered for the time being was that they were not in their vehicle or anywhere close by, as far as he could tell.

He and Amy were now within feet of the police car. The branches of one of the trees standing close by rattled in the breeze, making them both turn.

The dirt track beneath their feet was baked hard by days of unrelenting sunshine and the dust rose in small clouds as they stepped on the dry earth. It was difficult to walk in places because of the depth of the ruts that scarred the ground. But they moved on, within arms length of the car now.

Behind them on the highway a lorry roared past and they both spun round in the direction of the noise, hearts pounding.

Amy put a hand to her mouth and kept it there for a moment. When she lowered it she could see it shaking but her fear was secondary to her determination and she finally reached out and touched the warm metal of the patrol car's boot.

She tapped on it gently and waited.

David looked at the boot then at his wife.

Again she tapped on the metal.

Silence.

'Open it,' David said, looking around for any signs of movement close by. If the policemen weren't in the car they had to be around somewhere, possibly on their way back to the car even now.

'Open the boot,' David persisted.

Amy slid her fingers under the ridge on the back of the chassis, reaching for the latch that would open the rear of the vehicle. She looked at David when she found it, hesitating.

He nodded in encouragement.

She clenched her teeth, wanting to know what was inside and yet fearing what she might find. There was a click as she opened it, pushing the lid upwards so that the contents of the boot were on show. They both looked inside.

'Oh my God,' David gasped.

It was all Amy could do to stop herself screaming.

She stumbled away from the car, her eyes wide and fixed on the contents of the boot.

There were three bodies in there. All children. All aged between five and eight, although it was difficult to tell the age of one of the boys because most of his head was missing.

The stench that arose from the compartment was vile. A thick odour of sweat, blood, excrement and death that seemed to envelop David and Amy like a noxious cloud. The warmth of the air made the fetid odour more intense and both of them felt their stomachs contract. David took a step closer, his gaze moving over the scene of carnage before him. He could see that one of the bodies was naked, the flesh blackened and charred. In a number of places, the scorched skin had peeled right off to reveal twisted muscle beneath. The body was stiff and rigoured, the legs slightly open and the arms rigid by its sides.

The second one was fully dressed but it was that one which sported the worst damage to the skull. Everything from the lower jaw upwards was missing, blasted away by a gunshot. There were pieces of bone in the boot, spread around the remains of the pulverized head like portions of jigsaw puzzle.

Inside the boot itself, spattered with blood, one of the children was moving. She raised her head slightly to look at the two newcomers and Amy let out a gasp.

The girl was no more than eight. A small, wiry child with light brown hair and a thin face that made her look undernourished. There were tracks through the blood on her cheeks where tears had cut their way through the congealed gore. She wiped her face with one red stained hand and sniffed. She looked at Amy first and then at David, her eyes wide, bulging so wide in the sockets that they threatened to burst. Her whole face was smeared with blood, her hair matted with it in places. The clothes she wore were soaked in the crimson fluid. How much of it was hers Amy had no idea.

She moved towards the child who clambered up and out of the boot towards her. With a loud whimper, she stumbled across to Amy who enveloped her in her arms and held her tight.

David glanced around in trepidation, trying to catch sight of the policemen.

'Where are they?' he asked the girl. 'Where are the men who put you in here?'

She could only shake her head.

'I'm taking her back to the RV,' Amy said, her voice catching.

David hesitated for long seconds then nodded, watching as Amy half carried, half dragged the terrified child back towards the hard shoulder and the waiting RV.

Then he hurried round to the passenger side of the police car and pulled it open.

He saw the shotgun immediately.

It was a Remington 870 pump action model and it was standing bolt upright, secured between the two front seats.

Almost without thinking, David grabbed it, pulling it from its housing, surprised at the weight of the weapon. He pulled open the glove compartment nearest to him and found a box of cartridges inside. These he also took, surprising himself with his blatantly aberrant actions. He backed away from the car, eyes alert for any movement but still there was no sign of the policemen.

Close to his feet there was a piece of fallen tree branch. David picked it up in one hand, snapping off part of it so that it left a jagged point. Using all his strength he jammed the point into the front tyre of the police car. It punctured the rubber at the side of the tyre with ease and the loud hiss of escaping air accompanied the car's slight slump to one side. He did the same to the other front tyre then tossed the branch to one side and ran off down the dirt track back towards the highway, the Remington in one hand, the ammo in the other.

***

Exactly how long the child had been missing neither man knew.

The two policemen stood beside the stricken patrol car, one of them looking at the punctured front tyres, the other peering at the rear of the vehicle.

'The shotgun's missing,' the second man said. 'So's the ammunition.'

The man with the thick moustache nodded then walked towards the highway, glancing in both directions.

He stood there motionless for a moment then returned to the patrol car and slipped into the passenger seat, reaching for the two-way radio.

'Who are you calling?' the second man wanted to know.

'Wherever she is she can't get far,' the man with the moustache said.

'What about the bodies in the trunk?' the other man enquired.

'We'll take care of them. We have to find the girl.'

There was anger in his voice but also something that sounded like fear.

FORTY-ONE

The child was soaked in blood.

Her clothes were drenched, her hair matted and almost every visible area of skin was seemingly coated with the red fluid, much of it congealed now.

Amy looked helplessly at the child who simply stood in the rear of the swiftly moving RV gazing at her with eyes filled with fear.

'It's ok,' Amy told her, softly. 'You're safe now.'

The girl looked at Amy, her eyes still bulging in the sockets.

'Can you tell me what happened to you?' Amy asked, holding the child's hands.

The girl looked at her more intently and spoke one word.

'Chase,' she said, her voice catching.

Amy looked puzzled.

'Is that your name?' she asked.

'Chase,' the little girl said then promptly dissolved into floods of tears, flinging her arms around Amy's neck and pressing herself close. Amy felt her body shaking uncontrollably.

'It's OK, sweetie,' Amy cooed as she held the child, although, from the child's appearance and the way she was shaking everything quite obviously wasn't OK. It was as about as far from OK as things could get, Amy reasoned. 'Did those men hurt you?' Amy enquired but her question was met only by another barrage of sobs and wails as the girl clung on to her. Amy stroked her hair as she held her, blood from the girls matted locks smearing her hand. She could also feel it soaking into her own clothes as she held the child to her, trying to comfort her but knowing that it would take more than physical contact before this child ever felt anything approaching calm again.

David glanced back into the RV as he drove, seeing Amy holding the girl.

He sucked in a worried breath and glanced again in the wing mirrors of the RV, expecting at any moment to see a police car speeding up behind them.

Exactly what he was going to do if one did he wasn't sure. The shotgun he'd taken from the police car was lying on the floor of the RV close to his seat, the ammunition stuffed in the glove compartment. Every time he looked down at the weapon his heart beat a little faster, the magnitude of what had happened hitting him a little harder each time he allowed himself to consider it.

He decided it was best not to consider it. The repercussions were too much to bear at the moment, David told himself. He couldn't think straight. His only mission was to keep driving, to get them as far away from the disabled police car as possible. It wasn't worth thinking about anything else yet.

He could see that the girl had stopped crying and was now sitting on the edge of the bed with Amy kneeling beside her. He could hear Amy murmuring words quietly to the child but what they were he couldn't make out. He gripped the steering wheel more tightly and drove on, noticing that the clouds were growing darker and thicker up ahead.

He thought about flicking on the radio but then decided it might be better not to. There might be something on the news already about the child. Police reports that she'd been taken and that police were already closing roads in an effort to find her. David sucked in a worried breath. The vision of what he and Amy had seen in and around the boot of that police car suddenly filled his mind but it made no more sense to him now than it had when they first uncovered the grisly find. Three children stuffed into the boot of a car, two of them dead. David shook his head, his mind still spinning.

'She can't wear those clothes.'

The words startled him and he turned his head sharply.

Amy was standing behind him, her hand on his shoulder.

'We have to get her cleaned up,' she went on.

David nodded.

'She's calming down,' Amy went on. 'I think she's going to sleep. But the poor little thing needs some clean clothes and I want to get her into the shower to get that blood off her.'

'Has she said anything?' David wanted to know.

'Just the same thing over and over again,' Amy informed him. 'She just says "chase" and that's it.'

'What the hell does that mean?' he wondered aloud.

Amy merely shook her head.

'It's not her name, is it?' David persisted.

Again, Amy shook her head.

'I'll pull in to the next truck stop and we can get her some clothes,' David murmured, feeling Amy squeeze his shoulder gently.

'We did the right thing, David,' she said, leaning close to his ear. 'I know we did. Someone had to help her.'

David reached up to touch the hand on his shoulder and, as he did so, he noticed there was dried blood on Amy's fingers.

'They'll be looking for us you know,' he said, quietly.

'Let them look,' Amy said, flatly and moved away from him back towards the rear of the RV.

He glanced round and saw her once again kneeling beside the bed at the back of the vehicle. The little girl looked at him and smiled.

David's response was immediate and unhesitating. He smiled back.

FORTY-TWO

'She's sleeping.'

Amy sat down in the passenger seat, her gaze fixed on the horizon.

She ran a hand through her hair and exhaled wearily.

David glanced at his wife then concentrated on the road once again.

'Has she said anything else?' he enquired.

'She's probably still in shock,' Amy told him, shaking her head. 'I'm not surprised. David, why would they do that to three children?'

'I wish I knew,' David confessed, gripping the steering wheel more tightly.

'Why would they kill them?' she murmured, still gazing out of the windscreen. 'I don't understand.'

David swallowed hard and glanced again at Amy.

'What have we done?' he murmured.

'We've saved a child's life, David, that's what we've done,' she told him.

'I wonder if that's what the court will say.'

'What do you mean?'

'We took a child from a police car, then I disabled that car and stole their shotgun.'

'They would have come after us.'

'They'll come anyway, Amy.'

'We had to help her.'

'Because she reminded us of Daisy?'

Amy shot him an angry glance.

'Would we have done it if Daisy had still been alive?' David asked.

'But she's not. You keep reminding me of that, David. Well, that little girl is alive now because of us.' She hooked a thumb over her shoulder. 'We couldn't save our own daughter but we've saved her.'

'For how long? They'll come after us Amy.'

'I know.'

'They'll come after *her*.'

Amy didn't speak, she merely glanced over her shoulder in the direction of the sleeping child.

She waited a moment then got to her feet.

'What are you doing?' David wanted to know.

'I'm going to sit with her,' Amy told him. 'Is that ok with you?'

He caught the edge to her words and tried to concentrate on the road again as he heard Amy make her way towards the back of the RV.

It was as he peered out of the windscreen again that he saw someone on the highway about two hundred yards ahead. David blinked, wondering if his eyes were playing tricks on him but then he realized that there was indeed someone on the road, standing on the tarmac with arms upraised. Just beyond the figure there was a large vehicle that seemed to be parked half on and half off the highway.

'What the hell is this?' David murmured under his breath, his heart thumping hard against his ribs.

He could now see that the figure up ahead was a man and, the closer the RV got to him, the more frantically he began to wave. David eased up on the accelerator.

'What's happening?' Amy called from the rear of the RV. 'Why are you slowing down?'

'There's someone in the road,' he told her. 'I think he needs help.'

'Don't stop,' Amy said, sharply.

David pressed gently on the brake, slowing the speed of the RV even more. Now he could see that the vehicle ahead of him was indeed stopped with most of its considerable bulk on the highway. Just the red painted cab seemed to be on the hard shoulder. The driver, or the man David assumed was the driver, was close to the back of the truck, arms upraised. As David slowed down to a crawl he ran towards the RV, a smile spreading across his face.

'Hey there,' he called.

'Don't stop,' Amy said from the rear of the RV.

David ignored her, opening his side window as the truck driver hurried up to it.

'Hi,' the man said, smiling broadly. 'Thanks for stopping. Two cars have already driven passed me.'

'What's the problem?' David enquired, pointing towards the huge truck.

'Blow out,' the man informed him. 'One of my rear wheels.' He gestured towards the truck and David could see the black slicks of rubber on the highway where the rig had obviously skidded when the tyre burst. 'I need to call for help but I lost my goddam phone. I was wondering if I could borrow yours to make a call, get someone to help me out.'

'We don't have a phone with us,' David said, apologetically. 'I'm sorry. We're on our holiday, I mean our...vacation. We just wanted to get away from technology for a bit, leave the mobiles and the laptops behind.'

'There's a truck stop about ten miles right down this road,' the driver said, gesturing off into the distance. 'If I could hitch a ride with you I could make a call from there.'

David hesitated.

'It would really help me out, man,' the driver persisted. 'I usually have my phone with me but...'

'I thought you guys had CB radios,' David ventured.

'Not all of us,' the driver corrected him.

The man stood motionless on the highway, looking at David with a hopeful expression.

'Just a minute,' David said, closing his window. He turned in his seat to look at Amy.

'He wants a lift to the next truck stop,' David told her.

'No,' Amy said.

'Pull the curtain across,' David offered. 'He won't see you or the girl if you're quiet. It'll only take twenty minutes to get to the truck stop. All we have to do is drop him off.'

Amy got to her feet and slid the curtain across so that the rear part of the RV interior was masked from view. She slipped behind it and settled herself on the bed beside the sleeping child.

David waited a moment then turned back to the side window.

'I'll take you to the truck stop,' he told the waiting driver.

FORTY-THREE

David watched as the man made his way around to the side of the RV. He tapped gently on the door then let himself in, walking across to the passenger seat where he settled himself, stretching out a hand by way of greeting and gratitude.

'Thanks, man,' he said. 'I really appreciate this.'

David nodded and shook the offered hand.

'My wife's asleep,' he said, gesturing towards the curtain behind him.

'No problem,' the driver said. 'I'll be quiet.' He grinned. 'My name is Mike Cooper by the way. Good to meet you.'

'David Carson.'

'Where are you from?' the driver asked.

'England,' David told him.

'Cool. Where you headed?' Cooper enquired.

'We're just driving,' said David. 'We hadn't got anywhere in particular in mind. We just wanted to experience a bit of freedom and the wide-open spaces for a week or so.'

'Well, you got plenty of wide open spaces here in Colorado,' Cooper told him. 'Trust me, I've been driving a truck for fifteen years. And when you get into Nebraska and Idaho, there ain't nothing but open spaces.' He cracked out laughing, the sound reverberating inside the RV. He held up his hands in supplication, hoping he hadn't woken the two unseen passengers in the rear of the RV.

'Where are you from?' David asked.

'Texas originally but I live in Nevada now.'

'What happened to your lorry...your truck?' David enquired.

'One of the rear tyres just blew on me,' Cooper explained. 'It's a good job I'm not hauling anything perishable.'

'What are you carrying?'

'Beer,' Cooper laughed, the sound filling the RV once more. 'Enough to float a ship.'

'So you wouldn't have been thirsty while you were waiting to get picked up?' David offered.

'No, sir,' Cooper chuckled. He glanced around at the inside of the RV, his attention caught by the curtain drawn across the rear of the vehicle. 'The missis sleeping behind there?' he enquired.

David nodded.

'Is there just the two of you?' the other man went on.

David swallowed hard, a bead of perspiration trickling down his face.

'No,' he said, quickly. 'Our daughter's with us.'

'She sleeping too?'

David nodded again, his eyes fixed on the road ahead.

'How old is she?' Cooper persisted. 'Your daughter I mean, not your wife?' Again he cracked out laughing.

'She's eight,' David told him.

'And how old is your wife?' Cooper chuckled, leaning forward in his seat.

David didn't look but he was aware that the other man was looking at him.

'I'm just fooling, man,' Cooper continued.

David nodded.

'We Texans, we're just friendly,' Cooper said. 'Hope you don't mind.'

'Whereabouts in Texas are you from?'

'San Antonio.'

'That's where the Alamo is, isn't it?'

'Yes, sir.'

'Why did you leave Texas?'

'I was looking for work. What do you do to make ends meet?'

'Not much,' David smiled. 'I work for a clothing company and I write in my spare time.'

'A writer?'

'Well, I might be building my part a bit to call myself a writer.'

Cooper looked a little perplexed by David's answer then merely smiled.

'And what about the missis? What does she do?' he asked.

'She's a designer. Are you married?'

'Yes, sir. Nine years. My second time. I didn't learn the lessons first time around.' He laughed loudly.

'Any kids?'

'Two from my first marriage. None from this one yet, but we keep practising,' he nudged David. 'If you know what I mean.'

David nodded and forced a smile.

Cooper turned and looked again at the curtain that hid the rear of the RV from the view of those in the front.

'The missis tired?' he asked, jabbing a finger towards the makeshift partition.

David looked at him then nodded.

'Probably still jet-lagged,' he said. 'We only arrived a couple of days ago.'

The drone of the engine filled the vehicle as the two men sat in awkward silence for a moment.

David glanced at his new companion again and saw that the man was peering fixedly out of the windscreen. As he did so he tapped gently on the arm of the seat with what appeared to be unusually long finger nails. The sound became irritating very quickly David noted.

'So you say you lost your phone?' David asked, anxious to break the silence that was becoming oppressive.

Cooper nodded.

'You come to rely on it when you're driving,' he said. 'It can get kind of lonely out here.'

'I can believe that,' David said. 'Do you have much contact with the police or the highway patrol or whatever they are?'

'You only see them if you've broken the law,' the other man said. 'And I don't do that if I can help it.' He laughed again. A throaty sound that David was beginning to find irritating.

'We saw a patrol car a few miles back,' David said.

The other man nodded slowly.

'They sometimes sit at the roadside and set up speed traps,' he said.

'We didn't see any policemen in the car.'

'You never see them until they want you to see them,' Cooper laughed.

David swallowed hard.

'Hey, man, are you feeling OK?' Cooper asked.

'I'm all right, why do you ask?' David wanted to know.

'You're sweating. Maybe you should turn up the AC.'

David reached forward to do just that, his hand shaking slightly.

'You sure you're OK?' Cooper persisted.

'We're having trouble getting used to your temperatures,' David told him, wishing they would reach the truck stop so he could get this man out of the RV. Picking him up didn't seem such a good idea any more.

'You don't look so good,' Cooper reminded him.

'I'm fine,' David snapped.

'Take it easy,' the other man insisted. 'I was just asking.'

'I'm sorry,' David apologised. 'I think I'm still suffering from jet-lag too.'

'You should pull over or get the missis to drive for a while.'

'Where were you going when your tyre burst?'

'I was heading up to South Dakota.'

'How long will it take you?'

'Once that tyre's fixed it shouldn't take me more than two days to get up and back. I'll probably see you folks again on the road.' He laughed.

David raised his eyebrows.

'What's your daughter's name?'

The question took David by surprise.

'What?' he muttered, glancing at Cooper.

'Your daughter,' the other man went on. 'What's your daughter's name?'

'Er...it's er...Daisy,' David stuttered.

'I thought you'd forgotten,' Cooper laughed.

'I wasn't thinking,' muttered David. 'I'm sorry. Daisy. It's Daisy.'

'How old is she?'

'Eight.'

Cooper nodded.

'I heard on the radio that some children had been abducted from around here,' he offered. 'About that age too. You should be careful. Lots of freaks around.'

'You're right.'

'Kids are special, man,' Cooper went on. 'I still see mine every weekend. I couldn't imagine life without them.'

David nodded, wishing that he could coax more speed from the RV and arrive at the truck stop as quickly as possible. He wanted this man away from him.

'I don't even want to think about what it'd be like if I hadn't got them,' Cooper went on. 'The parents of these kids that have been abducted must be going crazy, man.'

Again David nodded.

'If I was one of them and I found the guy who'd taken my child, I'd blow his head off,' Cooper persisted. 'I wouldn't let anyone fuck with my kids.' He held up a hand. 'Excuse me.'

'I know what you mean,' David added. 'You don't have to apologise.'

'I can't think what it would be like to lose a child,' Cooper continued.

David gripped the steering wheel more tightly.

'And you'd blame yourself,' Cooper insisted. 'No matter what. If something happened to one of my kids, I'd blame myself. I mean, you're supposed to protect them as a parent. They're your responsibility.'

David glanced at Cooper.

Shut up. Just shut up.

'If you can't take care of them, you shouldn't have them,' Cooper continued.

Shut your mouth.

'Especially girls,' Cooper droned. 'I mean, they're even more special.'

Shut your fucking mouth.

David slammed on the brakes.

FORTY-FOUR

The RV skidded slightly as David hit the brakes but he kept control and guided it off the highway onto the road that led towards the truck stop.

'Nearly missed it,' he murmured, guiding the vehicle towards the group of buildings up ahead.

Cooper glanced at him but didn't speak, surprised by the speed of the manoeuvre.

'Where do you want to get out?' David said, flatly.

'Anywhere is fine,' Cooper told him. 'Thanks, man.'

David brought the RV to a halt in the parking lot of the truck stop, easing it into an empty space close to another similar vehicle and a pick-up truck.

'I appreciate your help,' Cooper told him, getting to his feet and extending a hand.

'You're welcome,' David told him.

'You have a good vacation,' Cooper offered.

David nodded and smiled.

The other man hesitated a moment longer then turned and headed towards the door of the RV, glancing towards the curtain across the rear of the vehicle before letting himself out. He closed the door behind him.

'I told you not to pick him up.'

The words came from Amy who emerged from behind the curtain and moved towards the cab of the RV, watching as their passenger made his way towards the buildings ahead.

'I felt as if he knew,' David said, watching as Cooper hurried on. 'All the time he was in here, it was as if he knew what we'd done.'

'He couldn't know,' Amy told him, sharply.

'I know he couldn't,' David snapped. 'I just felt as if he did.'

'I heard what he was saying.'

David nodded.

'He was right about protecting your children,' Amy went on.

'We did,' David reminded her.

'Not well enough.'

David glared at her.

'Is she still asleep?' he asked. 'I'll go inside and get what she needs.'

'You don't know what she needs.'

'So tell me,' he snapped. 'I'm not stupid.'

'She needs clothes. The ones she's wearing are...' Amy let the sentence trail off. 'I'll have to wash them for her.'

'They're not going to have much of a selection in there are they?' he noted, nodding towards the buildings ahead.

'Just get her some jeans, a couple of t-shirts, socks and underwear,' Amy instructed.

'Will you be ok in here?' he asked.

Amy nodded.

'What if she wakes up?' he wanted to know.

'I'll handle it, David,' Amy assured him. 'Go and get the clothes.'

He hesitated for a moment longer then got to his feet and left the RV.

'Lock this behind me and don't open it to anyone but me,' he said as he stepped outside.

Amy merely looked at him evenly, closing the door behind him. David hesitated until he heard the click of the lock then he set off across the wide parking lot. As he walked he glanced around him, seeing cars and trucks pulling in to or out of the truck stop. There were people milling about in most parts of the small complex and David felt as if every single one of them was looking at him questioningly. He felt as if each pair of eyes was fixed on him, boring into him. He brushed some sweat from his forehead and took a deep breath before moving inside.

The temperature within, due to the air conditioning, was startling compared to the heat outside and David shivered involuntarily as he made his way past a woman who was standing beside the ATM machine close to the entrance. She cast him a cursory glance then returned to her business as David headed into the area where he could see clothes hanging up on several tall rails.

He snatched up a couple of t-shirts and checked the sizes.

She's about the same size as Daisy. Imagine you're buying for her.

He picked up some packs of white socks. Two pairs of jeans. He didn't even check the prices he was so eager to get the products and get back to the RV. He hurried across to the check out counter and put his purchases down, watching as the young woman behind the counter scanned them, pushing each item into a plastic bag.

'Anything else I can help you with?' she asked, without the slightest shred of enthusiasm.

'No thanks,' David said, reaching into his pocket for his credit card.

He tried to stop his hand shaking as he pushed the card into the machine and he was aware of the young woman gazing at him.

She is looking isn't she? She is. She's staring.

She stifled a yawn, handed him his receipt and pushed the clothes towards him. David snatched them off the counter and headed for the exit.

She's watching you.

He hurried outside and back across the parking lot towards the RV, again glancing around him, feeling the heat beating down on him as he walked. Two huge trucks were pulling in. David wondered if Cooper had made his phone call yet. For a brief, panic stricken second he wondered if the man might come back seeking more help. He glanced around the parking lot almost expecting to see him bounding across the baked tarmac. David reached the RV and tapped lightly on the door, waiting for Amy to open it and let him back in.

There was no answer.

David grabbed the handle and tugged it but the door was still firmly locked as it had been when he left.

He banged harder this time.

There was still no answer.

FORTY-FIVE

David felt his heart beating more quickly as he pulled and pushed again at the handle of the RV door.

'Come on,' he murmured under his breath as he banged once more on the partition, forgetting that he himself had the keys to the vehicle.

'Amy,' he hissed, his head right against the metal of the door. 'It's me. Open up.'

The strident honking of a car hooter behind him caused him to spin round

momentarily and he dropped one of the bags he was carrying. Muttering to himself he snatched it up, preparing to strike the door again but, before he could, it was opened from inside. Amy looked quizzically at him then ushered him inside.

'What the hell were you doing?' he asked, irritably.

'I was busy,' Amy told him dismissively.

'Doing what?'

'She woke up,' Amy said, flatly. 'I finally managed to get her in the shower to get the poor little thing clean.'

David nodded and handed the bags of clothes to his wife who looked at each item and began removing the wrapping then she headed back to the rear of the RV, the sound of splashing and running water reaching David's ears.

'Has she said anything?' he wanted to know.

Amy shook her head.

'Only the same thing again,' she explained. 'She woke up, looked at me and just said "chase,"'

David frowned.

'What the hell does that mean?' he murmured.

Amy shrugged.

'A name?' she suggested. 'Someone she knows?'

David looked in the direction of the shower then caught his wife's glance again.

'We can't expect too much from her,' Amy said. 'Not so soon. She's in shock, not surprisingly.'

'We'd better get moving,' David said, heading to the cab of the

RV and slipping into the driver's seat. 'Are those clothes alright?' he asked.

'They'll do for now,' Amy told him. 'I'll wash the ones she was wearing but I could understand if she never wanted to put them on again. Every time she sees them they'll remind her of what happened.'

'Whatever it was,' David said, quietly.

'What do you mean?' Amy pressed.

'What the fuck did happen?' he went on. 'How did she end up the way we found her?'

'She'll tell us when she's ready.'

'I hope you're right.'

David started the engine.

'We should find somewhere to stop,' he called. 'It'll be dark in three hours and I'm not driving through the night.'

Amy didn't answer. She had already disappeared into the rear of the RV.

She stood outside the shower for a moment then used her nails to tap gently on the opaque door.

'Are you OK, sweetie?' she called, leaning closer. When she got no answer she tapped again and gently slid the door open.

The little girl was sitting beneath the shower spray on the floor of the cubicle, her chin resting on her knees and her dark hair hanging down around her shoulders like blackened, lifeless seaweed. As Amy looked down she could see the dark stain of blood washing away across the floor of the shower, spiralling down the plughole.

The girl looked up as she heard Amy, her eyes wide in their sockets. Amy smiled reassuringly at her, thinking how helpless the child looked.

Helpless. Wasn't that how Daisy looked just before the lorry hit the car?

Amy held up a towel and beckoned to the little girl.

'When you're finished you come out and I'll help you get dry,' she said, softly. 'We've got some clean clothes for you.'

The child didn't speak but lowered her head again until her chin was once more resting on her knees.

More congealed blood washed away from her back and swirled away down the plughole.

'Do you want some help?' Amy persisted but the child shook

her head.

Amy hesitated for a second longer then slid the shower door shut again.

She stood with her back against it for a moment then sat down opposite the shower stall, gazing at the door blankly, repeatedly stroking the material of the towel she held on her lap. Minutes passed and there was no movement from inside the shower stall.

'Are you ok?' Amy called again.

Still there was no answer.

FORTY-SIX

In the cab of the RV, David eased up on the accelerator slightly, settling in at an even fifty miles an hour. His heart was still thudding uncomfortably fast against his ribs and, no matter how high he turned the air conditioning inside the vehicle, he still seemed to be sweating profusely.

Fear can do that to you.

It was the feeling of uncertainty that he found particularly hard to deal with. The fear was understandable. After all, they had just effectively kidnapped a child from the boot of a Colorado policeman's patrol vehicle. Fear was to be expected he told himself but it was the fact that they had absolutely no idea where they were going or what they were going to do with this child that worried him so much. There had been no discussion about it. Nothing logical. No long conversation about what would transpire once the child was in their hands. He almost smiled. Almost. He had never been a spontaneous man. Never given to acting on impulse. Until now? Was this acting on impulse or was it just what it appeared to be? Namely an act of pure, unbridled lunacy.

David shook his head, unsettled by his own thoughts. He felt dizzy, as if his head was being inflated with air, growing slowly larger and larger. He took a deep breath and tried to hold it, convinced that he was about to have a panic attack. Not something he wanted to do while at the wheel. He opened his side window a touch more but the air that rushed in was warm. Everywhere was warm it seemed. There was no respite.

He glanced over his shoulder and beckoned to Amy who joined him, standing behind his seat with one hand on the back of it.

'Where is she?' he asked.

'Still in the shower,' his wife told him.

'Get her out and get her dressed,' David said, sharply.

Amy looked at him irritably.

'I'm still waiting for her,' she said. 'She's still in shock I would think.'

'I know how she feels,' David murmured.

'No, you don't,' Amy said, dismissively. 'You have absolutely no idea how she feels. Neither of us do. How can we know what she's feeling? Not after what she's been through.'

'She might not want to go with us,' he offered.

'You think she'd rather have stayed where she was?'

He wasn't slow to catch the sarcasm in her voice.

'They must know by now,' he intoned. 'They must know she's gone.'

'They don't know where, that's all that matters. They didn't see us. If they didn't see us they can't find us.'

'Don't be naïve.'

'They don't know where she's gone,' Amy snapped. 'They didn't see us or the RV so they've got no number plate to trace or track down. There were no cameras around so we're not on CCTV.'

'You've got it all worked out haven't you?'

'We've got time, David. Time to get away from them. Time to get *her* away.'

'Away to where, Amy? We can't just keep driving indefinitely.'

'We saved her,' she said. 'That's all that matters.'

'No, it isn't,' David protested.

'If we'd left her there they would have killed her, just like they did the others.'

'We don't know that,' he barked.

'We know enough,' Amy hissed.

'What do you think we're going to do now?' he went on. 'Where are we going to take her? How long do we keep her with us?'

'Does it matter?' she snarled, and when he looked into her eyes he saw something that resembled fury. 'I thought we were supposed to be helping her. Why do you keep putting obstacles in the way?'

'Obstacles like us breaking the law, you mean?' David snapped.

'You were the one who stole their gun and punctured their

tyres,' she told him.

'Thanks for the vote of confidence, Amy,' he said, wearily. 'What did you want me to do?'

'You *did* what I wanted you to do. You helped her.'

'Yes, we both helped.'

'Would you rather have left her there, David?'

He shook his head.

'I just want to know what happens next,' he said, wearily.

She had no answer for him.

FORTY-SEVEN

As the day ended and the sky became a little darker, the heat that had been so prevalent during the sunlit hours gradually dissipated.

David was grateful for that much. Even the smallest respite was to be welcomed. The heat had been unrelenting inside the RV despite the air conditioning and now he was glad to feel the air temperature dropping, albeit slowly. The countryside around the highway was still predominantly flat land stretching away into the distance in all directions but during the last thirty minutes, there had also been more uneven ground. Hills that had seemed nothing more than illusory for so long were now beginning to rise and swell on one side and sometimes both sides of the road.

Traffic travelling in both directions had been sparse but David had looked at each vehicle with something approaching panic. In every case that feeling had been unmerited. He had also not seen the police cars that he was expecting from minute to minute.

'When do you want to stop?'

Amy sat down in the passenger seat, gazing out at the landscape.

'Soon,' he told her.

'It might be better if we stayed away from hotels and motels tonight,' Amy suggested. 'We can sleep in here can't we?'

'That's what it was designed for,' David said, trying to mask the sarcasm in his tone but not quite managing it. Amy looked at him briefly then returned to gazing out of the window.

'Where is she?' David wanted to know.

'She's resting,' Amy told him. 'I got her cleaned up and dressed. She's still really tired. Emotionally drained.'

'She'll probably sleep through the night,' he offered.

'It would be good if she did,' Amy added, softly.

David nodded and suddenly pointed to something up ahead.

'What about there?' he said, gesturing towards a bend in the road that curved gently around and over a shallow river that snaked across the landscape. There were several narrow tracks leading off the highway into the countryside on either side of the wide expanse of water, trees growing thickly on both banks.

Amy nodded and he slowed the RV down, turning off the highway onto the sun baked track. Dust rose in thick clouds behind the vehicle as David guided it down the

gentle slope away from the tarmac.

'What if it's someone's land?' she asked.

'Then we'll move if they ask us to,' David said, gripping the wheel more tightly as the RV bumped over some particularly uneven ground. The track was little more than bare parched earth, large open cracks across it to prove how long it had been since the land had tasted rain. He finally brought the vehicle to a halt overlooking the river and switched off the engine.

'Let's have a look around,' he said and got to his feet, heading for the door of the RV.

Amy turned towards the rear of the RV but David shook his head.

'Let her sleep,' he said, quietly.

Amy hesitated a moment then followed him out of the stationary vehicle, feeling the cool breeze wash over her. It felt good after the humid claustrophobia of the RV and she took a deep breath, looking around her. They were no more than four or five hundred yards from the highway and yet the land looked completely different. Trees and bushes grew thickly in places and the grass looked lush despite the absence of rain for so long. The bank sloped down gently to the river and opposite, there was a steeper incline leading up to

more trees and scrub land. 'We'll stay here,' David announced, looking out over the shallow river. 'It'll be dark soon. No one will be able to see us from the road.'

'What's that on the other side of the river?' Amy asked, touching David's arm and pointing between a copse of trees.

He followed her pointing finger and saw the white washed structure she was indicating.

'It looks like a church,' he said, putting one hand, visor like, across his brow and squinting in the direction of the building.

'Out here?' Amy murmured.

'Well, I suppose they had to build it somewhere,' he said, glancing more intently at the battered structure. 'It looks as if it's seen better days though.' He glanced around and saw that the shallow river was easily fordable a little way downstream via a series of small islands that made crossing the waterway relatively simple. 'I might go and have a closer look later.'

'Why?' Amy wanted to know.

'I just want to have a look around.'

'No, David, stay here.'

He nodded slowly then turned and headed back towards the RV, Amy walking along beside him.

'I'll cook us something before we settle down for the night,' she said. 'Our...guest must be hungry too.'

'If she's got the stomach to eat,' David mused. 'I'm not sure I have.'

Amy squeezed his hand as they headed back up the slight incline to the waiting RV.

'There aren't any snakes out here are there?' she said, gazing around at the terrain warily.

'I doubt it,' David told her, also glancing around. 'Anyway, we'll be inside won't we? Don't worry about it.'

'There are rattlesnakes in this part of America, I'm sure there are.'

'I'd forgotten you were an expert,' he said, dismissively. 'Anyway, we've got enough to worry about without fucking snakes.'

As they drew closer to the RV they both saw the child standing in the doorway.

FORTY-EIGHT

The small dining table inside the RV was more than large enough for the three of them.

Amy sat on one side with the child while David sat opposite, his gaze alternating between the food Amy had placed before him, his wife and the child.

Outside, the sunshine and the warmth of the day had been

replaced by a dark sky and a chill breeze that occasionally whipped around the RV and rattled the windows on more than one occasion. Each time that happened, the girl would jerk her head around worriedly in the direction of the noise, on every occasion to be reassured by Amy that it was indeed nothing more than wind. There were sounds too but Amy was happy that the child had not asked what they were because she wasn't sure herself. She'd heard an owl a couple of times but other than that, the nocturnal chorus that was going on outside the RV was a combination of noises Amy could not decipher.

She glanced down at the little girl's plate, relieved to see that she'd eaten most of the food that she'd been given. As Amy watched she reached for her glass of milk and sipped from it.

'Did you enjoy that?' Amy asked.

The girl nodded.

'Are you feeling better?' Amy went on.

Again the girl nodded.

'We won't let anyone hurt you,' Amy told her. 'You're safe now.'

The girl reached for her glass and sipped at the milk again.

David glanced at Amy then at the girl.

'What's your name?' he asked her.

She merely raised her head and looked at him but she didn't answer.

'Don't you want to tell us?' David persisted. 'My name is David and this is my wife, Amy. Why don't you tell us your name too?'

The girl simply sipped her milk.

'She's probably still in shock,' Amy offered.

'Probably,' David murmured.

'Can you tell us where you're from?' Amy asked, gently stroking the girls arm.

The girl remained silent.

'That's OK,' Amy told her. 'You'll tell us when you're ready won't you?' She smiled at the girl who looked up at her and managed a thin smile by way of reply.

'Do you like your new clothes that we got you?' David enquired, pointing at the bright pink t-shirt the girl was wearing.

She smiled again and nodded.

Amy ruffled her hair and the girls' smile grew broader.

'What does "chase" mean?' David asked softly.

The girl's smile faded immediately.

'I think that's enough for now,' Amy told him, sliding her arm down to the girl's shoulder.

'You said "chase" David pressed. 'What did you mean?'

The girl shook her head almost imperceptibly.

'David,' Amy urged.

'Is it your name?' he went on. 'Is "chase" your name?'

The girl moved closer to Amy.

'Stop it,' Amy snapped. 'She doesn't want to tell us yet, you can see that.'

David sat back slightly, his eyes still fixed on the girl. He got to his feet and glanced in the direction of one of the RV windows. The blinds had been pulled in order to shut out the darkness and the wind blew strongly for a moment as he straightened up.

'Where are you going?' Amy wanted to know.

'For a walk,' David told her. 'Want to come?'

Amy shook her head.

'I'll stay here,' she nodded towards the girl. 'Make sure she's OK.'

David nodded and headed to the door of the RV, opening it and gazing out into the blackness beyond. The wind whipped again around the vehicle, shaking it momentarily. David reached for the light jacket on the back of one of the dining chairs. He pulled it on, paused a moment longer then stepped out into the night.

He was surprised at exactly how black the night was. Without the benefit of any kind of lighting, the landscape was bathed in darkness so total he could only see about ten or fifteen feet in front of him. The moon which he'd seen earlier and which had lit the land with a cold, white glow, had been smothered by the thick banks of dark cloud that filled the sky. Nevertheless, David dug his hands in his jacket pockets and set off away from the RV towards the riverbank, the sound of the swiftly flowing waterway clearly audible in the gloom. He slowed his pace slightly wondering if the bank close to the river was secure enough to take his weight. In such impenetrable blackness it was difficult to see if there were any potholes or rifts in the ground that might make his progress difficult or even dangerous. He moved further away from the bank, ensuring that he was always ten or fifteen feet from the water.

Exactly why the word snake suddenly surfaced in his mind he wasn't sure but he suddenly glanced around him, squinting in the gloom, aware that Amy had mentioned the reptiles earlier and also painfully conscious of the fact that most snakes were nocturnal hunters. He was reasonably sure that rattlesnakes were native to Colorado although, in the darkness and with this sudden fear of snakes building, he could probably have convinced himself that pythons were equally at home along this stretch of river.

He made his way further along the bank, the RV disappearing in the gloom behind him but he also noticed, with something akin to relief, that the moon was beginning to nudge its way out from behind the bank of thick cloud in the heavens. The cold silver light it cast at least illuminated the terrain around him. David stood still for a moment, gazing up at the moon and then around him at the shadow shrouded landscape. A fresh breeze swept across the land too and he shivered momentarily until it passed.

David stood motionless for a moment longer then decided to set off further down the river towards a series of small islands that looked like enlarged stepping stones in the water.

It was as he was standing there that he first caught sight of the figures on the far bank.

FORTY-NINE

At first he thought he was imagining things. Seeing images in the gloom. Tricks of the light.

But, as David walked slowly towards the riverbank and the trees, he squinted and peered towards the far bank, up the incline towards the low ridge that had suddenly become illuminated by the moonbeams. He moved among the trees, hidden by them and grateful for that because, he reasoned, if he could see someone moving about on the far bank then, logically, they could see him too. He held onto the trunk of one as he peered once more across the river and up the slope towards what had first caught his attention.

There were more figures there now.

He could see at least ten. Men and women of all ages.

David muttered something under his breath, wishing he could see more clearly. He stepped back from the enveloping trees and sprinted back towards the waiting RV, surprised at how fast he crossed the flat, dry ground.

As he reached the RV and hurried inside, Amy turned in surprise.

'I need the binoculars,' David told her.

'Why?' she asked.

'There's people out there,' he informed her, reaching into one of the cupboards and pulling out a small pair of binoculars. 'On the other side of the river, near that old church.'

The girl, who was sitting at the table with Amy, looked up quizzically at David.

'It might be their land, David,' Amy told him. 'Be careful.'

David nodded.

'They can't see me from where they are,' he assured her, heading out of the RV once again.

'I hope you're right,' she called after him.

David sprinted back across the open ground between the RV and the trees, grateful that the moon had momentarily been eclipsed by the thick clouds to give him cover. He ran sure-footed on the dry ground, concerned only with reaching the safety of the trees once again. Any thought of snakes, potholes or danger of any kind caused by the impenetrable blackness seemed to have left his mind, replaced only by his desire to get a better view of the figures across the river and what they were doing.

He raised the binoculars to his eyes and peered through them, adjusting the focus.

With the moon obscured, it was difficult to make out anything, let alone the shapes and outlines of people on the far bank. He swept the binoculars back and forth, trying to pick out some signs of movement but was thwarted by the blackness. He muttered something under his breath and lowered the glasses, looking up at the sky to see that one particularly dense bank of cloud was actually close to moving once more. He waited, raising the binoculars as the clouds rolled away. The familiar cold white light flooded the landscape once more and David squinted gratefully through the binoculars.

In the moons glow he could now see more people. They were moving around outside the church in twos and threes, occasionally alone. Exactly what they were doing he had no idea but he could see several vehicles parked near to the dilapidated structure too, some of which had their headlights on. He wondered briefly if the beams, cutting through the blackness, would pick him out but decided they wouldn't. Also, he told himself, no one knew he was watching, no one knew he was hiding there in the trees, they wouldn't be looking for him would they? And besides, why would they object to his presence? Unless, he thought with a shudder, he was trespassing. It was a cliché he knew but Americans were fond of firearms weren't they? What if they decided to shoot him? He shook his head, pushing the thought from his mind, annoyed with himself for even entertaining it.

He watched intently as the small groups of people gradually joined together outside what looked like the main entrance of the church and yet still more vehicles were approaching from the other side of the building, along a dirt track, their headlights cutting through the night.

Was there, he wondered, some kind of service being held in the church? It seemed unlikely at such a late hour (a glance at his watch had told him it was fast approaching 11.15). But, if that wasn't the case then why were so many people gathering outside the building. He counted at least twenty by now. The youngest he'd seen was in his twenties, the oldest was walking slowly and only with the aid of a stick.

David's curiosity was growing by the minute.

A particularly strong gust of wind rattled the tree branches above him and one of the lower ones brushed the top of his head. He spun round, his heart thudding harder against his ribs, muttering to himself when more clouds again hid the moon and robbed him of his only source of natural light. He peered again through the binoculars but could barely make out the figures across the river in the impenetrable gloom. He looked up, wishing that the clouds would clear so he could continue his vigil. Some of the vehicles parked close to the church had their headlights on still but the meagre beams weren't enough to aid visibility for David. He held the binoculars to his eyes and waited.

The flames that suddenly rose into the air cast a yellow glow all of their own.

FIFTY

David let out a low gasp as he saw the eruption of yellow and orange fire, puzzled and surprised both by its ferocity and also by its sudden appearance.

He swung the binoculars round to concentrate on the large plume of fire that seemed to have sprung from the very earth itself not more than fifteen or twenty feet from the main entrance of the dilapidated church. Adjusting the focus once more he saw that there was a deep hole dug in the parched earth before the building and it was from within that the fire had risen. There were several discarded tree branches and even a couple of petrol cans lying close to the edge of the pit.

He frowned, pondering the purpose of this huge bonfire. Smoke was belching upwards into the sky, thick grey smoke that periodically drifted across the landscape affecting visibility as surely as the darkness. A combination of the two would make it almost impossible to see what was happening but, for now, David was grateful that the moon remained uncloaked in the sky, its silvery light now competing with the fevered glow cast by the huge fire.

The people outside the church began to gather around the edges of the hole, seemingly oblivious to the leaping flames. They stood motionless, gazing either down into the fiery depths or staring blankly across the landscape.

Even when the main doors of the church opened they didn't move.

David adjusted the focus on the binoculars again, swinging them round to look at the church doors. He could see two men emerging, holding something between them. Although dragging would have been a more apt word. They were hauling something small between them, from the gloom of the church into the moon and fire illuminated landscape beyond.

It took David a moment to realize that what they were dragging between them was a child.

'Oh God,' he murmured, the breath catching in his throat.

For a moment he wondered if his eyes were playing tricks on him. It was like a waking nightmare. He trained the binoculars on the child and squinted through them.

She was five or six. No older. Her clothes, jeans and a yellow top, were torn and, David noticed to his horror and revulsion, stained with blood. As she lifted her head slightly he could see that there were several wounds on her face and he could see blood running from her mouth. Her hair was tied back, pulled off her face and he could see, even from such a distance, that she was crying. Her face was twisted into an expression of suffering and dismay as the two men on either side dragged her from the building.

Some of those gathered around the pit glanced in her direction but most merely kept their gaze on the flames.

High above him, the clouds once more closed around the moon, sending darkness spreading across the land. Only the glow from the fire illuminated what was happening and that was sadly inadequate compared to the celestial brightness the moon had offered. David muttered angrily under his breath, frustrated that he couldn't see what was unfolding across the river with greater clarity.

He glanced downstream, wondering if there was another area that might give him a better vantage point.

Across the river there were a number of low bushes that would offer him cover from those he was watching. It looked relatively simple to reach that new vantage point by using the series of islands across the waterway.

Are you absolutely insane?

He hesitated for a moment, peering again towards the church and the fire. And the child.

Another child.

David slipped from between the trees and hurried down the gentle slope towards the first of the islands, although he realized they were little more than mounds of earth that were poking through the surface of the water. Would they, he wondered, be able to take his weight.

He put one foot on the first of them and pressed down on it. It seemed solid enough. David stepped across on to the second one, feeling a cold breeze blow over him from the river. He moved across swiftly and sure-footedly, finally reaching the far bank with ease. He scrambled up towards the bushes and, as the moonlight rolled across the land once more, he raised the binoculars to his face and peered in the direction of the church and those standing outside it.

He couldn't see the child.

David swept the binoculars back and forth, searching around the flaming pit, studying the faces of those he was watching as closely as he could but of the child and the two men who had been holding her there was no sign. Some of the other onlookers had also moved away from the side of the hole, doubtless driven back by what looked like considerable heat. The flames were writhing and dancing in the breeze, sometimes dipping low and close to those gathered around them. David let out a breath and continued to look for the child.

As the moon emerged from behind the cloaking cloud he saw her.

'Oh Jesus,' he murmured.

She was being held aloft by a man who had emerged from the gloom. A large man who was dressed in dark clothes and who was staring ahead blankly as if he was in some kind of trance. He held the girl before him easily, his thick arms slightly bent to accommodate her negligible weight. The girl was motionless there, afraid to move.

David moved forward slightly, careful to keep behind the thick hedges that masked the approaches to the river from those close to the church. He adjusted the focus on the binoculars again, keeping them trained on the girl and the man who held her, wondering why there seemed to be something strangely familiar about the man. *How could there be?*

David frowned and raised himself up slightly anxious to see through some particularly thick branches poking up from the bushes.

I know that face, he told himself, even though that seemed like an impossibility. How could he know this man? Where could he possibly have seen him before? It was impossible. And yet.

He gasped. He *did* recognise the thick moustache and the thin features. It was the highway patrol man they'd seen back at the truck stop earlier. The man whose car they'd taken the girl from back down the road. Even out of his uniform he was a distinctive and recognisable individual, and David was unfailingly convinced that was who he was gazing at.

And that man was holding the child who'd been brought from the church closer and closer to the edge of the flaming pit.

David felt his heart hammering against his ribs.

'No,' he murmured.

The child was squirming in his powerful arms now, desperate to escape, to be away from the leaping flames.

David tried to swallow but his throat was too dry.

He trained the binoculars on the girls face and realized that she was screaming now.

The patrol man was saying something too, his words shouted from the expression on his face and the way he was gesticulating with his free hand. He held the girl in one powerful hand now, both of them close to the edge of the pit and those watching moved closer.

'No,' David whispered again, shaking his head. 'Let her go.'

He stood up.

'Don't hurt her,' he said, a little more loudly.

The patrol man made a wild gesture with his free hand.

With the other one, he lifted the girl by her throat, held her suspended there in mid-air for a moment then hurled her into the flames.

FIFTY-ONE

David felt his stomach contract. His entire body suddenly felt as if it had been dipped in freezing water.

'Oh my God,' he murmured, standing bolt upright, transfixed by what he'd seen.

As the moon was revealed, the clouds drifting aside like curtains before some emerging deity, white light flooded the landscape illuminating everything. He ducked back down into the bushes but his movement was too slow.

He could see at least two of the group gathered around the pit pointing in his direction.

For a second he froze. Unable or unwilling to accept that they could possibly have seen him. They were over two hundred yards away. How could they have seen him? But, even without the benefit of the binoculars he could see that more of them were jabbing fingers in his direction. Two men were actually moving across the dry ground towards where he was hiding.

David scrambled to his feet and sprinted towards the riverbank, glancing behind him in the process.

The two men had been joined by another. All three were heading in his direction now.

David dashed down the incline towards the river, grateful that the moon was still covering the land with its light. He didn't relish running across terrain like this in pitch blackness. He jumped down to the waters edge, overbalancing and almost pitching forward into the swiftly flowing water, cursing under his breath when one of his feet splashed into the river but he ran on, stumbling over the first of the small islands and through the water to the next, peering anxiously behind him once again.

He could hear raised voices now.

They were getting closer.

Again he looked behind him and saw several figures silhouetted against the top of the ridge.

David ran on, trying to reach the sanctuary of the trees he'd hidden in before crossing the river. If he could reach those, they might not be able to see him from the far bank. They might not come after him.

Thoughts tumbled through his mind. Visions he wanted to shake but couldn't. The patrol man. The girl in the yellow t-shirt. The fire. And, most unwelcome of all, the image of the girl being thrown into the flames. What the hell was going on? Who were these people? Why was the patrol man involved again?

David ran on, the muscles in his calves now beginning to throb. He wasn't used to prolonged exertion like this and his plight seemed to be making movement even more difficult. It was as if his joints had frozen as surely as his blood had when he realized he'd been spotted.

What would they do if they caught up with him, he wondered. If they had watched unmoved while a child was hurled into fire then his fate would be similarly untroubling to them he told himself as he stumbled on.

He shot another glance over his shoulder, now only ten or fifteen yards from the possible cover of the trees.

Two of the men were already heading down the bank opposite, leaping down to the waters edge just as David had done. The first of them landed heavily, fell backwards and shouted angrily. His companion was more sure-footed and hurtled across the islands in the water, pursuit the only thing on his mind it seemed. David knew that the trees would offer him no hiding place or shelter. His only hope now was to get back to the RV.

He sucked in a breath, realizing that the vehicle was parked more than two hundred yards away across open ground.

And he was sure the man was gaining on him.

The second figure also was hurrying across the river, splashing through it in places, sinking up to his knees on more than one occasion. As David ran, a third man dropped down, rushed across from the far bank and began chasing him. The breath was already catching in his throat as he ran, his feet pounding the dry ground.

He was still a hundred yards from the RV.

All three men were now on the same bank as David, two of them slowing their pace slightly. It was the leading man that concerned him. He was less than thirty yards away from David and he was gaining with every stride, his face twisted in an expression of rage. David tried to coax more speed from his already aching muscles. He felt pain at the back of his thigh and thought for a moment that he'd pulled a hamstring but he forced himself on, knowing that the leading pursuer was now uncomfortably close. He could hear words being shouted too, whether they came from the leading man or from those behind him he had no idea and he didn't intend turning to find out. Instead, he forced himself on towards the RV.

Fifty yards.

He could hear a low rumbling sound and wondered if it was the roaring of his own blood in his ears.

David hurdled a deep rut in the ground, thinking how lethal it would have been had the land still been bathed in blackness. Only the moon had enabled him to see and to avoid it. The man pursuing him wasn't so lucky. He tripped and went sprawling, grunting loudly as he hit the ground. David ran on.

Thirty yards.

Grateful for the slight respite, David hurtled onwards towards the RV, a tightness beginning to spread across his chest. He could still hear a low rumbling but still could not identify its source. Both his thighs were tightening up now and he knew he couldn't run for much longer but the man behind him was on his feet again and, despite the fact that he was moving a little slower than he had been before his fall, he was closing in once again. The other two men were following at a much more restrained pace but their progress was just as inexorable.

Twenty yards.

One of the men shouted something but David couldn't hear what it was. He was within reach of the RV now. He gritted his teeth against the pain that seemed to be enveloping his entire body. It felt as if his muscles were on fire. Every single one of them ablaze because of their prolonged exertion.

David gasped and headed for the door of the RV.

Behind him, the leading pursuer was almost upon him.

You're not going to make it.

He reached for the handle of the door, finally realizing what the low rumble was that he'd heard. It was the RV's engine.

As David grabbed for the door, the RV pulled away from him.

FIFTY-TWO

The vehicle moved forward, its back wheels spinning momentarily as they tried to gain purchase on the dry ground. Dust and parched earth sprayed upwards behind the RV which finally shot forward ten yards, leaving David clutching at empty air.

He ran after the vehicle, aware that his pursuer was gaining on him.

He actually heard the sound of the man's laboured breathing and turned, expecting to see that he was upon him. David prepared for the impact as the man grabbed for him.

It never came.

The RV suddenly shot backwards, jammed into reverse by Amy.

It slammed into David's pursuer and sent him flying, the impact lifting him off his feet, hurling him several feet through the air before he landed with a thud on his back, his arms and legs splayed.

David took one quick look at the man, saw the blood oozing from his slightly parted lips and grabbed again at the handle of the RV. This time he made it, wrenching it open and hauling himself inside.

'Come on,' Amy shouted, hunched over the steering wheel of the vehicle. In the passenger seat, the girl looked at David impassively.

David slammed the door behind him and tumbled into the RV which moved off

quickly, skidding across the ground as Amy pumped the accelerator.

'Get us out of here,' David called.

'That's what I'm doing,' Amy said. 'Who are they?'

'I don't know,' David said, trying to regain his breath. 'There's something going on across the river. A child was killed.'

'What?' Amy gasped.

'I saw a child killed,' David went on. 'A young girl.' He looked at the child in the passenger seat. 'Same age as her.'

'Are you sure?' Amy pressed.

'I wish I wasn't,' David sighed.

Amy pointed at two figures that had suddenly appeared ahead of them.

They looked as if they were trying to block the track, to slow the pace of the RV.

Amy put her foot down, watching as the two men leapt aside, hurling themselves away from the onrushing RV. David ran to the back of the RV and peered out of the wide rear window. Through it he could see more figures dashing across the dry ground towards the RV. He counted at least half a dozen, their faces contorted with rage. Some were still running after the RV, attempting to catch up with it. One or two had given up and were merely gazing in the direction of the vehicle.

He glanced towards the river and the ridge beyond, the vision of the young girl they'd had with them being hurled into the flames still strong in his mind.

The scream startled him and he spun around.

The girl in the passenger seat had let out the high-pitched sound and David stumbled back to the cab of the vehicle.

As he did, he heard several loud thuds as something slammed into the chassis of the RV.

Stones had hit it and more followed.

Amy gasped fearfully.

Another stone, much bigger, hit the windscreen.

The glass spider-webbed in one corner but, thankfully, didn't shatter.

'They're trying to stop us reaching the road,' David said, breathlessly.

Another rock slammed into the nearside headlight, splintering the housing. Pieces of broken plastic and glass skittered across the hard ground. Amy gripped the steering wheel more tightly.

The headlights of the RV had picked out the highway up ahead and Amy tried to coax more speed from the vehicle. There was a sharp turn coming up, the track snaking between two outcrops of trees and David realized that Amy was going to have to slow down to negotiate the turn safely. He shot an anxious glance in the wing mirror and saw that two of their pursuers were still running behind the RV. The manoeuvre Amy was going to be forced to execute might slow them down enough for the pursuers to catch them.

He crossed quickly to the RV door and ensured that it was locked. He did the same with the windows.

As he turned back towards the cab of the vehicle he heard a loud thump and spun round to see that one of those chasing, a wiry, dark haired, man in his thirties, had managed to clamber his way up onto the back of the RV.

He was pressed against the rear windscreen glaring in.

'Get him off,' Amy shouted.

David froze for precious seconds then moved towards the rear of the RV where the man was still clinging on. He was holding a large lump of fallen tree branch which he brought down with incredible force.

The loud crash and the explosion of glass startled David who recoiled violently, realizing that the dark-haired man had managed to smash the back windscreen. Cold air swept into the RV and the man shouted something incomprehensible at David who moved to stop him crawling inside the moving vehicle.

From the passenger seat, the girl screamed.

David snatched a frying pan from the stove and, hefting it like a weapon, he advanced across broken glass towards the dark-haired man who had now managed to get the upper half of his body, including the lump of wood he gripped, inside the speeding RV.

'Bastard,' David snarled and swung the frying pan as hard as he could.

The blow caught the man across the forearm and he tried to grab the implement from David who merely swung it again, this time with greater accuracy. The rim of the pan slashed the man's forehead open, blood spurting into the RV, some of it splashing David who struck again. This time there was a dull clang as the pan smacked savagely into the face of the dark-haired man. He lost his grip on the window frame of the RV, groaned and fell backwards, landing heavily on the dry earth below. David stood motionless for a moment, gazing out into the darkness, his eyes fixed on the fallen attacker, his own heart thudding so hard against his ribs he feared it would burst through.

The moment passed and he spun around, gazing through the windscreen as Amy drove on.

The headlights of the RV illuminated the narrow track they'd taken originally and David realized that they were close to the highway again.

'Come on,' he breathed as Amy too spotted the wide expanse of tarmac ahead.

She guided the RV onto the road and David squeezed her shoulder with one shaking hand.

The tyres got purchase on the road and the RV sped on.

David looked behind them but saw nothing.

Only darkness.

FIFTY-THREE

It was a long time before anyone spoke.

Amy remained in the driving seat, her foot pressed as hard to the accelerator as she dare, her eyes flicking constantly to the wing mirrors as she squinted through the darkness looking for lights behind them. Following them. Beside her, on the passenger seat, the girl huddled silently, not sure where to look or what to do as the RV hurtled along the night-shrouded highway.

In the rear of the vehicle, David gazed from the wide window, his eyes too alert for any signs of movement or lights that might indicate someone was following. He had no idea what time it was or how long they'd been driving. Time, like everything else, seemed to have lost its meaning in the last hour or so. What he's seen made no sense and what had happened to them made even less.

He tried to consider, rationally, what he had witnessed and the subsequent events but, no matter how many times he tried to run the events through his mind, they still baffled him. Who had those people been? Who was the girl who he'd seen thrown into the pit of flames? Why the attack on them?

David shook his head.

Why?

He turned and moved across to Amy, gripping her shoulder with one hand.

'Let me take over,' he said, quietly.

Amy thought about refusing but then merely nodded gently.

She checked her wing mirror yet again and pulled the RV over onto the hard shoulder, slumping back in the seat.

As she slid from behind the steering wheel, she pulled the girl towards her and hugged her.

David took up position behind the wheel and immediately edged the RV back onto the highway. His heart was thudding faster than it should have been, his eyes alert for the slightest sign of movement behind them on the road. There was none.

Amy slipped her arm around the girl's shoulders and pulled her close.

'Are you OK?' she asked.

The girl nodded and held her tightly.

'Where are we going?' Amy said, placing one hand on David's shoulder.

'I don't know,' he replied. 'I think we should keep moving though. Put as much distance as possible between ourselves and those...' He let the sentence trail off.

'What were they chasing us for?' Amy pressed.

'I told you,' David said. 'They killed a girl. They saw me. They must have known I'd seen what they did.'

Amy swallowed hard.

'Do you think it had anything to do with those policemen?' she murmured 'The kids bodies in the boot of that police car,' she continued. 'And now this? What the hell is going on?'

'I wish I knew,' David sighed. 'But I know we have to get away from here.'

'To where?'

'I don't know. Anywhere.' He swallowed hard. 'And there's damage to the RV that's going to need repairing. We need to get to a garage. I think we should try and make the next town as soon as we can.'

'But the next town could be miles away,' Amy reminded him.

'Check the map,' David instructed, motioning to the glove compartment on the other side of the RV's cab. Amy did as he said, pulling out the wad of paper that was inside, dragging the map free. She opened it, running her finger over the paper, trying to find their current location, muttering anxiously under her breath.

'I can't tell,' she snapped.

'There must be something,' David grunted.

'Well you find it then,' Amy rasped. 'I can't read maps. Just keep driving until you find somewhere to turn off.'

The girl approached, her eye fixed on the map spread out on Amy's lap.

'Chase,' she said, quietly.

Amy looked at her almost indulgently.

'What did you say?' she asked.

'Chase,' the girl repeated and Amy finally realized she was pointing at the map.

'Chase,' the girl said again.

She moved closer, now jabbing her index finger at the map, actually touching the paper.

Amy closed her hand gently around the girl's arm.

'What do you mean?' she asked.

'Chase,' the girl said again, more urgently this time.

Amy glanced at David and then back at the girl who suddenly pulled the map from her lap and raised it into the air, brandishing it like a weapon. She pressed her index finger to the map and thrust it towards Amy again.

'Chase,' she rasped through gritted teeth.

Amy looked at the map and saw where the girl was pointing.

'Oh my God,' Amy murmured. 'It's a place. It's on this map. Chase is a town.'

FIFTY-FOUR

David glanced round and looked at the girl who was standing motionless behind the passenger seat of the RV.

'Is that where you live?' he asked.

The girl said nothing.

'Is Chase the name of the town where you live?' David repeated.

The girl merely looked at him for a moment, holding his gaze.

'Is that where you want to go?' Amy added, squeezing the girl's hand.

She nodded.

'You want to go to Chase?' Amy repeated.

Again the girl nodded, this time moving closer to Amy who hugged her and held her close.

'Do you want us to take you there?' David enquired.

The girl smiled thinly at him and nodded once more.

David exhaled deeply and eased up slightly on the accelerator. He glanced in the wing mirror but saw nothing behind him other than darkness. For that he was grateful. The headlight beams cut through the night ahead and it felt as if the entire world had shrunk down to just the area illuminated by the cold white lights cutting through the blackness. David glanced at Amy and the girl then nodded towards the map again.

'How far is it?' he wanted to know. 'How far are we from Chase?'

'It's hard to tell,' Amy confessed, glancing at the map. 'Two, three hundred miles maybe. It could be more.'

David nodded.

'And where's the nearest town to where we are now?' he went on.

'I told you, I can't be sure,' Amy reminded him. 'But it looks like about ten or fifteen miles.'

David nodded again.

He glanced again into the wing mirror.

The lights he saw were tiny pin pricks in the gloom but he could still make them out in the blackness.

He pressed down on the accelerator slightly, the RV gaining speed.

Behind them, the lights grew larger. Whatever was following was gaining.

David felt his heart beginning to beat faster, thudding against his ribs as he watched the pursuing lights swell in size.

'Is that where you live?' Amy asked, softly, stroking the girl's hair.

The girl moved closer and lowered her head.

'What the hell was she doing so far away from home?' Amy murmured, her question directed at her husband who, by now, was far more interested in the growing lights he could see in the wing mirror.

Whatever was on the road behind them was now, David guessed, less than four or five hundred yards behind them.

He wondered if he should pull over and let the vehicle behind pass but that made no sense. If whoever was pursuing them was closing in then they wouldn't want to pass and slowing down would just make the inevitable arrive more quickly. David swallowed hard and glanced down at the gleaming bulk of the shotgun. It appeared huge in the cramped cab of the RV. The barrel yawned wide, the ribbed grip looked massive. He sucked in a deep breath and checked the wing mirror once more.

The lights were closer now.

'David,' Amy said, aware that her husband seemed more concerned with what he was seeing in the wing mirror than with what she was saying.

He didn't respond but she felt the RV accelerate.

'What is it?' Amy demanded.

Still David didn't answer.

She reached across and grabbed his arm but before she could speak again, without turning to face her, he spoke.

'There's something behind us,' he told her, quietly.

The girl also moved closer to Amy and David heard the low whimper of fear escape her.

Behind them, the lights of the approaching vehicle drew ever nearer.

David glanced down at the speedometer, the needle barely nudging seventy miles per hour but he knew that no matter how much harder he pressed on the accelerator, the vehicle couldn't reach much greater speed. Whoever was pursuing was already closing in. It was just a matter of time before they caught up.

And then?

He gripped the wheel tighter.

The headlights behind were now less than five hundred yards away, growing brighter and more intense as they seemed to swell upon the front of the chasing vehicle.

Four hundred yards.

David glanced ahead, looking for any way off the highway but, with only the subdued glow of the RV's headlights to cut through the thick blackness of the night, it was difficult seeing more than forty or fifty yards ahead. It was as if the night was sucking the light from the RV, ingesting it. David flicked the beams to high. Swathes of cold white light pierced the gloom.

Three hundred yards.

Amy got to her feet and moved towards the rear of the RV, the child trailing along behind her.

Through the back window of the vehicle, Amy too could see the lights.

Two hundred yards.

'Can you see what it is?' David called.

Amy shook her head, feeling the child clutching at her hand.

'Amy,' David called again.

One hundred yards.

'I can't see it,' Amy called.

David winced, the lights of the following vehicle were so bright. It must be less than fifty yards from his back bumper by now.

He pressed down helplessly on the accelerator and felt it crush against the floor of the RV. There was nothing else he could do now.

FIFTY-FIVE

David felt his heart thudding hard against his ribs and he shot an anxious glance towards the wing mirror then the rear view mirror as the blinding white lights of the pursuing vehicle seemed to fill his vision.

He held the steering wheel more tightly and waited.

Amy pulled the girl towards her, bracing herself against the back of David's seat.

They could all hear the roar of an engine alongside them and they realized that whatever was drawing up close by them was big.

David shot an anxious glance to his left, the sound roaring in his ears.

The truck that swept past was huge. An eighteen wheeler. A metal juggernaut that seemed to fill the road, it's lights cutting effortlessly through the night.

It overtook them then pulled in ahead and, for a second, he thought it was slowing down but then David saw it speeding away from them, the tail lights gradually disappearing into the gloom.

Darkness flooded across the highway once again. They were alone in the night shrouded expanse of open country. He checked the wing mirror again and saw nothing but impenetrable blackness. He eased gratefully off the accelerator, trying to swallow but finding that his throat was too dry to complete this seemingly simple action.

'Shit,' he murmured under his breath. The sound was a combination of relief and gratitude.

'Are you all right?' Amy wanted to know.

'We've got to pull over for the night,' he said, his voice catching.

'Where?' Amy asked.

'The first place we can,' he told her. 'We need to get off the road, rest for the night. We can find a town in the morning. If we set out early.' He nodded to himself, allowing the sentence to die away.

'How do we know it's safe?' Amy enquired.

'We'll be ok once we get off the highway.'

'How do you know that?'

'I don't. But what choice have we got.'

'Just keep going.'

'We can't drive all night, we've got to chance it,' David went on. 'I don't think they came after us.'

'How can you be sure? We don't know how crazy they are. They could be following us now and we wouldn't even know about it.'

He had no answer and that made him feel even more uneasy. Looking ahead he scanned the area to the left and right of the highway, hoping for anything that might allow them to get off the main road. There were no lights in evidence that suggested anything like a town within easy reach but David thought that was probably a good thing. He just wanted to get off the highway. It left them exposed, he felt.

Amy sat down in the passenger seat, the girl seated on her lap.

David glanced at them and thought how tired they both looked. The girl had her head on Amy's chest and was within minutes of dropping off to sleep. Amy looked pale and wan, her eyes bloodshot. She looked as if she hadn't slept for a week and he knew how she felt.

It was another thirty minutes before David finally saw a dirt track that veered off from the main highway.

He took it almost without hesitation, guiding the RV down the narrow road about a hundred yards. When he finally shut off the engine he looked across at Amy who met his gaze.

'You get some sleep,' he told her. 'I'll keep a look out.'

She hesitated for a moment then retreated towards the beds, carrying the child easily in her arms.

David contented himself with gazing out of the windscreen into the night.

Within fifteen minutes he too had fallen asleep, unable to fight off the crushing weariness that swept over him.

The blackness closed around the RV.

FIFTY-SIX

The sign above the garage said SHERMAN YOUNG AND SONS in bright red letters. David brought the RV to a halt and looked at the front of the building. It had a glass front overlooking a large expanse of concrete that was cracking in several places and reminded David of parched earth that was desperately in need of water. In the cloudless blue sky the early morning sun was already beating down and David could feel the heat through the windscreen.

'Do you think they're open,' Amy asked, peering towards the main door of the building.

'Let's find out,' David said and hit the hooter twice.

The strident wail echoed across the forecourt of the garage, slicing through the still morning air. Moments later, the sound of a barking dog filled the air and David nodded in the direction of a small mongrel that was bounding across the forecourt towards the RV.

It was followed a moment later by a tall, well-built man dressed in a Harley Davidson jacket, and jeans with both knees worn through. They looked as if they were only held together by the stains that covered them.

'Morning,' called the big man, waving exaggeratedly. 'My name's Sherman Young.' He pointed towards the sign over the garage. 'As you can probably tell. How can I help you?'

'We've got some damage to the RV,' David told him. 'We were hoping you could help us out.'

'Sure will,' the man beamed, glancing down at the dog which was barking constantly at the RV. 'Hey, shut up, these people will think we don't want them here.' He prodded the dog with the toe of one boot. The gesture did nothing to stop the barking.

'Could you check underneath too,' David asked. 'We've been over some pretty rough ground.'

'No problem,' Young told him. 'I'll get one of my boys to check everything. Do you want to sit in the office while we check it? We've got some damned fine coffee brewing.'

'Thank you,' David said.

The big man reached into his pocket and pulled out a small whistle which he blew loudly three times. Even before the last shrill blast had died away a youth in his early twenties emerged from the office wearing a pair of denim dungarees and a black t-shirt with JACK DANIELS emblazoned across the front of it.

'That's my son,' Young announced, gesturing towards the new arrival. 'Lyle. Check these people's vehicle will you?'

'Okay pop,' the boy said, advancing upon the RV.

David turned towards Amy.

'They said we could wait in the office while they checked it,' he told her.

Amy nodded, took the girl's hand and headed for the door of the RV. As she stepped out the barking of the dog intensified.

The girl froze.

'It's OK,' Amy said. 'It's just a noisy little dog.' She smiled reassuringly but the girl seemed reluctant to leave the confines of the RV. As she held the girls hand more tightly, Amy realized that she was shaking. She glanced at the girls face and saw that her eyes were bulging wide in their sockets.

'David, she's terrified,' Amy said, quietly.

David knelt beside the girl and looked into her pale face.

'It's OK,' he said, softly.

Outside the RV, the dog's barks had intensified both in volume and also in duration. The sound was non-stop now. An unending litany of yelping, punctuated only by growls and snarls.

Amy reached for the door handle and the barking suddenly stopped.

'See,' she said. 'It's fine. He's stopped now.'

The girl hesitated for a moment then stepped towards the door, standing behind Amy.

As Amy opened the door the dog looked up, its eyes fixed on her and the girl. It stood motionless, tongue lolling from its mouth. It growled deep in its throat.

Amy gripped the girls hand more tightly as they hesitated on the steps of the RV, waiting to step down onto the tarmac.

The dog was staring fixedly at them now.

'Is it safe?' Amy said, trying to force a smile. 'Your dog doesn't seem to like us.'

'He's a dumb dog,' Young said and prodded the animal once again with the toe of his boot. 'Don't take no notice of him.' He looked directly at the girl. 'There's nothing to be scared of little lady.'

The girl looked at Young then at the dog which was still standing motionless.

It had stopped barking too and the silence was somehow more menacing than the loud yelping had been.

Amy and the girl stepped down.

The dog's lips slid back from its teeth as it snarled, saliva dripping from its exposed canines.

'What the hell is the matter with you?' Young snapped.

The dog suddenly spun around and hurtled off across the tarmac, disappearing round the side of the garage, it's barks and yelps gradually dying away.

Young shook his head and smiled.

'Told you he was dumb,' he chuckled. 'You folks go on into the office and my wife will fix you some coffee while you wait. We shouldn't be too long seeing to your vehicle.'

David glanced at Amy and nodded almost imperceptibly then they headed across the tarmac towards the office.

Unseen by any of them, the dog watched. Silent now. The hairs on its back standing almost upright.

FIFTY-SEVEN

The office walls were decorated with posters of everything from makes of tyre, engine oil and brake pads to the latest stars of WWF.

There was a large desk to the rear of the room behind which was seated a blonde woman in a black t-shirt and faded jeans. The bottom of the jeans were tucked into a pair of cowboy boots that made her feet look enormous. As David, Amy and the girl walked in, the woman got to her feet, beamed a welcoming smile and ushered them in as if she was inviting them in to the foyer of a five star hotel.

'Hi, how are you doing?' she said. 'My name is Ashlynn Young. I hope my husband and my boy are taking care of you. Do you want coffee? Maybe a soda for your daughter?'

Amy smiled and nodded.

'Are you guys on vacation?' the woman asked.

It was David's turn to nod. He looked appraisingly at the woman and thought that, when she was younger she must have been a very attractive woman. She was still striking now, despite the fact she looked tired, her skin pale and washed out despite the heavy make-up she wore.

'Where are you heading?' Ashlynn Young wanted to know, handing out the drinks.

'We're just driving,' David told her, taking the drink. 'Enjoying the country.'

'Are you enjoying yourself, sweetie?' said Ashlynn, ducking down so she was looking directly into the girl's eyes. When the girl didn't answer she reached out a hand towards her.

The girl recoiled.

'I won't bite,' the woman laughed.

'She thought your dog was going to,' David said. 'He wouldn't stop growling.'

'Don't take no notice of him,' said Ashlynn. 'He's friendly enough but he's a good guard dog.'

'He ran off behind the office,' Amy explained.

'His kennel's back there,' the woman informed them. 'The

restrooms are back there too if you need to use them before you leave.'

'We probably will,' David offered.

'How long have you had this garage?' Amy asked, anxious, it seemed to repay the friendliness that the blonde woman was showing.

'Almost fifteen years,' Ashlynn told her. 'My husband used to be a speedway rider but he had a bad accident and he bought this place with the insurance money he got.'

'Does your son like helping?' Amy wanted to know.

'Well, boys like to be around their fathers at that age don't they?' the blonde woman smiled. 'Children need to be with their parents when they're growing up.'

Amy nodded.

'I bet you like having your girl around you don't you?' Ashlynn Young went on.

Amy nodded again, this time almost imperceptibly. She pulled the girl closer to her and squeezed her shoulder.

'Do you like having your mommy close, sweetie?' the blonde woman said, leaning towards the girl who promptly took a step back. The woman stood up and looked at Amy. 'Are you planning to have any more?'

Amy looked at David then shook her head.

'We haven't thought about it,' Amy told her.

'What about you?' David interjected, coming to his wife's rescue. 'Are you sticking with one?'

'We've got another one at home,' Ashlynn told him. 'He's only seven. About the same age as your daughter. My sister looks after him. She's got two of her own the same age.'

David crossed to the large picture window at the front of the office and glanced out. Young and his son were standing close to the RV pointing at the rear of the vehicle. The big man turned, saw David watching them and waved good-naturedly. Almost in spite of himself, David waved back. He watched as Young turned and strode back towards the office.

'What happened to your back window?' he asked as he walked in.

'We don't know,' David told him, glancing furtively at Amy. 'We didn't see the damage until we got back. Kids probably.'

'Well we don't carry replacements for that model of RV but I figured we could tape a windscreen across the gap then at least you'll still be able to see out the back.'

'That'll be great,' David told him.

'Where did you guys say you were headed?' Young asked, conversationally as he searched for something in the drawer of the desk on the far side of the room.

'Just driving,' David told him. 'Seeing the sites.'

'But you must be going somewhere,' Young persisted.

'The Rockies are beautiful at this time of the year,' Ashlynn added.

'Are we close?' Amy enquired.

'You're almost into the foothills,' the blonde woman told her. 'There are some beautiful spots. You could just park the RV and enjoy them.'

'Are there any wild animals we need to worry about?' Amy wanted to know.

'There used to be bears even low down in the foot hills but they're going to be more frightened of you than you are of them,' Young told them.

'I wouldn't count on it,' David said, trying to force a smile.

'How dangerous are they?' Amy wanted to know.

'Well,' Young said, sighing. 'There used to be grizzlies in these parts but no one's seen a grizzly bear around here for more than forty years. There are brown bears and black bears but as long as you stay clear of them you'll be fine. They're pretty shy.'

David nodded slowly but then, as Amy glanced at him she wondered why his face suddenly looked so pale.

For some reason he had suddenly begun to think about the shotgun lying in the cab of the RV. What if Young or his son saw it? David tried to swallow but his throat was dry. His heart was beating faster against his ribs as he tried to remember if the Remington was in view to anyone walking around the vehicle. He was sure it wasn't. But, even so, his heart continued to race.

FIFTY-EIGHT

It was just over an hour before Young and his son came back into the office, both of them looking pleased with themselves.

Young had a list of repairs that they'd carried out and he detailed these as David watched and listening, the big man explaining what had been done in each case and telling David the cost.

'I think we'll use the restrooms while you're finishing up,' Amy said and, accompanied by the girl, she headed out of the office around the side of the building in the direction Ashlynn had indicated earlier.

'Your daughter's a beautiful girl,' Ashlynn intoned, watching the child intently.

Amy felt herself blushing. Surprised at her own reaction to the comment but wondering if that particular reaction was attributable to something she could not identify. *Your daughter.* The words stuck in her mind like a splinter.

David glanced in her direction as she and the girl left the office, his attention drawn back again swiftly to Young and his inventory.

'Do you want to take a look before you drive off?' the big man asked. 'Make sure you're satisfied?'

'No, that's ok,' David said. 'I'm sure the work you and your son have done is fine.' He dug in his pocket for a credit card and handed it to Young. As he turned he noticed that the garage owner's son was gazing intently at him but he thought nothing of it. He tried to dismiss the stares of Ashlynn too but, when they continued to gaze at him he began to feel uncomfortable. Only when Young returned his card to him did he succeed in breaking the spell. The unwavering glances of the remainder of the Young clan however remained fixed on him. David wondered if he should say something but he tried to convince himself that his paranoia was somehow getting the better of him. All the same, he was hoping that Amy and the girl would return quickly from the rest rooms. He suddenly wanted to be away from here.

'What's her name?' Ashlynn asked, her gaze still fixed on him.

David looked blank.

'Your daughter,' the blonde woman went on. 'You didn't tell us her name.'

He hesitated.

'Daisy,' he muttered. Then, a little more loudly, more authoritatively. 'Her name's Daisy.'

'She doesn't look like you,' Ashlynn went on.

'Well, not all kids look like their parents do they?' David said, none too convincingly.

'Most do,' Young added. 'She doesn't look like either of you.'

David had no answer.

Well she wouldn't look like you or Amy would she? You have no idea who she looks like or where the hell she came from, do you? She's a complete stranger.

David walked towards the door of the office, pulling the keys from his pocket.

A complete stranger.

'Thanks very much for your help,' he said.

No one answered. All three members of the Young family were still gazing at him. David hesitated a moment longer then left without glancing back. He feared if he did he would see the whole family glued to the window watching him.

As he strode across the tarmac towards the RV he saw two other vehicles pulling into the forecourt. Both stopped but kept their engines running, the drivers looking in his direction. Judging by the amount of fumes belching from the exhaust of the green station wagon, David thought that the driver had left it longer than he should have to visit the garage for repairs. He smiled thinly to himself and tried to drive the thought from his mind that the drivers of both the station wagon and the red pick-up truck were still staring at him.

Weren't they?

David shook his head and swiftly opened the RV door, clambering inside.

They're not looking at you. Get a grip.

Sliding behind the steering wheel of the RV he started the engine, never even thinking to inspect the work that Young and his son had completed. It suddenly didn't seem so important. From where he sat he could still see the green station wagon and the red pick-up. He glanced across the tarmac wishing that Amy would hurry up.

When he saw her a moment later he wondered why she was alone. There was no sign of the girl.

'What the fuck...' David murmured.

Amy climbed into the RV and settled herself in the passenger seat.

'Where is she?' David snapped.

'She wanted to go to the toilet,' Amy explained. "I didn't want to leave her alone with everything that's going on but she didn't want me to stay."

'How do you know?' he rasped. 'She never fucking speaks.'

Amy looked at him with irritation in her eyes.

'She wanted a bit of privacy, David,' she told him. 'She didn't have to *tell* me. I'm not stupid. I can still remember what it was like with Daisy you know.'

He nodded.

'I wish she'd hurry up,' he went on, his gaze still fixed on the two vehicles parked on the garage forecourt. 'We need to get moving again.'

Amy glanced at him again and saw that his gaze was fixed on the green station wagon and the red pick-up. She glanced at them herself then back at her husband who was tapping agitatedly on the steering wheel.

'Go and check on her,' David urged.

'She's on her way,' Amy said, quietly.

'How do you know that? You don't know anything about her?'

Amy shot him an angry glance.

'What the hell is wrong with you?' she wanted to know.

'I just want to get out of here,' he snapped.

'And we will, as soon as she comes back,' Amy told him.

Again David glanced at the station wagon, his fingers beating out an agitated tattoo on the steering wheel.

FIFTY-NINE

When he finally caught sight of the girl walking unhurriedly across the forecourt, David let out a gasp of relief.

'About time,' he murmured under his breath.

Amy shot him an angry glance and got to her feet, crossing to the door of the RV to help the girl when she approached it. Amy had the door open before she knocked and the girl smiled happily up at her as she stepped into the vehicle.

'Are you all right?' Amy asked, putting an arm around her shoulders.

The girl nodded.

David stepped a little too hard on the accelerator, almost

causing them both to overbalance. He guided the RV out onto the road, glancing again in the wing mirror to gauge the whereabouts of the green station wagon and red pick-up that had so obsessed him. As he pressed harder on the accelerator he saw neither and for that he was thankful.

'Where were you?' he called to the girl. 'We wanted to get moving.' the girl didn't answer but merely moved closer to Amy who held her tightly and looked down at her.

'It's OK,' she said, soothingly. 'You're here now, that's all that matters.'

The girl held her and nodded.

As Amy looked down again she frowned, her attention caught by the girl's hands. There was something dark on her fingertips and Amy could see that it was blood. She knelt beside the girl, inspecting the stained digits more carefully.

'What happened?' she asked, holding one of the girls hands up.

The girl merely shook her head.

'What is it?' David called.

'I think she cut herself,' Amy told him.

The girl nodded.

Amy bustled through to the bathroom at the rear of the RV and pulled the girl gently with her. She filled the sink and pushed the girl's hands into the cool, clear water, watching as she rubbed them enthusiastically, the spots of blood coming off easily. The girl smiled and wiped her hands on a towel. Amy ruffled her hair and smiled back.

'Do you need a plaster?' she asked but the girl shook her head.

It was then that the first impact came.

Something slammed into the rear of the RV so violently that Amy was knocked off her feet by the collision. She toppled helplessly against the wall of the vehicle, the scream of the girl echoing in her ears.

'David,' she called, frantically. 'What's happening?'

The impact came again. This time to the side of the RV and even more thunderous than the first one. The vehicle skidded sideways, the scream of spinning tyres mingling with the roar of the engine. Amy grabbed for the girl and pulled her close, trying to protect her and wondering what the hell was happening. Had they hit something? Or, more to the point, had something hit them?

She scrambled towards the passenger seat and saw the fear and rage etched on her husband's face.

'He ran into us,' David snarled.

'Who?' Amy wanted to know.

'There's a green car behind us. I saw it back at the garage. I think it's been following us.'

'Why?'

'How the hell do I know?'

There was another impact and David gripped the steering wheel tightly, trying to maintain control of the vehicle. Amy shot a terrified glance out of the side window and saw the green station wagon swing out into the other lane. From where she was she couldn't see the driver's face.

'What's wrong with him?' she snarled, holding as tight as she could to the passenger seat as the station wagon swerved towards them again.

David pushed his foot down hard on the accelerator, trying to guide the RV away, to keep it clear of the next impact. The engine roared but he couldn't coax enough speed from the vehicle to force it away and the station wagon clipped the rear of the RV. It skidded and Amy wondered if it was going to tip over but David drove on, perspiration beading on his face.

He turned the wheel and sent the RV cutting across the other vehicle. The driver slammed on his brakes to avoid the collision and the green station wagon skidded across the road, smoke rising from its tyres as it left black smears of rubber on the tarmac beneath it. David's eyes were blazing, wide with fear and anger as he looked again towards the green car, trying to see what it was going to do next.

'Can't you get off the road?' Amy snapped, steadying herself as the car hurtled towards them again.

'Where?' David demanded. 'Where am I going to go?'

The car slammed into them again.

In the rear of the RV the girl screamed.

'Make sure she's all right,' David shouted, hunched over the steering wheel but hooking his thumb over his shoulder in the direction of the terrified girl.

Amy got to her feet, steadying herself against the walls of the

RV as she rose, watching fearfully for the next onslaught of the green car. It was only seconds before it came.

There was a shriek of what sounded like buckling metal as the station wagon smashed into the RV once more.

Amy hurried across to the cowering girl who was looking out of a side window towards the offending vehicle. Amy grabbed her and held her tightly.

'Oh Jesus,' David suddenly gasped, glancing in the wing mirror.

Speeding up behind them was the red pick-up truck he'd seen at the garage.

It was coming at a ferocious pace, aimed at the RV as surely as if it had been fired from a gun. Like a huge red projectile, it hurtled along the road, the driver intent on barrelling right through the RV. At the same time, the green station wagon prepared to swing into them once again.

David gripped the wheel more tightly and waited.

'Hold tight,' he roared.

The double impact was seconds away.

And David knew there was only one thing left to do.

SIXTY

'Take the wheel.'

Amy heard his frantic shout and looked at him almost incredulously.

'Now,' David snarled, still gripping the steering wheel but easing himself from the driver's seat. His eyes were wide, bulging in the sockets as if pushed from inside and Amy wasn't about to argue with him. She slid into the driver's seat and grabbed the wheel, pressing her foot down immediately on the accelerator.

'Just keep going as fast as you can,' David told her, squeezing her shoulder and moving behind her.

She realized that he was reaching for the shotgun.

'What are you going to do?' Amy wanted to know.

'Save our lives,' David told her, the Remington 870 held before him. 'They're trying to kill us.'

'You've never fired a gun in your life,' Amy reminded him, glancing at the swiftly approaching red pick-up that was still hurtling up behind them.

"Are you sure it's even loaded?"

David nodded and held the weapon so tightly that his knuckles turned white.

The shotgun felt reassuringly heavy in his grip as he turned towards the side window of the RV, glancing out at the swiftly moving green station wagon that was still hurtling along beside them. The driver was keeping away from them for the time being, swerving nearer every now and then as if to remind them that he could, at any moment, send the vehicle crashing into them once more. David could see that there were two occupants of the green car and he wondered what the hell was going through their minds as they sped along. What sort of people were they? They must, he decided, be insane.

David lowered the window slightly and raised the shotgun to his shoulder, pulling the stock in tight and grasping the pistol grip so tightly that his hand ached. The twenty inch barrel protruded out of the RV like a gleaming black pipe. David held it there, ensuring that the occupants of the car could see it. If he could get away without firing it then he would and he hoped that the mere sight of the fearsome weapon would cause them to drop back.

He saw the passenger gesturing towards the RV and, for precious seconds, the station wagon did indeed drop back a few yards and David felt hope surge through him briefly. But that hope faded just as quickly when the other vehicle drew level with them once more.

David remained where he was, his heart thumping so hard against his ribs he feared it would burst free.

He touched the trigger lightly, his hand shaking.

The station wagon swerved across towards the RV.

David fired.

The blast was deafening. The barrel of the Remington exploded in an orgasm of fire and lead as the first round erupted. The recoil was savage and slammed the butt of the shotgun hard against David's shoulder. So violent was the impact that his shoulder went numb momentarily and he feared that his collar bone may be cracked but he held the weapon in place, the smell of cordite filling his nostrils. Tiny black flecks of powder floated through the air as the massive blast subsided.

The shot hit the side of the station wagon on its rear passenger door and punched in the metal there with ease, blasting four or five fist size holes in the green door. The station wagon veered to one side as if struck by a huge invisible hammer and David wondered if the driver was going to lose control but he just about managed to keep the vehicle on the road, skidding slightly and careering onto the dusty area at the side of the tarmac. Stones and dust sprayed up as the station wagon regained the tarmac and roared on. As the blast died away, David heard the girl screaming. His ears were ringing from the shattering blast, the sound thunderous in such an enclosed area.

David prepared to fire again. He worked the slide, the spent cartridge case flying from the mechanism.

As he steadied himself, the red pick-up hit the rear of the RV.

David cursed under his breath and fell to his knees, momentarily knocked off his feet by the impact.

The RV swerved a little but Amy kept it aimed ahead and her foot on the accelerator.

David made his way to the rear of the vehicle where he hurriedly opened the back window, pushing it up to clear his field of fire. He could see the red pick-up only five or six yards from the RV's back bumper now and he instantly swung the shotgun up again and fired.

The blast hit the windscreen, shattered it and sent fragments of glass spraying back into the truck.

The girl, cowering close to Amy, screamed again.

David barely heard her. His attention was fixed on the pursuing pick-up which veered off the road and into the wooden fence beyond. He watched it for a moment but it didn't move and he guessed he had done it enough damage to prevent it pursuing further. He turned his attention back to the green station wagon which was hurtling back across the wide road towards the RV once more.

David pushed the barrel through the window and fired.

The first blast shattered a headlight, pieces of glass skidding across the road. The second, more by luck than judgement, hit the front offside tyre and obliterated it.

The station wagon lurched violently to one side, the driver losing control.

David saw the vehicle go into a spin and then flip. It rose several feet into the air as if an enormous spring beneath it had suddenly erupted upwards. The green car spun over and over, at least five or six times before landing on it's roof where it lay immobile.

David, his breath coming in gasps, worked the slide of the Remington once more and lowered the shotgun slowly, watching as the RV sped on, leaving the wreckage behind.

'Jesus,' he murmured, his ears ringing and sweat pouring down his face.

'David,' Amy called.

'Keep going,' he shouted back to her and she kept her foot pressed down hard.

Amy reached out a hand and gripped the girl by the shoulder, holding her tightly there as she drove, eyes alert for any other vehicles approaching in either direction. The girl touched her hand lightly. David joined them, slumping into the passenger seat, his breath still rasping in his throat.

Amy looked at him and saw how pale his face was beneath the sheen of sweat.

'How far is it to the next petrol station?' she wanted to know.

David could only shake his head.

'Why?' he wanted to know.

Amy gestured towards the petrol gauge.

'We've got about a quarter of a tank left,' she said. 'If we don't find somewhere in the next half hour we're in trouble.'

'I'll look at the map in a minute,' he breathed. 'See how close we are to somewhere we can get fuel.'

They sat in silence for a long time then Amy glanced at her husband.

'Did you kill them?' she wanted to know.

'I don't know,' he confessed. 'I hit them. Both of them. Hopefully they won't come after us again. I don't see how they can.'

Amy nodded.

'But if they don't, others might,' he said, quietly. 'We've got to be ready. I don't think this is over yet.'

'Why do you think others will come after us?'

David said nothing, he was peering out of the windscreen, gazing ahead at the empty road.

'David,' Amy persisted. 'Why were they trying to kill us? Because of what you saw back at that church? Because of what we've done?'

'I don't know,' he murmured. 'I really don't know.'

The words hung in the air as surely as the smoke from the shotgun blasts.

THE PURSUERS

'They've got to be stopped.'

The words seemed to fill the room.

A murmur of conversation followed, as the people gathered there could not restrain their thoughts and allowed them to spill out.

'And who's going to do it?' a voice demanded. 'We've already tried and they got away.'

'Then we try again and we keep trying until they're stopped,' the first man said, forcefully. 'It has to be done.'

'They've got a gun now,' someone else offered.

'They took it from your patrol car didn't they?' another called, angrily, jabbing a finger at the first man who'd spoken. 'Where else could they have got it?'

There was another rumble of conversation.

'It doesn't matter where they got it,' the first man said, raising his hands to quieten the others around him.

'The girl killed a dog at that garage where they stopped,' someone else shouted. 'Gutted it.'

More rumblings.

'Are you sure?' the first man asked.

'Sherman Young himself told me,' the voice went on. 'He found the dog an hour after they left. Torn apart at the back of his garage. He said it looked like some parts of it had been eaten.'

The entire room filled with nervous babbling for a moment, finally stilled by the first man who raised his voice to make himself heard above the noise.

'We knew this would happen,' the first man insisted.

'The girl ate the dog,' the other man repeated.

'Did they know?' someone close by demanded. 'Did they know what she did?'

'Who cares?' an angry voice snarled. 'They got her. That's all that matters. They're protecting her now.'

There was another chorus of shouts and calls.

'It's only a matter of time before we find them again,' the first man said, confidently. *'And when we do we'll take care of it. Of all of them.'*

'No, just the child,' someone shouted.

'It has to be all of them,' the first man insisted.

'They don't know what's happening,' another voice called.

'They must know,' a woman snapped.

'They know enough,' the first man intoned.

'I didn't figure on them using a gun,' another man shouted angrily.

'They're trying to stay alive,' the first man countered. *'What the hell did you expect? They're dangerous now. They're scared. Scared people do strange things. We have to be ready for anything when we catch up to them.'*

'Are you going to pull the trigger on them?' a woman wanted to know. *'When the time comes, will you kill them if you have to?'*

The first man nodded.

'It has to be done,' he confirmed. *'You know that. There's no turning back now. This is what we've been waiting for. The prophecy will be fulfilled.'*

SIXTY-ONE

'I don't think we should go into a petrol station,' David murmured, the map spread out before him.

'Why not?' Amy wanted to know. 'We're going to run out of fuel.'

'In case there are more of them around.'

'But we've got no choice...'

'They could be waiting for us,' he interrupted.

'How?'

'We don't know how many of them there are. Or who they are?'

'We don't know anything, David. We don't know why they were chasing us, trying to run us off the road.'

'Trying to kill us.'

She looked at him.

'If they've tried once they'll try again,' David murmured.

'But why would anyone do that? What have we done to make them come after us like that? Is it because of what you saw?'

'I don't know, Amy,' he snapped. 'I have no fucking idea why complete strangers would try and kill us. Just like I have no idea why someone would kill kids or shut them in the boot of a police car.' He looked at the girl who moved nearer to Amy.

A heavy silence descended.

'There's another fifty odd miles to the next filling station,' David finally said. 'And then it's another hundred or so until we get to Chase.' He jabbed the location on the map with his index finger.

'And then?' Amy asked.

David could only shrug.

Amy looked at the girl who was sitting close to the driver's seat looking up at her.

'Sweetie,' she said, touching the girl's hair gently. 'When we get to Chase, can you show us where you want to go?'

The girl nodded enthusiastically.

'Are we taking you home?' David enquired.

The girl looked at him and smiled.

'Chase,' she said, softly.

David nodded and then turned his attention to the vast open road that stretched away before them. There were no vehicles to be seen in either direction and he hoped that was how it continued.

'Do you want me to drive?' he asked, his attention still fixed on the sweeping vista before them.

'No,' Amy said, flatly. 'I'm all right. But we should think about what we're going to do when it gets dark. We're not going to reach Chase before night.'

'We'll pull off the road, find somewhere safe.'

Amy cast him a weary glance.

'Is anywhere safe now?' she murmured.

They drove on in silence for a while, time seemingly as meaningless as the huge open spaces they were passing through. David thought how it all looked so similar and how it didn't seem to even matter any more what the countryside looked like. Nothing mattered any more. Everything they had ever known or done was irrelevant. All that mattered was this moment. Their lives had been condensed into this moment and this vehicle. They might as well have been animals in a mobile cage. And, like animals, they were being hunted.

He glanced at the girl.

For what seemed like an eternity he sat gazing at her then he finally got to his feet and walked to the rear of the RV, peering out of the back window at the road they had left behind them. It too was empty of vehicles. For the time being. David put down the shotgun, ran some cold water into the sink then splashed his face with it, enjoying the coolness against his skin. He stood there motionless, his eyes closed, droplets of the clear fluid dripping from his face then he straightened up and headed back to the cab of the RV.

'I just saw a sign on the roadside for the filling station,' Amy told him. 'We'll be coming to it soon. What do you want me to do?'

David hesitated.

'We need petrol, David,' she reminded him. 'And we need food too.'

He nodded.

'All right,' he murmured. 'But let's be as quick we can. Just in case.'

He glanced up at the sky which was beginning to fill with clouds, heralding not just the approach of evening but also threatening a storm it seemed.

They drove on.

SIXTY-TWO

As Amy brought the RV to a stop in the huge car park of the truck stop both she and David looked around anxiously at the other vehicles halted there. There were a dozen or more. All colours and makes. None more immediately striking than the next. There were huge trucks parked further away in a separate designated area and David could see a couple of men standing beside one of them talking. Neither turned to look at the RV as it pulled in.

Amy sat behind the wheel for a moment as she turned the engine off, also peering out of the windscreen to inspect the complex of buildings ahead of them.

'We'll get something to eat first,' David suggested. 'Fill up with petrol when we leave.'

Amy nodded and got to her feet, putting her arm around the girl's shoulder as they approached the door of the RV. David let them out then followed, locking the door and tugging on it once or twice to check it was secure. They walked together towards the main entrance, eyes alert for any signs of movement.

Inside they sat down at the first available table, conscious of the glances from others inside the building. There were two men in their fifties seated at one of the tables. A man was sitting alone close to the cash register, his table covered with plates and cups. Another man in his thirties was leafing through a newspaper.

Within minutes of them sitting, a waitress emerged from the kitchen and bustled across to their table, smiling happily at them, an order pad gripped in one pudgy hand and some menus in the other. She laid the menus on the table and smiled a greeting.

'Can I get you some drinks?' she asked.

'Just some coffee please,' Amy told her, glancing at the little badge she wore on her overall. It revealed that her name was Chrissie. 'And a glass of milk here.' She pointed at the girl who looked up at the waitress and smiled.

'I'll get that while you decide what you'd like to eat,' the woman told them and she turned and headed back towards the kitchen.

David glanced at a framed plaque that was attached to the wooden partition behind the bench where Amy and the girl sat.

AMERICA IS NOT ANYTHING IF IT CONSISTS OF EACH OF US.

IT IS SOMETHING ONLY IF IT CONSISTS OF ALL OF US.

The quote was attributed to Woodrow Wilson, David noticed. He glanced around at the inside of the truck stop then returned his attention to the menu the waitress had left them. His stomach rumbled loudly as if to remind him that they hadn't eaten since the morning. With evening approaching he was ready for something. Shooting guns at people seemed to give you an appetite he thought, darkly. When the waitress returned they ordered and she scribbled it down on her pad before retreating once again to the kitchen. Again David watched her go, once more glancing at the two men nearby. He was sure one of them was looking at Amy.

Wasn't he?

Two more people walked in and seated themselves at a table towards the far end of the room. A man in his early thirties and a woman a little younger. David glanced at the woman who was looking in her handbag for something. He watched more intently as she rummaged inside the large bag.

What was she looking for?

David sat forward on his seat, his heart suddenly beating quicker.

'David.'

He was watching the woman more intently now and didn't answer Amy.

'David,' she said again.

The woman was saying something to the man she was with and David heard them both laugh, his gaze still fixed on what she was about to pull from the handbag.

It was an inhaler of some kind and David sighed as she finally found it and made use of it before slipping it back inside the bag. Only then was he aware of Amy's voice and he turned towards her.

'Couldn't we stay here for the night?' Amy enquired. 'Leave the RV in the car park and just sleep in it?'

'I want to get off the road,' David told her. 'Away from people. It'll be safer.'

'If we drive through the night we could make it to Chase before morning,' Amy told him.

'Chase? You're going to Chase?'

The waitress suddenly appeared beside them and her voice startled them both.

'You did just say that didn't you?' she went on, putting the plates of food they'd ordered down on the table before them. 'I couldn't help but hear.'

'Have you heard of it?' Amy wanted to know.

'I was born there,' Chrissie announced.

'Is it a big place?' Amy enquired.

'Not any more,' the waitress told her. 'People left there over the years.'

'Why?' asked David.

The waitress shrugged evasively.

'Why are you going there?' she wanted to know and David caught a slight edge to her voice.

David looked briefly at Amy then at the little girl who was sipping her milk.

'We'll be passing through it,' David said. 'That's all.'

'There's nothing to see there,' the waitress told him.

One of the men from a nearby table passed and the waitress

shot out a hand and gripped his arm, halting his progress.

'They're going to Chase,' she told him, nodding towards David and Amy.

'What the hell for?' the man snapped, looking at David with an expression of bewilderment.

'We're just visiting,' Amy offered.

'Well why don't you visit somewhere else?' the man snapped. 'Why would you want to go there?'

'You make it sound dangerous,' Amy told him.

The man and the waitress exchanged a brief glance.

'You got no business going there,' the man told her. 'There's plenty of other places you could visit. Stay away from Chase.'

'You still haven't told us why,' David reminded him.

The man and the waitress looked at each other for a moment and something seemed to pass between them.

'The town's changed a lot over the years,' the man said. 'Chrissie will tell you that.'

'Yes, she said she was born there,' Amy offered.

'I go through it every now and then,' the man went on. 'When I'm working.'

'You drive a truck?' Amy enquired and the man nodded.

'There was some trouble up there two or three years back,' he went on.

'Frank,' the waitress said, as if to stop him.

'It's OK,' he said, reassuringly. 'It won't do harm if they know. It's not like it's a secret is it?'

'What happened?' David enquired.

'People moved into Chase,' the man went on. 'Lots of them. There was talk of it being a cult or something like that.'

'Were they religious?' David wanted to know.

'They never really said,' the man explained. 'They just moved in and sort of took over. Some local people started moving out. The man in charge, their leader or whatever the hell they called him, he had some ideas...' The man allowed the words to fade away.

'About what?' David wanted to know.

'I don't know,' the man confessed. 'Word started to spread about what they were doing there. People said this man claimed he'd found a way of removing evil from the world.'

David frowned.

'I know it sounds crazy,' the man continued. 'But they believed him. Children started to go missing in the town. At least that was what people said. Children all around the same ages.' He nodded in the direction of the girl. 'All about the same age as your daughter there.'

'Why?' Amy asked, her expression darkening.

'Word was that they were sacrificed,' the man told her. 'Killed for some reason that the leader of that cult talked about. He believed, like the Apache used to, that the end of the world would be brought about by the evil carried inside a child. He and his...followers believed that they could stop that evil by destroying it while it was inside a child. Purifying it.'

'How did they do that?' Amy enquired.

'They'd take a child and torture it to death,' the man said, quietly. 'All of them standing around watching like it was a goddam baseball game.'

Amy swallowed hard and glanced at the girl who seemed to be listening as intently as she and David were.

'Police went in there but they couldn't do anything,' the man continued. 'Word was that one of the cult members was a lawman himself. No one would speak. No one would say what had been happening.'

'So there were no arrests?' David asked.

The man shook his head. 'Most didn't want to speak out and the rest didn't dare,' he said, flatly.

'So what happened?' Amy insisted.

'They're still there,' the man told her. 'There and in a few other places in the State. Chase wasn't the only place they settled,' said the man. 'This cult or whatever the hell it is, they had people in other towns. If you believe the stories.'

'Do *you*?' David wanted to know.

'I've heard things over the years,' the man confessed. 'Me and others. You hear things often enough, it gets so you believe.'

'How many children did they kill?' David asked, unaware that Amy was glaring at him now.

'Who knows?' the truck driver confessed. 'Like I said, no one was ever arrested. The leader killed himself they say. Shot himself in the head.'

'Why?' Amy asked.

'Perhaps he realized what he'd done,' the waitress interjected. 'Maybe he couldn't stand it any more.'

'How did they do it?' David persisted.

'David,' Amy snapped, pulling the girl closer to her.

'How did they kill them?'

'However they wanted,' the man said, flatly. 'However they could inflict the most pain.'

'You still going there?' the waitress wanted to know. 'Or you heard enough to put you off?'

David reached for his coffee and took a sip.

'What did you mean about them believing what the Apache believed?' he said, finally.

'It might just be a legend,' the driver sighed. 'But some Apache's in this area used to believe that if they killed children they could stop the end of the world coming, or the end of *their* world anyhow. It's just what they believed. When they attacked homesteads around here they killed the children or kidnapped them.'

'Why?' David wanted to know.

'Most of the settlers around here were from other parts,' the driver went on. 'Immigrants. Foreigners. From different countries. They were outsiders. The Apache called them '*the ones who didn't belong*' and they blamed them for bringing evil here with them I guess.'

'And this cult followed those ideas?' David said, softly.

'That's why they moved in to Chase in the beginning,' the man informed him. 'Back in 1886, it was a small town, newly settled. Apaches rode in one day and killed every one who lived there. They took the children with them. The army found them a week later. Every one of them butchered. They'd hung the babies on the branches of trees like Christmas ornaments. Jammed them onto sharpened branches and left them there for the buzzards. When they finished with the other kids they threw them into a pit and burned them alive.'

SIXTY-THREE

David felt the hairs on the back of his neck rise.

'I think we've heard enough,' Amy said, looking first at the older man and then at her husband.

'He wanted to know,' the man said flatly, pointing at David. He hesitated a moment longer then headed back to his table where his companion was waiting.

The waitress too turned and left them, more concerned with the two people who had just walked in. She seated them and handed them menus, glancing occasionally across at David, Amy and the girl.

'Did you have to ask him everything?' Amy said, irritably. 'About the children...' She let the words trail off, her anger evident from her expression.

David looked at the girl and saw the anxious expression on her face but she seemed to relax a little when the waitress and the man moved away and now, as he glanced at her, she ate her food hungrily. Apparently unworried by what she'd heard.

'I thought it was important,' David told her. 'It sounds as if we should keep away from there.'

'We have to take her back,' Amy offered, slipping an arm around the girl's shoulders. 'It's where she wants to go.'

'Knowing what we just heard?' David hissed.

'We promised we'd take her,' Amy went on.

'No we didn't,' David reminded her.

Amy didn't speak. She picked disinterestedly at her own food while the girl consumed everything on the plate before her. David, who had been hungry when they first sat down, contented himself with sipping at his coffee and taking occasional mouthfuls of his food. As he chewed he kept glancing across in the direction of the man they'd been speaking to. There was much that he still wanted to ask. Questions tumbling through his mind that needed answering and he felt the older man may well have those answers. Whether he would get the chance to ask them or not remained to be seen.

When David saw the man and his companion get to their feet he felt a stab of concern.

Amy saw his reaction and she too looked in the direction of the two men, both of whom were heading out of the dining area. David swung himself free of the booth where they were sitting and followed them, aware Amy was glaring at him.

'Excuse me,' David called, hurrying after the two men, as one turned off towards the rest rooms.

He caught up with the older man as he drew near to the ATM, close to the main exit of the truck stop. The man looked round at him and recognised him, eyeing him up and down appraisingly.

'I'm kind of in a hurry,' the man told him. 'And I need to get some money.' He smiled humourlessly and nodded towards the ATM.

'I just wanted to ask you a couple more questions,' David told him. 'If that's all right.'

The man raised his eyebrows.

'This cult you were talking about,' David began. 'Did they ever burn any children?'

'Why do you want to know?' the man snapped. 'You seem pretty damn interested. Why?'

'Something happened a day or two ago,' David confessed. 'I saw something. I wasn't sure what it was until I heard you talking earlier.'

'What the hell you talking about, man?'

'I saw something...I...I'm not sure what it was. I think it was a child being killed. She was thrown into a bonfire.'

The man regarded him warily.

'A bonfire?' he muttered.

'A funeral pyre,' David snapped. 'A fire.'

'They killed her,' David went on. 'There were a group of people. They were all gathered around and then one of them threw this girl into a pit where they'd lit a fire. That was what you said the Apaches did to the children they captured.'

'These people you saw weren't Indians though?'

'No, of course not. But you said this cult did to children what the Apache used to do.'

The man nodded.

'So it could have been them?' David persisted. 'It's a little coincidental isn't it?'

'How old was the girl?'

'I'm not sure. Eight or nine. Maybe younger.'

'What did you do?'

'There was nothing I *could* do. She would have been dead before I reached her. There was no way I could have saved her.'

'Did you report it?'

'Who the hell would believe it?'

The man nodded gently.

'And what happened?' he asked.

'They chased us. I think they're still after us. Earlier on, someone tried to run us off the road. I think it was them.'

'You think it's this cult?'

'You said they were in other parts of the state as well as Chase.'

'And you think they're trying to kill you?'

'Because of what I saw, yes.'

'Where did this happen?'

'I don't know the exact location. About a hundred miles South of here. We've been moving North since we got on the free-way. I'm not sure of the place where it happened. There was a church, that's all I know.'

'I ain't an expert, mister. I was just telling you the stories I heard. You need to go to the police.'

The man headed towards the rest rooms and David followed. As the man entered, David touched him on the shoulder.

'I need to know what you know,' he snapped.

'And I need to use the john,' the man rasped, glaring angrily at him. He disappeared into one of the cubicles and slammed the door behind him. David hesitated a moment then crossed to the door, determined not to miss the man when he left. He stood there with his arms folded, watching the door. Another man glanced at him as he left but David didn't meet his gaze, his attention fixed instead on the cubicle where his quarry was. When he emerged a minute or two later he saw David moving back towards him and sighed wearily.

'You don't give up easy do you, man,' he grunted, washing his hands in one of the basins nearby. 'I can't tell you any more.'

'Can't or won't?'

The man shook his head, moved across to the hand dryer and stuck his hands beneath it. The rest room was filled by the loud roar of the dryer and he rubbed his hands together beneath the warm air.

'I already told you everything I know,' he snapped.

'Children have been going missing around here haven't they?' David insisted. 'My wife and I heard it on a news programme a few days ago. Do you think they could have anything to do with this cult?'

The man merely shrugged.

'What you told us, is it common knowledge around here?' David demanded.

'You hear things when you drive a truck. People talk.'

'About cults and missing children?'

The man held David's gaze for a moment.

'There are things a man needs to know and things he's better off not knowing,' he said.

'Very philosophical,' David sighed, dismissively. 'You said the leader of this cult shot himself. When did that happen?'

'A couple of weeks ago.'

'Where?'

'In Denver. At the airport as a matter of fact.'

'Do you know his name?'

'I told you, I ain't no expert.' He finished drying his hands and headed for the exit, pursued by David. As they reached the doors that led out into the parking lot the man turned and looked at David. 'Look, man. I got a long drive ahead of me. If you got any sense you'll keep driving too. Right past Chase. Don't go anywhere near it. Just keep driving.'

'And what about what I saw?' David called as the man set off towards his waiting truck.

'Report it,' the man called over his shoulder. 'And keep the hell away from that town.'

His words drifted on the air until they were finally swallowed by the chill breeze that was blowing across the wide open area. The sky was darkening, clouds bulging and filling the heavens. In the distance, the first dull rumbles of thunder began to sound.

David waited a moment then turned and headed back inside the building, glancing back at the mottled sky.

The storm that had been threatening was drawing closer.

SIXTY-FOUR

As David walked back into the dining area he slowed his pace slightly, wondering if his eyes were somehow playing tricks on him. As he moved further inside he realized they weren't. Amy and the girl were no longer sitting at the table where he'd left them.

There was no sign of them.

Panic gripped him. He glanced at the other tables and saw that most of the people who had been there before he left were still present. Eating. Talking. Resting. Everyone was there except Amy and the girl. David walked hurriedly back towards their table. Exactly why he did that he didn't know and, of course, it was a fruitless exercise. He turned around and caught sight of the waitress emerging from the kitchen. He hurried across to her, his face pale.

'Where's my wife?' he wanted to know, reaching for her arm and almost causing her to drop one of the plates she was carrying.

'I don't know,' she said, more irritation than bewilderment in her voice.

'She was here when I went out.'

'I didn't see her go.'

David continued to block her path and she frowned, trying to move around him towards the couple who were waiting for their food.

'I have customers waiting, sir,' she reminded him. 'Do you mind?'

'Did she say anything to you before she left?' David snapped.

'No.' Again she tried to step around him and, once more, David blocked her path to the table beyond.

They stood facing each other for a moment longer then David moved aside and she swept past him irritably, muttering something under her breath.

'Have you seen my wife?' David said, turning towards a man sitting alone at another table near by. 'She's about five foot two, brown hair, slim. She's wearing jeans and a black top. She's got a young girl with her.'

The man shook his head.

'I haven't seen anyone, buddy,' the man said. 'I just walked in.'

'She was sitting there,' David snapped, jabbing an impatient finger in the direction of the table where they'd been seated.

'I told you,' the man repeated. 'I haven't seen her.'

David spun round, his heart beating faster now. He hurried away from the man at the table, moving towards the waitress once more.

'You must have seen her,' he said, grabbing the woman's arm. 'Where did she go?'

She shook loose angrily.

'I told you,' she snapped. 'I didn't see her. Now leave me alone will you? I'll call the manager if you don't.'

'I need your help. I've got to find her,' David protested. 'You must help me.'

'Hey, what's your problem?' the man sitting at the table intoned. 'She said she didn't know where your wife was. Let it go.'

'Mind your own fucking business,' David snarled.

Taken aback by the ferocity of David's response, the man sat back slightly and raised a hand in supplication. He looked at the Englishman warily for a moment, seeing the fury and desperation in his eyes.

'She might be in the rest room,' the waitress offered.

David shot her an angry glance too then headed off, his heart thudding hard. He found the women's rest rooms and stood uneasily outside the door for a moment, shifting nervously from one foot to the other. Finally, unable to restrain himself any longer he pushed the door open and walked in, glancing around.

He was lucky that no one was in there but that was the least of his problems at the moment. David moved along the line of cubicles, peering beneath the doors where they were closed, hoping to catch sight of Amy's feet. Anything to tell him that she was inside.

There was no one in the room except him and he spun round and headed for the exit, almost colliding with a young woman who entered and gave him a puzzled look, wondering what this wild-eyed man was doing in the ladies room. She had no time to ask him because David blundered past her and out into the corridor beyond, his eyes darting to the right and left as he desperately sought a glimpse of Amy or the girl. He tried in the shop but was similarly disappointed.

'Did a woman with a little girl come in here?' he asked the attendant behind the counter.

He could only shrug.

'A woman with brown hair,' David went on. 'She would have had a girl with her. The girl's got dark hair. The woman is in her twenties. She's wearing jeans.'

The attendant shook his head.

David glared at him for a moment as if he was personally

responsible for Amy's disappearance then he hurried out of the shop and across the entryway to the main exit doors. He started off across the parking lot towards the RV, fear and desperation now filling him.

Where the hell else could they be?

As he approached the vehicle he slowed his pace slightly, something catching his eye.

The offside headlight was broken. Not just cracked but shattered. There was broken glass lying on the tarmac in front of the RV. The other headlight had also been struck but the destruction wasn't as total. But this damage had been done recently, David realized. this was no legacy of their flight along the highway. No damage caused by some stray piece of gravel during the furious chase. Someone had deliberately broken the headlights. There looked like purpose behind this destruction and it made David even more frightened.

He put his hand on the door of the RV and moved his ear closer to it, listening for any sounds from inside.

He heard none and glanced around the parking lot before finally pulling the door open and slipping inside where it was almost pitch black. The blinds had been closed to shut out what remained of the fading light. And yet, David could still see Amy standing to the rear of the vehicle, her arms around the child who stood before her.

David was overwhelmed with relief as he saw them and he was about to speak when he felt something cold against the back of his neck and he knew instinctively that it was the barrel of the shotgun.

The voice that spoke and lanced through the gloom was shaky, uneven. Fearful. But the words were unmistakeable.

'If you move I'll kill you first and then the woman.'

SIXTY-FIVE

'Please,' David breathed, raising his hands slightly. 'Please don't hurt us.'

He felt the barrel of the Remington pushed harder against his skull and he began to tremble, his mouth dry with fear.

'We don't want to hurt you.'

The voice that spoke next came from the front of the RV, from the second figure that David had not noticed when he first stepped inside the vehicle. Cloaked by the gloom, the second man had been almost invisible, just another part of the thick blackness that filled the RV and seemed to be seeping in from the night beyond.

'We just want the child,' the second man told him.

David could see now that the newcomer was in his late thirties, possibly older. He was a well-built man with short dark hair and a thin moustache that looked as if it had taken months to grow.

Despite his own terror, David could detect the same unease and concern in the voice of the second man. He too sounded nervous, frightened even.

'You're not having her,' Amy told the second man.

'We're taking the child,' the second man insisted.

'We'll kill you if we have to,' the first man snapped, pushing the shotgun barrel hard against David's head. 'I'll blow his head off.'

'All right, all right,' David gasped. 'Just calm down.'

The man jabbed the barrel against the base of his skull even harder.

'Don't tell me what to do,' he hissed. 'I'll kill you.'

The second man raised a hand towards his companion to calm him, aware that everyone inside the RV was now equally agitated and afraid.

'Why do you want her?' Amy asked.

'She belongs with us,' the first man announced.

'No,' Amy snapped.

'You don't know shit, lady,' the first man told her, taking a step towards them both.

'I know you're not taking her,' said Amy, defiantly. 'I won't let you.'

The man extended one hand towards her.

'Just let her go,' he murmured. 'We'll be on our way.'

'And you'll let us go?' Amy chuckled, the sound hollow and mirthless. 'You really think we're that stupid? You kidnap this girl and then just let us go?'

'We're taking her back,' the second man insisted.

'We'd go to the police as soon as we could. You know that.'

'We don't care.'

'Who chased us?' David enquired. 'Someone chased us. Was that you?'

The second man looked at him.

'Someone came after us,' David went on. 'Tried to run us off the road. Was that you?'

'No,' the man confessed. 'Not us. People we know.'

'You tried to kill them,' the first man rasped.

'We were defending ourselves,' David told him.

'We don't care,' the first man said. 'Give us the girl now.'

David looked helplessly towards Amy who still had her hands on the girl's shoulders but then, as they watched, the girl herself took a step away from Amy, moving towards the second man.

'That's it,' he said, almost smiling. 'You come to me and this will all be over real quick.' He saw Amy take a step forward to and raised his hand to halt her. 'Not you, you stay where you are or your husband dies. Understand? Both of you, just stay where you are.'

The girl took another step towards the man and, even in the darkness of the RV, David could see the fear and uncertainty on the second man's face. He put out both hands now to greet her, looking as if he was about to sweep her up into his arms. The girl shuffled forward, watched by Amy who was shaking her head gently.

'That's it,' the first man said, quietly. 'Keep coming.'

He dug one hand into the pocket of his jeans and pulled a length of rope free.

'Don't hurt her,' Amy said, helplessly.

The man didn't answer. Instead he took a step forward too, moving closer to the girl who was looking up into his face, her own features expressionless. David watched, impotent rage and helplessness filling him.

You can't just stand there and watch while they take her. You gutless bastard. Do something.

He felt the gun barrel still at the back of his head.

What can I do?

The girl took another pace forward and she was within reach of the second man who unwound the rope more fully. One end of it dangled on the floor.

'That's it,' he whispered, his voice cracking. David could see that his hands were shaking as he reached for the girl.

She looked into his face, her features suddenly twisting into a look of pure fury. She grabbed his right hand and sank her teeth into it, biting hard into the base of his thumb. He shouted in pain, surprised by the sudden attack. As she clung on furiously, David could see blood beginning to seep from the wound but still the girl kept her teeth fastened in his flesh, determined it seemed to keep going until she reached bone. He tried to pull free, dragging at her hair, yanking her head backwards but still unable to release the vice-like grip on his hand. Blood and spittle dripped onto the floor of the RV and now, finally, David felt the barrel of the shotgun removed from against the back of his head as the man behind him turned his attention to the girl and his struggling companion.

Amy moved forward, sliding open one of the drawers in the unit close to the rear of the RV. She pulled out a long kitchen knife and gripped the handle tightly, advancing towards the girl and the second man.

David saw what she'd done but he was more concerned with the struggle before him. The girl was clinging on to the second man's arm with both hands, her teeth still buried in his hand, determined that no amount of shaking would dislodge her. Like a predator clinging to its prey, the girl held on furiously, grunting and whimpering as blood continued to pour down her chin from the increasingly vicious wound she was inflicting.

'Bitch,' the second man roared and slammed his free hand into her face, finally breaking the grip and knocking her against the side of the RV. The girl dropped like a stone but before the second man could react, Amy had run at him, swinging the knife upwards.

Still confused by the pain the girl had inflicted, he was off balance and unprepared for Amy's onslaught. She drove the blade into his stomach, tore it free and struck again, slicing through his left forearm almost as deep as the bone. Blood from the first wound began to pour freely, some spattering Amy, but most of it soaking into his clothes or gushing on to the floor of the RV.

He let out a horrified gasp and tried to parry the other blows Amy rained down upon him but it was useless. The next blow sent the blade slicing through his left palm, almost severing the index finger. Another tore deep into his left shoulder, cracking the collar bone such was its power.

'No, please,' he gasped, frightened by the sight of so much of his own blood.

The second man backed off but Amy advanced angrily, now using savage downward strokes. One of them caught him in the face, laying his right cheek open to the bone and exposing the network of muscles beneath. The flap of skin yawned open like a red smeared mouth and, as the man tried to scream, Amy struck again.

The blade sheared through his mouth, ripping open the top lip, slicing part of his tongue and smashing two teeth.

Fresh blood jetted onto Amy.

David heard the man behind him gasp weakly and he knew that he was swinging the shotgun up again.

Driven more by desperation than valour, David spun round and grabbed the barrel of the shotgun, pushing it to one side as he threw his weight into the first man. They overbalanced and crashed against the side of the RV, David trying to wrestle the weapon from the other man's grip. His frantic efforts were more effective and he succeeded in pinning the man against the wall, bringing his knee up sharply into his groin with such power he felt it slam into the others pelvic bone. The man groaned as white hot agony lanced through him and the pain was sufficient to make him loosen his hold on the Remington. David dragged the it from his grasp, the shotgun falling to the floor of the RV.

'You son of a bitch,' the man grunted.

Hunched over slightly due to the pain in his groin, he lashed out and caught David in the face, a blow that staggered him and caused blood to spill warmly from his nostrils. He tasted it in his mouth too and drove one foot hard into the man's thigh, then his shin. David had never been in a fight in his life and his efforts were driven by fear not expertise. He grabbed the first man by the shoulders and slammed him up against the wall of the RV once again, desperate to keep him away from the shotgun.

He dropped to his knees, one hand reaching out for the weapon but not finding it.

As he turned he saw that Amy had picked it up. She was standing with the weapon levelled at the first man, one hand on the slide the other with her index finger curled around the trigger.

'No,' the first man gasped, peering at the yawning barrel and then at Amy's face. She was spattered with blood from her attack on the other man, her eyes wide and blazing.

David saw her too, her eyes gleaming, looking almost luminescent in the gloom within the RV. He could see tears running down her cheeks, cutting through the dark, and rapidly congealing blood that had sprayed her only moments earlier.

She was still crying when she pulled the trigger.

SIXTY-SIX

The roar was deafening.

The barrel of the Remington flamed and an orgasm of fire and lead erupted from the weapon.

From such close range, Amy didn't need to be a marksman. The massive blast caught the man in the upper chest and face, the buckshot slamming into him with incredible force. It obliterated part of his bottom jaw, ripping through the zygomatic and sphenoid bones, pulverizing them. Blood and fragments of shattered bone erupted from the ruins of the man's face and portions of sticky brain matter exploded from the rear of the skull, spraying the wall of the RV.

He slumped to the ground, one eye still open and bulging in the bloodied socket.

David gasped as he felt an eruption of blood and viscera drench him and it was all he could do to stop himself vomiting. Amy lowered the shotgun, the tip scraping on the floor of the vehicle. She glanced at the girl who was cowering on the floor, and then in the direction of the second man who was slumped between the front seats of the RV, hands weakly clutching the stab wounds in his shoulder and face. Blood was coursing madly through his shaking fingers. He looked in Amy's direction, his breath coming in gasps, his eyes wide with pain and fear.

'Please,' he murmured.

Amy and David barely heard him. The massive report from the shotgun had momentarily deafened them both.

Amy looked at David and then at the desperately injured second man.

'Please, help,' he gasped again, the words distorted by the fact that the tip of his tongue was missing and his mouth was full of blood.

Amy swung the shotgun up once more, levelled it at him and squeezed the trigger.

The blast tore through the man's chest, splintering ribs, rupturing his lungs and tearing through his aorta before exploding from his back. Several large gobbets of lung and torn flesh erupted from the exit wounds and sprayed the inside of the windscreen.

The man fell back and David quickly grabbed his ankles, dragging him away from the cab of the RV. He then slid into the driving seat, started the engine and stepped on the accelerator, sending the RV speeding out of the parking lot towards the highway beyond. As he drove he squinted into the darkness, aware all too quickly that the broken headlights of the RV were not providing sufficient light to guide him. One of them was still functioning despite the damage inflicted on its housing but the other one was completely destroyed and about as useful as a blind eye. David gripped the steering wheel tightly, glancing feverishly at the wing mirrors to see if anything was pursuing them. Surely someone inside the truck stop had heard the thunderous explosions of sound when the shotgun was fired.

It seemed as if it would be only a matter of time before others came after them. Again he checked the mirrors but there was nothing visible in the blackness behind them.

Two or three vehicles drove past them going in the other direction, one of which flashed its headlights to alert David that something was wrong with his own vehicle. He nodded to himself, only too aware of the problem. As he drove he was also becoming increasingly aware of the stench beginning to fill the RV. A combination of odours that made him retch such was their intensity. There was a dominant coppery smell that he realized was blood but it was matched by a rancid scent that he was all too aware was excrement. He had read once that bodies sometimes defecate during death and that shred of information bubbled into the forefront of his mind as he wrinkled his nose and gasped at the vile smell. The air was also thick with the pungent odour of gunpowder and cordite, a legacy of the shotgun blasts. The combination was a heady and repulsive mixture and David hastily lowered the window, hoping that some of the cold night air might dispel the smell that was clogging his nostrils.

'Where are we going?' Amy asked him, her voice low and strained.

'I can't drive for very long like this,' David told her. 'I can hardly see where I'm going. We're going to have to pull over.'

'Where?' Amy wanted to know.

David shook his head by way of an answer.

'We have to get rid of these as well,' he grunted, nodding in the direction of the corpses.

Amy said nothing but merely glanced at the two dead men expressionlessly.

'Get us off the road and we will,' she said, flatly.

David let out a long sigh and returned his attention to the darkened road ahead. The puddle of light provided by the one remaining headlight was barely adequate and, more than once, he almost veered off the highway, the tyres sending small stones and dust spraying up each time he did. Amy had retreated to the rear of the vehicle, taking the girl with her. David assumed they were going to change their clothes as both of them were spattered with blood. He knew how they felt. The blood and human debris that had soaked into his clothes was beginning to stiffen and congeal, causing the material to rub uncomfortably against his skin. He wanted a wash most of all. He wanted to scrub the blood and mess from himself and be clean again.

And he wanted a drink.

The raging desire was more than just the need to slake his thirst. His throat and mouth were parched, that much was true, but it was the taste and texture and everything else about alcohol that he wanted to experience now. He wanted to feel the fiery fluid burn its way down his throat. He wanted to drink until he passed out. Perhaps then, when he woke up, this entire twisted nightmare would be over.

David smiled bitterly to himself. If only it was that simple. As he drove, peering myopically into the night, forced to look through a mist of blood and fragments of human viscera that was painted on the inside of the windscreen, he felt the pain gripping the base of his skull. The headache was growing quickly and savagely. He wanted a drink but he also wanted to rest, to lay down and sleep if that was possible. Anything that would involve oblivion seemed attractive at the moment. But the world seemed to have collapsed into this cramped and confined space. His entire life, both of their lives, were contained within the reeking confines of the RV now. He wasn't even sure any more if there *was* anything beyond it.

The night looked blacker than he'd ever seen before. It was like driving off the edge of the world.

SIXTY-SEVEN

Exactly how long he'd been driving when Amy returned to him he had no idea. It felt like a long time. A soul crushing feeling of exhaustion was beginning to envelope him. He'd heard the sound of running water as Amy showered and that only served to make him more acutely aware of how much he wanted to wash the blood from his own skin and clothes.

She squeezed his shoulder gently and he felt her other hand ruffle his hair. It was a gesture of affection that almost made him weep. When she touched his cheek, congealed blood came away on her fingertips but she ignored it, remaining where she was for a moment longer before sitting down in the passenger seat.

'She's asleep,' Amy breathed. 'I got her to settle down after she showered.'

David nodded.

'She's lucky,' he said, softly, still gazing out into the night.

Amy turned her head and looked at him.

'When we stop I'll clean up,' she told him. 'You get rid of *them*.' She gestured over her shoulder towards the two corpses. 'We should burn our clothes. There's too much...blood on them.'

They rode a little further in silence then Amy spoke again.

'They would have killed her, David,' she murmured. 'We had to stop them.'

He didn't speak.

'They would have killed us too,' Amy went on.

'How many more?' David murmured. 'How many more are going to die?'

'We were defending ourselves. They were going to kill our...'

'Our what?' David snapped, glancing at her. 'Our daughter? Only she's not our daughter is she, Amy?'

'Keep your voice down,' Amy told him, angrily. 'You'll wake her up.'

David looked at her with fury in his eyes.

'You killed two men,' he snapped.

'Men who would have killed us. What the hell did you expect me to do? You shot at those cars before. What if one of the people inside them was killed? We were defending ourselves, David. They attacked us first. They would have hurt us. All of us.'

'They only wanted *her*.'

'Our daughter died because of me. Because I did nothing to save her. I'm not going to let this girl die too.'

'Daisy's death wasn't your fault,' he snarled.

'I think it was,' Amy rasped.

'So if we get this girl to Chase then that'll cure your guilt will it?'

'It'll help.'

'And what do we do when we get there? Just drop her off, drive away, return the RV, get on a plane and head back to England as if nothing's happened?'

Amy was gazing distractedly out of the windscreen into the night.

'The police will be waiting for us,' David persisted.

'The same police that had her locked in the boot of a car with two dead children?' Amy snapped.

He didn't answer.

'What do you want to do, David?' Amy demanded. 'Stop the RV now? Leave her on the roadside? Leave her there until they come and find her and kill her?'

'She's not our daughter, Amy,' he breathed, quietly.

'I'll tell you what, David. Stop the fucking RV now and *you* get out.'

He shot her an irritated glance.

'You don't want to help her any more then that's fine,' Amy went on. 'Get out. Leave us. I'll drive her to Chase. I'll get her back safely. You go. You can even tell them that it was me who killed these men. You can tell them what you like if you think it'll help *you*.'

'Don't be stupid,' he grunted.

'I'm not being stupid. I'm just telling you what you can do if you want to. Because I'm not going to stop until I get her back home.'

'We don't even know what's there.'

'We'll find out and whatever it is we'll be ready for it.'

'Even if it means killing more people?'

'Yes.'

There wasn't a seconds hesitation in Amy's reply and as David looked at her he didn't doubt her for one moment.

They didn't speak again until he pulled the RV off the highway, another twenty miles further on. Completely enveloped by the blackness of the night, the vehicle was invisible from the main road, hidden also by the trees which grew thickly around the place where David brought it to a halt.

'How do we know it's safe?'

It was just after midnight.

SIXTY-EIGHT

David propped the torch in the branches of a bush, ensuring that its beam played across the dark earth.

Once that was done he used a thick branch to scrape that same earth aside, labouring for over an hour to create a makeshift grave that, even when finished, was less than two feet deep. More than once he stopped, gasping for air and exhausted by his exertions but, finally, the first hole was ready and he stepped down into it as if to test that the depth was sufficient. It probably wasn't he reasoned but he didn't feel that he could achieve much more with such a rudimentary tool. There had been nothing in the RV but, David reasoned, most people who rented the vehicle probably didn't need to dispose of bodies in the dead of night. He smiled to himself. Exactly why he had no idea because there was absolutely no humour in this situation.

He stood motionless for a moment, wiping his dirt covered hands on his jeans then he

stepped out of the hole, looking down into it for a moment as if to congratulate himself on what he'd created.

It would take the same amount of time, if not longer due to his growing fatigue, to dig the second one.

David sat down on the edge of the first grave, glancing around him into the darkness, the only light coming from the torch. It's sickly yellow light illuminated the area where he'd been working. It was about a hundred yards from where he'd parked the RV which was barely visible from where he sat.

He knew that inside it, Amy was busily cleaning blood from the walls and floor in a desperate attempt to make the vehicle look pristine once more. David finally got to his feet and trudged back towards it.

They'd dragged the bodies out of the RV as soon as they parked. Both of them now lay on the dirt near the rear of the vehicle looking like blood spattered mannequins. David hesitated a moment then grabbed the ankles of the first man, dragging him with considerable difficulty across the stony ground towards the site of the makeshift grave. The weight of the body was extraordinary. David looked at the man and guessed that he was about twelve or thirteen stone but it felt as if he was dragging twice that weight. When he finally reached the dirt rimmed hole, David let go of the man's legs and dropped to his haunches, sweat soaking through his clothes as readily as the blood had earlier on. He was gasping for breath due to his exertions and he began to wonder how likely he was to suffer a heart attack. He had never endured physical exertion like this and he hoped that it didn't take a toll on him. Although, he thought fleetingly, perhaps a quick death out here in the middle of nowhere would be preferable to what might be in store for him. If he and Amy were caught they would be charged with murder, surely. And after that? Did they execute in Colorado? He tried to swallow but couldn't.

As he knelt there, trying to suck some air into his tortured lungs he heard a soft hissing noise and turned his head trying to find its source.

Was it some animal of some kind? Was some creature watching him?

David snatched up the torch and shone it around, looking for the source of the sound.

It came again.,

A harsh, rattling, sucking noise that sounded as if air was being drawn through liquid.

Again he flashed the torch back and forth. Could it be a predator of some kind? Attracted to the smell of the blood and the corpse? David had no idea what kind of animals frequented this part of Colorado but he was becoming increasingly convinced that one of them was very close to him now. He looked for movement in the bushes and trees but could pick out none in the blackness. Even partially lit by the torch, the foliage looked impenetrable. Anything could have been hiding inside or behind it. A coyote. A wolf. A bear. A puma. Did any of those creatures make their home in this state? He knew that if they did, all of them were more than capable of doing him damage if they chose to attack. He spun round again, desperate to find where the sound was coming from.

He heard it again.

That vile, liquescent noise that sounded like laboured, painful breathing.

And in that second it struck him where the sound was coming from and the realization almost made him vomit.

It was coming from the corpse. Air was rushing through the punctured lung, hissing and slurping through the gaping wound every time a breath was taken. Doctors who had treated it on a battlefield called it a 'sucking wound.' As the victim tried to swallow air to keep them alive, the desperately needed oxygen rattled in and out through the hole in the lung. The realization hit David like a sledgehammer because he now knew that the man lying at his feet was still desperately clinging to life, trying to suck air into lungs already torn by a shotgun blast. Somehow, this man was still alive. Stabbed and shot, almost dead from loss of blood and shock, he had managed to cling to life somehow and now, his dying breaths were echoing around David as they rasped through his death wounds.

He reached out a hand and grasped David's ankle.

There was no strength in the grip and as David shone the torch towards the man's face he could see that his lips were fluttering gently as if he were trying to form words but even that effort was just beyond him. The strength had drained from him as had his life fluid, which had streamed out from the wounds that had brought him so close to death.

David stood staring fixedly at the man's face for long moments, listening to the sucking sound coming from the wounds in the lungs as the man attempted to breathe. He couldn't hear the words the man was trying to say. He didn't want to hear them. The large lump of wood he'd used as a makeshift tool to dig the grave was lying nearby and David suddenly snatched it up, standing over the dying man, the branch held above his head as if he was about to bring it crashing down. Should he strike until he smashed the man's head in? Ensure that he was finally dead when a knife and shotgun hadn't been able to accomplish the task? David stood there for interminable seconds then finally dropped the lump of wood, his own breath coming in frantic gasps now.

He used his foot to roll the body into the shallow grave, hearing the man whimpering and groaning as he tried to move over on to his back in the narrow hole.

David stared down at him, seeing him accomplish this task, one hand upraised towards the edges of the grave, the fingers shaking.

The man tried to speak again but only a combination of sobs and hisses escaped him. He kept his hand in the air, as if hoping that David would suddenly grasp it and haul him free of the dark earth into which he'd been pushed.

Instead David began kicking earth on to him, dropping on to his knees to push it with his bare hands when the grave didn't fill up quickly enough. He shovelled the dirt with his hands, pushing it onto the dying man, watching as he spat some of it away from his mouth but swallowed other smaller lumps of it. And now, the man in the shallow hole found the voice for something more than mere whimpers. He began to cry, the sound as strident and penetrative as if it had been a laser beam through fog. David felt that the noise was digging into his soul. Still he pushed earth onto the man, so much of it now that it had covered his face and chest. When he screamed the noise was muffled.

David kept on pushing the earth onto the dying man, eager to cover him completely and cut out the sounds of those muted and desperate shrieks. Perhaps they were for help or maybe they were just the last exhortations of a man who knew that finally, he had run out of time.

David pushed the rest of the earth onto the grave and stamped down on it, flattening it. He pulled several branches and some pieces of twig over the freshly turned earth, trying to camouflage the last resting place of the man who was, even now, slowly suffocating beneath him. David could still hear muffled screams of terror and desperation.

He waited almost an hour before he headed back to the RV. It took him even longer to bury the second body

By that time, the night was silent once again.

SIXTY-NINE

When David finally returned to the RV, pulling open the door wearily and with something like trepidation, he saw three black plastic bags close to the door. They were stuffed with towels and cloths, every one soaked through with blood.

He looked around at the interior of the vehicle and was amazed to discover that

the mess had been expunged from view far more efficiently than he had ever thought possible. Amy looked blankly at him and then gestured towards the bags.

'We should bury them or burn them or something,' she suggested.

David nodded.

'David,' she persisted.

'I heard you,' he snapped, crossing to the driver's seat and slumping into it.

'She helped me clean up,' Amy murmured, moving across to the passenger seat and sitting down.

He looked at her, his face expressionless.

'Daisy helped me,' Amy continued. 'She helped me clean...'

'Don't call her that,' David interrupted. 'Don't call her Daisy. She isn't Daisy. She isn't our daughter.'

'What do you want me to call her?'

'Call her what you like but she isn't our daughter. She never will be.'

'Then what is she, David?'

He merely shook his head by way of an answer.

'That's the trouble,' he said, quietly. 'We don't know who she is do we?'

'She's a little girl who needs our help,' Amy snapped.

'Who we've killed for.'

'They would have killed *us*,' Amy reminded him.

'And they'll try again. They'll keep trying until we get her back to Chase.'

'And after that?'

David glanced at her quizzically.

'When we get her to Chase,' Amy continued. 'What then? We just leave her in the middle of a street and drive off? Leave her to fend for herself?'

'We get her back there. That's what we set out to do.'

'And then it's not our problem, is that what you're saying?'

'We're taking her back to a place where she might be in even more danger,' David mused. 'That's where the cult is based. The cult that kills children.'

'What are you talking about?'

'The guy we spoke to at the last service station said that the cult was based in Chase. They...'

'He was mad,' Amy snapped, her tone so dismissive it bordered on contempt.

'What if he wasn't?' David went on. 'What if the stories are true?'

'She wants to go back to Chase and that's where we're taking her.'

David nodded.

'That's fine with me,' he said. 'I just want to get this finished. One way or the other.'

'She needs us, David. Just like Daisy needed us.'

'She's not our daughter,' David said, softly without looking at his wife.

'I know that but I'm not going to turn my back on her. Not now.'

'She's not our daughter,' he said again, this time gazing out of the windscreen into the black and impenetrable night.

'I know,' Amy shouted.

Her voice reverberated inside the vehicle and David turned and looked at his wife, all too aware of the pain etched so deeply into her features.

'Do you think I'm going to forget what happened to our daughter, David?' she said, her voice losing some of its volume. 'Do you think I'm *ever* going to forget?'

Amy turned slightly in her seat, distracted by movement towards the rear of the RV. The girl was standing there gazing towards them with a blank expression on her face.

Amy smiled reassuringly and put out her arms to the girl who ran across to her

and David watched as she swept her up and held her close. He watched as she gently stroked the girl's dark hair.

'Did we wake you up?' Amy asked, softly.

The girl sat contentedly on her lap.

'We should all get some sleep,' David murmured. 'It'll be light in a few hours. We'll need to move on.'

The girl turned and looked at him and he saw that there was a slight smile on her face. He met her gaze and saw the smile broaden. She reached out tenderly and touched his hand, ignoring the mud and blood that stained it. When he looked at her face again he could see that there were tears in her eyes.

Almost in spite of himself, David reached out and gently touched her hand and again she smiled.

Was it gratitude? Relief? Or something else?

He had no idea but, at this precise moment in time, it didn't really seem to matter that much. When the girl moved towards him, snaking her arms around his neck and holding him tightly, he welcomed the action and he felt tears trickle slowly from his eyes, cutting through the grime and gore on his cheeks.

His words came to him like a beacon lost in a patch of fog.

She's not our daughter.

The girl seemed to tighten her grip on him and he responded, holding her closer.

She's not our daughter.

David closed his eyes for a second and the words seemed to recede slightly.

Amy reached out and touched the girl.

'Back to bed,' she whispered and the girl released her grip on David, allowing herself to be lifted by Amy and carried back to the rear of the RV. As David watched, the girl waved to him. He waved back without even thinking about it. And in that second he missed Daisy as much as he ever had. He would have given anything to be able to hold his own daughter just once more like that. To feel her close to him, to tell her how much he loved her. David gritted his teeth, trying to drive the thoughts from his mind, all too aware that to dwell on such fantasies was pointless and painful.

And he'd already seen enough pain today.

Amy returned and seated herself in the passenger seat once again. The two of them sat in silence, gazing out into the blackness, lost in their own thoughts. It was Amy who finally broke the stillness.

'She's sleeping again,' she murmured. 'She was exhausted.'

David nodded, his eyes still scanning the gloom beyond. When he finally looked at her again she had slumped low in the chair.

'Amy,' he murmured and she looked at him.

He wanted to tell her that he feared there was more pain ahead of them. More suffering to come. But the words wouldn't come. He couldn't force them out. Instead, he slid down further in his seat, aware of the crushing weariness that was sweeping over him in unstoppable waves. This time, he didn't fight it.

SEVENTY

The early morning sun was a pleasing sight both for the warmth with which it carpeted the ground but also for its golden rays that spread across the heavens and banished the last vestiges of night. Blue sky and white cloud replaced the mottled black and unsettled firmament of the previous night and with its light it also brought something else. Something that touched the soul as surely as the warmth touched the skin.

As David stepped from the RV he took several deep lungfuls of fresh air, enjoying the scents of the surrounding countryside. Birds were singing in the trees, heralding the daylight hours that had now spread completely across the sky. He blinked hard, closed the door gently behind him and set off down the narrow track, glancing around him to ensure that the RV was still indeed the only vehicle around. Behind him he could hear the distant sound of engines as other cars sped along the highway but they were so far away they were out of sight. David felt as if he was the only person on earth as he strode further away from the RV, glancing back at it every now and then.

When he was twenty yards away he concentrated on the area in front of him, picking his way across the uneven ground and past some bushes until he came to the area he sought. He could see that the earth was darker in places where it had been turned the previous night. Once he reached the darker dirt he snapped off several large pieces of bush which he then swept across the ground, disturbing the other dusty soil so that the darker patches were covered and camouflaged. He was still engaged in this particular task when he heard footsteps close behind him.

David spun round and saw that he had company.

The girl was standing about ten yards away, her dark hair blowing in the early morning breeze.

David looked at her for a moment, wondering why she had left the RV.

'Is everything alright?' he asked and, by way of an answer the girl merely smiled, nodded and hurried across to him.

'Did Amy tell you to come out here?' he wanted to know.

The girl shook her head and looked up at him.

Almost despite himself, David put one hand on her shoulder and she moved closer to him as they walked. There was something curiously calming about the scene, David thought and he felt a serenity he had not experienced for many months, certainly not since Daisy's death. He glanced down at the girl. She was so similar to Daisy in build and appearance it was uncanny.

She could be your daughter.

David shook his head, dismissing the voice inside his head.

She could be but she isn't is she? She's not your daughter and she never will be. Your daughter is dead. As dead as those men you buried last night.

The girl moved away from him momentarily and picked up a long branch, waving it in front of her like a gnarled sword. She dashed ahead, towards the patches of dark earth that David now fixed his gaze upon. He sighed and noted that they didn't appear as invisible as he'd first thought. He picked up a branch himself and began sweeping dust and stones over the shallow graves, attempting to further disguise their presence. If anyone passed this way he didn't want their attention to be attracted by the hastily dug resting places. The girl watched him for a second then started to mimic him, kicking dry dirt onto the area where David was. He glanced at her, grateful for her help, wondering what thoughts were tumbling through her mind now. Memories of what she'd seen? Of the horrors she had witnessed the previous night? Or of further back? He could only imagine what had gone through her mind when she was locked in the boot of that police car, trapped there with two corpses.

She moved about looking untroubled now. Enjoying the warming sunlight as much as he was.

Who are you? David thought as he glanced at her.

He was still thinking that when he felt the ground move beneath his feet.

He turned, looking down to see that the dark earth was rising in a couple of places that looked like mole hills. Seconds later, a hand burst through, pushing the earth aside and reaching upwards towards the sun like a flower. But this flower was shaped like a bloodied hand, the soil and blood smeared digits twitching as more of the arm now appeared.

David took a step back, watching in terror as another hand burst through the thin blanket of dirt. It was followed by a face, the features contorted with fury and hatred. The face of the first man he'd buried the night before.

The corpse sat up, dirt dropping from its shoulders.

David stood motionless for a moment, rooted to the spot, paralysed by the sight of the body which was now rising slowly to its feet, its movements uneven and jerky. The girl too was looking at the figure but with barely any expression on her face. She watched it with the detached eye of an observer and nothing more.

'Get back to the RV,' David snapped but she stood still, gazing at the corpse which was still trying to get up. It was now on all fours, it's head bowed.

As David watched, the girl bent and picked up a large rock, took two or three purposeful steps towards the crouching body and then slammed the rock down hard on its head twice. The impact sent it crashing back to the earth and the girl used the rock again, striking hard. The head burst like an overripe peach, thick gobs of brain spilling out onto the earth that was already becoming saturated with blood. She kept hitting the head despite the fact that the cranium was now gaping open, portions of splintered skull actually having fallen away to expose the jellied mass within. Finally the girl dropped the stone, her arms as high as the elbows drenched with reeking crimson fluid.

David felt his stomach contract but the girl merely looked at him and smiled.

Then she dug one hand into the greyish-red brain matter, gripped some of the slippery matter and raised it to her mouth. As he watched, she pushed some into her mouth, chewing it hungrily like a starving man who has just been unleashed on a banquet. There were lumps of the chewed brain falling from her mouth, thick dark blood dribbling down her chin as she looked at him.

It was then that he vomited.

SEVENTY-ONE

David sat up with a grunt, his head turning rapidly from side to side, his mind struggling to come to terms with the fact that he'd been dreaming. And dreaming so vividly. He could still see the residue of the images in his mind's eye. The girl using the stone as a weapon, smashing the skull open. Eating the glistening, swollen contents. He let out another deep breath, anxious to drive the last vestiges of the nightmare from his mind. As he moved he could feel how stiff his clothes were. The material hardened by the congealed blood that covered it. He rubbed his face with both hands and looked around once more.

'Are you all right?' Amy wanted to know.

'I think so,' David told her. 'Where is she?' he asked, looking around.

Amy looked vaguely at him for a moment then gestured over her shoulder.

'She's still sleeping, why?' she wanted to know.

'I...I just wondered...I was having a nightmare and...' The words faded away.

'I know, I heard you,' Amy told him. 'What was it about?'

'I can't remember,' he lied, his voice cracking.

Amy looked intently at him for a moment longer.

Only now did David glance out of the windscreen of the RV and he could see that the first traces of dawn were beginning to colour the heavens pink. He shivered and sat forward, suddenly aware of how cold it was inside the vehicle.

'Did you sleep?' he wanted to know.

'For a few hours,' Amy confessed. 'I think I could have slept standing up I was so tired.'

'Not really surprising is it?'

He reached out and squeezed her hand, holding it tightly as if he feared that she would pull away at any second.

'We should move on,' he decided, finally.

'If we can.'

'What do you mean?'

'Last night when we stopped, we never got fuel like we said we would.'

'Oh Jesus, that's right. Start it up. Let's see how much we've got.'

Amy did as he instructed and the engine burst into life. They both cast worried looks towards the needle on the petrol gauge which rose a little way but not far enough. It signalled that the tank was less than a quarter full.

'Enough to get us to Chase?' Amy wondered.

'I wish I knew,' David murmured.

'It's another hundred miles. Do we risk it?'

'We either push on or go back to that truck stop and fill up.'

They sat in silence for a moment, considering the options open to them.

'If we move on we could make it,' Amy said.

'And if we run out of fuel before we get there we're stranded.'

'Do you want to go back?'

He shook his head. 'No I don't but what choice have we got? We need to get that headlight fixed too.'

'We can make it to Chase before it's dark again if we leave now.'

'I hope you're right.'

'We should risk it,' Amy insisted. 'Push on. Get to Chase.'

'If we can,' David interrupted. 'If they're following us and we run out of petrol then it's just a matter of time before they catch up. All we'd be able to do is sit and wait for them to get us.'

Another heavy silence descended, again broken by Amy.

'They've caught up with us before,' she said, flatly. 'And we're still here.'

David looked at her for a second then nodded.

'There must be somewhere between here and Chase,' he said, quietly. 'Another truck stop. A diner. Something where we can fill up.'

'Let's find out.'

'Are you all right to drive?'

Amy smiled at him by way of answer. 'Why shouldn't I be?' she wanted to know.

'I was just checking,' he told her, softly.

'So, we're going on?' she murmured.

Again David nodded.

'You need to get cleaned up,' Amy told him.

He hesitated a moment, watching as she turned the wheel and guided the RV back along the narrow track towards the highway. The sky was turning blue now, the luminescent panoply flecked with thick white clouds. It all seemed welcoming compared to the thick, menacing blackness the previous night. If David had been that way inclined he might even have thought that the day promised much. But he dare not think that way. Not yet.

As Amy sent the RV speeding back onto the highway he headed towards the rear of the vehicle, anxious to rid himself of the blood drenched clothes that were sticking to him.

There was a thin, cotton curtain between the shower area and the beds at the rear of the RV and David glanced through the curtain briefly before undressing. He could see that the girl was still fast asleep, tucked snugly in beneath the sheets and blankets. Satisfied that she was unlikely to awaken just yet, David hastily undressed and stepped into the shower, the streams of water splashing over him. He looked down to see the blood washing away down the plughole, swirling and twisting around the circular hole before it disappeared.

He wished he could wash memories away as easily.

SEVENTY-TWO

The sunlight was dazzling.

The traces of early morning mist had been burned away by the searing heat of the golden orb hanging in the cloudless blue sky. Amy put on her sunglasses as she drove, careful to shield her eyes from the bright rays. The countryside spread out around her, hillier and more heavily wooded than it had been during the earlier part of the journey. There also seemed to be more curves to the highway as it snaked through the brightly lit landscape. It was no longer just an endless stretch of perfectly straight tarmac but it seemed to Amy more like a blackened tongue now, lolling and turning through the greenery around it, lapping at the gently rising hills in places.

She guided the RV over a low bridge, glancing to one side to see the shallow stream beneath her. Despite what she'd seen and been through the night before, she began to feel as if the warming rays of the sun were actually having some kind of positive effect on her. She managed a smile. The arrival of a new day, she hoped, might bring the kind of joy that had been absent from their lives for too long now. As she looked up she caught sight of her own reflection in the rear-view mirror and her smile faded rapidly. Her skin looked pale. Her face wan. She tilted the mirror down slightly as if the fact that she couldn't see herself would actually cause her appearance to improve.

She drove on, checking the wing mirrors for anything that might be following, glancing at each vehicle that approached from the other direction, fearful that any one of them might just veer across the lanes and smash into the RV. Fortunately there wasn't much traffic on the road yet. Half a dozen cars and some trucks had passed going in the other direction but not much else. She knew there would be more as the day progressed but for now, she was happy with the relative solitude.

Almost unconsciously she glanced down at the petrol gauge.

The needle was just above the E.

Amy sucked in a worried breath. She had no idea how much further they would be able to drive before the fuel tank finally emptied completely. And then what?

She let out a sigh and drove on, slowing down slightly as if that simple action was going to use less fuel.

The road was turning again, a huge curve that cut through some low, wooded hills before straightening out across another bridge.

The road across the bridge was blocked. There was a white car and what looked like a black transit van stationary across the highway blocking both lanes. There were black marks on the tarmac behind the transit and Amy wondered if there had been an accident but it didn't make her feel any less anxious. She pressed gently on the brake, her heart thumping faster now. There didn't appear to be anyone near to the abandoned vehicles. The ground sloped away sharply beneath the bridge, down towards a wide but shallow river.

'David,' Amy called, her eyes fixed on the vehicles ahead.

He joined her almost immediately, standing behind the driver's seat, his own attention now drawn to the transit and the white car. But it wasn't just the abandoned vehicles he was looking at, it was the yellow tape that had been drawn across the bridge approach that caught his attention. The tape that displayed the words;

POLICE LINE; DO NOT CROSS

'Stop here,' David told her.

She brought the vehicle gently to a halt about two hundred yards from the blocked bridge, the engine idling.

'I'd better have a look,' he told her.

'No, don't go out there,' Amy snapped. 'We can get through. I can get the RV between the two of them if I'm careful. Don't go out there. You don't know who might be around.'

'Like the police who put that tape across the road?' he murmured.

'It looks like an accident. You can see the tyre marks on the road. The white car looks as if it skidded.'

'That's what I thought but how can we be sure?'

David swallowed and scanned the scene before them once again.

'I wonder where the police are?'

As they continued to gaze at the makeshift road-block, both of them heard footsteps behind them in the RV. The girl joined them, moving around David towards the passenger seat but Amy held out a hand to stop her.

'Stay out of sight, sweetie,' she said, softly.

The girl nodded and backed off, away from the RV's cab and back into the vehicle, pausing beside the door. David reached for the shotgun and swung it up before him, working the slide to chamber a round.

'Just in case,' he murmured, licking his lips which were dry and beginning to stick together. 'Good job I re-loaded.'

Amy eased her foot from the brake and the RV moved forward slowly, trundling towards the bridge and the vehicles that blocked it.

Like Amy had done before him, David now glanced to his right and left, checking for any signs of movement anywhere on or around the bridge. If this had been an accident then why were there no passengers around? If the white car had gone out of control and crashed into the transit then had anyone been injured? And if they had, where the hell were they now? Or, he wondered fleetingly, had the accident happened some time ago and the emergency services had already ferried any injured to a nearby hospital? Questions tumbled through his mind, each one unanswered and fuelled, with each passing second, by more paranoia.

If the accident had been staged just to stop them, he told himself, then it was an elaborate ruse. But, he thought as the RV crawled along, it had worked in as far as it had slowed them down. Set them up as targets?

He glanced around once more, tension growing within him.

'Do you seen anyone?' he wanted to know.

Amy shook her head, her attention fixed on the vehicles ahead. She could see a small gap between the front bumper of one and the rear of the other and she was sure that she could nudge the RV through that gap when the time came.

'Be careful,' David said, quietly, touching her on the shoulder with one hand, his eyes never leaving the road. The other hand gripped the shotgun tightly. His fingers curled around the pistol grip, he could feel the sweat forming on his palm. He tried to control his own increasingly laboured breathing.

Amy could also feel perspiration forming on her forehead as she drove slowly along the road towards the bridge and its obstacles. The warm weather she had welcomed earlier in the day was now a hindrance, making her feel even more uncomfortable. She felt one single bead of sweat trickle down her face. How much was induced by the heat and how much by her growing fear she could only guess. She gripped the steering wheel more tightly, removing her hands one at a time to wipe her palms on her jeans.

She glanced down at the fuel gauge again. Then at the speedometer.

She was doing less than ten miles an hour. It felt as if the RV was barely moving.

They were now twenty yards from the approach to the bridge. The two stricken vehicles were more or less in the middle of it.

Fifteen yards.

David sat down in the passenger seat, glancing round briefly at the girl.

'You sit down,' he said, smiling at her and the girl returned the gesture, settling herself on the floor of the vehicle just behind Amy's seat. David returned his attention to the road ahead.

Ten yards before they reached the ramp that led onto the parapet of the bridge and Amy pressed a little harder on the accelerator. The engine roared for a second as the RV rolled on.

Accident or ambush?

David sat forward in his seat, eyes alert for the slightest movement ahead or around them, the same unanswered question whirling round and round inside his head.

Five yards.

Amy was driving straight for the gap between the two vehicles, guiding the RV

towards the narrow space that would allow them passage. If it meant bumping into one or both of the other vehicles then so be it, she thought. She pressed a little harder on the accelerator, her t-shirt sticking to her back now.

There was a loud crack that seemed to reverberate even inside the RV. It echoed across the landscape and, before it died away, the side window of the slowly moving vehicle was punched in, shattered glass showering David who raised one hand to shield his face.

It took him only seconds to realize that it was a bullet that had smashed the window.

Another followed it, slamming into the side of the RV, exploding into it and punching a hole the size of a fist.

The girl screamed and ducked down to the floor, covering her head.

'Go,' David shouted.

Amy stepped on the accelerator.

SEVENTY-THREE

The RV sped forward, accelerating as Amy pressed her foot down on the gas, gripping the steering wheel tightly.

As the vehicle moved towards the transit and the white car Amy wondered, fleetingly, if the impact would be sufficient to push them aside. She was still wondering when another shot cracked against the windscreen, causing the glass to spider-web in several places.

David peered fearfully towards the sound of the shot, trying to catch sight of who might have fired it, wondering where the next one would come from. He ducked down a little lower, all too aware that whoever was shooting at them was probably in a position to pick them off at will. But, he reasoned, it was harder to hit a moving target. The RV was still picking up speed, ready to smash into the vehicles blocking the bridge.

Amy was hunched over the wheel, her eyes fixed on the gap between the

black transit and the white car. The needle on the speedometer nudged sixty and she gripped the steering wheel tightly.

Another shot smashed into the side of the RV.

There was a screech of buckling metal as the RV hit the back of the transit and knocked it aside, ploughing through the small gap between the two vehicles, shattering one of its headlights and denting the radiator grille. It cut the yellow tape like a sprinter dashing across the finish line, the ends flapping in the air. The RV skidded slightly but Amy pressed her foot down harder and kept it there as the larger vehicle careened onwards, clipping the white car too. David heard the squeal of brakes and gripped the edge of his seat, bracing himself when the impact came.

Behind the driver's seat, the girl was crouched on the floor, her hands clasped over her head as if hoping they would act as some kind of protection. When the vehicle accelerated away, she rose up, glancing out of the windscreen to see that the road ahead was open and empty.

David looked into the wing mirror and was delighted to see that they were putting more and more distance between themselves and the vehicles on the bridge but, as he continued to look, he saw two men running towards the black transit. Another man sprinting for the white car. They had appeared from the thick trees on either side of the bridge approaches and David could see others now. Some were gesturing angrily towards the escaping RV. He could see a woman in her thirties pointing towards them, yelling something unintelligible but, even from a distance he could see the expression of anger and fear on her face.

'They're coming,' he gasped, still gazing into the mirror.

He saw the transit reverse and then turn sharply, the white car following. Both vehicles now speeding after the RV.

'We can't outrun them,' Amy gasped, also seeing the pursuing vehicles drawing closer as she glanced in her own wing mirror.

'I know,' David conceded.

He hefted the shotgun before him, his hands shaking.

'Shall I try and get off the road?' Amy wanted to know.

'No. Just keep driving.'

He moved towards the rear of the vehicle, glancing at the girl as he passed.

'You get in the passenger seat and strap yourself in,' he told her. She nodded and scrambled forward to do as she was told.

Peering through the back window of the RV, David could see that the other two vehicles were still pursuing but, he realized, they were making no attempt to close the gap between themselves and the RV. Even when they were joined by a motorbike that roared out of the trees on the other side of the bridge, they didn't appear to be increasing their speed and none of them made any attempt to get closer to their fleeing quarry. He wondered why.

Both the transit and the white car looked capable of matching if not excelling any speed that could be coaxed from the RV and yet they were content to remain twenty or thirty yards behind, one behind the other. There seemed to be no urgency to their pursuit and David couldn't understand why.

For a full five minutes he stood gazing at the pursuing vehicles and they did nothing more than retain their distance.

'Amy,' he called. 'Slow down a bit.'

'Why?' she shouted back.

'Just do it, will you?'

Amy eased up on the gas slightly, their speed falling to just above fifty.

Still the pursuing vehicles made no attempt to get closer.

What if they don't need to get closer? What if they're just waiting to pick all three of you off with a high-powered rifle?

David let out a worried breath, realizing that option was probably open to their pursuers. Were they just waiting for their moment? Was there a section of road ahead that would lend itself more readily to that? Were they driving into another trap? One that, this time they wouldn't be able to extricate themselves from?

The thoughts and possibilities tumbled through his mind, none of them with satisfactory answers.

Why wait? If their pursuers wanted them dead why not just keep shooting into the RV until they had achieved that aim?

'David.'

Amy's shout broke his train of thought and sent him hurrying to the cab of the RV.

She was gesturing forward when he got there, pointing at something in the distance. It took David a moment or two to realize that there were vehicles coming the other way too.

Were their pursuers trying to box them in? Attempting to cut off the road in both directions?

He watched as the sun glinted on the chassis of the vehicles heading towards them and he realized with a brief feeling of relief, that whatever they were, they were on the opposite side of the highway. He'd thought originally that the approaching cars had been heading straight for them.

Behind, the transit and the white car kept their distance. Even the motorbike was resisting the temptation to speed ahead and catch them up.

What the hell are you playing at? What's coming next?

The vehicles heading towards them were close enough to identify now and David could see a large silver grey truck leading the way. It seemed to loom out of the distance, a massive moving edifice that appeared to tower above the highway and the blue car that followed it.

Both vehicles swept past on the opposite side of the road and David looked around again to check the progress of those following.

They were still there. Still keeping the same, almost respectful, distance and not attempting to catch up. They were like vultures tracking dying prey. Just waiting for it to stumble or fall before they moved in, David mused. Why should they hurry? They knew that the RV couldn't outrun them. It was just a matter of time.

SEVENTY-FOUR

'We're nearly out of petrol.'

Amy's voice lanced through the hot and clammy interior of the

RV and David glanced at the fuel gauge, his eyes fixed on the needle there.

'David,' Amy went on, her voice catching.

'I can see,' he told her.

'I don't know how much further we can go now,' Amy told him.

As she spoke she glanced in the wing mirror and saw the black transit and the white car still trundling along, the motorbike moving in and out of them, occasionally taking the lead. The little procession had not drawn one foot closer to the RV during the entire duration of the chase.

'What are they doing?' Amy groaned. 'What are they waiting for? It's like they know we're running out of petrol. They're just waiting until we stop.'

David didn't speak, he merely glanced back and forth from the rapidly falling needle on the fuel gauge to the vehicles tracking them.

There was a loud, strident sound that cut through the sunlit morning air and seemed to shake the RV and David turned again, trying to find its source, wondering what was about to happen. It was the unmistakeable blast of an air horn and it was coming from behind them. Amy glanced at him worriedly and he made his way towards the rear of the RV as the sound came again.

He could see the truck further back, behind the black transit and the white car. It was a massive blue and chrome juggernaut that was pulling out and overtaking the other vehicles as it thundered along the highway. The horn sounded again and the truck sped on, swinging back into the lane behind the RV. The sound of the huge engine was deafening and David could see the driver perched high up in the cab of the metal leviathan.

As the air horn sounded again the truck pulled out once more, roaring past the RV. David watched as it sped by, the huge black rig it was hauling glinting in the sunlight. He just saw the word FLAMMABLE on the container as the lorry finally accelerated away from them, exhaust fumes billowing into the air. He could smell hot oil and rubber as the truck passed, moving back into the lane ahead of the RV and then speeding away with another blast of its air horn.

Behind them, the black transit and the white car kept up their steady pursuit, never attempting to draw closer.

There was a sign on the side of the road ahead of them and Amy glanced towards it, her attention drawn away from the pursuing vehicles for a moment.

As the RV got nearer she could see the white words on the green sign more clearly.

There were three locations highlighted on the sign but it was the one at the top that caught her attention.

CHASE 12

'David,' she called, gesturing towards the sign. 'We're nearly there.'

Even as she spoke she glanced down at the fuel gauge again.

'But are we going to make it?' David breathed and the words hung on the air like the stink of hot oil.

The girl sat forward excitedly now, peering out of the windscreen as if she was looking at something no one else could see.

'You're nearly home,' Amy said to her, a smile touching her lips.

The girl looked at her and grinned more broadly.

'Can you show us where to go?' David wanted to know. 'When we get to Chase, can you show us how to get to your home?'

Again the girl nodded excitedly, the grin spreading even more widely across her face.

Suddenly, from behind them, there was a roar and David shot a worried glance in the direction of the sound. Seconds later, the motorbike swept past them, the passenger turning to peer in the direction of the RV, but the bike only remained level with the vehicle for a moment before roaring off along the road, seemingly uninterested in the RV or it's passengers. David wished that was the case but he watched as the motorbike sped off, disappearing into the distance.

'Are they planning something else further up the road?' Amy murmured, the same thoughts tumbling through her mind too.

David didn't answer but moved towards the rear of the RV, checking the progress of the other pursuing vehicles and not surprised to see that both were still continuing on their way, still seemingly determined not to get any closer than they were now.

He walked back to the cab, glancing at the needle on the fuel gauge once more.

Twelve miles to Chase. It might as well, David thought, have been a thousand miles.

Ahead of them they could see that the road forked off to the right as well as continuing on straight ahead. There were signs across the road as well as on the side of the thoroughfare that indicated they were closer to Chase. Amy checked the wing mirror and guided the RV towards the off-ramp that would take them clear of the free-way. This new arterial road turned sharply, disappearing into some low hills and more densely planted trees. Amy glanced up at David who merely watched as they drew nearer to the road that would take them to their destination.

Behind them, the black transit and the white car retained their distance as if it had been measured for them. When the RV pulled off the highway they both followed, their pursuit inexorable.

THE HOUSE

The house wasn't quite in the middle of nowhere but it was pretty close.

Approachable only by a single track that cut practically straight across the countryside for almost five hundred yards once it branched off the service road, it stood in a slight dip in the ground that made it almost invisible until any visitors were within fifty yards of its front door. This, coupled with the trees that grew on three sides of the structure, helped to make it look as if it were hiding from the world. Something that might be an admirable quality to some but might hamper its sale to others.

Solitude was one thing but isolation was something quite different and the distance from the nearest town might be something that would make the house difficult to sell.

The house had been empty for more than a year and whoever had lived there had obviously never had the approaches to the building levelled to provide a smoother driving surface but this was appalling.

Off to the right there was a small building that might have been used as a stable but it was windowless and the tiles on the roof were discoloured and missing in many places. There was an air of neglect and decay about the whole place that was impossible to hide. The area directly in front of the house was overgrown, the grass and weeds almost knee high in most places.

The sunshine reflected off the filthy windows, rays seemingly unable to penetrate the layers of grime and dust that had built up like cataracts on blind eyes.

And from behind those dirty windows, hidden from the prying stares of

those who might pass by, they watched. Curious and expectant gazes peered outwards at the sunlit landscape and the long driveway that led up to the house.
They watched.
And waited.

SEVENTY-FIVE

As Amy swung the RV off the freeway, her attention was fixed more on the rapidly falling level of fuel they possessed than on the road itself. She expected that, at any minute, the vehicle would judder to a halt, warning lights flashing and glinting all over the dashboard. She did, however, manage to look at the child who was sitting forward on her seat, gazing out raptly at the countryside ahead and around them with a look on her face that Amy could best describe as bliss. She obviously recognised the area they were passing through, that much was evident.

'Can you tell me where to go, sweetie?' she said, reaching out to touch the girls arm gently.

The girl nodded enthusiastically and pointed straight ahead.

About five hundred yards further on the road split again, the left-hand fork leading towards the town of Chance itself, the right hand one curving away into the hills and woods. It was that right hand fork which the girl indicated and Amy did as she was instructed, guiding the RV along that more isolated route while David moved back and forth between the cab of the vehicle and the rear, checking on the progress of their pursuers.

Needless to say, they were still there.

'Are you sure?' Amy asked the girl as they drove on.

The girl nodded, her gaze never leaving the road ahead. The smile had faded a little from her face but she still looked happy and excitable, Amy mused.

Directed by the girl she took another turning, the road, she noticed, now becoming narrower and bumpier.

Behind them, the pursuing vehicles were falling back.

David gripped the shotgun more tightly, wondering why they were stopping. What next in this insanity, he wondered? What kind of game were they playing now?

He thought about telling Amy that their pursuers had left them but decided to let her concentrate on the road ahead. The sun, hanging high above, was blazing with even greater intensity now and the temperature inside the RV was rising by the minute it seemed.

'Oh God.'

He heard Amy's voice and hurried back to the cab of the RV just in time to see her pointing at the dashboard.

There was a red light flashing just above the fuel gauge.

David said nothing. What could he say? It was what they had feared for so long now.

The RV juddered once but kept going.

'Keep going as long as you can,' David told Amy, checking the wing mirrors for any sign of activity behind them but relieved to see that there was none. As they continued along the narrower road he could see houses and barns beyond, some linked to this road by even more rudimentary tracks and pathways. There were fences in some places, protecting fields but, for the most part, the area next to the road was open. In some places, trees grew right up to the road side. Dust rose all around the RV as Amy drove on, still guided by the girl who continued to point straight ahead, seemingly unperturbed by the fact that they were now virtually out of fuel.

'Have we got much further to go?' Amy asked her and she shook her head.

Amy didn't know if she was relieved at that revelation or not. She gripped the steering wheel more tightly, pressing down gently on the brake as the RV began to head down into a sharp dip in the road. There was a small bridge at the bottom of it and she guided the RV across it, the sides of the vehicle almost brushing against the wooden parapet of the bridge. Below the bridge was a shallow river that seemed to have mostly dried up, only a trickle of what Amy guessed had once been a more substantial flow now visible between the rocks and boulders on the river bottom. Some birds that had been drinking there took off as the RV rolled over the bridge, their bodies black against the perfect blueness of the sky.

Amy drove on, slowing down as much as she dared as if that would prevent the petrol loss which was already irreversible. It was only a matter of time before the RV stopped completely but whether that time could be measured in minutes or moments she had no idea.

The RV was bumping over the uneven ground and Amy was shaken unceremoniously from side to side as she drove. On more than one occasion she turned the wheel to avoid particularly large and jagged looking rocks that littered the narrow track, fearing that to run over one may well cause a puncture. It was bad enough running out of fuel but the prospect of having to change a tyre was even less enticing. In fact, Amy thought that a couple of the rocks in the road looked capable of smashing an axle let alone puncturing a tyre. She steered carefully around them where she could, even sending the vehicle off the road a couple of times. David steadied himself behind her seat as she drove on.

The hills were rising on both sides of the road and ahead was what appeared to be a low ridge that the road climbed. What awaited them on the other side Amy could only imagine.

The RV juddered violently twice, rolled on another fifty or so yards and then slid to a halt.

The dashboard seemed to explode in a dazzling array of lights.

The petrol had finally run out completely.

'That's it,' Amy said, her mouth dry, perspiration beading on her face and neck.

David crossed to the door of the RV and looked out. They were alone it seemed and for that at least he was grateful. Straining his ears to hear any sound, he detected nothing and came to the conclusion that there was no movement for quite a distance around them either in front or behind. Exactly how far off the main road they had come he had no idea but there was no sign of life anywhere he looked.

'Is it much further to your home?' Amy asked the girl who shook her head and pointed at the low ridge ahead of them, making a semi-circular gesture with her other hand.

'Over the hill?' Amy said, attempting to interpret the gesture. 'Your home is over that hill?'

The girl looked directly at her, smiled and nodded then got to her feet. She was heading for the door of the RV before Amy could stop her.

SEVENTY-SIX

David also saw the girl bolt for the door but he too could not stop her and he watched helplessly as she jumped out of the RV down onto the dusty track beneath.

Amy hauled herself from the driver's seat and ran after her but the girl was walking unhurriedly along the track towards the ridge, apparently untroubled by the two adults pursuing her.

'We said we'd take her home,' David told Amy, joining her on the dusty track. 'That's what we'll do.'

Amy paused and looked at him for a moment then set off again after the girl.

Both of them looked around as they walked, scanning the landscape for any sign of movement but there was nothing to be seen except the girl who was leading them closer to the summit of the low ridge. David and Amy caught up with her about a hundred yards from the crest. She looked up at each of them in turn, smiling happily.

The little procession moved on, the warmth from the blazing sun enveloping them. A slight breeze was also blowing but it brought a welcome respite from the heat and David wiped his forehead with the back of one hand as he walked, peering around him constantly, the shotgun gripped in one fist. How he was going to explain it to anyone beyond the crest of the ridge he had no idea but that didn't seem to bother him as he trudged on, keeping pace with Amy and the girl.

As they reached the crest of the ridge, David slowed his pace, looking down into the shallow valley beyond. There was one single house down there, standing alone in the dusty surroundings.

The girl looked up at them and grinned.

'Is that your home?' Amy asked and she nodded wildly.

David glanced at his wife then back at the large building below them, his brow furrowing a little. The three of them continued on their way, moving down the reverse slope of the ridge, moving as unhurriedly as if they'd been out on a morning stroll. David and Amy looked around them constantly but the girl kept her eyes fixed on the house ahead, her happiness increasing, it seemed, with every step. She ran a little way ahead of them but neither attempted to restrain her.

'That's what we've killed for? To bring her back to this?' David said, nodding in the direction of the house.

Amy didn't answer. She was also peering at the building, watching for any sign of movement inside or around it.

'It doesn't look like anyone's lived here for years,' Amy murmured.

'Could she be mistaken?' David asked.

'She's not going to forget where she lives is she?'

'But we found her hundreds of miles from here. What the hell was she doing there?'

'What do you mean?'

'She was in that police car miles away from here. How did she get there?'

'She was kidnapped, David. We don't know how long she'd been in there or where they snatched her from. The other kids in that boot might have come from miles away too but they weren't alive to tell us were they?'

They walked on, watching as the girl began to run towards the house, running up the flight of steps that led to the front door. David and Amy both hurried after her, seeing her standing before the main entrance to the building.

As they drew closer they could both see that the windows of the house were sealed. Some with thick tape, others with nails.

David slowed his pace, confused and unsettled by what he was seeing.

'No one lives here,' he murmured, his voice catching.

Amy also saw the electrical tape that had been stretched across every single inch of window frame. It was dusty and covered with the accumulated filth and neglect of what seemed to be years.

The girl was standing in front of the door, waiting for them to reach her. Amy frowned as she drew nearer, seeing that the blissful expression that had been on the girls face before had faded to be replaced by one of growing concern. She was now looking up at the house with fear etched across her features. Amy rushed to join her. David glanced around them once more, looking for any sign of movement on the open ground but he saw none. As he drew closer to the girl he too saw the look on her face had changed and the hairs on the back of his neck rose.

'What's wrong?' Amy asked, kneeling close to her.

The girl merely shook her head.

David walked to one of the windows and ran his index finger along the strips of tape sealing it.

'What the hell is this?' he murmured.

'Is there anyone inside?' Amy asked the girl who shook her head.

'No one lives here do they?' David said, flatly

Again the girl shook her head.

'Why did you bring us here?' he continued.

The girl moved to the door, grabbed the handle and shook it, slamming it up and down as if she was trying to open it. Then she turned helplessly towards them.

'You want to go inside?' Amy asked.

The girl nodded.

David stepped towards the door, steadied himself then drove one foot against the battered partition. It didn't budge and the sound of the impact echoed across the empty landscape. He struck it again, pieces of paint flaking away under the impact. He used the butt of the shotgun on the handle but still it wouldn't give. More flakes of paint fell or drifted to the ground, piling up like discoloured confetti.

The girl moved closer to Amy who snaked both arms around her as she watched David battering at the recalcitrant door. Finally, he swung the shotgun up and fired twice into the area around the handle.

The shotgun made two huge holes in the rotting wood, the handle dropping to the ground with a loud clang. Again he kicked the door and, this time, it swung open, creaking on rusted hinges that hadn't tasted oil for years. For long seconds he stood motionless, peering into the gloom beyond. Motes of dust turned in the rays of sunlight filling the hallway of the house and David took a step closer, looking into the blackness. The girl looked at him and smiled then she pulled free of Amy and walked towards the doorway, stepping across the threshold into the house.

David and Amy waited a moment then joined her.

SEVENTY-SEVEN

Despite the warmth of the sun outside, the interior of the house was as cold as the grave. The chill wrapped itself around David and Amy as they entered, as though someone had draped them with freezing blankets.

To their right was a large, wide staircase that rose to the upper floors of the house. To their left were several closed doors, one of which the girl approached. Across the wide hallway there was another door, also closed. It was towards that door that David advanced.

'Did you live here with your parents?' Amy asked, a little puzzled when the girl shook her head dismissively.

She pushed the door open, dust rising from the floor before it, swirling and twisting like noxious fog. The girl waited a moment then stepped over the threshold into the room beyond. Amy hesitated a moment then followed her, discovering that they were in what had once been a sitting room or at least she guessed it had due to the furniture that was still on the bare floor. There were a couple of chairs, a battered sofa and two coffee tables, one of which had a cracked dish upon it. Amy looked around the room and saw that no one had been inside it for a long time. The dust was several inches thick on the floor and, as she followed the girl through the room, it rose with each footfall until she had to shield her nose from the particles that clogged her nostrils when she tried to breathe. The whole place smelled of neglect. Amy headed back to the door briefly to see that David was heading back across the hallway to join them, making his way into the sitting room, blinking as his vision became more accustomed to the dull interior.

'What's she doing?' he wanted to know.

Amy shook her head by way of reply.

'No one's been here for years by the look of it,' David mused, glancing around again, then stepping back as the girl hurried past them and back out into the hallway.

This time she made for the door on the far side of the open space, passing through it quickly. Amy and David followed.

'If this was where she lived it had been a long time ago,' he muttered.

The room they advanced in to was, or at least had been, a

kitchen. Blinds had been pulled shut in this room too and despite the blazing sunshine outside, it was still gloomy and oppressive inside. A large wooden table occupied the centre of the room but there was no other furniture to be seen.

The girl wasn't interested in the kitchen however, she hurried across to the door at the far side of the room, tugging on the handle while David and Amy watched her but she couldn't move the recalcitrant handle. She turned to them and gestured at the door, an expression of despair on her face.

'What the hell is behind that?' David murmured.

'Open it and find out,' Amy told him., moving across to the door with her husband who drove the butt of the shotgun against the handle until it finally dropped to the ground. The door swung open and a blast of cold, rancid air swept out to greet them.

'It smells like something died down there,' Amy gasped, covering her nose and mouth.

'An animal might have got in,' David suggested.

The girl stood motionless for a moment then moved towards what were clearly stone steps. They led down, flanked on both sides by bare stone walls. David reached out to stop her but she was already making her way slowly down the steps.

Amy moved after her, choosing her steps carefully so she didn't slip on the cold stone.

The stench that they had first noticed was just as strong.

When the girl reached the bottom of the steps she walked forward to the centre of the subterranean room and stood motionless.

As Amy joined her, she glanced around in the darkness, her footsteps echoing inside the gloomy space. She could tell from the reverberations that the cellar or basement was large. There was a small window high up in one wall but, despite it being covered with black tape like so many of the windows were, there was still enough light spilling inside to enable Amy to see the layout of the room.

As David joined her she glanced around. He put one hand on her shoulder and they both stood gazing at the girl who was still standing in the centre of the room motionless.

'Why did you want to come here?' David asked, his voice echoing inside the cavernous underground room.

The girl turned her head slightly in his direction.

'This is where they kept us,' she said.

David and Amy weren't sure if it was the sound of her voice or the very fact that she had actually uttered words that shocked them. Her voice echoed around the subterranean space.

'What did you say?' Amy asked, her own voice quivering.

'This is where they kept us,' the girl repeated.

'You can speak,' Amy said, incredulously. 'Why didn't you speak to us before?'

The girl didn't answer.

'Who kept you here?' David wanted to know.

'I don't know who they were,' the girl murmured.

'Why did they keep you down here?' Amy wanted to know, moving towards the girl but David held out a hand to restrain her, his eyes fixed on the immobile figure of the girl who was still standing in the centre of the floor.

'There were chains,' she said, softly. 'Or they tied us up.'

'Why did they do that?' David enquired.

'So they could hurt us,' the girl told him.

'But who were they? Why did they want to hurt you?'

The girl could only shake her head.

'If they hurt you why did you want us to bring you back here?' Amy asked.

The girl was silent then and turned to look at them.

'Because they told me to,' she said, flatly. 'They said they'd kill my brother and my family if I didn't. I had to do what they said.'

The blackness and silence inside the cellar seemed to form into one nearly tangible entity. Before the girl could speak again, another sound seemed to fill the space.

Above them they suddenly heard muted, furtive movement and they realized that could mean only one thing.

Someone else was inside the house.

SEVENTY-EIGHT

David looked up anxiously.

Amy, too, heard the commotion and glanced first at her husband and then at the child who was still standing in the middle of the room, her head bowed slightly.

'They know we're down here,' David said, quietly, his heart thudding hard against his ribs. He looked at the girl. 'They know don't they?'

She turned and looked blankly at him then nodded gently, almost apologetically.

David moved towards the stone steps that led back up to the kitchen, climbing two of them, his ears filled with the sounds from above. There were many footsteps now. He could only guess at how many people were in the house.

'Come on,' he urged, signalling to Amy and the girl to follow him, Amy beckoned the girl to join her.

'I'm sorry,' the girl said, softly.

Amy swallowed hard and wanted to say something. She wanted to tell the girl how angry she was. That she felt betrayed. But the words would not come. Instead she just pulled the girl closer to her as they climbed the stone steps behind David.

He had reached the doorway by now and he peered into the kitchen beyond, checking that it was empty. He beckoned to Amy to join him and she hurried up the last few stairs.

They could hear voices now.

In the hallway beyond and also in the sitting room. There was more movement above them, on the stairs.

David led the way, moving slowly through the kitchen towards the door that opened out into the hallway beyond.

He gripped the shotgun more tightly, pausing to push a hand into his pocket where he'd stuffed some spare shells before they left the RV. There were four inside the weapon now and he guessed another five in his pocket.

Would it be enough?

He put a hand on the cold metal door knob and stood motionless, aware that Amy was gazing at him, able to hear the voices beyond as clearly as he could. She was thinking the same as he was. How many were waiting out there for them? What could they do to get past the intruders? Thoughts tumbled through both their minds as David's grip on the door knob tightened. He turned it and pushed the door, stepping across the threshold.

The four people in the hallway froze.

David lowered the shotgun and jabbed the barrel towards them.

As he did, several more figures descended the staircase to his right, eyes peering towards him and Amy as if they were visitors at a zoo inspecting some exotic specimen.

The closest of the people was a tall man in his forties and he slowly raised one hand, motioning towards the front door of the building.

'Stay back and no one will get hurt,' David said, trying to inject some strength into his voice.

'We want the child,' the tall man said.

'She told us,' Amy informed him. 'She told us that you made her do it.'

The man looked momentarily puzzled then smiled thinly.

'You can't get away,' he told them. 'There are too many of us.'

David raised the shotgun slightly.

'I'll kill anyone who tries to stop us,' he breathed. 'I mean it.'

'I guess that you do,' the tall man intoned, glancing towards the yawning barrel of the Remington.

'You don't understand,' said a dark-haired woman who was standing close to the front door.

'Yes, we do,' David told her. 'We know who you are. What you believe. We know what you do to children. I saw some of your friends murder a girl a couple of nights ago.'

'Who told you about us?' the tall man wanted to know.

'Does it matter?' David challenged. 'We know about your...cult. Your twisted ideas and beliefs. You think that by killing this girl you're going prevent the end of the world don't you?' He spoke the last two or three words through clenched teeth.

The tall man shook his head.

'You don't understand,' he murmured.

'I understand that we're walking out of here now,' David went on. 'And if you or anyone else tries to stop us I'll kill you.'

The dark-haired woman stepped away from the front door, moving further back as Amy advanced towards it and pulled it open.

What she saw beyond made her gasp.

There were four or five hundred people gathered outside the house, every face turned expectantly towards it.

'We've been expecting you,' the tall man told her.

'As you can see,' the dark-haired woman added. 'There's nowhere to run now.'

David moved out onto the front porch of the house, looking at the array of people before him, all standing silently and expectantly. As he looked more closely he could see that, almost without exception, they were carrying weapons. Knives. Hatchets. Machetes. Shovels. He saw a scythe. Close to the front of the throng a man was holding a chainsaw. Another brandished an antique looking sword, the blade broad and wickedly sharp. One was holding a crossbow. Two others gripped long bows.

'Listen to what we have to say,' the tall man offered, his voice calm and unworried.

'The wisdom of your cult?' David said, dismissively, his mouth dry with fear.

'Some call us a cult,' the tall man informed him. 'The ignorant. The uninformed.'

'You murder children,' Amy rasped.

'We cleanse,' the tall man said, quietly.

'You're insane,' David told him. 'All of you.'

'We have our beliefs,' the tall man went on. 'We don't expect everyone to understand them.'

'Now you've got the child, what are you going to do with her?' Amy demanded.

The tall man smiled but there was no warmth in the gesture.

'That child?' he said, pointing towards the girl. 'That isn't the child we want. It never was.' He looked directly at Amy, one index finger pointing at her stomach. 'We want *your* child. You're pregnant.'

SEVENTY-NINE

David looked at the tall man and then at Amy. He shook his head disbelievingly. Amy met his gaze, her eyes wide with fear and confusion.

'You're pregnant aren't you?' the tall man insisted.

'I can't be,' Amy told him. 'It's too soon to know.'

'You are,' he snapped.

'You can't deny it,' the dark-haired woman added.

'The child is the one we seek,' said the tall man, defiantly.

'It was foretold,' the dark-haired woman offered.

'You really *are* insane,' David breathed.

'Your child is the one that was prophesied.'

The newest voice came from the crowd of people gathered before the house.

'You can save the world,' someone else called.

'You can stop evil entering,' another voice howled.

'This was foretold,' shouted a man close to the front of the crowd.

'Stay with us,' the dark-haired woman said. 'We can help you.'

David shook his head.

'You need our help,' the tall man told them.

'You keep away from us,' David snapped. 'All of you.'

Amy moved closer to him.

'We can't let you leave,' the tall man said, flatly. 'The child cannot be allowed to flourish.'

'I'm not pregnant,' Amy insisted. 'I can't be.'

'You are,' the dark-haired woman told her, her tone assured.

'A child conceived in rage,' said the tall man.

'In pain,' the dark-haired woman added.

'A child of suffering,' a woman in the crowd called.

'A child conceived from loss,' offered a man close to them.

'A child of outsiders,' another man called.

David looked at the faces before him, his breath coming in low gasps.

'What the hell are you talking about?' he rasped.

'The child your wife is carrying is all of those things,' the dark-haired woman insisted. 'All the things we were told to expect.'

'This is the child we've been waiting for,' the tall man went on.

David pulled Amy closer to him, holding the Remington by it's pistol grip, the barrel aimed at the tall man.

'What about the others that you killed?' David snarled.

'Does it matter?' the tall man challenged. 'Do *they* matter?' He shook his head. 'There won't be any more. Not now. There's no need.'

'Your child is different,' the dark-haired woman continued.

'It would be powerful,' someone called.

'The most powerful of all,' a woman shouted.

'It cannot be allowed to flourish,' the tall man insisted.

'What do you think you're going to do?' David demanded. 'Kill it? You think we'd allow that?'

'You have no choice,' the tall man told him. 'This matter is beyond you.'

David shook his head.

'We're leaving here,' he said. 'Anyone who tries to stop us is going to die.'

The tall man merely shook his head.

'Where are you going to go?' he asked, quietly.

'The child must die,' the dark-haired woman told them. 'If not now then some other time. It cannot be allowed to grow.'

'Its evil will destroy the world,' a voice from the crowd shouted.

'You don't know what you're talking about,' Amy snapped. 'You're mad. All of you.'

The tall man took a step closer.

David worked the slide on the shotgun, chambering a round.

'I'm warning you,' he snarled.

'Even if you kill me there are too many of us for you,' he said, smugly. 'You can't kill us all.'

'Do you know what will happen if the child is born?' the dark-haired woman interjected. 'It will mean the end of this world as we know it. Everything will be destroyed. Swept away by the evil that child will bring.'

Amy shook her head.

'It's a little child,' she said, tears forming in her eyes. 'That's all. Nothing more. Just a child.'

The tall man shook his head and smiled patronisingly.

'I wish that was true,' he said, quietly.

'Why do you think your daughter died?' the dark-haired woman asked.

Amy glared at her.

'Your daughter died because this child needed to live,' the other woman continued. 'It was prophesied.'

Amy shook her head.

'If Daisy was still alive this wouldn't be happening,' said the dark-haired woman.

Tears were rolling down Amy's cheeks now.

'Don't talk about her,' she gasped, her voice catching. 'Don't you dare.'

'How did you know?' David demanded. 'How *could* you know?'

The tall man smiled again.

David squeezed the trigger of the shotgun, gripping the weapon as it roared, the recoil slamming the weapon back into his shoulder so hard it felt as if the collar bone had been cracked. The sound was thunderous. Smoke drifted in a grey cloud from the barrel, rising towards the pure blue heavens.

The tall man dropped like a stone, hit in the chest and face by the blast.

He lay in a supine position, motionless. Blood forming an ever-widening pool around him.

David pumped the slide, the sound echoing though the warm air.

'That's not the way,' the dark-haired woman chided. 'You can't save yourselves or the child.'

As David and Amy turned towards the crowd they saw it part and, in the centre of the throng of people, they caught sight of something else. Something new.

It was a deep hole in the earth. Twenty feet long and perhaps half that across. From it flames were rising, adding to the heat of an already sweltering day. Smoke billowed upwards too, thick and black. Noxious fumes that sometimes blotted out the sun for those standing close to the pit and its leaping fire.

And now the crowd were advancing towards them with slow, measured steps and David understood what the pit was for.

'Purified by fire,' the dark-haired woman said, her eyes glancing in the direction of the pit and then back to David and Amy. 'You will all be purified. And this world will be safe.'

David shot her too.

And then they ran.

EIGHTY

They didn't know where they were running to. Deep inside them, the logical parts of their minds told them that there was no way they could escape this place or this crowd but they ran anyway because every human being's most basic instinct is survival. Logic doesn't enter into it when someone's life is at stake. All that surfaces is the screaming desire to stay alive. No matter what. So they ran, pursued by the crowd who came on with the same inexorable approach of an incoming tide sweeping towards the shore.

David turned and fired at them twice and if he'd stopped to look he would have seen that he'd brought three more of them down but what use was three when there were hundreds to replace them?

Many among their pursuers were older and David and Amy outpaced them with ease but a large number were their age and younger and they raced on with determination, knowing it was just a matter of time before their prey ran out of energy.

As they reached the top of the ridge they could see the RV below them but they knew that it offered no means of escape, drained as it had been of petrol. Their only hope was to get inside, to use it as a bastion of sorts. And then?

And then what? Sit and wait until their pursuers got inside?

No matter where they ran, there was no escape but they ran on, breath searing in their lungs, muscles tightening and aching, throats dry with the effort of sucking in air as they dashed onwards.

Behind them, the crowd were closing in.

Looking back from the top of the ridge, the flames from the pit looked bright orange as they leapt and danced.

David was still musing on that when the first of the arrows hit him in the left thigh.

The fibreglass shaft tore through his leg, slicing easily through the abductor magnus muscle, the shaft and tip of the arrow erupting a full six inches from the vastus lateralis muscle at the front of the thigh. Luckily for David, it missed both his femur and also his femoral artery but, as he pitched forward, searing pain filling him, he was concerned only with the length of arrow that had skewered his right leg and left him helpless. The shotgun fell from his grip and skittered away a few feet on the hard ground.

Amy groaned helplessly and tried to help him up but he could put very little weight on the punctured leg.

She grabbed the shotgun, looking around to see that the crowd were now closing in. The leading pursuers were less than fifty yards away.

David gripped his leg, staring down in terror and pain at the arrow that had ripped right through it.

Amy fired the shotgun but the blast went high and hit no one.

David tried to hobble on but it was useless. As Amy fired again, he was forced to drop to one knee, moaning in agony when he accidentally knocked the shaft of the arrow with his left hand. Fresh pain filled him and he saw blood pouring swiftly from the wound.

The crowd, almost as one, had slowed their pace and were now just shuffling forward, knowing that Amy and David were going no further.

Amy kept the shotgun aimed at the approaching pursuers but even the sight of the yawning barrel did nothing to deter them. When they were ten yards away, as if a signal had been given by some invisible watcher, they stopped as one. Despite their numbers, they were silent.

High above, the sun shone down with seemingly increased brilliance. Its heat was intense and the entire landscape was bathed in a welcoming glow.

And beyond the crowd, the flames inside that deep pit burned brightly.

David felt sick. The pain from his injured leg was intense and that, combined with blood loss, was making him feel faint but he clung to consciousness, shaking his head in the hope that it would dispel the onrushing oblivion. Every time he moved his leg fresh agony lanced through the limb. He noted with disgust that there was a large piece of skin on the tip of the arrow and that observation alone was almost enough to make him vomit.

'It's over,' one of the crowd called.

'You can't get away,' another shouted.

And yet still they didn't advance.

Helped by Amy, David tried to struggle to his feet, wincing each time he put weight on his right leg. They stood side by side, facing their pursuers, sweating in the sun. Exhausted by their flight, the breath rasping in their throats when they breathed.

'If you're going to kill us then get it over with,' David shouted, angrily.

Still the crowd of people remained where they were, twenty yards away. None moving closer. There was no need to hurry. Like a spider with its prey secured firmly at the centre of its web, the whole group advanced with grim deliberation.

The sun glinted on the array of weapons they carried. David

caught sight of a man with a bow and wondered if he was the one who had fired the arrow jammed in his leg. He fought off another wave of sickness, supported by Amy who held the shotgun in one hand, gripping the pistol grip firmly , despite the weight of the weapon. There was sweat pouring down her face but she looked relatively calm as she faced the watching crowd.

Close to the front of the throng of people she could see the girl.

She was standing with a slim blonde woman and a heavier set man who was gazing unblinkingly in the direction of David and Amy.

Amy was sure the girl was smiling.

For what seemed like an eternity they stood there on the top of the ridge, the crowd facing them, reluctant it seemed to move nearer. Beneath the blazing sun they stood like sentinels. Waiting.

David looked at the rows of faces before them. There was little emotion on any of them. Just the same kind of blank indifference worn by scavengers waiting for a dying animal go give up its hold on life before they moved in for a feast.

He gritted his teeth against the pain he was feeling and also against the waves of nausea and faintness that were sweeping over him. A combination of the heat, exhaustion and his wound were pushing him closer to unconsciousness and, despite his battle against it, he was losing control.

Amy glanced at him and saw his eyes roll upwards in their sockets and she too knew that the end was in sight. She gripped the shotgun in both hands and held it, the barrel levelled at the hordes facing them.

Again she saw the girl in the front row of the crowd, gazing at her dispassionately.

She was the first to throw a stone.

Snatching it up from the rough ground, the girl hurled it towards Amy, it missed and struck close to her left foot.

More children in the crowd followed her example. Within seconds, rocks and stones were raining down and it was only a matter of time before one hit her. It caught her a glancing blow on the temple and Amy gasped at the sudden pain, feeling warm blood trickling down her face from the cut that had been opened there.

She reeled uncertainly, aware that David too was falling.

For some reason, the image of Daisy appeared in her mind and Amy felt a sudden sadness fill her.

More stones hurtled through the air, some striking her, some hitting David but most slamming into the dry earth around them.

Then a larger rock struck her head and there was nothing but darkness.

EIGHTY-ONE

It was hard to tell whether the heat was coming from the blazing sun or from the flames that were still rising from the pit.

As David opened his eyes all he was aware of was the enveloping warmth. His body was sheathed in sweat and he could feel his clothes sticking to him. For a fleeting second he felt no pain as he awoke, but then, when he looked down towards his leg he was suddenly aware once more of his punctured thigh. The arrow, however, had been removed and the wound bandaged. He could feel as well as see the thick gauze wrapped around the place on his thigh where the shaft had penetrated. For that at least he was grateful.

As his head cleared a little more he also became aware that he was alone.

There was no sign of Amy, and that realization caused him to look around frantically.

He tried to move, but as he did he felt his wrists slam against restraints and, as he glanced up, he saw that he was firmly tied to a cross beam, forcing his arms into a cruciform position that was causing pain in both his shoulders. His feet were bound, secured to the upright post of the crude structure. David felt a sudden and intense stab of fear and his eyes became fixed on the flames before him.

'There was no other way.'

The voice came from behind him but even when he turned his head he couldn't see the face of the man who spoke the words.

'Where's my wife?' David asked, his voice cracking.

'She's with us,' the man told him.

David tried to swallow but his throat was dry. A combination of fear and the extreme heat.

'Why did you bother taking the arrow out of my leg if you're going to kill me anyway?' he wanted to know.

'Does it matter?' the voice murmured.

David turned his head to the other side in an effort to see the man.

'Please don't hurt her,' he said, quietly. 'Don't hurt my wife.'

The man stepped in front of him and ran appraising eyes over him.

'The child she's carrying has to die,' the man told him. For the first time, David could see that he was carrying a large double bladed knife, the razor sharp edges glinting in the sunlight.

'For God's sake,' David gasped, helplessly. 'Not this again. She can't be pregnant and even if she is...' The words faded as he bowed his head.

The man stood for a moment just looking at David who finally raised his head once again to stare at him.

'Where are the others?' he wanted to know. 'Aren't they going to watch too?'

'They don't need to,' the man told him. 'Not this time.'

'You'll never get away with this.'

The man raised his eyebrows.

'Do you believe in God?' he asked.

David looked puzzled.

'In *your* God,' the man went on. 'Do you believe?'

David allowed his head to loll back against the upright part of the beam.

'Does it matter?' he sighed.

'Everyone should believe in something.'

'Like you believe that killing my wife and I will stop your world from being destroyed.' He laughed bitterly. 'You're fucking idiots. All of you.'

'It was foretold,' the man insisted. 'That is what we believe. We have to stop that prophecy from coming true. Destroying your child is the only way we can be sure.'

Again David shook his head.

'And after us?' he grunted. 'How many more will there be? How many more will you murder?'

'There won't be any more,' the man said, flatly. 'There doesn't have to be. The only one that matters is your child. Once it dies this is over.'

'What if you're wrong,' David gasped.

The thought didn't seem to have occurred to the man before now and David was sure he saw a flicker of uncertainty cross his face. It was a small, brief second of victory.

The man held his gaze for a second longer then drew the knife swiftly across David's throat. Even before the blood had finished spurting from the savage wound, he cut the ropes that held David to the wooden beams, pushing his body forward into the flames.

Shock and blood loss ensured that David was spared the agony of the flames. He was unconscious before his body reached the fire. Dead before the flames began to devour him.

The man stood for a moment looking down into the pit, watching the flames leap and dance. Then he turned and walked away, glancing up occasionally at the pure blue sky.

There wasn't a cloud to be seen and, as he watched, he saw the dark outline of a hawk against the heavens. It was a good omen. He hoped the bird would still be circling when they brought the woman out.

He glanced down at his knife and decided it needed sharpening as well as cleaning before he used it again. The man nodded and glanced up once again in the direction of the hawk.

He could hear its strident call and he smiled.

It really was a beautiful day.

'Someone has to die in order that the rest of us value life more.'
Virginia Woolf.